THE LORD
OF THE STOΝ
MOUNTAIN

CW00337494

Antony Swithin was born in England but now lives in Canada. While still a child, the mysterious Atlantic island of Rockall came to haunt his imagination; and it has done so ever since. Over the years, his concepts of the island have evolved into a whole imaginative tapestry, rich in detail — of its geography, its fauna and flora, and the history of its peoples, so that the island emerges in his writing as a land as real as any to be found on our maps.

The Lords of the Stoney Mountains is the second volume in a series of novels about Rockall. The first was *Princes of Sandastre* and the third will be *The Winds of the Wastelands*.

THE LORDS
OF THE
STONEY MOUNTAINS

The Perilous Quest for Lyonesse

BOOK TWO

Antony Swithin

Fontana
An Imprint of HarperCollins*Publishers*

A FONTANA ORIGINAL

First published in Great Britain in 1991 by Fontana,
an imprint of HarperCollins Publishers,
77/85 Fulham Palace Road,
Hammersmith, London W6 8JB.

9 8 7 6 5 4 3 2 1

Printed and bound in Great Britain by
HarperCollins Manufacturing, Glasgow

To
Rachel Penelope and Juliet Katherine,
respectively the first auditor
and one of the first readers
of the tales from Rockall,
for their critical enthusiasm.

CENTRAL AND SOUTHERN

ROCKALL

in the Year of Our Lord 1404

HEIGHT OF LAND

2,500 – 3,000 m. (8,200 – 9,840 ft.)

2,000 – 2,500 m (6,560 – 8,200 ft.)

1,500 – 2,000 m (4,920 – 6,560 ft.)

1,000 – 1,500 m (3,280 – 4,920 ft.)

500 – 1,000 m (1,640 – 3,280 ft.)

200 – 500 m (660 – 1,640 ft.)

100 – 200 m (330 – 660 ft.)

0 – 100 m (0 – 330 ft.)

statute miles

kilometres

CONTENTS

ILLUSTRATIONS

Chapter One

THE SNAKE IN THE TREE

A ride in heavy rain is rarely an exhilarating experience. Grey skies, charcoaled darker by the edges of clouds; the sting of raindrops on one's cheeks; the steady drip, drip, drip of moisture from the trees and from one's cloak; the slippery-wet saddle between one's thighs and the damp hide of one's mount rubbing against one's knees — those are constant liabilities. To make matters worse, southern Rockall is warm even in January; within minutes of setting forth, one found oneself perspiring so much that the shelter of a cloak was more a disadvantage than a benefit. Moreover, our mounts were sevdreyen, not horses. A sevdru is so mentally in tune with its rider that it shares and reflects his mood, jogging along merrily enough when he is cheerful but going reluctantly and with drooping horns when he is dismal. One needs to be in good spirits to endure such a ride with equanimity.

Unfortunately, after my parting with Ilven Estantesec, princess of Sandastre and my affianced love, I was in the very lowest of spirits. To be sure this expedition was, in the last analysis, of my own designing. The party of soldiers among whom I was riding had been advertised as an embassy to the Kingdom of Temecula, with Avran Estantesec, Ilven's brother and my good friend, as its leader. In truth, however, it was merely a cloak to conceal the purposes of Avran and me and to protect us during the first few leagues of our journey. Soon Avran and I would be shedding that protective cloak and venturing northwards on our own particular quest — the quest for the land of Lyonesse.

That was the refuge to which my father and brother had fled, after the high hopes of the followers of Henry Hotspur had died with him on the battlefield of Shrewsbury in that

1

sad summer of 1403. Because my father had loved me for my own sake and as a remembrance of the slim, dark-haired mother I resembled so much, he had striven to guide me into the safe career of a clerk of holy orders, not the perilous one of a squire. In consequence, I had been given no instruction in martial skills. However, I had not wished to follow the path of life he intended for me. To avoid it, I had taught myself in a fashion not only to use lance and sword, but also to shoot with a bow with most un-knightly skill. In addition, I had my own special weapon, the throwing-knife, in whose use a wandering Genoese had first instructed me.

When father had fled to Rockall with Richard, in his farewell message he had presented me with three alternatives: to seek a personal peacemaking with the victorious King Henry, to enter the sanctuary of the church or, if I were brave enough, to follow them to Lyonesse, the land of their refuge. Since I had been yearning so long for adventure, I had not hesitated, even for a moment, before choosing the third alternative. Yet, though I had made that choice in part to prove to my father that his younger son was quite as capable of knightly attainments as his elder, in larger measure it was made through sheer love of them both.

The trouble was that my love for my father and brother had become eclipsed by my greater love for Ilven. Through fortunate chance, I had been able twice to save the life of Avran, third son of the eslef (the ruling prince) of Sandastre. During our voyage to his father's capital, Sandarro, we had become firm friends. Moreover, through the small services I had been able to perform in preventing a potentially bloody rebellion, I had been made centenar in the armies of Sandastre and accepted as a worthy enough husband for its princess. Not that I, mere Simon Branthwaite of Hallamshire, could ever truly deserve the hand of one so high-born and so lovely . . .

However, I had been supremely foolish — or so, in the black depression of those days, I considered. Even in the moment of our betrothal, I had reminded Ilven of my quest and stressed to her my determination to carry it through. Her father Prince Vindicon, perceiving how perilous that quest must be, had ruled that our marriage might not take place, nor even our betrothal be announced, until I returned safely and successfully to Sandarro. That had indeed been a bitter moment for us both. Ever since then I had been torn two ways, at once wishing to be gone quickly, so that the journey and its perils would be soon over, and desiring not to leave at all, but to remain forever in Sandarro with my love. Yet, self-committed and honour-bound as I was to my quest, how might I have stayed?

Avran had long since decided he would accompany me, in part through friendship, in part because of his sheer craving for adventure. Planning our journey had been a difficult enough task, when neither of us knew where we were going. None of the savants of Sandastre had heard of Lyonesse, even as a faint echo of English legend. However, they thought it might well be among the forests of central Rockall, where Englishmen and Gascons who were fugitives from earlier wars had certainly settled. So, to those forests we would travel, if we could succeed in crossing the perilous grasslands of Montariot that lay between.

Our route decided, it was Avran who had set our departure date and undertaken most of the preparations. However, the stratagem of suggesting we were departing on embassy to Temecula had been that of his father's secretary, wily Enar Servessil. It was Enar who had assembled our company and chosen old Berim Andracanth to be its true leader. I had done little save acquiesce in all the suggestions of Avran and Enar. Our setting forth on Avbalet Ava, as the first of January is styled in the Sandastrian tongue, was their idea, not mine. Left to myself, I reflected bitterly, I might have delayed our departure for many weeks more. I might yet be with Ilven, laughing with her, embracing her . . .

Why had I ever proclaimed to her my quest? With the excuse that no-one in Sandastre knew of Lyonesse, might I not have forgotten it and persuaded Avran to forget it also? After all, Avran's commitment was only to me. If I had decided not to fulfil my vow — a vow, after all, that I had made only to myself, for father and Richard could not be aware I had made it — Avran would have acquiesced in that decision and been spared great peril thereby. I might then have settled contentedly into Ilven's land of Sandastre, so different from — and so much happier than — strife-ridden England!

3

Yet *could* I have been content, knowing I had never even attempted to reach Lyonesse? Would not Avran have properly despised me as an oath-breaker? Would I not have despised myself?

Yes, I was in the very lowest of spirits. Avran perceived and understood my mood and, with consummate tact, did not try to jolly me out of it. When he rode with me, he would remain silent except when he saw need to point out some feature of the landscape about us. However, since his own cheerfulness was unquenched by the rain, he preferred to leave me in the taciturn company of Berim Andracanth, riding instead for much of the time with the soldiers.

As he laughed with them, joked with them and joined in their songs, I felt a sullen resentment that was the product more of my mood and a vague jealousy than of any logic — though I convinced myself I was being logical. Surely it was poor discipline for a leader to mingle thus with his men? Surely Berim Andracanth ought to reprimand Avran for such behaviour? Yet Berim did no such thing, perceiving — as, in my dismal emotional state, I could not — that Avran was keeping up the soldiers' spirits very effectively on this drenching ride, in conditions when there might else have been much grumbling. So I rode along, surrounded by my personal aura of despondency and hating life the more because those about me were so cheerful.

Nor, during these days, did Rascal ease my temper. The little vasian had once belonged to Prince Brandar Estantesec, the murdered second brother of Avran and Ilven. However, upon my arrival in Sandarro, he had firmly attached himself to me. This astonished everyone since, upon the death of its owner, a vasian normally pines away and dies. Indeed, Rascal's acceptance of me had been a factor in my own acceptance by the Estantesecs. By now, Rascal reflected my moods even more closely than did my sevdru, Rokh. When I was so depressed and bitter, I could scarcely expect Rascal to be bright and cheery. Nor was he; he sat atop the pack-sack behind me and clung to my shoulders, a mere hump under my cloak, hating the weather as much as I. Unlike me, however, Rascal was fortunate in being able to sleep throughout much of each of those wet days. Nevertheless, even in the evenings he seemed subdued. Obviously he was too affected by my gloom to be capable of lightening it.

Since this was a trade route, there were plenty of inns along the way. Each one occupied some defensive position, high on a river cliff perhaps or in the crook of a river meander, where earth had been heaped to lift the building clear of floodwaters. The inns themselves were built of stone, sometimes a tough white flagstone but more often a rather crumbly brown sandstone, much like the ironstone of Northamptonshire. Each had the basic circular shape of a Sandarrovian padarn, but the ring of buildings was often broken by a watchtower or even by a couple of towers, one looking toward the hills and one toward the river. This land might be at peace, but it was ever in a state of defence.

Each evening, on arrival at the inn, we would unload our pack-saddles from our sevdreyen before releasing them into the forest. There the sevdreyen would browse and keep their own watch; the weather did not greatly trouble them.

I would walk among the trees with Rascal until he discovered one whose leaves were to his taste; then I would wait beneath it while he browsed also. Once his cheek-pouches were full, he would descend onto my shoulder and hum contentedly to himself as we returned to the inn. Usually, by that time, dinner was ready. After discarding cloak and boots, I would arrive late to the repast and be spared overmuch participation in the conversation. Thereafter I would retire to my blankets as early as the company allowed.

As one day followed another, we traversed the lands of Beldevard and Stormavard into those of Bredennavard, crossing the River Siskeven by a great stone bridge about whose pillars clay-brown waters swirled in spate.

Sometimes we had the roads and inns to ourselves, but often enough we encountered other travellers — soldiers on fleet sevdreyen, carrying messages; merchants with their servants and trains of pack animals; minstrels with stringed instruments on their shoulders, protected from the rain by leathern covers; storytellers, higglers, priests touring the smaller communities, or men and — to my surprise — women also, who were simply footloose and eager to see more of their homeland. Though most of the travellers carried arms, this was not from fear of robbers, for crime was rare and justice swift in this land, while raiders from over its borders did not penetrate so far. Rather they were armed because so many fell creatures yet roamed its forests.

I was reminded of this on the fourth day, when a great brown beast broke from a riverside covert and charged us. I was sunk deep in my dismal musings, but was jerked out of them by the sudden mental warning from Rokh. As my mount leapt nimbly aside, the huge animal crashed snortingly by us. I glimpsed a red, rolling eye, as angry as an infuriated bull's, and a pair of immense cone-shaped horns with tips sharp as lances. Then it was past and lumbering away into the trees.

Though the soldiers had scattered at its charge, no arrows were shot and no spears thrown. When I expressed my surprise at this to Berim Andracanth, he in turn seemed surprised.

'Why, it was only an old bavalin,' he rumbled. 'It did us no harm; just woke us up a little. No need to kill the creature!'

Avran and the others were laughing meantime at a soldier who, in his surprise, had fallen off his sevdru into the river mud; and the incident was soon forgotten.

Other life was to be seen a-plenty as we rode. Thorn-backed fishes leapt from the river waters and fell splashing back; birds thronged the trees, many of them come south for the winter, their songs stilled and their bright colours subdued by the rain; and small, bright-eyed animals skittered across our path or chattered among the trees. Once we glimpsed a group of plump grey creatures plunging and snorting among the mid-river waters. Avran called them galikheyen, water-hogs, and told me they were poor eating but made amusing pets. They dived from sight at our approach. Another time, a pair of slim antelopes with spiralling brow-horns leapt in fright from our paths and ran away uphill at a speed which even a sevdru could not have matched; but Avran was not by me then and, later, I forgot to ask him about them.

On the seventh day we crossed another stone bridge spanning the Bildilin, a swifter-flowing tributary of the flood-sluggish Siskeven, and entered a terrain where the lands of the Aradars marched with those of the Menavedras. Thereabouts the waters of the Siskeven had been diverted into many little ditches, each planted with bushes much like withies. Their branches

6

were used for basket-making, the particular art of western Menavedravard. In such weather, all the channels were brimming and a-croak with little red or green frogs. The road oozed mud between its stones and even the normally sure-footed sevdreyen slipped or skidded sometimes. The soldiers and Avran laughed at such happenings, but I cursed the mud and the rain and huddled deeper into my cloak.

There were two days of this slippery riding before we left those irrigated lands behind. Crossing another bridge, over a tributary river of the Siskeven whose name I did not catch, we passed into the lands of Brantavard.

Here, beside the river, was a huge mound of stones, a hundred feet tall or higher, with the ruins of walls at its summit. I noted, in the muddy soil beside the trail, fragments of pottery curiously patterned with red chevrons and whorls. Avran told me that this mound was the ruin of one of the great sun-temples of the long-vanished Empire. About its foot there were other ruins, with great trees growing over and within them. Evidently this had once been a city, but it had died so long ago that Avran knew neither its history nor even its name.

One of the great trees had fallen, so completely blocking the trail with its branches that there was only room to pass under in single file. Berim Andracanth was riding ahead and we after him. As the way narrowed, I caused Rokh to fall back so that Avran could go before me.

Old Berim had passed without trouble, but Avran was taller and rode higher in the saddle than the soldier. A branch of the fallen tree arched low over the trail. Not troubling to duck, Avran thrust it aside impatiently. As he did so, a little yellow-and-green snake was precipitated onto his shoulders and wrapped itself hissing about his neck.

Avran gave a yell and his sevdru, startled, began to buck. Thus shaken, the snake clung tighter about my friend's throat, its evil little head swinging from side to side. Avran groped for it, lost balance on his mount and fell sideways into a tangle of branches.

Perhaps that fall saved him. The snake, jolted by the impact, did not strike at once. Already I had a knife in my hand, drawn from the shoulder sheath beneath my cloak. As the snake reared its head to strike at Avran's face, I threw.

The blades of my knives had been whetted to razor-sharpness during those last days in Sandarro; fortunately so, for this one, aimed truly, decapitated the snake. Its body convulsed, then relaxed in death.

In a moment I had leapt down from my mount, to unwind the reptile's body from Avran's neck and throw the limp coils disgustedly aside. Berim had dismounted also and helped me lift Avran out onto the path. His eyes were closed and his chest heaving, for the snake's convulsions had come close to strangling him. The other soldiers rode past us and then gathered on the path beyond the fallen tree, exchanging shocked comments.

Slowly Avran's breathing became steadier and he opened his eyes. He shivered convulsively, then said gaspingly: '*Vakhast*, what a horrible experience! I thought I was finished, then. My, how my neck hurts . . . Whoever killed that creature has my deepest gratitude!'

It was Berim who explained what had happened. Avran reached up and clasped my hand, his cheeks creasing into a smile. 'Is it always your destiny thus to guard over me, Simon my brother? Yet again, I thank you.'

My eyes seemed hot and all my ill-feelings were gone now. 'Avran, is all well with you now? That was a heavy fall you took.'

He sat up and flexed his shoulders. 'Ow! Yes, I have a few bruises, but I think all else is well.' Stretching his legs, he winced. 'At least, comparatively well; though I don't believe I'll be swallowing or riding comfortably for a few days!'

I bent to retrieve my knife from among the branches. As I straightened, I was surprised to find myself being pushed firmly aside. Avran's sevdru, Zembelen, had returned and wished to approach him. The poor animal, having lost his rider, seemed apologetic, even embarrassed.

Avran scratched the sevdru's muzzle and caressed the bases of his brow-horns. 'Not your fault, old fellow!' he said affectionately. 'Well, time for me to stand up.'

As he rose painfully to his feet, the soldiers exchanged words of profound relief. The snake, it seemed, had been a zikadath, a tree snake rarely encountered but known to have a deadly bite and much feared in Sandastre.

Soon we were on our way again and, if Avran winced

anew at each jolt, at least he could still ride. As I rode beside him, I found myself chattering cheerfully; and old Berim looked back at us and smiled. Though it was raining quite as hard as ever, my personal cloud of despondency had faded wholly away.

Chapter Two

THE GREY RIDERS

Soon the ruins vanished into the trees behind us and our road began slowly to climb away from the riverside, up onto the valley flanks. As we jogged along, Avran told me that we would be spending that evening in Peratenay, the town of the Brantvuts. This would be the first Sandastrian town, other than Sandarro, that I had ever seen. In my new mood, the prospect filled me with excitement.

However, Peratenay proved to be only a tiny place. On a high ridge jutting out into the valley of the Siskeven was a tall tower of brown sandstone within a shell-keep. About and below this, the castle bailey formed a sort of apron, fringed by towers and striped by five close-set rows of padin, the circular houses so typical of Sandastre. Avran told me that each padarn was linked to the next by two high walls with a narrow passageway between, and that each line of padin was connected by a tunnel to the castle itself — a defensive design echoing on smaller scale the plan of the city of Sandarro.

That day there was no thought of war, for it was market day. The gates stood open and the four streets between the padin were thronged with merchants and their customers.

About the block of streets and within the walls was a green space of grasses and shrubs, where sevdreyen and hasedain might be kept at need. However, presently there was no such need. We left our beasts outside the walls and walked into the town, exchanging cheerful greetings with the folk and inspecting the piles of fruit, vegetables and handiwork offered for sale.

That night we slept, not in an inn but in the castle. There we received a genial welcome from Kerem Brantvut, vardaf of Brantavard. I had encountered him before in Sandarro, during his attendance at sessions of the Dakhvardavat, the Ruling Council, and I had liked him — a tubby man whose beardless cheeks were creased with laughter-lines. That day he was wearing a silver-cloth robe, making him look oddly like an ewer given life by some magician. Vigorous life, indeed; for he seemed ever in energetic movement, attended by an equally tubby, beaming wife and a swarm of merry children whose exact number I was never able to estimate accurately, so rapid and incessant were their runnings about.

Berim Andracanth, Avran and I dined with the vardaf and his other guests in a room high in the central tower. Through its series of arrow-slit windows — *asekleyin*, I told myself dutifully, remembering Ilven's tuition — there would earlier have been a view of the higher ridges of the Trantevrin Hills; but, so late in the evening and in such cloudy weather, there was nothing to be seen. We seemed suspended in a bright, cheerful place above a black abyss.

It was an evening of much music and much laughter. Rascal's spirits had risen with mine and his capers caused the children immense delight. However, when they had been sent to bed, Kerem Brantvut ushered away his other guests and returned to us serious-faced. Picking up his goblet, he toyed with it awhile and then spoke with evident hesitation.

'Prince Avran, tell me honestly; is it your purpose to go to Temecula? So I have heard rumoured; yet I find this hard to comprehend, for the Ruling Council has approved no such embassy. Indeed, I can perceive no good cause for one at this time.'

Avran paused awhile before responding, looking at Berim and then at me as if seeking guidance. 'Well, yes, such a word has been spread; yet it is not altogether the truth. Our friend Berim here, and his soldiers, they will indeed be travelling into that land — to Darransgar at least and perhaps to Verumest. But Simon and I, no. We are headed for — oh, let's merely say a very different destination. Tomorrow, indeed, we plan to quit the party and turn away northward.'

'Thus your rumoured purpose was just another of Enar Servessil's schemes, a ploy to divert the attention of enemies? So I guessed and so, I fear, have others guessed also. Are you aware that you are being followed and your progress watched?'

12

Avran was startled, as also were Berim and I. 'No, we never suspected it! How do you know?'

The vardaf's grim expression relaxed into a chuckle. 'Really, it's rather amusing! Your watchers have been taking such elaborate precautions not to be seen by you that they've attracted everyone else's attention! If farmers notice strangers wallowing along through the mud of field paths, when a good road is nearby, they are sure to wonder why; and if innkeepers with vacant rooms learn that, in such weather, men have been camping nearby under the dripping trees, naturally they will gossip! Really, it isn't the right weather in which to be successfully surreptitious; poor things, what a waste of effort! Of course, the Menavedras were watching them and, of course, they passed word to us. As you know, such tidings travel faster than sevdreyen.'

Avran was grinning also. 'So they do, indeed! Nor do I doubt that you have gained full particulars of our pursuers. Please tell us all you know.'

'Well, at the outset ten riders were on your trail; but after crossing the Bildilin, the party divided. Six are still following you as cautiously as ever, but four others have ridden ahead faster. They passed you while you were sleeping in the inn two nights agone. Theirs must have been a wearisome ride in such weather; my people tell me their mounts were covered in mud from pastern to withers!'

He chuckled again, then gazed reflectively into his goblet before continuing: 'Two of those four riders crossed the Siskeven by the bridge beyond this town and went off into the lands of Marexavard. The Marrecs, of course, are no friends of yours or of ours. I've little prospect of determining what happened to those two, but I don't doubt they'd find some of that vard still ripe for mischief, even after Draklin Grassad's fall. The other two remained on this bank; they appear to be keeping an advance watch on your party. Indeed, it wouldn't surprise me if they are staying in Peratenay this night; if not, they'll be somewhere close by. I have men keeping watch on them; I'll learn more in the morning.'

The vardaf took a swig from his goblet and swirled the remaining wine awhile, in a fashion suggesting puzzlement. Then he spoke again.

'So that's *where* they are, Prince Avran; two ahead of you,

13

six behind you. As for *who* they are, that's a harder question. Your pursuers ride hooded and cloaked; they bear neither emblems nor any other tokens to tell us their identity; and, though they must talk, none of my folk has heard them doing so. We may be sure, at least, that they don't hail from these parts. If they did, never would they have chosen such bad ways across the wetlands.'

'Six behind us and two, at least, ahead of us!' Avran spoke pensively. 'Not enough to challenge twenty soldiers; but eight men might cause problems for you and me, eh, Simon? I believe they are waiting for us to leave the party, don't you? And then, a quiet little murder . . . What must we do?'

Kerem coughed discreetly. 'Well, I might arrange to have them rounded up and brought into this castle — always happy to oblige my friends, you know! I have no least doubt that they'd claim to be innocent travellers and I'd need to release them fairly soon, but it would set back their plans. Simple enough — leave it to me!' He beamed at us cheerfully.

I was thinking hard. 'The problem is that they'd guess this was where our party split up. All too soon, they'd be after us again. And those two that rode away into Marexavard; I wonder what they're doing? Perhaps there'll be other watchers, unknown to us. Surely there must be some better alternative . . . Ah, I have it!'

My mind had gone back to the earlier deception I had played. (Whatever *had* happened to poor cousin Hector?) I turned eagerly to the vardaf.

'Sir, I can conceive of one means by which we might confuse those earnest pursuers of ours. However, we will require your help. Have you two trustworthy men, one as little and dark as me and the other as big and redheaded as Prince Avran? The likeness of the first one to me need not be close, for no-one here knows me; but the other would need to be very like Prince Avran, for I'm sure *he* is well known, even so far from Sandarro as this. Moreover, it is surely Avran, and not I, in whom they're most interested.'

I did not add that it was surely he whom they most desired to slay, for we all realized that was so. But already Berim Andracanth had grasped my idea. He laughed.

'So you are thinking of a substitution? Excellent! We would

14

need to take my men into our confidence, but I'll vow they're all trustworthy — indeed, they'd enjoy the game!'

Kerem Brantvut was considering swiftly. 'As you say, Simon, a substitute for you may be easily found — but for Prince Avran . . . Ah, I have an idea! There is a cousin of mine, fresh come into town for the market. He is an educated man, but he chooses to live as a hunter. Since he dwells high in the Trantevrins, he is not well known hereabouts. He is not like enough to you, Prince Avran, to deceive at close view anyone who knows you. However, if clad in your garments and seen from a distance, I'm sure that in this grey, rainy weather, he would pass. He talks a lot, too — just like you, Prince Avran, just like you! Excellent idea, Simon! I'm confident that we can befuzzle and bedazzle these pursuers of yours — leave it to me!'

Beaming with renewed pleasure at the prospect of such amiable stratagems, he drained his goblet and hustled us off to our beds.

When I awoke next morning, there was only a dim light in my chamber. Upon gazing out from its window I found I could see little, for the town below and the valley beyond were submerged from view under pale waves of mist. Such a prospect made me, not depressed, but joyous; dismal weather for travelling, certainly, yet ideal for our purposes.

By design, we had a leisurely breakfast and Berim Andracanth made no haste about gathering the soldiers together for departure. Our walk down through the streets of the little town was also leisurely. Kerem Brantvut accompanied us and, by his deferential addresses to Prince Avran whenever a crowd was about us, made it very sure that my friend would be identified. Moreover, three times during that promenade Avran was addressed by men who knew him — two Brantvuts and an Aradar — and once I was surprised by being accosted cheerfully by one of my former pupil archers, a Derresdem presently journeying back to Sandarro. Should they enquire, the men following us would be left in no doubt that we two had visited Peratenay!

Our sevdreyen, summoned by our thoughts as usual, met us at the gate. While they were being groomed and cosseted — for their coats were wet and tangled after a night abroad in such weather — and the pack-saddles strapped on anew, we chatted with Kerem Brantvut a while longer, making loud reference to our journey to Temecula in hope of further bemusing any hostile listeners. It was mid-morning ere we mounted and rode away from Peratenay.

On this eastern side the road led us quite steeply down into the valley, where broad meadowlands bordered the river. The hanging mist gave us swift isolation from the town behind and little prospect of what lay ahead. The very sound of our passage seemed to be absorbed by the water-laden air.

In such conditions, a smaller party might successfully ambush a larger. Berim drew his soldiers compactly about Avran and me; after last night's warning, he intended to guarantee our safety at least up to the moment of parting.

A sudden tumult from our left caused us to draw up sharply, but it was only a sounder of gelikheyen, water-hogs, startled by our passage and rushing pell-mell for the river.

When we were a few furlongs farther on our road, the shapes of riders loomed out of the mist and caused us to reach for our swords. However, that proved a false alarm also, merely a group of merchants from Trantevar leading laden hasedain. We exchanged cheerful greetings, then they passed on into the mist. After that we jogged along steadily and, though conditions improved not at all, the tension that had gripped us slowly eased. Nevertheless, when one of the soldiers began a song, he was swiftly hushed by Berim.

After an hour or so of riding we found the road swinging away from the river, in part to avoid a marsh, in part to ascend a spur stretching out from the hills. As we rode up it, we could hear the sound of a waterfall somewhere below us. Soon we found ourselves among trees, each one a pool of greater darkness in the mist. These were ideal circumstances for an ambush. Berim, in his new mood of caution, held us back while four of the soldiers went ahead to prospect our path. Only when they reported that all was well did we ride on.

At the point where the road crossed the rock spur there was an open space. A blackened ring of stones showed that many fires had been lit here by parties encamped at this point, while other stones, arranged about the fireplace, made convenient seats. Here we halted to have our midday repast; but, for the first time, Berim felt it necessary to set out sentries while we did so. The sevdreyen were released to browse among the trees and Rascal fed also.

As we ate and drank, Berim explained my plan to his men, who greeted it with chuckling approval. When our meal had ended, Avran and I bade farewell to the soldiers, for this was the parting of our ways. Then we remounted and, accompanied only by Berim, turned left off the road and rode uphill into the trees.

The mist was so thick and the undergrowth now so dense that, despite our caution, we did not see the party waiting for us until we were challenged by them. Four men were squatting in the lee of a massive ikhoras tree. Two were soldiers, their blue uniforms and cloaks bearing the leaping silver sevdru that was the device of the Brantvuts. However, it was the two others that held my attention. Both wore the simple brown-leather cloaks, tunics and boots of hunters, but their similarity extended no further. One was a slim, dark youth, like me in build if not in feature and with hair that, like mine, was trimmed unusually short for a Sandastrian; the other was as solid and smiling as Avran, and as redheaded. He spoke first.

'Eledrin Brantvut at your service, Prince Avran and gentlemen! And this burly giant beside me is my distant cousin Lerened, come also to your aid. We gather that we are, as it were, to exchange skins with you! These other gentlemen' — he waved airily at the soldiers — 'courteously came along to act, as it were, as our shepherds; to make sure that we would not stray from our way and miss this merry meeting. Yet they roused us unduly early and made us ride unduly fast. It has been a long and' — he gave a consciously conspicuous shiver — 'wet wait in this dreary woodland!'

Yes indeed, this man *did* talk a lot — and in a fashion much like Avran! I found myself chuckling and, though Berim Andracanth seemed inclined to be disapproving, Avran was smiling also.

'Such complaints, cousin!' he replied as we dismounted. 'Well, on the next occasion I'll bear in mind the thin blood of the Brantvuts. Be sure that I'll send along furs and earthenware hot-water bottles, to keep you warmer!'

17

Eledrin Brantvut bowed with mock solemnity. 'I shall be honoured on that future occasion, as always I am to serve you, my prince. Yet, bethink you — would not a tent and couches be also proper significations of your munificence? Of course, for common soldiers like these' — he gestured again at them — 'a little hardship is appropriate — welcome, even. But we hunters, we like our comfort!'

At this, I found myself laughing outright; even Berim was struggling to hide a smile. However, the two soldiers were clearly rather shocked, and the dark man seemed embarrassed, by such levity.

Perceiving this, Berim Andracanth spoke brusquely. 'No time for talk now! We must be on the road soon. Please make your exchange of garments as expeditiously as you may, gentlemen!'

Eledrin Brantvut pulled a wry face at this and muttered: 'It is always the tardy who are in greatest haste!' Yet, even as he spoke, he was unfastening his cloak and soon he had exchanged it for Avran's orange one. Lerened Brantvut, in contrast, was not at all talkative. Indeed, while we swapped cloaks and tunics he spoke not a word, though he smiled at Rascal and aroused crooning approval by gently tweaking the vasian's ears.

When we were done, the bushes rustled and two sevdreyen appeared. They were like enough to Zembelen and Rokh in colour to pass any casual inspection and bore bundles similar to ours in all particulars. There were even staves like our bowstaves (though, I noted, not of the same woods) strapped beside each saddle. Evidently the people of Brantavard were observant of details and reported them accurately, for the vardaf himself had not seen us on our mounts until late morning. With such eyes watching, no wonder those men following us had been so swiftly noticed!

To further the deception, Lerened Brantvut tied atop his pack a small bundle. When he had mounted and tucked it within his cloak, this looked surprisingly like Rascal did when huddled beneath my cloak. For his part, Eledrin Brantvut bestrode his sevdru in a fashion carefully modelled upon Avran's. It was again he who spoke, his voice prim but a big grin on his face.

'It is, of course, always delightful to take time properly to

18

develop a new acquaintanceship. Nevertheless, in view of this — er — extreme need for haste, my dear Berim Andracanth, I wonder that you linger so! Should we not be rushing away to rejoin those patiently waiting soldiers of yours, before any travellers pass? Haste, centenar, haste!'

Berim stiffened, his face mottling with anger: 'You're most impudent, young man! Yet indeed we should make haste. Your pardon, Prince Avran and Simon, but I consider that we should leave here before you do. Travel safely and swiftly; be watchful; and may God bless and guide your path! Come then, gentlemen!'

He turned and, as the sevdreyen of the two Brantvuts fell into step behind his, rode away down the ridge into the mist. Just before the three faded from our view, Eledrin Brantvut waved us a jaunty farewell.

Avran turned to the soldiers. 'I take it you have mounts? Good; then summon them, please. Simon, we must prepare to ride also.' As two more sevdreyen emerged from the bushes, he spoke again to the soldiers. 'Did your lord the vardaf send us any message, about our path or any other matter?'

'Aye, he did, Your Highness. He said you should ride on up this shoulder of the hill we're on, leaving it not at all till you attain the high moor. About four hours' ride, that is; and not easy going, mind! Just past the edge of the trees you'll find a stoney knoll, and on it an old tower. 'Twas a signal-tower in the Arctorran wars, but none use it now. There you'll find a messenger waiting. Doubtless he'll be telling you where to head next. More than that I can't say.'

'Good enough; that seems clear. Now, have you heard our party is being followed? Just so; it seems common knowledge among you Brantvuts! Well then, our pursuers seem anxious to avoid the main highway whenever they can. Is there any other road that they might be travelling?'

The soldiers conferred in undertones, then the same one spoke. 'Aye, there's two ways. There's a riverside path, but that's rank bad. In this weather it'll be fetlock-deep in clay and no sevdru could follow it far. But there's another road as well. 'Tis used by woodmen for their carts in summer and autumn, but no folk travel that way at this season, for the road winds too much and climbs too high. Likely enough your followers have chosen that way, for 'tis shown on all the charts. Aye, I reckon that'd be the road they'd favour.'

'Good, then please lead us to it. Quietly and cautiously, mind! — I don't desire either that we should surprise them or that they should surprise us.'

Despite Avran's words and despite the route-finding skill of sevdreyen in woodland, it proved neither an easy nor a very quiet ride up the shoulder of the hill. There was no semblance of a path and our mounts had to thrust their way through dense underbrush. Since every branch and every leaf was water-laden after so many days of rain and mist, it was wet work. The leather cloaks and tunics that Avran and I wore did not permit the moisture to penetrate, but we were soon sweating so much that they afforded us no real advantage. As for the azure-blue cloaks and tunics of the soldiers, they were soon darkened and dripping.

As we climbed higher, the trees became taller and crowded closer together, their canopies blocking from our view the grey sky. The roof of branches overhead was broken briefly where an outcrop of sandstone traversed the slope, but the sevdreyen had no trouble in scrambling up this. Elsewhere, starved of light, the underbrush diminished and we were able to travel more quietly.

We were riding in single file, the silent soldier in front. I wriggled my shoulders to shake some of the moisture from my cloak and, as I did so, the first soldier stopped. The second soldier drew up alongside him and, turning, said: 'The logging road is just ahead, masters.'

'Thank you,' responded Avran. 'Simon, you're more skilled than I at reading tracks. Can you try to determine whether any riders have passed this way today? Don't ride onto the road, if you can avoid it; I don't desire that our own hoofprints be seen.'

Urging Rokh forward, I passed the others and rode on a few more paces. Yes, there was the track — two furrows deeply gouged by years of passage of logging carts, with a hump between. After a few months of disuse, many weeds had sprouted and I knew at a glance, by the even cover of dew droplets on their leaves, that no riders could have travelled that road today.

Yet what was that? Surely I heard a whisper of sound,

away to my left? Yes indeed, I was not mistaken. If no riders had passed earlier, unquestionably some were approaching now! Hastily I returned to the others.

At this tiding, Avran dismounted. 'If this be they, then we're fortunate, for we'll have the chance of determining who they are! Come with me, Simon; and gentlemen, would you mind concealing the sevdreyen and yourselves in the trees back there?'

While the four beasts and two soldiers withdrew, Avran and I crawled forward to a point of vantage close to the trail. Here, anciently, a tree had fallen and given access to light to a cluster of saplings. Their energetic growth furnished excellent cover for us.

As we took refuge among them, the sound of approaching riders grew from a whisper to a murmur. A shape appeared indistinctly in the mist and progressively took firmer form: a tall man on sevdru-back, cloaked and hooded in grey garments that were only a little darker than the mist about him. The knob of a sword-hilt gleamed at his waist. As that rider passed us, another took shape behind him; then another, and another. Six riders in all, just as Kerem Brantvut had said; each one silent, each hooded and cloaked in grey, each on a dun-coloured sevdru without distinguishing marks. None bore any emblem and none seemed to me to afford any indication of identity — save, perhaps, the third. It so chanced that his cloak had become caught up, unnoticed, on his sword-hilt. Even so, all that could be seen beneath was the scabbard itself, chased in silver in an elaborately serpentine pattern, and a riding-boot with pointed toe and turned-over top, tooled with what seemed to be the shape of a rayed sun.

As he glimpsed this, Avran gave a low whistle of surprise. However, he said nothing; nor did he move till the last rider had vanished into the mist and the sound of their passage faded entirely away.

'Well, Avran, what do you think?' I asked at last, impatiently. 'Who are they — Baroddans, Arctorrans, Grassads? Can you tell?'

Avran shook his head puzzledly. 'How can I say, Simon? Under those cloaks and hoods, they might be Arctorrans, Grassads — anyone! Yet that scabbard — I've never seen a scabbard chased in silver in quite that pattern. The Fachnese love to decorate their weapons, but never to my knowledge in such a style . . . And the emblem stamped into the leather of his boot . . . It's ridiculous, but — Simon, that was an echo of long ago, the rising-sun emblem of the evil Empire that was overwhelmed by the sea! You may still observe it in the stonework of their temples, but its use has long been prohibited everywhere in southern Rockall. I wonder who dares to wear it again now, after more than a thousand years?'

Chapter Three

THE TOWER

We returned to where the soldiers and our mounts were waiting. Quickly Avran described what we had seen. The soldiers undertook to pass word of this to Kerem Brantvut and, through him, to Enar Servessil. Then we bade them Godspeed and watched them ride away down the hill into the mist.

For our own part, we must continue up toward the high moors, but also we must try to evade any pursuit. If our careful deceptions should fail to mislead them as we hoped, it was all too likely that the grey riders would back-track and seek for us. The tracks of the sevdreyen between this position and the main road would be hard to interpret, since the two soldiers, the two hunters and Berim had ridden up and down that part of the slope as well as we. It was our onward tracks that mattered; we must strive to obscure these. Moreover, we had yet to cross the logging road. How might that be done, without our passage of it becoming obvious?

The first problem was quickly solved. We rode downhill a little way to the point where the sandstone outcrop intersected our tracks. There Avran instructed Zembelen, and I in my turn instructed Rokh, to leap sideways. After that we made sure that our mounts kept to the sandstone — their hooves slipped sometimes, but they managed quite well — for fifty yards or so, until it disappeared beneath the soil. The rock surface would show no clear traces of our passage and it would require imagination on the part of any pursuer to guess what we had done.

From that point we rode on along the flank of the hill. Without realizing it, we were still following the line of the sandstone. This was fortunate, for it cropped out again as a ridge. Through this, the descending logging road cut a deep, narrow hollow. Our sevdreyen were able to leap easily across from the rock on one side of this gully to the rock on the other, thus leaving no traces visible from the road.

Fair enough; but, as we made our way back toward the crest of the ridge, our mounts were soon thrusting once more through shoulder-deep vegetation and leaving tracks that would be very easy to see. However, Avran was confident that we had no cause for further apprehension, since our two detours would suffice to bemuse any pursuer. For the moment, I was content to share his optimism — and, after all, I could think of no other means for throwing off pursuit.

Just as we regained the ridge-crest, we were given a fright. Avran almost rode upon a large bird. The noise of its taking to flight, with a whirring of wings, seemed as loud as a cannonshot. Zembelen reared up so suddenly that my friend was almost thrown. As the bird flew away, its call was so much like the 'Go-back, go-back' of a red grouse that I was reminded of my native moorlands; but the tail of this bird was longer and its colouring more sombre. Avran, who had been too busy retaining his seat to see it properly, could not name the bird for me.

Paradoxically, this brief incident served not to enhance, but rather to relax, our tensions. Moreover, it was pleasant to be on the ridge again. Not only was the undergrowth less dense there than under the trees, but also a rising current of air dissipated the mist and extended our view, wherever the tree-trunks permitted, to a hundred yards or more. We were able to ride along side by side, talking relaxedly and even singing a little. After so many days of riding amid a throng of soldiers and travelling at their pace, the sense of freedom was suddenly pleasant; and, for me, the completeness of my reconciliation to my friend brought a new optimism. Maybe, after all, our journey might turn out neither so long nor so dangerous as I had feared!

For more than two hours we rode steadily uphill through this woodland, the slope progressively slackening and the ridge broadening as it neared the main crest of the Trantevrin Hills. For much of that distance, visibility was not severely restricted. However, as the ridge broadened, so did the current of air slacken. Mist thickened anew, not at first forming a solid blanket but instead creating pockets of dense vapour amid clearer air. For a few minutes, we would be able to see deep into the aisles of trees; then the mist would close about us so that only the nearest trunks were visible. It was as if some spirit of the air was playing a 'Now you see it, now you don't' game with us. Our singing ceased and, as we rode on, our conversation lapsed also.

When we had reached and passed the hillcrest, the trees became fewer and there were more bushes. However, these were neither so numerous nor so dense as the undergrowth of the hill slopes and we might have made fast progress. The trouble was that the current of air was quite gone and the mist weaving itself into a dense blanket. We knew we must be approaching the moor.

When we had heard them, the soldiers' instructions had seemed explicit enough: 'just past the edge of the trees . . . an old tower on a stoney knoll.' Yet where *was* the edge of the trees? They were becoming fewer, but there was no distinct margin to the woodland. Moreover, the ground beneath the hooves of our sevdreyen had become quite flat; the ridge had been left behind and we were on a hill-top plateau.

Was this the last tree? No; there in the mist ahead was another. Was *that* the last? No; off to the left was another tree and after that, dimly to be seen, yet another to the right.

After a few hundred yards of such corkscrewing, we knew we had lost our line. We consulted, then followed our own tracks backward until the trees closed together again. This time we proceeded more sensibly and systematically. While I waited and watched, Avran would ride ahead in as straight a line as he might manage. At the point when he was barely in view, I would call out to him; then I would ride up to and past him until, in my turn, I was fading from his sight. In this fashion, turn and turn about, we contrived more or less to follow a straight path from the end of the ridge up onto the plateau — and we were not at all surprised that this new path did not even intersect our original meandering tracks.

Since we were now so high in the Trantevrin Hills and the day was ending, it was becoming cold. Both of us were still soaked with sweat after our long ride through the wet woods and, despite our leather cloaks, we found ourselves shivering. The mist became more opaque as the light diminished; we could see no more than a few yards ahead. Twice we heard the sound of drumming hooves as herds of unidentified animals ran past us; and once a rabbit-sized creature scurried between Avran and me, too swiftly and unexpectedly for me to gain any real view of it. In general, though, there was a silence and a pervasive sense of loneliness that made the minutes of our careful progress seem to stretch into hours.

It chanced that I was ahead when the land began to rise again; and soon there were rocks thrusting up through the grass. As we climbed, the vegetation became sparser and loose stones abundant, the hooves of our tired mounts slipping and sliding on them. Since there was real danger of a fall that might injure them or us, we dismounted and led them up the hill, a newly awakened Rascal sitting unhappily on my shoulder.

It was becoming dark all about us, but ahead there loomed a greater darkness. Ah, good! — there it was, the tower at last! — a great mass of masonry that seemed to solidify before us as we approached it.

There was no entrance on this side. We turned arbitrarily to our left and walked clockwise about the base of a structure that seemed to grow from the ground like a stone tree. Not until we had almost circumnavigated the tower did we discover, at last, a flight of stone stairs. They were too steep for our sevdreyen to climb, narrow and without balustrades.

I was again ahead of Avran and should have begun climbing them immediately, in quest for the messenger who was presumably awaiting us above. However, I hesitated to do so — whether through Rascal's prescience or my own, I do not know. Instead I walked back to Rokh's side and unfastened my bowstave from the straps that held it to the pack-saddle. I attached the quiver of arrows to my belt and, taking the bowstring from the pouch at my belt, bent the stave and strung it.

By now Avran had caught me up and was watching me with surprise. 'Whatever is the matter, Simon my friend?' he asked.

'I don't truly know,' I answered hesitantly. 'Yet something is wrong — I feel it.' As I spoke, my thoughts were clarifying.

'Listen, Avran. If one of the Brantvut's soldiers were waiting for us up there, would he not have lit a fire — to warm the place up, to provide some light? After all, he would realize we'd have trouble in traversing the moor in such weather. This tower — it's too dark, too silent. I don't like it at all. And Rascal — he's not happy either.'

Avran's expression tightened. He nodded and, summoning Zembelen to him, strung his own bow. As he attached the quiver to his belt, he said quietly: 'Simon, normally I'd prefer to climb first up those stairs, but you're the better bowman. I believe you should take the lead. Would you do so?'

That was a hair-prickling ascent. The mist had not thinned as we climbed the knoll and the light was fading fast. The moon had not yet risen and, after yesterday, I doubted whether we would ever have its light that night. Would I be able to see into the tower, when I reached the entrance? If I could, what might I see? All the horror stories I had heard in childhood, of murder, mystery and madness, seemed to be crawling out from the recesses of my mind as I went upward.

How steep these steps were, and how winding! They were circling the tower in an ascending corkscrew; already I had circuited it twice as I climbed. Assuredly no fire could have been lit inside the tower, not even any torches; by now I would have seen any least gleam of light. No light, certainly; but did I hear a sound above me? Yes indeed — but what was it? There was something familiar, yet something unpleasant, about it . . .

I continued climbing, each step a conscious effort of will. I recognized the sound now — a growling, worrying and tearing, like a hound with a bone at the fireside. Some beast was feeding in the chamber above us. As to what it was feeding on, I did not care to speculate.

Ahead and to my right, I could now perceive a high stone door-post. Above it, a mighty carven lintel could be glimpsed in the fading light. The unpleasant sounds were becoming louder. I stopped and Avran came up behind me.

'I hear the beast also,' he breathed quietly into my ear. 'Go carefully now, brother Simon, and have your weapon ready. I believe we are in great peril.'

I fitted arrow to string and drew breath. Then, my heart

pounding, I began the ascent of those last few steps. As I did so, the sounds ceased entirely and all I could hear was the thumping of my own heart.

Now I could peer into the doorway, into an abyss of blackness. Yet there were two bright gleams in that blackness — two orange eyes that seemed to find, and bore into, mine. Staring into those eyes, I took one further step upward, two, three . . .

There came a slavering, snarling noise. A great shape seemed to gather itself together in the gloom and rush toward me. I could not see my target properly, yet I dared not wait. Holding my bow at an angle, I drew back the string and loosed; then I dropped into a crouch against the stone stairs.

A horrid, gurgling yowl told me that my arrow had struck, yet it had not halted the rush of the beast. Still it was hurtling toward me — almost it was upon me! Below, Avran straightened and loosed his own arrow up and past me — so close! I glimpsed a mighty form above me and spreading claws eager to tear me; and I crouched in terror, sure I was about to be slain.

There came an ear-rending cry as Avran's arrow hit home. Its force deflected the creature's leap and its shadow fell away from me. There was a scrabbling sound and a wail as, missing the stone steps, it dropped into the darkness beyond; the sound of its impact on the stones below; then silence.

I was trembling as I straightened; but, in a moment, Avran's arm was about my shoulders. 'A close thing, Simon. I'm glad you taught me how to use the long-bow; I would not have cared to tackle that beast with a sword!'

'What was it, Avran?'

'I'm not sure, but I think it was a thassak. They're one of the few creatures in our land that attack at sight. When aged or injured, often they become man-killers. Moreover, they climb readily. I fear for our messenger; but let us see. Attend a moment and I'll strike a light.'

He felt in the pocket of his tunic and produced a cloth roll, containing the flints and the roll of dried moss that serve as fire-starters in Sandastre. A stub of wax candle soon was lit and, reluctantly, we went upward into the tower.

Avran's fears were fully realized. I will not describe what we saw, for it was a sickening spectacle. Suffice it to say that whatever message Kerem Brantvut had sent could never be transmitted to us. Its bearer may have died swiftly enough, but the great beast had fed well and the remains of its feeding were unpleasant. Moreover, apparently it had laired in the tower for several months, for there were gruesome relics of numerous earlier kills.

We found the body of the creature below the tower, with my arrow in its shoulder and Avran's in its flank. It was indeed a thassak, a creature much like the heraldic depictions of a leopard. However, it was more massive, with a hide that was silver-grey, not saffron, and with larger dark splotches in an irregular pattern that, at the times of its hunting at dusk and dawn, would confuse any eye. Two huge, curving tusks arched downward from its upper jaw, as sharp and pointed as sickles. There was blood on them; I was glad only that it was not ours.

Though it was so cold and so damp out there in the mist, we preferred to spend the night outside than in the tower.

Chapter Four

A RIDGE RIDE IN THE TRANTEVRINS

Wrapped in my cloak, I was asleep soon enough, but my dreams were uneasy. My awakening, however, was a delight. The clouds were gone after so many days and the whole landscape had that particular shimmering brilliance which one sees only when sunshine follows much rain. I noticed a spider's web on the grass close to where I was lying, each strand of it laden with dewdrops that, like tiny mirrors, collected and reflected the light dazzlingly. A bee was buzzing with sleepy anxiety as it climbed a moisture-laden grass-stem and a fly with green-veined wings suddenly took flight from a seed-head close to my nose. In such conditions, the adventure of last evening retained no more reality than a fading nightmare.

I sat up and saw the stone tower above me. This morning, however, it was no dark threat but merely an ageing pile of honey-brown stone. The dead beast huddled at its foot was just another pattern of tints in a colourful scene.

Avran was awake already and had made a little fire, whose grey strand of smoke was spiralling up to the sky. He was using the point of an arrow to toast a hunk of the crusty nut-meal bread that is a staple of Sandastrian travellers. He called a cheery greeting to me and soon we were breakfasting together. Rascal was awake also and blinking in the sunlight; after a while, he began to groom himself with busy fingers and tongue. The sevdreyen had drifted away to browse in the forest, but we knew they would return swiftly when summoned.

After breakfast we climbed the stone steps again. The massive door to the tower had been left wedged open — most unfortunately, since that had enabled the thassak to make its lair within. We closed the door firmly, but then we paused on the step outside.

This was an excellent viewpoint — and designedly so. During the Arctorran wars a soldier would have been stationed here, to keep watch northeastward for the beacon fires that would warn of an invasion. In clear weather he would be able to see for twenty miles or more, with the wooded southeastern slope of the Trantevrin Hills to his right and the moorlands on their high tops to his left. Another tower was to be seen in the middle distance, five miles or more away.

Having no word as to any future rendezvous with another messenger, we must choose our own route; and indeed, we had discussed and decided it during breakfast. If the weather had remained as dolorously misty as yesterday, we would have crossed the ridge of the Trantevrins as speedily as we might and would have descended into the gorge of the Argrelen River, to follow its steep course toward Argray. However, in this clearer weather, it would be quicker to ride in the direction the Sandastrians call *salnen*. (They recognize eight, not four, major directions — *salis*, north; *ebra*, northwest; *ustres*, west; *atra*, southwest; *marnis*, south; *felbra*, southeast; *baeldis*, east, and *nendra*, northeast. Intermediate points have intermediate names and *salnen* is thus what we would call, more clumsily, north-northeast). By this means we might avoid the lands of Argravard altogether and travel directly into those of Estantegard. The openness of the moorland — really parkland, for there were scattered groves of trees in its dells — would render it easier for us to spot any pursuers than in the valley. Moreover, such pursuers might well assume that we would head for Argray; this other route would be unexpected.

We had called our mounts already by the usual mental summons. As we descended that winding stairway I saw below us a whole group of sevdreyen, not just our two. However, the other animals — sixteen of them — became uneasy when they glimpsed us and were in flight before we reached the tower foot.

Avran was quite unsurprised by this. Wild sevdreyen, he told me, were common enough on those uplands and, though rarely hunted — they were regarded as a valuable stock with which domesticated beasts might be interbred, with benefit, from time to time — they distrusted and avoided men.

The fire had been stamped out already. The pack-saddles were quickly put onto our two beasts and the bowstaves — kept handy, though unstrung, overnight — were returned to their straps. Thankfully we folded our cloaks and tied them to the saddles, for this promised to be the first day since leaving Sandarro on which cloaks would not be needed. Within minutes we were on sevdru-back again and riding down the gentler northern face of the knoll onto the flat moorland below. The dark traces left in the dew by the hooves of our mounts would fade quickly as the sun rose. Only an exceptionally expert tracker would be able to trace our course across the tussocky grass.

Since the uplands were unsuitable for grazing by domesticated sevdreyen or hasedain, they belonged to no particular vard and were not permanently settled. The route used by travellers from Peratenay to Argray lay further to the west. Consequently, these hills were visited only by a few hunters. In mid-morning we glimpsed a solitary rider far away north of us, but he manifested no interest in us. We saw no other humans all day. Twice, herds of sevdreyen ran past in the distance, causing our mounts to prick up their ears, and once we saw a shaggy-furred, roly-poly brown creature that Avran called an urut; he told me that it had broad claws and lived by digging for ants and beetles. There were many lizards basking in the sunshine, in livery of brown and green, yellow or even red, and several times we glimpsed the flicker of a furry tail as some other small creature dived into its hole.

The dark apprehension of pursuers that we had felt in the rain and gloom of yesterday seemed ridiculous in this bright warmth. There seemed no need to hasten; why not take our ride easily and enjoy the sunshine? The sky was blue and bedecked only by the smallest and fluffiest of clouds; birds were singing high overhead and grasshoppers stridulating among the grass-roots. We were content to ride along slowly, singing in turn the songs of our two countries or conversing cheerfully. Though, by the short day's end, we had ridden no more than twenty miles, we felt contented enough by this modest achievement.

For our night's rest we found a sheltered spot under a cluster of gnarled trees. While the two sevdreyen browsed nearby and Rascal skipped cheerfully around in the branches overhead, we ate our own meal at leisure. We watched the stars appear and the nighthawks winging over the moors in the moonlight, then rolled ourselves in our cloaks. Our sleep was long and our dreams benign.

The next morning proved sunny also, but with enough wind to give it exhilaration. While we breakfasted, Avran told me that we were now almost due east of the lakeside town of Argray and might expect, by midday, to be descending from the ridge of the Trantevrins into the forested lands of Estantegard. At the prospect, his countenance was bright with delight.

'Why, Simon, those are real trees!' he said. 'They're truly huge; a man might make a comfortable home for his family within a fallen trunk. And when they're growing — why, they reach up to the sky — oh, a hundred ells or more. You've never seen such trees! The oaks of England, the ebelmeks of Sandarro — they're mere bushes in comparison. Oh Simon, it lifts my heart to think that I'll soon be showing you the lands of my own vard!'

When we were mounted, he smiled at me mischievously. 'I wish to see those trees soon. Come on, now, Simon, let's ride fast; let's race! You're a good rider now; see if you can catch me!'

At those words, he gave Zembelen's neck a pat. In a moment, sevdru and rider were speeding away, out from the grove of trees and along the ridge crest.

I laughed joyously and started in pursuit. Rokh, catching my mood as always, was prepared to give of his best. He was not so fleet as my beloved Whitebrow, but he was capable of a good pace — better, I thought, than Zembelen. Moreover, Avran was heavier than me; we should catch them easily! Rascal, clinging to my shoulders, was chittering to himself disapprovingly but Rokh and I, in the sunshine and the wind, were enjoying the special exhilaration of speed.

Up onto the ridge we raced, where the soil was thin and plant growth meagre. Thin soil and stony ground; good footing. Avran had a long start and was at least a hundred yards ahead, but we'd be up with him soon. The wind was behind us and seemed to be blowing us along light as a leaf; this was glorious! Faster, Rokh, faster!

Ahead of us, the ridge tilted up into crags and ended;

Avran had headed his mount to the left, down from the ridge-crest, and was gaining on us. A long, long descent it was, into the deeper grass of the moorland. Further to the left was a scatter of animals in flight — wild sevdreyen? I could only glance and guess, for Rokh's stride was lengthening as the slope gave him impetus.

Down, down we went. Surely, now, we must be gaining on Avran? Yes indeed; for the slope was easing and the herbage becoming denser, a disadvantage to a heavier mount and rider but favouring Rokh and me.

Avran turned in his saddle, laughing and waving, then urged Zembelen to even greater efforts. Yet we were over-hauling them quickly now! The gap closed to twenty yards, ten, five; one last effort, and we'd do it. Come on now, Rokh; faster, faster! In a moment, I'll be able to reach out and touch Zembelen. One pace, two paces more . . .

But ah! What was happening? Rokh had caught a forehoof in a concealed hole and was falling, forward and sideways. His frantic distress, and Rascal's alarm, were screaming into my brain. I grasped the sevdru's horn-bases and threw myself off him, landing heavily but managing to roll clear before he fell on me. At the same moment, Rascal leapt from my shoulders to the grass.

I lay still for a moment, then sat up experimentally. No bones broken but ow! how my shoulders were bruised! Rascal was hopping up and down, chittering frantically but quite uninjured. I gathered him into my arms as I got to my feet, then went to look at Rokh. The poor beast was lying awkwardly, his body twisted to the right and his left foreleg tucked under him, at such a strange angle that I knew it must be broken. Dolefully I knelt beside him and stroked his muzzle, feeling all the affection and misery of a mother with an injured child, when she knows her heedlessness has caused the injury.

Avran arrived beside me and dismounted. He was contrite. 'Simon, I led us into an unwise escapade and I'm sorry. A ride like that — it's fun when one is close to home, but it's silly when one is journeying. I ought never to have suggested it. Well, let's give proper attention to this animal of yours. Can you persuade him to rise?'

With a horse it might have been impossible; with a

sevdru, it was done readily. As well as understanding my desire, Rokh read the compassion and concern in my mind. There was a shiver down his spine, a scrabbling of hind legs and a lurch. His hindquarters rose and then, taking the weight of his forequarters on his good foreleg, somehow he was on his feet again, panting and trembling. I put my arm about his neck and, with head tilted to keep the horns away from me, he rubbed the side of his muzzle against my cheek.

That other foreleg, though, was dangling uselessly. Avran examined it briefly. 'Yes, this is broken; you'll ride no further on him. Yet it's a clean break; I believe I can fix a splint that will hold the bone together for a while. Look, there's a grove of asalbeks in the hollow over there. I'll ride over and cut a couple of branches. No, don't bother to come, Simon; stay with your beast.'

While Avran was gone I unstrapped the pack-saddle from Rokh's back — with difficulty, for the straps had twisted awry when he fell — and talked to him soothingly. Though he was shivering from shock and pain, my sevdru stood still and patient while Avran hacked off two suitable branches with his sword, trimmed them and carried them back. My friend had brought twine and bandages in his pack.

It is hard to put splints on a horse or a dog, for they feel only the discomfort and cannot understand that the splints will be beneficial. The mental links to a sevdru, in contrast, make the task easy. When the job was done, Rokh was persuaded into movement. It was a heavy sort of limping walk — a sad contrast to the swift, bird-flight-like ride that had so recently ended — but it was a brave effort and a tribute to Avran's veterinary skill.

'Well and good,' said my friend. 'Yet Rokh can't travel far and obviously you can't ride him, Simon. If only I hadn't been so foolish as to suggest that stupid ride . . . But, as you Englishmen say, it's no use weeping over spilled wine. The fortunate point is that we're not so very far from the lands of my vard. If we'd ridden just a few miles further on, we'd have been down in the valley of the Dalirond. Trantevar is only about five leagues up-valley; we might seek help there but I don't wish to, in view of our need to travel secretly. The lands of Estantegard are down-valley and not much more distant. Our problem is that we can't hope to get Rokh so far, even if you were to walk and lead him.'

My mind was made up already. 'Well, I'm not leaving him. Obviously I must remain here while you go for help.'

Clearly Avran was relieved by this suggestion. 'I cannot be back before midday tomorrow, at the very earliest. Might it not be better to move over into the trees? No, *not* the thicket where I cut the splints; see, over there, that bigger clump, just below where the crags end? That will be easier for me to locate and, tonight, you and Rascal should be able to roost in safety among the rocks. Be vigilant, though. I don't believe you'll encounter another thassak — certainly I pray that you don't! — but there are other dangerous creatures about. Of course, even if you do sleep, Rascal will keep watch, so you should be safe enough.'

He mounted quickly and, with a cheery 'Farewell till tomorrow!', rode off down the slope at a pace not much less than when we were racing.

After Avran had passed from view, I took my bowstave in hand to serve as a staff, shouldered the pack-saddle and made a slow way over to the grove Avran had pointed out, with Rascal hopping along beside me through the grass. Poor Rokh followed stumblingly. Avran was right; we could never have got Rokh to Trantevar unaided.

Below the last and highest crag there was a deep hollow, rimmed by a horseshoe-shaped ridge. Since there was a scar beneath the crag and a ruckle of stones topping the ridge, I guessed there'd been a landslip here — oh, fifty years or so ago, for the trees on the ridge and in the hollow were well grown. Most of them were asalbeks, with short trunks from which a cup of stiff branches rose upwards, bearing spearhead-shaped leaves and sour black fruits. However, saplings of a less familiar, taller tree were growing among them, broader-leaved and with cherry-like clusters of pale blue berries. These, it seemed, provided more attractive provender for animals. Soon Rokh was stretching upward to crop the leaves and Rascal climbing among the branches, selecting berries and buds with his usual fastidious care.

I sat for a while, watching the two animals and enjoying the sunshine, then decided to seek for some game. It would be wise, in any case, to have my bow in full readiness, so

I strung it and set the quiver of arrows to my belt. As I made my way up the horseshoe ridge, a covey of plump partridge-like birds flew up in alarm. Like partridges, however, they did not fly far. After a short stalk, I brought one down at my first arrow-loosing. Excellent! — it should make me a good supper.

The rest of the day was passed idly. In the early afternoon I climbed the rocks above the coppice and looked out northward, but by then there was too much haze for me to see far. I clambered around for an hour or so to use up some of my energy and then, after descending, used up more of it by exercising with my sword and throwing-knives. After that I was content to laze in a sunny spot, watching birds among the trees and lizards among the rocks. It was an enjoyable day, despite the lack of human company.

At the afternoon's end I lit a small fire down in the hollow and, having plucked the bird I had shot, cooked it on an improvised spit. Accompanied by hunks of bread, its meat tasted well enough, even though a little charred in places. Afterwards I sat on a stone by the fire and watched the stars come out in the darkening sky. The flames were burning lower; I threw on a couple of dead branches and watched them take light. A bat circuited the hollow several times, flying so close by me that I saw its eyes glowing red in the firelight. As it flickered away into the night I heard the coughing bark of some hunting animal.

Whether because of that sound or for some other reason, I found myself becoming uneasy. The night seemed suddenly colder and more hostile. What was the matter? Was it merely that my loneliness was affecting me? Rascal was uneasy also; I could feel his mood changing with mine — or was his special perception altering my mood?

Rokh was standing under a tree some distance away; I saw now that his head was turning restlessly. He moved toward the fire, then seemed to change his mind and instead hobbled deeper into the shade of the trees.

My eyes followed him awhile, then shifted back toward the ridge. The moon, now almost at its fullest, was rising behind it. The trees crowning the ridge gave an odd effect, making the moon appear like a white saucer held up in the fingers of some scullery-maid, with thumb set behind and four fingers before it. I smiled at this conceit — and then stiffened. One of those finger-shadows was moving, coming toward me!

Carelessly I had set my bow down a few paces from me. With my eyes fixed upon that approaching form, I rose to my feet and went forward to pick up my weapon. The shape was resolving itself into a rider mounted on a sevdru. I could see the animal's horns, but I could not distinguish any other details. Was the rider's cloak dark, or did it merely seem so because of the brightness of the moon behind him?

Rascal made an abrupt leap and ran up onto my shoulder. His mental warning was urgent now — danger, danger! I set the arrow to my bowstring and drew it back.

Yet the rider was approaching me so slowly and so steadily that I was reluctant to loose. The moon had risen above the ridge now, but he was looming taller as he approached and its light was still masking him from me. I could discern neither his face nor the colour of his cloak, but his sword was still in its scabbard. Was he foe or was he friend?

Suddenly he addressed me — an unfamiliar voice, yet speaking not in any Rockalese tongue but in English. 'Lower your bow, lad. Ye might harm me, maybe, but ye'd be dead yourself soon enough. Look about you, lad, look about you!'

So wholly had my attention been engaged by him that I had not looked elsewhere. I had been shamefully impercipient. Other riders were converging upon me from all sides; five, six, seven of them, all in grey cloaks. How could they have come so close without my being aware of them? Though the first rider had not drawn any weapon, these others had. Between the horns of each sevdru was the band of a sasayin, drawn back at full tension. The moonlight gleamed on the sharp edges of seven sasial darts, all aimed at me.

The first rider was closer now, his hood thrown back. In the firelight, his teeth were gleaming whitely as he smiled. 'Aye, lad, ye do see now, don't ye? Little sense is there in trying to fight. You're fairly caught!'

Chapter Five

AMONG THE GREY RIDERS

Well, it was better to be captured than killed out of
hand; I had no desire to be cut to pieces by sasial
darts. Despondently I lowered my bow and returned
my arrow to its quiver, cursing my own lack of watchfulness.
Why had I kept that fire so long alight, making myself so
conspicuous to any attacker? Why had I not followed Avran's
advice and roosted up among the rocks? What a fool I had
been!

In a tongue wholly unfamiliar to me, the first man —
evidently the leader of the grey riders — gave swift orders.
My bow was taken from me, my sword, and also my belt
with its quiver of arrows and its six sheathed knives. (These
latter seemed to puzzle my captors, for I heard low-voiced
comments that, even to my uncomprehending ear, indicated
wonder.) Only then were the sasayin ribbons allowed to
slacken and the sharp sasialin returned to their sheaths.

I was not searched further. Instead, my hands were seized
and roped together behind my back. I was left standing by
the fire under the watchful eyes of two of the riders, while
others searched for the sevdru they knew must be nearby.
Rokh was found swiftly enough and his condition noted, as
was made evident when the leader spoke to me again.

'Ah, so your mount took a fall among the stones, did he?
We wondered why ye travelled so small a distance. And you
with your bright fire and all, hoping a friend might come by!'

I could see his face clearly for the first time; a lean, dark
man he was, with black hair grizzled at the temples and a
curling black moustache and beard, both trimmed in the
French fashion. So dark in colour and complexion, yet with
pale blue eyes; I did not like those eyes . . . His voice had
a caressing, lilting quality that might have been appealing

41

but somehow was not. He was no Englishman, of that I was sure, yet I did not think he could be Rockalese. An Irishman, perhaps, or a Scot?

He was speaking again now. 'Well, maybe after all a friend *did* come by; and you in such deep trouble, with the young Prince dead behind ye, killed by the beast in the tower, and your sevdru broken-legged so that there's no riding him! Well, soon we'll be taking ye along with us for a little journey. Sorry I am that it's so late in the evening, and you so tired and all, but we've a way to go. And since ye'll have to be sharing a mount with me, I'm sure ye'll not be minding, will ye now, if we make sure ye don't fall off? Sure, that would be a terrible thing to happen to a lad!' His smile was mocking.

His tone changed as he gave further swift orders, in the same unfamiliar language as before. I was seized again and my hands unbound briefly; then I was lifted bodily and set before the leader on his sevdru. My wrists were bound anew to the bases of its two brow-horns.

When I was first captured, Rascal had been on my shoulder; but he had leapt away so swiftly that he had passed unnoticed. Now, however, he was bounding up and down on the rock and chittering with indignation. The leader looked down at him in surprise.

'A strange pet ye have, lad! Some sort of monkey, is he? — I've heard tell of such creatures. Ach, well, I'm not one to sunder a man from any beast that is his; one of my men shall carry him along.'

I spoke for the first time since my capture. 'No, let him go. He'll find enough food here. He'd be merely a nuisance on the ride.'

So these men did not recognize a vasian, nor know its special abilities! Certainly they were not Sandastrians; but where *could* they be from? With all the mental concentration I could muster after so many shocks, I gave instructions to Rascal: *Go to the trees. Hide till Avran comes, then make him seek me! Haste now!* Almost on the instant, Rascal obeyed. As he hopped away into the shadows, I sensed his message of anxious farewell.

The leader spoke again; this time, though, he sounded uneasy. 'Strange it is, that the beast ups and goes just as we speak of it. Ye wouldn't be a warlock, my lad, and that creature your familiar?'

I laughed bitterly. 'If I were, do you suppose you'd have me roped to your sevdru? I'd be flying away over the treetops, for sure, and you and your men would have been blasted to cinders!'

He chuckled in response. 'Aye, that's true enough; and ye've got some spirit in ye, me boyo! Well, that's a thing I like. Time enough later for talk; we must away.'

More quick, incomprehensible orders. The fire was quenched with earth, my pack taken up by one rider and my belt and weapons, in a bundle, fixed to the saddle of another. I noticed now that all the sevdreyen bore pack-saddles only a little different from those the Sandastrians used. All save the leader's, that is; which must be why he would be carrying me, rather than one of his men. Or — since he might surely have changed saddles — was it that he did not altogether trust them, even with a prisoner?

Out of the darkened hollow we rode in single file, two riders ahead of the leader and me, the others behind us. Once on the open moor, however, the grey riders spread out into a formation like a flattened W, with the leader's mount at front centre. I could count only seven of them now; where was the eighth? Oh yes, there he was following along behind us — as a rearguard, maybe?

As minute followed minute and the minutes grew into hours, we rode across the moonlit moor in a silence that gave the ride a dreamlike — or, rather, a nightmare-like — quality. Sevdreyen are capable of very silent running; they do not need to be shod like horses, for the two hooves on each foot are circular, with a hard rim and a central, cushioning pad. The riders, wrapped in their grey cloaks, seemed more phantoms than men. Even the leader, so close behind me, was shrouded and hooded now, nor did he speak any further word.

Yet that was not all. Other, more sinister shapes were moving around and about us in the air as we rode. About the riders to left and right of me were swooping and circling the dark shapes of bats! I remembered the bat that had circuited the fire and I shivered. Had it been spying on me? What sort of men had bats as servants? Were these not men, after all, but demons? Was I being carried away to Hell?

43

A sick terror of the unknown rose up in me, clouding my thoughts and causing me to shiver with panic. Fervently and fearfully I prayed for release from this nightmare and for the preservation, if not of my body, at least of my soul!

However, nothing particular happened. The ride went on, my wrists beginning to ache and my back also, for this hunched-forward position was far from pleasant. With time and discomfort my spirits began, paradoxically perhaps, to rise again and my mind to reassert itself. The leader, at least, was no demon; why, the very idea that I might be a warlock had disturbed him! And if he was human, so also were his men. Moreover, they had not searched me thoroughly and might not do so; I had other knives hidden, about which they knew nothing. I might escape them yet!

Furthermore it was evident that, knowing nothing of any messengers, they had mistaken the poor corpse in the tower for the body of my friend. They could not know that Avran would be returning to seek me. With or without any message from Rascal — and I was doubtful whether Rascal could communicate lucidly with anyone but me — I was confident Avran would follow us. The tracks of so large a party should surely be distinguishable, even across this tussocky moor!

However, as hour followed hour and I became ever more weary, that tide of confidence ebbed. Avran might be returning only with another sevdru for me to ride, or perhaps with a couple of other men to look after Rokh. How could he hope to rescue me from eight armed riders? He was rash enough, of course, to make the attempt even against such odds — and might forfeit his own life thereby. Moreover, should I contrive to escape, I could not travel far without a mount. On these open uplands, I would be as readily discovered as a snowball on a green lawn. Soon enough, they'd either recapture me or kill me.

What direction were we travelling, anyway? Surely we should have been off these hills by now. Oh, of course, we must be heading directly eastwards, going from the Trantevrin Hills onto the broader uplands of the Sandastrian Hills — country about which I knew little.

Did these riders never tire? Would this journey never end? Into my weary mind there rose uncomfortable memories of stories I had heard, of Herne the Hunter and his host, condemned to expiate their sins by riding forever under the moon. Had I been captured by such earthbound, evil spirits? No, of course not; pull yourself together, Simon! Yet, as I hung against the sevdru's neck, my wrists throbbing, my body an ache of weariness, and as I saw the grey shapes and black bats all about me, it was hard to expel such thoughts from my mind.

When the ride did end, so utterly exhausted was I that I was scarcely aware of being lifted from the leader's mount, laid down on the ground and covered perfunctorily with a cloak. Shaken and battered though I was, with wrists and ankles bound anew, I fell straight into sleep like a stone dropped into a millpond.

We had ridden through the night and I, at least, slept through the day. The sun was already sinking in the southwest when I awoke — or, rather, was awakened. One of the grey riders was bending over me, untying my wrists, while another with a sword stood guard. I swallowed, groaned at the stiffness of my limbs and, helped by the first rider, sat up. My legs had been freed already, but my feet and ankles were throbbing from cramp. Peremptorily I was urged to stand up — I understood the gesture, not the words — but I was quite unable to do so until the first rider, grunting with impatience, had massaged my limbs back to life.

While he was doing this, I blinked my sleep-gummed eyes more fully open and looked about me. The overnight halt had been made in a gully high on a broad hill, a gully so shallow that I could see beyond it. A covert of long-leaved, spiny bushes grew in the deepest shelter, to my left, and there the sevdreyen were still feeding, with a tugging unenthusiasm that suggested harsh provender. Beyond, other hills rolled to the horizon, cloaked in coarse blue-leaved grasses and other plants so short as to afford no cover. Only the higher ridge behind me blocked part of the view, and that was to the eastward. No riders from the west could approach unseen.

Looking around, I found a scene so familiar that the last of my night fears left me. These men might be evil but at least they *were* men, not ghosts or demons from Hell! In the fashion of Rockalese soldiers, the riders had taken the pack-saddles from their mounts for use as seats or pillows. Several, indeed, were still resting, their cloaks serving as a blanket. Broad-featured, rather squat men they were, with coarse brown hair and beards, not prepossessing but nothing like so forbidding as their cloaks had made them seem. A small fire had been lit, over which a pot was boiling while two men prepared food.

Yet there *was* something odd about the scene, after all. In a normal camp there would have been talk, banter, even songs. This camp was far too silent. The men in grey — for, indeed, their tunics were of the same hue as their cloaks — seemed unrelaxed and withdrawn, quite lacking the easy friendliness that is usual among comrades travelling and working together. It was not of me that they were distrustful, but of each other.

The leader was sitting on a stone at the rim of the hollow, watching the scene in the ever-attentive fashion of one who intends to miss nothing. I was raised to my feet and walked toward him stumblingly, steadied by the reluctant arm of the first rider and with the second following watchfully. It was only about thirty paces, yet I was grateful when allowed to subside again to a sitting position at his feet.

'Well, now, Simon Vasianavar, what a sleepyhead ye are!' he said banteringly, 'Yes, ye see I know your name — such a strange name, for an Englishman! Belike ye'll be telling me your born name, for ye were given *that* one in Sandastre, were ye not? No need to be fearful, now; King Henry is far away!'

It was disturbing, not only that he knew who I was but also that he had guessed so accurately my reason for being in Rockall. 'Simon Vasianavar will do,' I said shortly. 'My old name is left far behind; why trouble with it now?'

He grinned at me. 'Ah, well, I thought ye were on the run! And sure, this is a good place to run to, as many have found before you. The Kings of England and France — aye, and the rulers of Scotland and Ireland too — can't ever reach out so far, even when striving to grasp a man! Yet ye've a new problem now, have ye not? Blithe those Sand-astrians were when you demonstrated to them the long-bow,

46

and pretty indeed your shooting is — two arrows through that thassak while it was leaping! Yet I doubt ye'll ever again find a welcome in Sandarro, with the son of the Prince dead in the tower and you off and away!'

Had the facts indeed been as he believed, I might well have feared to return to Prince Vindicon's castle; and my apparent flight would certainly have made matters worse for me. I contrived to look up at him open-mouthed, as if startled and aghast, and his smile broadened. He was a handsome man, no doubt of it, yet that smile was about as enticing to me as a cat's to a mouse.

'Aye, ye'd best be considering carefully, me young Simon! And it is time I told ye my own name. Dermot Fitzstephen I am, of Leinster once but now a soldier of the world. I'll fight for any man that can pay me in good yellow gold; and there are some on this island' — his lips twitched — 'who can do just that! Well, now, ye'll be needing a drink and a mouthful of food. Time enough to talk when you've eaten.'

He clapped his hands and motioned. At this, one of the men by the fire rose and brought me over a hunk of bread and a bowlful of broth. I was ravenously hungry; the broth was too hot to drink, but I managed well enough by dipping the bread in it and biting off hunks. The broth contained a rich mixture of nuts, meat and fruit made (as I learned later) from sun-dried cakes that were easily carried and would dissolve in water — excellent fare for a traveller. Afterwards I was given a sip of wine from a hide-covered flask. I would have liked more, but the flask was snatched away all too quickly.

While I ate, most of the other riders were eating also; but Dermot Fitzstephen and my two guards must have had their meal already, for they took nothing. The guards gave me their unrelenting attention, but Fitzstephen turned away to watch the sun going down behind the hills. Only when I had finished did he look again at me.

'Aye, so ye're what they call a fugitive from justice; and since I am one also, why cannot we be friends? Mind you, it was my own lords in Ireland that did not love me, and they my own kin, curse them for a poor-spirited bunch! Whereas your own cause, I would guess, was lost with the

47

Hotspur? Ah, I thought so! — and you so young to be fightin' and fleein'!'

He gave me a look of amused commiseration, which broadened into a smile. 'Ah, well, a man can leave bad fortune behind him. I've served Scottish lordlings who would swindle a man of his last penny and fat Flemish burghers more productive of promises than pay. But my present masters, why, they're as generous with gold as any Englishman could wish! And sure, I'm blithe to serve them in any way I can. Yet, when they desired a man that might teach the use of the long-bow, I couldn't assist them. I was born a gentleman, and that's neither a gentleman's nor an Irishman's weapon.'

He perceived that I resented this condescension, all too familiar though it was to me, for he went quickly on: 'Of course, now, maybe men think differently in England. And so, when they learned of your skill, my masters sent me along with these fellows here' — he gestured at his men — 'to, er, persuade ye into our service.'

So it was I whom the grey riders had been pursuing, and not Avran. That was news indeed!

'A fine lot of persuading you did!' I responded bitterly. 'Trussed up I was, like a sack of corn on a donkey's back. My bones still ache from it.'

He threw back his head and laughed uproariously, then said: 'Aye, well, ye're a lad of spirit; that I can see. Sure, you and me, we can be good friends. Maybe it wasn't such an easy ride for ye, but last night we needed to move fast and far — and I wasn't just sure that ye desired to accompany us! Tonight we'll be needin' to travel just as far, for we've quite a long way to go yet; but, if ye'll be sensible, mayhap we can make ye more comfortable. I've given ye the offer; will ye join us?'

'You've given me no offer at all,' I replied stoutly. 'And who are "us" anyway? Who are these nameless men that hold the purse-strings? You've told me nothing about them. The Grassads, maybe? Yet I don't think they love me too much. Rather than hire with the Grassads, I might as well have my throat cut now, for surely it'd happen later.'

He gave me a crooked smile. 'I do not serve the Grassads. Ye may have my word on that.'

I noticed again the emblem of the rising sun, stamped into

48

the leather of his boot-tops and repeated in the buckle of his sword-belt. 'No, I do not believe the Grassads would use your emblem, the emblem of that Empire of long ago. Who does?'

The smile had faded from his lips. 'Well, now, let's say that it's a group of men who would like to see southern Rockall at peace under one rule. Time enough for ye to learn their names.'

'Time enough also, then, for me to decide whether to join you! I will not commit myself to the employment of folk whose very name, whose country even, I do not know. It's not a fair offer you're making. You're asking me to give a blind commitment, and that I won't do.'

I could see that my words had put him in a quandary. When he was sent out to capture me, he and his masters had expected to be dealing with a mere prisoner, unwilling and recalcitrant maybe but capable of being coerced into obedience. However, following his discovery of what he believed to be Avran's body in the tower, Dermot Fitzstephen considered me to be in a very difficult situation and open to deals. He was astute enough to perceive that a willing colleague would be a better teacher of the art of the long-bow than any prisoner under compulsion. Yet he had not been empowered to negotiate any terms with me, of that I was sure; nor dared he divulge more than a minimum of information. He was sitting hunched forward on the stone now, the fingers of his right hand tapping his sword hilt.

'Come now,' I urged softly. 'You and I are the only two here that speak English, are we not? Surely you can tell me more?'

He glanced at me sharply. 'No, I'm not so sure . . . No, the secret is not mine alone. Ye must wait till our journey is ended. The offer will be liberal, very liberal; more gold than ye'd ever gain in England, I'll be bound! Yet I can't tell ye more; ye must wait.'

Mentally I had completed that first sentence for him. So he was not certain that we were the only English-speakers and he dared not say more, for fear of being overheard and reported as a traitor! Indeed, I had been conscious that the men watching me were watching their leader also. Was our conversation being understood and remembered?

Fitzstephen rose to his feet and prowled up and down restlessly awhile, his eyes avoiding mine. The light was fading fast now and the other grey riders were busy strapping the pack-saddles onto the backs of the sevdreyen. The little fire was out, stamped to embers.

The Irishman turned and gazed at me again, his face in shadow but his eyes gleaming palely. 'We must ride,' he said abruptly. 'Yet I see no reason why ye should be discomfortable. If I leave your hands free, will ye promise to behave?'

It was not a hard undertaking to give, for I foresaw no way of escaping while on sevdru-back, in the midst of a bunch of riders and on such open hillsides. Nevertheless I qualified it: 'Most certainly I'll pledge you my word that I'll cause you no problems during the ride.'

The same W-formation was adopted as last night. As our sevdreyen ascended southeastward out of the gully — yes, I was watching the direction carefully — a cloud of bats rose from the low shrubs to circle about us in the fading light. Almost at that moment, a nighthawk stooped down from the sky — the silver-plumaged bird that was the emblem of Sandastre. In a blur of motion, the bird slew with its talons one of the bats and carried it away. A grey rider struck upward with his sword at the hawk, but missed it entirely.

That little happening seemed to me an omen. It comforted me greatly.

Chapter Six

A NIGHT OF ALARMS

I noticed that, when Dermot Fitzstephen mounted, he spoke an order to his sevdru — '*Ksashassat!*' — which I presumed meant 'Be still!' When he wished to be moving, he said: '*Ksakeren!*' Belatedly I recalled that the starting of his sevdru yesterday had been controlled by similar words.

Since Dermot did not address me at all during the ride — nor, indeed, did any of the riders speak — I had ample time to ponder. Neither of those words was known to me; I was sure they could not be Sandastrian. Yet they *did* use the same imperative form — the 'ksa' prefix — with which I was familiar. This must be a Rockalese language, then; and it could not be Dedestan or Mentonese, for (as Enar Servessil had told me) the structure of those languages was wholly different. Was it Baroddan, perhaps? No, for that was only a variant, little more than a dialect, of Sandastrian. Could it be Arctorran, maybe, or Temeculan, or one of the several tongues of Salastre?

It was only afterwards that a second point struck me. Dermot Fitzstephen had *spoken* to his mount. Why need he do so? Surely a mental order would have been enough? Was it that he had established no mental link with his sevdru? Avran and Ilven, by their praise of my own abilities, had made it clear that those abilities were exceptional for an Englishman. Could it be that Fitzstephen did not share them? Might I succeed where he had failed? If so, then the sevdru might come to be under my command, not his!

Well, it was worth attempting. How I did this is hard to describe to a reader who has never forged a true mental link with any animal, but I must try. Suffice it to say that I reached out my thoughts to the sevdru on whose forequarters I was riding. It was a gentle reaching, as tentative as the probing of a tongue-tip into a hollow, aching tooth and with the same preparedness for rapid retraction. Very quickly I realized that the sevdru's mind was unused to such approaches, unaware even that they were possible, since its usual rider made none. However, when my approach was perceived, it was welcomed and the mental door opened. Indeed, I sensed a relief in the creature and an immediate happiness, like that of a maltreated dog who has at last received and recognized kindness.

Predictably I felt a reciprocal surge of pleasure and affection. Soon I was beginning to receive from our mount the same signals of warning, of a swerve or a slight jump necessitated by the rough terrain of the hillsides, that I would have obtained from Whitebrow or Rokh.

At first I was afraid that Dermot Fitzstephen might detect our interchange, but he did not. Indeed, I was made swiftly aware that the sevdru had never received anything other than spoken orders from him. Moreover, I was confident that Fitzstephen would not expect any rapport to be attained between his mount and me. After all, I was English, not Rockalese, and he as an Irishman could not achieve such a rapport himself.

This meant also that, though there was a certain loyalty between mount and rider, there was no strong bond. I found I knew the animal's name — Yerezinth — though Fitzstephen himself neither used, nor had ever heard, it.

After a while I tried giving a mental order, albeit a gentle one; that Yerezinth should swerve to the right. Immediately he did so; and I knew I could control him at will. This was a considerable achievement, for now I had a mount I might use if I were to escape.

There is little else to tell of that second night's ride, for it was very much a repetition of the first and across similar terrain. However, I was much more comfortable and, despite the circling bats, no longer so scared. Indeed, assured that I would be sustained by Yerezinth and steadied at need by Dermot Fitzstephen, I allowed myself to fall asleep in the saddle.

Before and after I fell asleep, the ride followed the same steady course, southeastward into the highest ranges of the Sandastrian Hills. It was a route chosen, as I realized later, to avoid the high pasturelands of Derresdavard by keeping south of them, through country where only the wild sevdreyen ranged.

I was awakened by a slackening in Yerezinth's pace, to find we were descending from a stoney ridge into a broad dell at the head of a marshy valley. On the upper skirts of this marsh was a grove of asalbeks which would furnish fodder of a sort for the sevdreyen. I was sure Dermot Fitzstephen would decide to stop here, for the valley was too open to permit any threat that assailants might approach unperceived; and so he did. He dismounted easily, lifted me down — I was pretending to be very drowsy — and called over one of the other riders.

'Simon, I fear ye're to be trussed up again,' he said almost apologetically. 'As yet, ye're not committed to us and I cannot risk trustin' ye yet. Your freedom will come soon enough, should ye decide properly; be sure of that.'

I pretended to be sleep-dazed, simulating a yawn and then nodding acquiescently as if only semi-awake. Nevertheless, when the other rider roped my wrists together before me, I contrived to hold them far enough apart to ensure those bonds were slack. I was taken into the shadow of one of the outermost ebelmeks and laid down. My ankles were tied together — again rather slackly, for the rider was too weary to be careful — and the rope looped and fastened about the base of the tree-trunk. I turned onto my side and pretended to fall into instant sleep, even before a cloak was thrown over me. The grey rider stood by me for a few minutes and then, satisfied that I was indeed slumbering, walked heavily away.

I was grateful that I had been put down in shadow, for the moon was bright. However, I did not wish to risk movement until the camp had quietened down. For the moment, the unstrapping of pack-saddles was still proceeding and sleeping-places were being chosen. It was a time, not for action, but for the testing of the mental links I had forged with Yerezinth. I concentrated hard on the instructions I needed to give him; *Eat swiftly and well, for we need to ride again soon. Be ready for a call; do not stray far from me.*

Again and again I strove to transmit that message; but it was a little complex and sevdreyen are not good at comprehending advance instructions. Had it been understood? I could not know yet. My next problem would be to free myself. However, I must not attempt this too soon, for I would surely be under regular inspection by guards and must know when.

The minutes seemed to crawl by; and yes, after twenty minutes a grey-cloaked figure, naked sword in hand, came to inspect me. As he bent over me to check that my bonds were secure, I realized it was the leader, Dermot Fitzstephen himself. I simulated the steady, quiet snore of deep sleep. Grunting in satisfaction, he straightened and walked away.

Cautiously I continued to lie still; and this was well, for I heard new footsteps. That time, however, the watcher — was it Fitzstephen again? — gave me only the briefest of inspections before turning away.

Now was my opportunity to act, but this was not to prove easy. Though there were still knives in my shoulder-sheaths, I could not raise my bound wrists far enough to reach them, wriggle though I might. However, there was my other secret. At my request, the Bristol cobbler had made a sheath for a throwing-knife in the shanks of each of my boots, the head of the knife being concealed by the turned-over boot-top. I blessed my choice of those boots, not the softer Sandastrian ones, for this journey!

Even so, it was no easy task to get at those knives, for I lay stretched out with roped limbs under the heavy cloak. It took much arduous bending and wriggling before, almost suffocated under the heavy cloth, I was in a position to grasp and turn upward my boot-top. With bound hands, the withdrawing of the knife was awkward, for it fitted tightly into its sheath. Then I dropped the knife and had to grope about for it. Scarcely had I located and grasped it when I heard further footsteps and must hastily wriggle back to my original position.

When the guard had again gone, I tried to hold the knife in such fashion as to enable me to saw through my wrist-bonds. In the end I managed this by thrusting the blade down between my two palms, gripping the handle with my left fingertips and, with motions of my right hand, rubbing the rope against the sharp edge of the blade.

It seemed an interminable time before the rope was severed;

and how I contrived to avoid cutting my wrist, I cannot imagine. Then I dropped the knife again and, even though my hands were free, took many minutes to locate it beneath the cloak. (I could have used a knife from a shoulder-sheath by then, of course; but, in my frantic gropings, that thought never occurred to me.) Once the knife was found, my ankle-bonds were discreetly cut. Then, with another patrol due, I lay back in my original position.

With relief I noticed that the sky was clouding over; in a short while, the moon would be hidden. Urgently I sent out a new call to Yerezinth: *Come toward me, slowly, quietly. Browse as you come; do not hurry.* Then, hearing the approaching footsteps of the guard, I closed my eyes and pretended again to snore. However, my nerves were tense and I had the knife in my hands, ready to be thrown at need.

No such need arose; the man seemed barely to glance at me before turning about. He would be moving away from me steadily for the next while. Since I had glimpsed no circling bats, I presumed they were not being used as additional guards; probably they were away feeding. The high-sailing moon was veiled already by thin cloud streamers; soon it would be masked by deeper cloud. The time was ripe for flight. Anxiously I waited. Would Yerezinth come?

Sevdreyen move so silently that it was his mental contact, not any sound, that told me of Yerezinth's approach. I crept out from under the cloak and arranged some fallen branches beneath it to simulate my sleeping shape. The knife was quickly returned to my boot and the boot-top folded back over it. Then, with a skip of excitement at my heart, I mounted.

From this greater height I peered out from the tree's shade. Only the one guard was pacing about and he was looking down-valley, not toward me. A fold of land to my right was already in deep shadow; if we reached it and followed it to the hill-crest, we would not be seen. Ah, the moon was diving into deeper cloud; this was the time! Quietly, Yerezinth, quietly — but swiftly now!

We were not perceived by the guard, of that I was sure. It would be a quarter-hour before he returned to inspect me again. Even then, if the moon remained cloud-covered, he might not penetrate my deception and realize I was gone.

It had not occurred to me that Dermot Fitzstephen might have stationed a second guard on the hill-crest, but so he had. Since that guard was looking out southward, I was upon him before he saw my mount and me. He raised his sword and opened his mouth to shout a warning, but I was too swift for him. I grabbed a knife from my left shoulder-sheath and threw without properly aiming. Yet I did not miss; the knife buried deep into his chest and he collapsed without uttering any cry.

Now the fat was truly in the fire! I did not know how long it would be before the time of that guard's relief, but I suspected it would be less than an hour. So soon as that, then, the pursuit might begin!

We were on a high hilltop now, with other hills about us in all directions and no moon to give any view. However, that did not concern me, for my night rides while bat-hunting had given me great confidence in sevdreyen. My mental order was, simply, *Back the way we came — and swiftly!* Even though I did not know that way, I was sure Yerezinth would find it.

Tired though he must be after so many hours of carrying a double burden and so brief a rest, Yerezinth responded magnificently. Indeed, he was the finest and strongest of the eight sevdreyen and I so small as to make him a light burden.

The questions were: How far could Yerezinth travel before he became exhausted? How readily might the grey riders find our trail in darkness? Would they use their bats to locate us? How I wished I had a nighthawk on my wrist, as on so many other night rides! Given such a hawk, I need fear no bats.

As we raced down a long, shadowed slope, a herd of wild sevdreyen started up about us. This startled me greatly but afterwards it pleased me, for their tracks would be confused with Yerezinth's. In glints of moonlight between the clouds, I saw their dark shapes scudding alongside us. Indeed, they ran with us for quite twenty minutes before turning away southeastward.

It was a night of alarms. A few miles after they had left us, Yerezinth, with a minimal warning to me, reared up and then leapt sideways. There was a vicious hiss and a dark shape launched itself at us; but Yerezinth gave another great bound and we were past the creature. It gave a yowl of anger and frustration, but it could not match our speed and soon was left behind.

Scarcely had my heart-beats calmed to a normal pace before the hunting howl of some other creature set them racing again. I glimpsed a dark shape and baleful green eyes. Fortunately, however, that creature was pursuing other prey and ran swiftly by us, away into the darkness. A fourth shock came when our rapid approach scared some other, smaller animals into rapid flight. I have no idea what they were, but their departing hoofbeats sounded as loud as a drum-roll in the quiet night.

Hour upon hour we raced onward through the short-grass hills, sometimes following a ridge, sometimes a hill flank, sometimes plunging down into a hollow or up out of one. Yerezinth never paused, never hesitated, confident of his route even in the deep darkness; for indeed, we saw little more of the moon that night. It was a wild ride and wildly exhilarating, yet it had also a strange quality of timelessness. I began to feel that my mount and I were still and that the hills were flowing toward and past us, as the foaming waters of a torrent flow past a rock in mid-stream.

At last there was a lightening in the sky behind us; dawn was upon us. The rising sun was hidden by clouds, as was the waning moon. As the light increased, rain began to fall lightly but steadily.

At first this was refreshing. Soon, however, it became chilling, for I had no cloak now. There was little shelter to be found in these bare hills and, in any case, we dared not pause. Yerezinth seemed tireless. On we sped, while the rain turned into a drizzle and then into a wet mist that hugged those high places and reduced our view to a matter of yards.

In such conditions, neither the sevdru nor I was aware that there were riders ahead till we were almost upon them. They saw us at the same moment; two men only, but with swords swiftly drawn to bar our passing. Both were cloaked and hooded against the rain, their faces hidden. Only when I heard his words: 'Halt! Who are you that rides so fast?' did I know that one of them was Avran.

Chapter Seven

THE SKIRMISH IN THE MIST

'Avran! Thank God. It's me, Simon!'

'Simon! It's a joy to see you again; but what happened? We feared the grey riders had taken you.'

'So they did. They caught me on the evening after you left. However, I was lucky, I escaped them — so far, though I fear they're pursuing me by now.'

'Are they indeed? How many of them? And how far behind?'

'Well, as you know there were eight originally, but I'm reasonably sure that I've slain one of them. Seven left, then, all armed with swords and sasayin; and I have neither sword nor bow. As to how close they are, I've no idea. I've been fleeing them for — oh, six hours or more. I fear they'll have been pursuing me for at least five of those hours.'

'We'd better turn about, then, and make all the haste we may. We were seeking you, of course. Here's your vasian under my cloak — Mekret — what do you call him? Oh yes, Rascal. We found him hiding in the trees and he acted as our guide. He led us toward you, straight as a die. Whenever we diverted from your trail, he uttered indignant cries till we found it again!'

And there indeed was Rascal, clambering up onto Avran's shoulder, squeaking with ecstatic joy. I held out my arms to him and he leapt into them, from sevdru to sevdru, as lightly and accurately as a squirrel between branches. Soon he was on my shoulder and his happy croon delighting my ear.

The other rider had thrown back his hood. He was sandy-haired and bearded, lean-faced and with the cobweb of wrinkles that are produced by years of hard weather. His eyes were blue and merry.

'Avran is too distracted to introduce me,' he asserted

cheerfully, 'so I'll do so myself. Lednar Estantesec at your service.'

As I rode closer to exchange hand-clasps, Avran said: 'Cousin Lednar is a hunter and knows these hills well. Mayhap he'll tell us what we might do to evade the grey riders — if there *is* anything to be done, other than fleeing from them!'

Lednar considered briefly, then replied: 'I think we must rely on flight. These hills afford no safe refuges. Moreover, Avran, you'll recall that we sent cousin Esenar back to seek aid. I'm certain that, by now, there must be quite a party of friends with weapons on their way to join us. We must trust that they do so before the grey riders catch us.'

'So be it. Yet I wish the day were clearer. This accursed mist is the very worst of all conditions in which to keep watch for riders in grey cloaks! Moreover, I'm concerned about your mount, Simon. You've ridden him far already and, strong though he must be, he can't go on forever. Well, all we can do is to keep riding and hold our hopes high!'

We rode along westward into the mist, maintaining a steady pace. Avran was on my left and Lednar on my right. Both of them were anxious for an account of my last two days. In particular, they desired a description of the grey riders, but what I told them merely added to their puzzlement.

'You're perfectly correct, Simon,' said Avran. 'They cannot be Baroddans; you'd have picked up some phrases, at least. Repeat those two words again, please!'

I repeated the two words of command given to his sevdru by Dermot Fitzstephen.

'*Ksashassat, ksakeren*,' Avran echoed reflectively. 'No, they mean nothing to me — or to you either, Lednar? The Temeculan people and the Arctorrans speak different variants of Sandastrian; so do the Fachnese and the Salatrins, for that matter. Yet there are other peoples in Salastre. The northern Salastrian tribes speak a language called Serren, like to Sandastrian and yet unlike. Then there are the Peredins and Dupratnese, who live in lands beyond Arcturus down in the southeasternmost corner of Rockall. They have their own languages, understood by few outsiders; indeed, I doubt if there's a single person in Sandastre who knows those tongues.'

He paused reflectively, then continued: 'I can only presume

60

this must be another Arctorran plot. As you know already, Simon, the Arctorrans have long wished to be masters of all southern Rockall. They might well have recruited these peoples — whoever they may be — as allies. There are three Peredin earldoms, Selettnar, Zufrendina and Presetécala if I recall correctly, all three extremely reluctant adherents of the King of Salastre. The men of Duprata have never acknowledged any master. They've fought both with and against the Arctorrans in bygone wars; I've no concept of their present allegiance. Yet this is all most surprising. Enar Servessil's network of intelligence is usually reliable, but we've been given no least indication of any new Arctorran scheming.'

'Might it be our old friends the Ranverems?' Lednar suggested. 'As we all know, they've long had imperial ambitions. Following the downfall of the Grassads, Ranverevard may be perceiving a new opportunity.'

'Oh yes, the Ranverems are ambitious enough. Yet why should they wish to seize Simon, when he's been teaching the long-bow to all we Sandastrians already? That makes no sense. And why need they despatch a party of foreigners to capture him, when their own people know this land so much better and would be so much less conspicuous?'

'Mayhap it was their supposed allies, acting unbeknown to the Ranverems,' I suggested. 'You'll remember how the Baroddans sought to murder me, even though allied to the Grassads? Dermot Fitzstephen, of course, is a mere hireling; yet it was quite evident that he considered his own men capable of betraying him. Mayhap they're all striving to cheat one another; mayhap these Dupratnese or Peredins want the long-bow for themselves.'

Avran sighed. 'Well, 'tis a pretty problem. We must wait and hope for more information. A further question is how they succeeded in locating you so speedily. I must confess that I believed we were safe from the grey riders for several days, at least. After those two Brantvut cousins had substituted for us and after the precautions we took to hide our tracks when leaving the valley, I was confident that we'd evaded any pursuit.'

I had considered this question already. 'Yet you know, Avran, we quite mistook the purpose of that pursuit. Both of us — and Kerem Brantvut also — assumed it was you

61

that they were pursuing, not I! Consequently, Kerem ensured that the substitute chosen for you should resemble you very closely indeed. Eledrin Brantvut not only looked like you but, if anything, talked even more! On the other hand, we thought it sufficient that my substitute should be merely vaguely like me in appearance. Lerened Brantvut is my size, certainly, and dark-haired also, but that's where the resemblance ends. As soon as any of the grey riders obtained a good view of him, the deception would fall flat. I would guess that happened on the evening after we slipped away — at the very next inn.'

Avran considered this idea. 'Yes, probably you're correct. Yet even then, how did they contrive to find you so quickly? They must have begun pursuing us that same night.'

'I don't know. Mayhap their bats sought for me and found me by the tower? Mayhap the riders have night sight so good that they can read our tracks in darkness? After all, they do seem to be creatures of the night. Or mayhap they used magic?'

'They cannot be very brilliant trackers, you know,' Lednar commented thoughtfully. 'After all, it is evident that they neither noticed Avran's tracks across the hills nor even recognized that you two had camped together on the night after your adventure in the tower. It must have been either the bats or magic that found you, friend Simon.'

Avran made a wry face. 'I must confess not to liking either of those ideas much! Yet Simon, I remain profoundly grateful that you escaped them. We'll strive to ensure that you're not taken again.'

After that, we rode along in silence. The rain dwindled to a drizzle and soon ceased altogether, but there was no break either in the cloud overhead or in the mist about us. Sometimes that mist thinned so that we could see before us for almost a furlong, sometimes it thickened until we could scarcely see beyond the noses of our sevdreyen. It was densest in the hollows, whereas on the ridges there was a slight stirring in the air that suggested the beginnings of wind. Perhaps the air might clear imminently, but that was not happening yet.

Ere another hour had passed, it was becoming painfully evident to me that Yerezinth was tiring at last. Since he had carried a double burden eastward for at least six hours and then, after a rest of scarcely an hour, borne a lighter one westward at a greater pace for at least nine more hours, the sevdru's stamina had been already truly remarkable. His pace dropped from a brisk run to a trot, then to a walk.

Avran and Lednar slowed their mounts to keep pace with us, but they were exchanging anxious glances. We must keep going as long as we could, that was evident. However, at this diminishing rate of progress, the grey riders must inevitably be gaining on us, unless they had lost my trail among the tracks of the wild sevdreyen. I mentioned this possibility, but my two comrades were doubtful.

'Certainly that might have confused them, slowed them down even,' responded Lednar thoughtfully, 'but, when confronted with so many tracks, any intelligent hunter would watch for the odd track striking off on its own. The darkness must have caused them problems, though. Even in daylight, it's difficult enough to follow a solitary track over the rough ground of these hills. It would be very difficult in moonlight and last night was one of cloud. Indeed, though I don't question that these grey riders must have good night sight, I believe they'd have found it pretty nigh impossible. As for the bats, why, they couldn't fly fast enough to catch you when you were riding apace — and I cannot picture a bat, however well trained, reading tracks! I trust and believe we have a good lead on the grey riders. Our problem is that it must now be dwindling.'

For a further hour and a half, we continued to ride steadily northwestward — steadily but oh! so slowly. The mist seemed decidedly whiter; the time must be approaching noon and the sun high in the sky, if we could but see it. Instead we proceeded doggedly on through the opaque, moist cloud that was clinging to those high tops, our nerves at high tension in the apprehension that, at any moment, the grey riders might burst out of the mist upon us. Both Avran and Lednar had unsheathed their swords again; their glances behind were ever more frequent.

Poor Yerezinth was extremely game, but he was moving even more slowly. When I dropped from the saddle to walk beside him, our pace was scarcely affected; nor did the lack of any burden appear to benefit the sevdru, so exhausted was he.

We were still travelling over the blue grasses of the Sandastrian Hills, but our altitude was lower now and the terrain a series of gentle rises and steeper descents, like stacked slices of bread that had toppled over. After a hasty consultation with his cousin, Avran announced that we must be only a few leagues south of Trantevar.

'I believe we should strike northward after all,' he said. 'There's a chance we might meet some other travellers. What is your opinion, Lednar?'

His cousin considered. 'The decision is not an easy one. If only it were sunny, I would concur; but, in this mist, we might pass within only a few paces of other riders and not see them. Moreover, if we divert from our outward trail, our friends are not going to locate us so readily — and, after all, they furnish our best hope. In these conditions, we might be slain at the very gates of Trantevar without anyone in the town being even aware of it.'

However, I was becoming increasingly concerned about Yerezinth. His steps were ever more stumbling and he was beginning to weave in his walk.

'Yerezinth is almost done,' I said decisively, 'and your own mounts are too tired, I'm sure, to carry a double burden. We have no choice; we must find a refuge.'

Lednar drew in his breath, then let it out slowly. 'Very well,' he said reluctantly. 'I can call to memory no good shelter, but there ought to be rocks somewhere over to our left where we might make a stand at need. I'll ride ahead and seek out the way. Wait for me here.' His sevdru and he hastened off into the mist.

While we waited, I caressed Yerezinth's muzzle and ears and talked to him softly. Avran sheathed his sword, leapt down from his mount and began unfastening the straps that held his bowstave in place.

'You should not be weaponless, Simon,' he said briskly, 'and you're a much better bowman than I. Please take this. Have you your own bowstring still? Good; but you'll require my arrows, of course.'

Having no belt, I fastened the quiver to Yerezinth's saddle before bending and stringing the bow. I did this somewhat reluctantly, for no sensible archer keeps his bow strung in such moist weather. Still, it felt comforting to be armed again with a weapon more effective than my knives! Avran's bow was slightly larger and heavier than my own; I flexed it a few times to become used to its weight, for such small differences are crucial to accuracy. Then I gave my attention again to Yerezinth.

It was fully fifteen minutes before Lednar rejoined us. 'We're considerably further east than I thought — curse this fog! Yet I've found us a refuge — and a better one than I remembered. Follow me and I'll show you.'

Even so brief a rest had given Yerezinth some measure of extra strength. He stepped out quite briskly as, with the bow on one shoulder and Rascal on the other, I followed Lednar's sevdru into the wall of mist. Avran, mounted again and with drawn sword in hand, had dropped a few paces behind. Soon I realized we were following a shallow declivity upward, a scatter of stones between tufts of spiky marsh-grass suggesting it might become a stream-bed in still wetter weather. The slope grew steeper and the stones larger, with water trickling between them. I was having to watch my footing and poor Yerezinth was flagging again.

The mist moved about us and, in a sudden shift, thinned. Ahead of us was a broad ridge from which a bite had been taken by some past landslip. There was a little patch of marshland about a spring and, above the spring, what seemed at first to be an irregular crag of limestone extending up onto the crown of the ridge.

When we drew closer, this resolved itself into two components. Atop the ridge was the tumbled ruin of a building. Immediately beneath it, and just above the marshy spring, was the tiny quarry from which the blocks of limestone used in making that building must have been cut. It was as if a giant fingernail had been pressed against the ridge, hollowing out the quarry and squeezing upward the rickle of stones that was the ruin. As we skirted the marsh and rode up into the quarry, the mist swirled back and became again opaque.

Lednar dismounted. 'We can leave the sevdreyen here,' he informed us, 'but we ourselves must climb up higher. I don't know what the old building was — an old sun temple from pagan days, maybe — but it surmounts the highest point hereabouts. The land falls away beyond into the valley of a stream that feeds the Dalirond. Quite an extensive view there

65

would be, on a clear day; but in these conditions . . . Well, the best we can contrive is to roost in the ruin and be watchful.'

The little quarry was spacious enough, not only to contain our three mounts but also to conceal them from view from below. Yerezinth walked unsteadily into its innermost recess and sank to his knees, resting his muzzle against the stone; I had never seen a sevdru so visibly exhausted and my heart went out to him. The other two beasts, Avran's Gedreylen and Lednar's mount, moved in beside him but stayed watchfully on their feet. They understood the peril as well as we.

At the back of the quarry, a flight of steps had been cut into the rock, enabling an easy ascent to the ruin — easy for men but impossible, I guessed, for a sevdru. The collapsed building had been circular in plan. Its walls had been high and thick, like those of a fortress, but there was a square black stone at the centre that had surely served as an altar; this must indeed have been a temple. There had been a doorway on its northern side, but its lintels had fallen in and there were large gaps in the walls themselves. If you bunch your five fingers together, leaving an inch of space at centre, you will see roughly what the ruin looked like and how big, relatively, were those gaps. The highest stretches of the wall — your three middle fingers — were on the northern and western sides, the two lower stretches on the southern and eastern sides, immediately above the quarry. The sevdreyen would warn us of any approach from those two flanks; it was the northern and western sides that we must guard.

Lednar stationed himself in the northern gap, where the gateway had been, Avran took up position in the western gap, while I scrambled up onto the wall between them, taking the bow and quiver with me. I seated myself on the topmost stone, with Rascal perched beside and below me. Thereafter the four of us gazed outward into the mist, waiting for the assault we were sure must come.

Despite this watchfulness, our pursuers were upon us almost before we knew it. I do not know how they found us, but I suspect they had simply assumed me to be heading directly for Trantevar and had taken a line that would intersect such a route. Certainly, since they did not come from the quarry side, they could not have been following our tracks. Moreover, it was soon evident that they thought me to be still alone.

Rascal was aware of them first, but a moment later I saw them also. The seven grey riders seemed to materialize out of the mist, as if its menace had been given substance. They converged upon the tower, each man hooded and silent, each with drawn sword in hand. No, they had not noticed Avran and Lednar; their attention was wholly upon me.

The rider closest below me threw back his hood. 'Ah, I see that we have treed our marten!' he called up mockingly; yes, it was Dermot Fitzstephen. 'Simon, Simon, what a mischievous nuisance ye are — killing one of my men, stealing my sevdru and all! Well, your games are over now. Better come down, like a good boy!'

'I'm sorry, gentle sir,' I shouted back, 'but I've decided not to enter your service. I fear the opportunities are not sufficiently attractive to tempt me. Please don't trouble to wait, for I won't be riding with you.'

He laughed shortly. 'We'll see about that! Truly, Simon, I'd advise ye to come down. I'd hate to have to — er — hurt ye.'

He spoke a quick order and I saw several of the riders fitting sasial darts to the sasayin between the brow-horns of their sevdreyen. However, that did not worry me much, for I knew Dermot was seeking to take me alive. Moreover, I was aware that sasayin darts could not be shot steeply upward with any great accuracy.

I stood up, balancing easily on the wall, so that they could see my drawn long-bow. 'My regrets to you, Master Fitz-stephen, but my decision is final. Better go away; for my part, I'd hate to have to hurt *you*!'

Quite evidently Dermot was greatly startled by the sight of my weapon. Shouting some brief, incomprehensible order, he wheeled his mount about, donning his hood again, and all seven riders went back into the mist like fading shadows. Yet I was sure they were not done with me.

Nor were they. Suddenly there were again five riders in view, all of them coming toward me with sasayins drawn down and back. So they would shoot me from my perch, would they? My arrow was already at the string. I aimed and loosed, the rider directly below me toppling from his sevdru. There was a hum of sasial darts; one pinged against a stone close to my feet, the others fell amply short.

Already I had fitted another arrow to my bow. This second shot was less accurate; I missed the rider at whom I had aimed, but I hit his mount. It staggered and collapsed sideways, impaled through the neck. Its rider was thrown heavily. As the sevdru fell, two bats detached themselves from its saddle and winged away into the greyness.

There came another whizzing sound as three more sasial darts were loosed at me. One plucked at my sleeve and a second flew past my shoulder; I have no idea where the third went. It was stupid of me, still to be standing erect and making so excellent a target! I dropped into a crouch and, as I did so, loosed my third arrow. A clean miss; but the remaining riders were wheeling away again, back into the mist. The man whose sevdru I had slain had risen and was hobbling after them. Easily might I have killed him, but I let him go. After all, he was in flight.

Belatedly I became aware of the clash of swords below me. While I had been engaged, the two other riders had ridden into the gaps on either side of my wall, unexpectedly to encounter Avran and Lednar. One had been so completely taken unaware by Lednar's attack that he was dead already and his sevdru wandering loose within the ruin.

The other rider had been warier. Not only had he fought off Avran's assault, but he had driven my friend backward into the ruin. It is hard indeed for a man on foot to fight one who is mounted.

As I watched, Avran backed against the black altarstone and seemed to stumble. My heart leapt in anxiety for him and I set an arrow to string hastily. However, all was well. As the grey rider bore down on him, Avran leapt forward and struck upward with his sword. Sandastrians hate to kill sevdreyen, but Avran had to equalize the contest if he were to survive.

The sevdru reared and fell backward, but its rider leapt nimbly clear. In a moment he was crossing swords with Avran again.

At that point I had to turn away, for I must watch out for the other riders. I turned not a moment too soon, for

68

already they were converging upon me. This time they were not relying upon sasayin. Instead, weapons of some other kind were gleaming in their upraised hands — short javelins, surely! So, in this assault, they were intending not merely to maim, but to kill me!

Holding my bow almost horizontally I loosed another arrow, then ducked down. A javelin passed over me with a vicious swish, while another clattered against the stones. Two of the riders swung away, back into the mist again; the third lay dead below me, his sevdru running free.

I glanced back into the tower. Avran and his opponent were evenly matched. Their swords clashed in a brisk cut-and-thrust sequence bewildering to the eye, but neither seemed able to penetrate the guard of the other. Lednar had turned away and was again on watch at the gap in the wall.

Almost at that moment, with the suddenness with which such events happen in high country, the mist lifted and faded, like smoke blown away in a wind-gust. As the sun broke through, I looked westward and gave a shout of joy. Yes, there were two grey riders still on their mounts, with a third on foot beside them. However, as the landscape was unveiled, I could see in the valley beyond and below them a group of at least thirty other riders, coming apace toward us. Surely these must be Sandastrians, by their colourful garb — and, equally surely, they must be friends!

The grey riders saw them also. The man on the ground was given a hasty hand up on to the mount of one of his fellows and the two sevdreyen, one now with a double load, raced away eastward. The two other sevdreyen that were wandering loose hesitated, tossed their horns, and followed.

The rising of the mist had startled the battlers in the ruin. Avran and his assailant had leapt apart, swords still upraised. At my shout, both of them looked upward.

'Our friends are coming!' I called. 'Our troubles are over!'

Lednar, sword in hand, joined Avran and they turned questioningly upon Avran's opponent. The grey-clad man lowered his sword in seeming surrender and they relaxed — too soon, for the man leapt suddenly away, ran to the sevdru of his fallen comrade and vaulted onto its back. A shouted order and the sevdru was running at speed, not toward my friends but toward the unguarded eastern gap.

The rider and his mount cascaded — there is no other word for that descent — down into the quarry, between Avran's sevdru and Lednar's. Viciously the rider struck out right-handedly with his sword, felling Lednar's poor beast; then he was splashing through the marsh and speeding away after his already fleeing comrades.

The menace of the grey riders was a thing of mist and darkness; the bright sunlight diminished them. As I watched them riding away in defeat, it was not merely increasing distance that caused them to shrink in my vision.

Chapter Eight

A SOJOURN IN TALESTANT

The approaching party had speeded up on sighting me. I waved to them and gestured toward the fleeing grey riders, but it was not necessary. The Sandastrians had divided already. Twenty set off at full pelt in pursuit, while the ten others continued more sedately toward the ruined temple. Seizing the bow and quiver, I clambered down from the wall to join my friends.

During the fight, Rascal had wisely kept clear of me and hidden himself, but now he leapt onto my shoulder, crooning rapturously. Avran gave us a crooked smile.

'It was well that the mist lifted, Simon; my opponent was a better swordsman than I. Your friend Dermot Fitzstephen himself, I presume?'

I had known this from the moment Dermot shouted his order to the sevdru. 'Yes, indeed; but Lednar, I'm grieved to tell you that he struck down your beast as he rode away. I hope she's not badly injured.'

'She's dead,' Lednar said quietly. 'She was a friend of many years and I shall miss her.'

So it was true, a rider did know immediately when his sevdru was slain — for Lednar had not looked down into the quarry. He sighed, then went on: 'Yet we must give thanks to God that, against odds of numbers and weapons, we three are not merely alive but unhurt.'

'We owe much to Simon's marksmanship, I suspect, since only two riders reached these walls. How many did you account for, friend?'

'Well, I brought down three; but one was not injured, for he was able to ride away.'

'And you finished another, Lednar, whilst the best I could manage was to kill that unfortunate animal.' Avran gestured

71

at the dead sevdru. 'I hated having to do it, but Dermot would have ridden me down otherwise. Well, let's sally forth and meet our friends.'

The ten approaching riders were understandably unsure of their reception and each rode sword in hand. However, as soon as they saw us there was a chorus of joy and a swift sheathing of weapons. Their leader was burlier than Lednar, but otherwise so much like him that I recognized at once Esenar Estantesec. Seven of the others were Estantesecs also, and there were two Derresdems in the party; I remember all their names, but there is no need to recount them.

Within minutes we were seated on fallen blocks of stone in the sunshine, sharing a repast of dried meat, bread and fruit. It was almost a full day since I had eaten; I was voraciously hungry, but I welcomed even more the wine that was shared so generously. Nor were our sevdreyen neglected. One of the Estantesecs went away to cut and bring fodder for Yerezinth and Zembelen, while another fetched them water from the spring.

Over the meal Avran recounted our adventures, paying me tributes so excessively generous that several times he caused me to blush. There was discussion about the identity of the grey riders, but no new suggestions were forthcoming. Afterwards, a close examination was made of the bodies and accoutrements of the three who had been slain, in the hope that this might furnish useful information. It did not. The three men were personally unknown to the Sandastrians and not sufficiently distinctive in colouring or build to be of any obvious origin. They carried no papers and, apart from the rising-sun emblem stamped into their boot-tops and repeated on belt-buckles and cloak-clasps, bore no identifying marks.

The examination of the two dead sevdreyen and their gear was no more informative, but it did furnish me with unexpected good fortune. The beast slain by my arrowshot from the wall chanced to be bearing the bundle containing my belt and weapons. Moreover, my bowstave had survived the sevdru's fall unbroken. With particular relief I resumed my belt, with its array of sheathed knives, for these were virtually irreplaceable. Though one knife, of course, was lost, I had twelve again, including the little Italian knife my tutor had given me. It was a pleasure also to have back my own sword and

72

quiver of arrows. However, my pack, with the good brown pelican I had bought in Bristol, was never found.

While our investigations were in progress the two Derresdems had ridden away, to follow and make contact with the party pursuing the grey riders. The other eleven of us decided to stay where we were for that night. In the bright sunshine, the old temple on its hilltop was a pleasant enough place. When evening came, there was cheerful talk and singing around a bright fire. If the temple held any ghosts, they did not trouble our sleep.

The next morning was one of sunshine and dew-sparkle, making the hills continue to seem a friendly place; it was only in mist that they became alien and hostile. As we breakfasted, two messengers arrived from the pursuing party, bringing a captured sevdru and news.

The animal, it seemed, was one of the two whose riders I had killed, the other having been taken over by the grey rider whose sevdru had been slain. I had thought that the Estantesec party would have caught up speedily with the fleeing grey riders, but of course they also had been riding through the night; pursuers and pursued were thus evenly matched and the gap between them had not closed.

Just before nightfall yesterday the grey riders had divided, two heading southeastward and two to the northeast. The Estantesec party had likewise divided, the two messengers being sent back at that point. The messengers had met and directed onward the Derresdems; then they had rested for a few hours before coming to the ruins.

Their arrival, therefore, left us still uncertain as to the fate of the grey riders, but it did furnish us with a mount for Lednar. The captured sevdru was a male, as grey in hue as the riders' cloaks. Lednar tried him and pronounced him satisfactory, but he was clearly not much enthused by his new acquisition. However, he managed well enough when, in mid-morning, we rode away. The two messengers, with two other Estantesecs, were left resting by the ruins; later they would go east to rejoin their colleagues.

It was a relaxed and merry ride that day. After sixteen hours of recuperation, Yerezinth was full of energy again and touchingly affectionate. With Rascal crooningly content on the pack-saddle behind me and Avran chattering happily to

73

his cousins close or distant, I felt wholly free of the tensions that had gripped me during three frightening days. Once again I could notice the birds, the flowers and the little lizards among the rocks, enjoy the sunshine and feel the pleasure of travelling through new country. I had no particular desire to talk, but I found myself humming as cheerfully as Rascal.

There was no reason now to go to Trantevar and we did not even glimpse that town. Around midday, however, we turned north and began the leisurely descent into the valley of the Dalirond. I saw many trees below us, appearing so big that I presumed they must be already close. However, though they stood ever taller before us, we seemed to take a surprising time in reaching them . . . Oh, of course! These must be the huge trees of which Avran had spoken. How high had he said they were? A hundred ells — why, that was three hundred and seventy-five feet! Surely no trees could be so tall?

Yet, as they towered ever higher before and then about us, I admitted to myself that Avran had not exaggerated. Truly these trees were giants, their very trunks as large in circumference as a church tower — and so much taller! Their bark was thick and of a creamy-brown colour, full of little holes, like the crust which forms on solidifying honey. (Later I found that it was strangely soft and yet resilient; one could hit it hard without injury to one's fist and without leaving any marks.) The lowest branches were high overhead and, since the great trees did not crowd one another, there was not only space, but even sunlight between them. We rode through a dapple pattern of lightness and shade, with plants and smaller trees crowding the sunnier spaces.

In the glades hasedain were grazing, under the watchful eyes of herd-boys whose merry whistles and cheerful greetings enlivened our passage. Twice I saw fallen trunks that had been turned into hasedain-sheds and several times we passed hasedu-drawn carts made from hollowed-out half-trunks. In the bigger glades there were padin much like those on the flanks of Sandarro hill. However, each was built wholly from wood, each decorated by careful carpentry into elaborate geometric or natural patterns, and each painted in cheerful

74

colours, green, scarlet, yellow, brown or azure blue. They were the gayest houses that ever I had seen.

'I like these padin,' I observed to Avran. 'Yours must be a happy people, to live in such habitations and to maintain them so well. Yet, if you were attacked, what would happen? Are there no fortresses, no strong-points, in Estantegard?'

Avran laughed. 'Why, our strong-points are all about you! No, I don't mean the padin; I mean the trees. Those are our defensive towers, our refuges from aggressors. There are ladders up them, tunnels in them, platforms high in their branches, lookout points at their tops. And you must understand also that an invader could not even use fire against us. The bark, the very wood of these trees is proof against flames. Only the lesser vegetation would burn; our trees, our residences even, would be safe enough. It is many years since any enemy entered the forests of Estantegard and, believe me, they gained much pain but little profit!'

'Why don't you abandon your castles, then, and grow such trees everywhere? If you did, presumably all of Sandastre would be impregnable!'

He laughed. 'I doubt that; the ingenuity of evil and ambitious men is boundless! Yet it wouldn't work, anyway. These trees, the great pevenekar, will grow only in the lands about Lake Vanadha. We've tried planting their seeds elsewhere; they sprout, but they never flourish. You'll discover that their seeds are tiny and even the cones are no bigger than the end of your thumb. Odd, to think something so mighty can grow from something so very small.'

I was remembering my early days in Sandarro. 'It was these forests, then, that your artists were remembering when they decorated the fifth level of your father's castle?'

'Yes, of course; and that is why we Estantesecs chose to have our rooms there. When we are so far from our own lands, those corridors make us feel at home. Yet not all the peoples of my vard live in these forests. Some live in the hill country north of Lake Vanadha — and not even in Sandastre, but in Denniffey and Pravan. They're venturesome people — they need to be, in those troubled lands. And they, Simon, will be very useful to us when we venture on northward.'

For some time we had been riding along a road through

75

the big trees — but it was not a straight, cobbled track like the old Roman roads that still traversed the moors near my home, nor yet one made of cut and fitted stones like those about Sandarro. Instead, this road was made of logs hewn from lesser trees, set at the level of the surrounding forest humus and laid transversely to the line of the road itself — if one might call it a 'line', for the road meandered intricately about and between the massive boles of the peveneks. If the trees were to become strong-points, such a road would bemuse and bring many hazards to any invader. Certainly it was not designed for folk in a hurry!

Eventually the road began to swing toward the north, not in a single turn but in a series of curves. I noticed that it was beginning to rise above the surrounding land — or, rather, that the road was maintaining its level and the land falling away. We passed through a belt of lesser trees, then into open meadowlands with many grazing hasedain, the road rising ever higher above those fields. Soon we were ascending a steep ramp leading to a broad bridge. As we traversed it, the waters of the Dalirond sparkled beneath us in the sunshine. A little scarlet, spear-billed bird, much like a kingfisher, flew upstream with the speed of an arrow.

'Why is this bridge built so high?' I asked. 'Why, we must be five full ells above the water!'

It was Lednar who answered. 'On a sunny day like this, yes, it must seem strange indeed. But picture to yourself that you are here instead on a day of storms, with pevenekar being brought down into the Dalirond by lightning or by the undermining of river banks. Such great logs, floating downstream, would sweep away any bridge of lower span — as, indeed, our ancestors found, at much cost in effort!'

'And you must understand, Simon, this bridge is made from the trunks of just two pevenekar,' contributed the rumbling voice of Esenar. 'My grandfather described to me how it was done. They built two sloping mounds of earth from either side of the Dalirond, when the river was at summer ebb. Then the trunks were tugged and heaved up till they met in mid-river and could be bound together. It took much effort, but the bridge has lasted, why! eighty years and more already. See, we're approaching midpoint now. That's the line where the trunks are joined.'

76

Beyond the bridge and the meadowlands, the road forked into three. The two cousins and we took the west fork and were quickly back among the great trees again, but the other Estantesecs bade us farewell here, four going north and two east to seek homes nearby. Nor were we far from the ending of our own journey. Twenty minutes of steady jogging followed, with the big trees ever fewer and farther apart until we were again among lesser trees. Mostly these were the slim-leaved estelens that the Estantesecs chose long ago as emblem for their vard, in modest preference to the giant peveneks. Already the estelens were in yellow bud, promising the golden glory of their spring flowering. Many sevdreyen browsed contentedly among them. Ever cheerfully at the call of their masters or mistresses, they required no herd-boys to keep them from straying.

We were riding slowly upward now. Ahead was a flat-topped hillock with a group of padin set upon it — two, three, no, five of them — arranged in stellate pattern about a central, large structure that seemed to be a sort of hall. The arrangement was reminiscent of the plan of Sandarro Castle, but here were no stone defence-works: instead, these wooden houses were gay with paint, sky-blue, red and gold, as cheerful as booths at a fair and about as menacing!

Avran drew his sword, tossed it high in the air, caught it by the hilt and flourished it. 'Home at last — truly home, after so many years! Here, my family lived for centuries before they became princes in Sandarro and here we'll return when we shed the burden of ruling. Welcome to Talestant, Simon!'

As we rose up the last rise, I saw beyond the padin a steep grassy descent, a curve of brown sand, and the blue waters of a great lake — Lake Vanadha.

It chanced that, though Ilven had taken me on visits to shops and inns in Sandarro, I had neither stayed in nor even entered any typical padarn — that is, one used as residence by a family. I cannot call it a house, for a padarn is more than that. Rather, it is like a group of small connected houses, set not in a row as are so many English cottages, but in a circle about a central open space. At opposite sides are two gateways, closed at need by massive doors. Normally the outer wall is high and windowless. At the top of that wall is a steep, outwardly-sloping rampart and within this is a circular walkway extending all the way round the padarn, on which defenders may patrol at times of need. Within the walkway, a roof slopes gently inward, with regularly spaced grooves that convey rainwater down into a gutter. The rainwater then drains down into two large, covered tanks, one for humans and one for beasts, furnishing an ample drinking-water supply for times of siege. Altogether, the padarn is a defensive design; even the garden at centre, stocked as it is with vegetable beds, fruit-trees and fodder-bushes for sevdreyen, is a part of that design.

The padin of the region about Lake Vanadha accord in general with that pattern, but the differences are significant. The circular walkway is bounded upon its outer side only by a fence, not by a solid rampart. Moreover, it has seats at intervals, so that its inhabitants may be at ease while enjoying the view. There are windows in the outer wall, with many little panes of thin, polished horn to admit the light and yet keep out cold winter winds. The gardens contain more flowers than feed-plants and the padin never have gates. Of course, they are inhabited only when the land is at peace; at times of war, as Avran had told me, the Estantesecs and their neighbours take refuge in the great trees. All in all, whilst the padin of Sandarro are pleasant enough, those of Estantegard have a joyousness and lightheartedness of design that quite charmed me.

Whether in Sandarro or on the shores of Lake Vanadha, each padarn is divided into a number of units, set about the central garden like the spokes of a cartwheel. Each unit, or aspadarn, is comparable with an English town-dweller's house of two storeys. The ground floor has a kitchen and retiring room at the back beside the outer wall and a living room on the garden side, whilst the second floor has three or more bedrooms and is connected to the kitchen by a steep staircase or ladder. However, in sunny weather, life is largely lived in the garden, where there are tables and seats.

Most often a padarn belongs to a single large family, grandparents living in two of the aspadin, their children and grandchildren in the others. Sometimes one padarn may be shared by two or more smaller families or by a group of unmarried men or women.

In an English castle, only the nobility have private quarters and even they must spend much of their lives in the hall. A padarn, in contrast, gives a choice of communal or private activities to all that live in it.

The padarn belonging to Avran's own family was one of the two on the lakeside. Since the prince's family must necessarily reside in Sandarro, it was used only during periodic summer visits and taken care of by the families in the neighbouring padin. In midwinter, the time of our visit, it had long been closed up; nor did we intend to stay in Talestant long enough to justify its being opened for us.

Instead, we resided with Lednar and Esenar Estantesec in a padarn on the forest side of Talestant. We were welcomed by their grandparents (great-uncles and aunts of Avran and Ilven), all four healthy and hearty; by Esenar's wife and six lively children; and by two other brothers and their families. Since Lednar the hunter was unmarried, it was in his aspadarn that we slept, though all our meals were taken in other aspadin.

These were cheerful, energetic and industrious people, whom I came to like very much. Yet, in my English fashion, I considered it strange and wonderful that members of the ruling family of Sandastre should be content to live so far from that land's capital city and so simply. When Avran told me that both great-uncles had formerly held high positions in Sandarro and that Esenar had been a quincentenar in the army of that land, my wonderment only increased.

I was delighted to find Rokh browsing cheerfully among the estelen trees close by. He had been brought back there by cart, I learned. His broken leg had been examined and redressed by Esenar's wife, a skilled animal doctor, and promised to heal wholly within a few weeks.

Yet, fond though I was of Rokh, I could not await the healing of his forelimb; my quest was too urgent for that. Moreover, I had Yerezinth now. Remembering my indcbtedness to Lednar, I offered Rokh to the hunter. This was a transfer of ownership that delighted our friend, since the grey rider's sevdru had proved uncongenial to him — and it was accepted readily enough by Rokh.

We stayed in Talestant for six days — six relaxing days, spent talking or singing in the garden, sauntering among the great trees (though I was given no chance to explore their 'fortifications'), lazing on the quiet shore of Lake Vanadha or swimming in its waters. I took the opportunity to write a long letter to Ilven, shaping my letters carefully so as to show how I had profited from her tuition. Though I told her something of our doings, much of that letter was an expression of love and of longing. Indeed, it was painful to think that our journey had yet barely begun. Much though I liked Talestant, I was eager to be leaving.

Avran, in contrast, was disposed to linger. He was happy to be back in the lands of his vard, of course, but he was eager also for news. Had Dermot Fitzstephen and his three associates been captured? If so, might Dermot be persuaded to forget his loyalties and name his employers? Already Avran had transmitted the information he had gained about the grey riders to his father the Prince, by way of the system of royal messengers whose swift passage binds together the bundle of vardlands that is Sandastre. Might the riddle of the riders be solved for us from Sandarro?

It was on the fourth day that we received an answer to the first question and on the sixth day that messages came from Sandarro. For both pursuing parties, the trail of the grey riders had proved a long one. While we were resting in the ruined temple, the Sandastrians had continued that pursuit until the fall of night prevented any further reading of tracks. The grey riders must have rested also and, though they were up and away earlier, their tracks were soon refound. And so the hunt had resumed. It was to continue throughout much of the day on which we rode to Talestant.

By the afternoon, the gap between the pursuers and the two grey riders who had headed southeastward was closing fast. In a gully somewhere above the lands of Indravard, they turned at bay. An invitation to surrender was spurned. Instead, there had been an exchange of darts from sasayin during which two of the Estantesecs were injured and one of the riders killed. Again there was a call to surrender, but the surviving grey rider ignored it. Desperately he charged his pursuers. When his sevdru was cut from under him, he fell on his own sword rather than be taken. Neither of the dead men was Dermot Fitzstephen.

It was Dermot and a companion, then, who had turned

northeastward, riding so desperately fast that they were not even sighted by the other pursuing party till late afternoon on the second day. By then they were in a region of crags and broken rocks, where tracking was difficult and a passage not easy even for sevdreyen. The gap between pursuers and pursued had not closed before darkness again fell.

Next morning, the Sandastrians discovered the tracks of the grey riders' sevdreyen only after much trouble. They followed and eventually caught up with those animals, only to discover that both were now riderless. Somewhere among the rocks, Dermot and his companion had slipped away. Though the Sandastrians alerted the surrounding vardai — Derresdavard, Kevessvard, Indravard, even Predaravard on the shore of Arcturus Bay — no trace was found of those two.

Nor did the message from Sandarro furnish any new information, for Prince Vindicon and his councillors knew nothing either of the grey riders or of any new plot against the realm of Sandastre. They were quite as puzzled as we and even more uneasy.

The messages to Avran, then, brought him no comfort. In contrast, a message sent to me by Ilven occasioned me great contentment. Though I remember exactly what she wrote, I shall not divulge her words, for they were written for my eyes alone.

Chapter Nine

THE FORGOTTEN CITY

So it was that, seven mornings after we had reached Talestant, Avran was persuaded to journey forth again with me. We had decided we would be wise to continue to wear soldiers' garb, for wandering mercenaries are common enough in the lands to which we were going. Both Zembelen and Yerezinth were joyous at being on the road once more but Rascal, squatting atop my new pack-saddle, was sulking. I was not sure whether this was through resentment at leaving those luscious estelen groves or through a consciousness that, ere long, he and I must part. (The latter thought caused *me* no joy, for that matter.) Soon the steady jogging sent him to sleep; and, when he awoke, he was cheerful enough.

After discussions with Avran's cousins, we had decided to ride northward into Denniffey rather than northeastward through Pravan and Volendar. Since the lands of the Estantesecs extend further into Denniffey than into Pravan, our decision may seem an obvious one. Quite evidently we would wish to remain as long as possible among people who were our friends. Elsewhere in those realms, there was little indeed upon which to put any trust.

However, there were other reasons also. Pravan's ruler, styled an earl, had taken to himself the powers of a petty king of the worst sort. He lived in tarnished state among servile courtiers and plundered whenever and wherever he might. The Estantesecs, with their powerful southern connexions, tended to be left alone, but beyond their lands there was no safety for travellers. Volendar was equally unsafe. It was a tiny realm beyond Pravan on the edge of the plains, with a Temeculan ruling family uneasily governing a handful of Montariotan subjects who, having given up nomadic life, were perpetually under threat from their wandering kinsmen.

Emphatically it was not the place from which to begin a crossing of the plains and, with Antomalata and Sapandella at war close by, we would be unwise indeed to choose the northeastern route.

Denniffey was a naradat, a republic somewhat on the ancient Athenian model about which my tutor had taught me. In theory at least, the narat, its ruler, was elected on the death or resignation of his predecessor by free vote of all adult citizens. The idea was attractive and I was disappointed to learn that practice fell far short of precept.

For almost two centuries, each successive narat had been a member of the powerful Abaletsen family. Since no other candidates had dared to stand in opposition, naturally there had been no need for elections! Yet the long rule of the Abaletsens had not been benign. Long ago Denniffey had been a rich and densely populated land, powerful enough even to rival Sandastre. However, years of almost incessant warring with adjacent realms to east, west and south and repeated attacks from the north by Montariotan marauders had pushed Denniffey into a long decline. Presently, however, Denniffey was at peace. Although, with neighbouring Darrinnett in fiery revolt against the Fachnese, that peace looked fragile, we trusted we might traverse Denniffey without incident and be beyond its frontiers before any new conflict flared up.

The sunshine continued through the next three days. After a few hours of riding through pasturelands beside Lake Vanadha, with brown sands at our left where shore-birds probed for food and peeped plaintively, we crossed another high-arched bridge to enter the realm of Denniffey. This frontier was not guarded, for were not both banks within the lands of Estantegard? Onward we rode, north up the narrow valley of the swift-flowing Demdelet, under the intermittent shade of giant pevenekar. On that night and the one following, we slept in padin as colourful as those of Talestant. The evenings were passed in song and celebration. Even if Avran's rank was being discreetly ignored, was he not an Estantesec and thus a visiting relative?

On the third morning, however, the character of the landscape began to change. The Demdelet, narrower and more turbulent now, was still at our right, but the huge pevenekar were succeeded by lesser trees and even those became ever fewer and smaller. There were sevdreyen browsing among these trees, but always under the eye of a heavily armed guard watchful, not for beasts of prey, but for marauding men. The padarn we slept in that night was built of stone and set high on a crag.

Our host was Senraidar Estantesec, a man in part of Temeculan descent, as his first name indicated. (Senraidar had been a name borne by many of the Earls of Stavrasard, one of whom became the first King of Temecula). He was tall, lean and wiry, with a nervous watchfulness evoked by years on the uneasy edge of the Estantesecs' lands. His wife was prematurely grey and his children were too steady and sedate for their years. However, his two sons played happily with Rascal and his daughter seemed especially enthralled by the little vasian.

We watched the children's games and talked relaxedly till the children were taken away to bed. Thereafter we began questioning our host about his land, for there was much we needed urgently to know.·

'Yes, indeed, there were once many people living hereabouts,' Senraidar said, in response to an enquiry from Avran. 'This would be yet a good land for men and beasts, if people might but rest in peace. But the folk of Denniffey, why, it seems they can never be easy. There's always soldiers being sent out from Doriolupata to enlist recruits or collect taxes for some new war — a campaign against Volendar or Siasaph, maybe, or what they style a retaliatory raid against those accursed nomads of the plains. Yes, sometimes there *is* a campaign, but more often the taxes disappear into the coffers of the narat and the soldiers are employed merely to extort more money. So why should folk trouble overmuch to grow bigger crops or breed larger herds of beasts, when it'd simply mean paying higher taxes to those money-grabbing Abaletsens?'

'Well, you're Estantesecs; doesn't that help?'

'Aye, of course it does — if you're down in the forests, with the pevenekar about you and Sandastre nearby. Up here, though, it's not so handy. It's just too easy for them soldiers to pick up a man and carry him off to Doriolupata, where he must explain to the narat and his fat cronies exactly why the taxes fell short, on pain of being clapped into prison if

85

they don't like his answers. Or else there's what they call an unfortunate accident, and you're found with a hunting-spear embedded in your spine. And then, look at our neighbours, if one can honour them with that title! The Sambrelans down on the lake-shore, they're not bad folk; but those Vaghats over to our west are a perverse bunch. If they don't chance to be fighting the Baroddans, you may be sure they'll be quarrelling with someone else. And you'll know all about the Lenavvars, I'm sure; I could do without that thieving, traitorous crew nearby.'

Avran did indeed know of the Lenavvars, who had played a black part in the history of southern Rockall. 'I wonder that you stay on up here, when the problems are so great.'

Senraidar's lined face creased into a smile. 'Well now, it does make life interesting, you know. And' — his eyes twinkled — 'I won't say but that the Lenavvars and Vaghats don't lose the odd beast on occasion!'

Avran laughed heartily. 'Why, you old battler, you! Well now, can you tell us what's happening in Doriolupata these days? As I mentioned, we're bound northward. We must somehow find our way across the River Werenthin and the plains beyond.'

Our host grimaced. 'Crossing that river's difficult enough. It's wide and there are neither bridges nor ferries, as well you must know. And traversing the plains — well, you *might* manage it, but I wouldn't give two asalbek berries for your chances! Best turn back while there's yet time. As for Doriolupata, it's the same old brew of politics and corruption that ever it was. Our beloved President Vizien Abaletsen' — he spat disgustedly — 'is just the right spice for such a brew.'

Senraidar helped us to more wine, but he would not say more about his land and its ruler. Instead, he told us much about the Montariotans, against whom he had fought during past years and about whom he knew much more than had Enar Servessil and his colleagues.

On more immediate matters, he gave us specific advice in two regards; that I should send back Rascal to Sandarro forthwith and that Avran and I should henceforward conceal our familiarity with the long-bow. Concerning Rascal he pointed out, firstly, that fodder trees for vasianar would become ever harder to find as we rode northward and, secondly, that a vasian would attract overmuch attention in lands where such beasts were scarcely known. Concerning our long-bows, he commented that word of my doings in Sandarro had spread widely already. To be seen carrying a strung long-bow would not only identify us irrevocably, but might well cause us to be pressed into teaching the use of that weapon to the soldiers of Denniffey.

Senraidar was able to be helpful in both regards. He offered to furnish us each with one of the light game-hunting bows of southern Rockall, as explanation for the quivers of arrows we carried. The long-bow staves, he suggested, might be passed off as sticks for quarterstaff combats, which are as common an amusement among the Temeculan tribes as they are in England.

As for Rascal, Senraidar had an excellent proposal to make. The children of Estantesec families resident outside Sandastre are quite regularly sent to Sandarro, there to gain education of a quality not available in these borderlands. Senraidar's daughter and elder son, along with children from several neighbouring padin, would be travelling south within two days under strong escort. Why should not Rascal travel with them? The children would be thrilled to have him in their charge; they would take care of him well and deliver him safely to Ilven.

This idea I found both comforting and disquieting. I knew that a parting from my vasian could not be long delayed, but I had become so fond of him that the prospect dismayed me greatly. However, the offer was too good to be refused; I summoned up a smile of thanks and accepted.

When I sought my bed that night, I had to undertake the task of mentally explaining his future to Rascal. Somehow this was managed. Though I could feel his pain, I perceived also that my vasian had been anticipating the parting and was ready for it. Even more strangely I became aware that, though Rascal would miss my company, he would not pine. Instead he would wait for me, certain that I would be returning to him some day. The confidence and trust of that little animal were both astonishing and humbling. Though I found I had tears in my eyes, at the same time I experienced a lift of my heart.

Nor, next morning, was the actual parting difficult. Certainly

Rascal's ears were drooping a little and, when I gave him a farewell hug, he was reluctant to be loosed. However, when I handed him over to Senraidar's little daughter, he settled on her shoulder without any sign of sulking or dolour. Though certainly saddened by that parting, I rode away in better spirits than I had expected.

It was well that my spirits were good, for the day was a bleak one. The sky was leaden-grey and the clouds lowering. A strong, cold wind from the northeast bowed the grassheads and stirred the dead leaves by the gate of the padarn into a dance. The path down the crag was both steep and exposed; our sevdreyen and we were glad to reach the shelter of the Demdelet valley again.

Not that this served us as protection for long. Soon the river was dividing into smaller, swifter tributary streams, the deep slots of whose channels were too narrow to allow the passage of riders. We were forced instead to endure the wind, following an ill-maintained road across uplands where tumbled walls divided abandoned fields. Here and there, heaps of stones marked the former positions of buildings so completely collapsed that their character could no longer be determined. It was all too evident how the population of Denniffey had dwindled, when so much cultivable land had fallen into such complete neglect.

Yet, though so desolate, this landscape was not depressing, even on such a bitter day; perhaps because grasses and weeds had grown up so luxuriantly about those tumbled stones, perhaps merely because the structures were so long fallen that they had lost the poignancy of recent ruins.

By then we had left the lands of the Estantesecs and were riding through the western fringes of those of the Lenavvars. Several times we saw, away to the east, herds of hasedain or sevdreyen grazing among the overgrown fields, under the watchful eye of some cloak-huddled warrior. However, in these lands there were no songs, no merry calls, to greet our passing; only a silent, suspicious watchfulness. A few birds fought the wind in brief flights from covert to covert, but the cold had subdued their songs also. All other wild creatures were keeping safe within shelter.

Around midday we found ourselves approaching what once had been a padarn — a larger ruin, set on a mound built from the earth and stone rubble excavated from a surrounding ditch. The ditch was still water-filled, though green now with weed, and three walls of the padarn still stood, although blackened by the smoke of its burning long ago. Since they promised shelter from the relentless wind, it was within those walls that we decided to take our noon repast. Green grasses stood high in the lee of the ruin.

As we rode up onto the mound, some small animal grunted in fright and hastened away unglimpsed, the grasses rippling at its passing like water about a submerged swimmer.

Senraidar's wife had furnished us with a generous store of food; compact rations for the days to come and cheeses, salads and fruits for this first day. Once out of the wind, we were warm enough to enjoy our repast in comfort. While we ate and talked, our two sevdreyen foraged contentedly among the tall weeds that grew round about. However, I found myself missing Rascal's happy crooning — and not for the last time.

Our afternoon road led us ever upward, onto the main mass of the looping Heights of Denniffey. The ruined field walls became fewer and more widely spaced; the vegetation became less green and progressively sparser; and soon we were traversing moorland that was stonier and more barren than even the Trantevrin Hills. Our uphill ride was ever more of a fight against the bleak wind. I found this familiar and exhilarating, for it reminded me of days on the windy moors of the Pennines; but Avran, accustomed to the benign climate of Sandastre, was shivering and the sevdreyen were cold and unhappy.

As we topped a minor ridge I was reminded again of my homeland. Ahead was a sandstone cliff which seemed to have been shaped by wind and weather into masses and pillars, much like the gritstone crags of Wharncliffe close to my Hallamshire home. Below were ridges of rubble and scattered larger blocks of sandstone, some square, some rounded. These also recalled Wharncliffe where, for uncounted centuries, men had shaped the coarse gritstone into querns and millstones for grinding corn.

However, as we rode closer, I saw that these blocks and mounds were not the residue of a stone-trimming industry but the tumbled ruins of a town. What I had thought to be crags were the crumbling towers and broken walls of the ridge-top castle that had once watched over that town. Below them, the whole broad face of the sandstone had, at some distant time, been elaborately graven and polished.

Though the stone had flaked or discoloured in places and lichens and mosses had rooted wherever they might, the theme of these carvings remained evident. A triumphal procession was depicted, of warriors returning from victory. Their helmets were wreathed with blossoms, their spears bedecked with flowers, and the horns of their sevdreyen caparisoned with feathers. Behind the warriors, to our right as we looked at the cliff, were depicted hasedain laden with booty and led by servants or prisoners (it was not clear which), while captured sevdreyen, roped together in threes, followed. Shown at lesser scale below the victorious warriors was a line of onlookers, men, women and children, their gestures expressing their joy.

Above the carvings, an inscription in archaic Sandastrian characters was yet decipherable, even though worn away in places. As we threaded our way through the ruins and drew closer to the rock face, Avran strove with furrowed brow to read those characters.

'I cannot clearly understand it,' he remarked at last. 'The words are like ours, yet unlike. However, I think this must, long ago, have been a fortress city of the Kingdom of Elvenost. Nowadays Elvenost is a very minor realm, just one of several small states huddled along the border of Temecula. There was a time, however, when Elvenost grew great and powerful, holding in thrall most of the lands about Sandastre.'

'I've barely even heard of it,' I confessed. 'How long ago was that?'

He laughed. 'Oh, quite a long time — twelve hundred years or so. We Rockalese have long memories, you know! But I remember Elvenost particularly because its most powerful king had the same name as my eldest brother — Helburnet. Helburnet the Triumphant, his people called him in the days of his greatness; and I presume that this carving must commemorate his conquest of Denniffey. If his luck had held, he might have conquered Sandastre also; our eslef of that time, Falco Serrad I Vednetren, was a devious man but without the qualities of a warleader. However, Helburnet was

90

assassinated — by one of his generals, I believe — and his whole empire collapsed almost overnight.'

Avran looked more intently at the carvings, then pointed. 'You see the figure over there — the rider on the unusually large sevdru? The rock has flaked badly, but he appears to be wearing a crown of Temeculan style. I presume that must be Helburnet. Odd, isn't it, that his figure should be the most severely damaged of all?' He paused, then added reflectively: 'Yet mayhap that is appropriate enough, since his own demise preceded the fading of his empire. And now, from all those conquests, nothing remains but a few ruins and these crumbling carvings.'

'What was this city called?' I wondered.

Avran shrugged. 'I've no idea. I doubt if even the Denniffeyens recall its name. What does it matter? Its only inhabitants now are lizards and other small beasts, and they have no language.'

Since the fortifications occupied the whole ridge, it was necessary to find a way through them. This proved easy enough. A steep earthen ramp led up to where an ancient gate once had stood, its arch now fallen in. Beyond was the courtyard of the old castle, grass-grown now and with a few bedraggled bushes rooting among its stone flags. Beyond again there was a second gate, its arch substantially intact but its doors long vanished. There had been a moat on its outer, northern side; this was dry now and overgrown, but still bridged by an arch of carven stone. This we rode over with some trepidation, but fortunately it remained solid.

However, now we were again riding into the teeth of the wind, which seemed yet more biting after the temporary shelter. A long slope of moorland was before us, affording no prospect of further protection for many leagues. Beyond, indeed, there was only the grey sky.

After about a quarter of an hour of dogged riding, Avran slowed his mount and addressed me. 'I've had quite enough of this. There's a refuge of a sort behind us, but none at all ahead. It would be stupid to go on. Let's turn back and spend our night in the old city.'

I hesitated. What Avran said made sense, yet his proposal made me uneasy. Or was it Yerezinth who was uneasy?

91

'Very well,' I said reluctantly; and we turned our mounts about.

Riding into the wind had been hard; riding with the wind behind us was delightful. Avran turned a laughing face to me. 'This is splendid! Come on, Simon, we'll race you back to the ruins!'

In a moment, Zembelen was galloping away at full pelt, with Avran shouting in joy and urging him to yet greater speed.

After my earlier misadventure, I did not truly strive to match Avran's pace; but since Yerezinth was a bigger animal than Rokh and his stride longer, we were soon catching up. Within minutes we were approaching the castle again. Yerezinth was only a few paces behind Zembelen when we crossed the stone bridge and yet closer as we traversed the grass-grown courtyard. Through the broken gate we rode neck and neck, to cascade down the steep slope beyond, warm now, breathless and laughing.

Yet, for a second time, the gay abandon of speed had carried us into trouble. When we had left the ruins of King Helburnet's city, it had indeed been populated only by lizards and other small beasts. In our unwisdom, we had presumed all would remain unchanged. Now, however, it was aswarm with soldiers.

They seemed to rise about us from all sides, burly men in jupons and hose as brown as the tumbled stone, with surcoats as green as the weeds and with drawn swords or axes in their hands.

Any resistance would clearly be futile. Avran raised his arms outward and forward, in the Rockalese gesture of surrender that shows no weapon is held.

As I followed suit, I noticed on each surcoat a heraldic device and read it automatically. '*Per bend argent and vert, a cockatrice sejant purpure,*' I muttered to myself — an obliquely divided shield, silver and green, bearing in purple the device of a sitting creature that looked like the cockatrice of legend. My studies in Sandastre had not been in vain. Even before Avran could tell me so, I knew that we were surrounded by soldiers of Denniffey.

Chapter Ten

CAPTIVES IN THE RAIN

However, those soldiers' intentions towards us did not seem hostile. Their swords were drawn, certainly, but they seemed more startled than threatening. An immense man, clad beneath his surcoat in rather rusty chain mail and with the cockatrice device repeated on his iron helmet, appeared to be their leader. It was he that addressed us.

'Why so hasty, brothers? Be ye in pursuit or in flight? Neither beast nor man has passed hereby. What is it that ye are about?'

His voice was a sort of dry roar, like waves breaking on a pebble-bank. Its inflexions were hard to read, yet I thought it indeed contained more of puzzlement than of threat.

'Might I ask, sir, whom I am addressing?' Avran enquired, breathlessly but politely.

'I am Burak Ekonar, quincentenar of the army of Denniffey. I am warden of these lands under the authority of the narat and responsible for all deeds done here or left undone. Who be ye, that come as strangers?'

Avran laughed gaily and lowered his hands. 'Why then, it is you whom we were seeking! My companion and I are soldiers of fortune. We are come to find employment in this land, for we are told that you welcome good warriors and offer them high rewards.'

The soldier eyed him suspiciously from under brows as shaggy as old thatch. 'Indeed! So ye were seeking us, were ye? Yet ye seemed greatly surprised at finding us!'

'True enough,' Avran responded easily. 'We thought you were many leagues away to the west. That was the cause of our surprise, for we had not reckoned on encountering you so soon; and it was the cause of our haste also, for we were trusting to locate you before sunset. There is little shelter in this land. We hoped to find refuge in your camp, for the wind is cold!'

'It is that.' The massive head was nodding slowly. 'A bleak day it has been, one of the hardest I remember. Where be ye from, may I ask, and what be your name?'

Avran's smile vanished like a chalk-mark wiped from a slate; he spoke very coldly now. 'As to where I am from, let us just say, from the south; and it is enough to add that my forename is Avran. My surname I mislike, ever since they placed a prefix before it; so I will not quote it.'

At this the listening soldiers smiled or even chuckled, perceiving that Avran was referring to the 'biek' placed before the vard name of a convicted Sandastrian criminal. Their leader said drily: 'Ay, well, we'll not press you for it. And your friend?'

'His name is Simon and he's from the east.' (True enough, for is not England far to the east of Denniffey?) 'He has a surname so barbarously strange that I cannot set my tongue to it. What is it, Simon? Bransait? Branthait?'

'Branthwaite,' I managed to respond gravely, though I was bubbling internally with amusement at Avran's adroit deceptions.

Their leader considered this, his brows knotting. 'A difficult name indeed, and not one that ever I have heard. Certainly not Temeculan, nor Salastrian either. You must come from beyond the Arctorran lands, I guess?'

I assented solemnly; and why not, for that was true! 'To my own people, such names are commonplace. However, you will surely find it easier to call me just Simon, as does Avran. Among comrades, there is no need for formality. If you accept our services, soon we shall be comrades indeed!'

Burak Ekonar had lowered his sword by now, as had the other soldiers. However, none of those swords had yet been sheathed and the huge soldier still appeared dubious. His brows had relaxed, but his rather small, palely brown eyes were busily assessing us.

'Well, as to that,' he rumbled, 'it is not for me to decide. Tonight you may remain with us, but you will be under guard. We return tomorrow to Doriolupata, where our commander can decide your fate. Maybe, indeed, you'll be recruited to the service of the narat — who knows? Yield to me your swords, please, and dismount.'

Our swords were examined with interest, for they were better blades than are commonly carried by Rockalese soldiers. In consequence, they earned us further suspicious looks from the massive quincentenar. However, our bowstaves were not examined, nor were we searched.

Moreover, though certainly we were watched, we were treated well enough that evening. Indeed, these soldiers were travelling in comparative luxury. The soldiers and we fed well on broth that had been heated in a big iron pot, hunks of bread (rather dry, but tasty enough when dipped in the broth) and beakers of ale freshly tapped from a wooden cask. The soldiers' pack-hasedain carried not only bedding and provisions, but also fodder and water for their sevdreyen. Thus Yerezinth and Zembelen were treated as well as we. However, they were likewise kept under guard, for Burak Ekonar understood fully the abilities of a sevdru and was taking no chances.

The soldiers themselves were a pretty rough bunch. A few were Denniffeyens of the lower sort, but the majority were mercenaries coming, it seemed, from most parts of southern Rockall — Arctorrans, Baroddans, Fachnese, and men from several Temeculan and Salastrian tribes. Avran told me later that the surname of their leader showed him to be from Skayarock, a realm north of Fachane and now reluctantly under the governance of that kingdom.

Only the strength and force of personality of Burak Ekonar maintained any coherence or discipline in this motley band. And indeed, on that first evening the discipline seemed tight enough. Though Avran's ready tongue and easy humour elicited both attention and laughter from the soldiers sharing our shelter, their watchfulness never ceased. That night, we went to sleep wrapped warmly in blankets, beneath a shelter of hides erected in the lee of one of the more substantial ruins. However, we slept under the steady eyes of guards and, when we woke next morning, new guards were watching us with equal vigilance.

That morning was a grey one. The wind had veered overnight and now was blowing from the southwest. It was a much warmer wind, but the massing, hastening clouds were an augury of rain soon to come. Under this threat, the soldiers and we breakfasted with such speed that, within forty minutes of our rising, the shelters were down and the hasedain being loaded. Even so, as we were mounting our sevdreyen the rain began.

Only at this time did Avran and I realize we were not the only prisoners. Two other men were enduring a much more rigorous confinement. Each had been bound to the pack-saddle on which he was mounted, the ropes being further tied to the pack-saddles of soldiers on either side.

One of these men was dark-bearded, with eyes deeply shadowed by lowering brows; he was almost as massive as Burak Ekonar and was guarded by two of the strongest of the soldiers. However, he appeared so wrapped in gloom as to be unaware of them. The other prisoner, a lean man of middle height whose bright red hair was somewhat muted in hue by the onset of greyness, was in contrast looking about him sharply. When he perceived Avran, I saw him start in surprise. However, he made no comment and instantly looked away.

There were around fifty soldiers in Burak Ekonar's band. They rode in the formation of an open wedge, with their leader, riding the biggest sevdru I had ever seen, in the van — at the point, as it were. Avran and I, though still without our swords, were not under any restraint; however, we were placed firmly at the centre of the wedge. The two captives and their guards were some way behind us. At the back — the blunt end — of the wedge, the pack-hasedain patiently trotted along in line abreast.

In such open country, our placement among the soldiers left us no chance of escaping; yet it had its advantage, for we were protected somewhat from the rain. This came in large drops, driven obliquely by gusty wind buffets that set the soldiers — especially those to our left, who bore the brunt of the weather — grumbling and cursing. Like them, Avran and I were wearing cloaks and had pulled the hoods forward over our heads. Our cloaks were good, yet the wind-driven rain found its way into and beneath our garb in warm runnels until our necks, arms and legs were soaked. Not since those days of riding to Bristol had I been so thoroughly uncomfortable.

Moreover, this day's ride was infinitely more boring, for the press of surrounding soldiers prevented any extensive view of the moorland about us. The distant prospects were, in any case, veiled by cloud. Even so, I was aware that we were heading northwestward, obliquely down the long northern flank of the Heights of Denniffey.

During the first three hours of riding, the surface beneath us changed little; but after that the stones became ever fewer till they vanished amid a deeper, greener herbage. Once we picked our way across a marsh, the wedge of soldiers and beasts narrowing before and widening after it in hourglass fashion; and twice we splashed through the waters of shallow, swift streams. There were increasing numbers of bushes and I began to glimpse, through the wet mist, dark shapes that must be small trees. The wind was blowing more steadily by then and the rain coming at us ever more drenchingly.

In such conditions, the vigilance of the soldiers was understandably diminished. Avran was riding quite close by me and we were able to talk in low tones. He was inclined to self-recrimination.

'Brrh! What weather!' he said, shaking his head so that the water spattered from his hood. 'And what a fool I am, plunging us into this mire of trouble! After that earlier episode, I ought to have known better than to race along so heedlessly. It serves *me* right, but I grieve at having brought you into such a predicament.'

'Actually, I thought you did us pretty well, Avran,' I responded honestly. 'I'm sure the soldiers truly believe you to be a criminal on the run and me, just some harmless wanderer with an appetite for adventure. If they realized who we were, matters might be much more serious. As things are, the worst that can happen is that we might be forced to serve awhile in the Denniffeyen army; and surely we'll be able to slip away soon and smartly.'

Avran snorted and gave another angry toss of his head. 'As to that, it might not be so easy, from what I've heard of the walls of Doriolupata. However, there's worse yet. Do you know who those prisoners are?'

'No. I presumed they were just farmers who'd fallen foul of the narat and his cronies.'

'It's much more serious than that, I regret to say. The

97

redheaded man is an Estantesec, a distant cousin of mine; Darolayn is his name, a member of our vard who lives in Denniffey just a few leagues east of Senraidar's home. Before you awoke two mornings back, I was talking with Senraidar and he told me that cousin Darolayn has been dabbling in politics. It seems that there are signs, at long last, of an uprising against the Abaletsens. Darolayn is in the very forefront of the discontented, so much so indeed that the narat has outlawed him and set a price upon his head. Senraidar was rather gleeful about that — he was sure they'd never catch Darolayn! He was wrong; they've caught him. The other man they've captured is less important, just a bodyguard, I would guess. However, without Darolayn, the uprising may collapse — and, Heaven knows, it's past time that the Abaletsens were overthrown.'

I whistled dolefully. 'Sad tidings, indeed. How did they catch him?'

'I don't know yet; I'll strive to find out. Yet there's another problem. Darolayn knows me well; he's been to Talestant several times and also to Sandarro. He wouldn't denounce me willingly but, if the narat's torturers should get at him, he might do so involuntarily; and I'm quite sure that Vizien Abaletsen would love to have me in his dungeons. He's well aware that my father dislikes his rule, even though Sandastre has never interfered in the affairs of Denniffey. Think how the narat might use me, either to secure a ransom or, more likely, to obtain political favours for his accursed family!' He groaned at the very thought.

I tried to respond bracingly. 'Well, that's not happened yet, so keep in good heart! Much may chance ere we reach Doriolupata. How far is it, anyway?'

He considered briefly, then shouted to the nearest soldier: 'How much longer must we endure this rain, friend? Shall we reach Doriolupata tonight?'

'Not we!' came a growled response. 'Given decent weather, we'd be there by noon tomorrow. In such conditions as these, who can say? It's my belief we ought to be seeking shelter, not riding on and on across these accursed hills.'

Avran gave me a covert smile and muttered: 'Grant that the rain continues, then!' Aloud, he said: 'Quite right, friend. You're soldiers — fighting men, not festikieren.' (The festikier is a common waterbird of southern Rockall.) 'Why endure this weather, when there's no enemy to be attacked and no other reason for haste?'

'Aye, that's right enough!' the soldier said; and he rode over to one of his fellows to pass on the comment. Indeed, they were becoming ever more restive. The close formation in which we had ridden forth was becoming ever looser, as the soldiers straggled or clotted into grumbling groups. Burak Ekonar's tight discipline was dissolving progressively in the steady downpour.

At the soldier's going, Avran addressed me again. 'Well enough; but all that may gain us is a wet night in some meagre shelter. I see small hope of our escaping and none at all of our freeing Darolayn.'

I tried a second time to cheer him. 'Don't be so glum, Avran, friend. We've been fortunate before; maybe we'll be so again!'

Almost as I spoke, the whole column of riders came to an irregular halt and a message was passed back that cheered the soldiers immensely. The one whom Avran had addressed hastened back toward us.

'Ah, now, here's good tidings!' he crowed. 'There's a stand of trees not far ahead where we can find shelter. We'll be camping there till tomorrow's morn or whenever this infernal rain stops. Burak Ekonar's no sort of a fool, after all!'

Nor was he, for he had sensed the mood of his rabble of followers and, being well aware how slight was their loyalty in any adversity, had adjusted his plans accordingly, as a sea-captain trims his sails to the wind. Though the rain did not abate, it was with a new enthusiasm that the ride was resumed.

Within another hour we were descending a slippery, rock-strewn slope into a saucer-shaped depression. Once there might have been a lake here, but if so its waters had long since drained away. Now it was overgrown densely by trees of a sort I had not seen before, with dark-green foliage opening out above their trunks as abruptly — and in much the same fashion — as does an open fan above its handle. (Avran called the trees tavelnekar and told me their bitter yellow berries were used in Sandastre to cure agues.) Though, to be sure, the trees could not keep out all the rain, they formed a welcome protection from the wind and allowed the hide shelters to be erected without much effort in their lee.

Since dry wood had been brought along in the hasedain packs, fires were soon burning and the stewpots bubbling merrily. About each of the fires, four shelters were set in an inwardly-facing ring so that the soldiers might each enjoy the warmth. As food and drink began to circulate, their spirits picked up and the talk became loud and cheerful.

Accepted into the communalty of one such circle, Avran and I, though in theory still prisoners under guard, were in practice being increasingly treated as equals. Avran's good-humoured badinage made him ever more popular and brought a corresponding increase in tolerance for me.

The two other captives were very much less fortunate. Each had been roped to a tree and, though fed and given water, left to find what shelter he might in the lee of its trunk. I could not see the dark-bearded man, but the red-haired captive, Avran's cousin, was not far distant from our tent. Technically, indeed, he was under the surveillance of the soldiers in our shelter-ring. It must have been a thoroughly miserable afternoon for both prisoners; and, though the rain continued steadily into the evening, they were afforded neither coverings nor any other protection from the weather.

On the excuse of a call of nature, I left our shelter shortly after dinner. I did not dare to stray far, for I was still under observation. However, the two soldiers appointed to the task of watching me were not disposed to follow me out into the rain. Moreover, they were much more interested in a game of chance, played with octahedral garnets on whose faces numbers had been scratched, that was in progress by the fireside.

The red-haired prisoner was reclining wearily in his ropes, about twenty yards away. Though the sky was darkening now, he saw me against the fire-glow and looked toward me appealingly, half-rising. However, the guards were also looking toward me and I did not dare approach him. Instead, I turned away. As I did so, I saw him slump back despairingly.

The daylight was fading now and the background of trees dark. I was sure that the guards, though still able to see me, could not perceive all my movements. As I turned back toward the shelter, swiftly I snatched one of my throwing-knives from its shoulder-sheath and hurled it toward the prisoner.

I heard the slight thwuck as the knife plunged into the soil somewhere by him in the gloom, but I could not determine how accurate that hasty throw had been. Nor did I dare attempt to check. Instead, with the haste appropriate to such wet weather, I returned to the shelter.

The game was at a tense stage; the two guards, distracted by it already, noted my return with relief and switched their entire attention to the rolling garnets. I sat down by Avran, my heart beating fast. Had the knife been thrown far enough? Would Darolayn Estantesec be able to reach it? Had he sufficient skill to free himself and escape the soldiers? Would he have sense enough to take the knife with him, so that his escape was not laid to my account?

As for Avran and me, no chance of escape was afforded us. Within minutes, the massive figure of Burak Ekonar followed me into the hide shelter. He had come to ensure that, in such cramped quarters, Avran and I were separated for the night and kept under close guard; and he arranged a rota of hourly inspection for the other two prisoners. When he left the shelter, he was accompanied by a disconsolate Avran and the two soldiers charged with guarding him.

That night, again I slept with two guards watching me; nor, on this occasion, did I find sleep quickly. Our capture by the Denniffeyen mercenaries had delayed our quest already; and, if their guarding of us continued to be so careful, it might be long ere we were able to evade them and resume our search for Lyonesse. Well, at present we were not in any real danger; be content, Simon, be content . . . And I slipped away into deep slumber.

Chapter Eleven

THE WALLS OF DORIOLUPATA

A clamour of voices awakened me. Burak Ekonar was standing close by our shelter-ring, roaring with fury, and other soldiers were shouting feverish responses, transmitting his orders or giving their own.

It was natural enough that I should ask my guards what was the matter. Their answer startled me. Not one, but both of the other prisoners had escaped!

That much, at least, was clear; but otherwise no-one seemed to comprehend quite what had happened. One theory seemed to be that the big black-haired man had burst his bonds, released his comrade and, after felling several guards, fled with him. Another was that both men had been freed by a rescuing party after a bloody — but mysteriously silent! — affray; and a third was that they had been treacherously released by one of their guards during the night.

Whatever the truth of the matter, the soldiers were as stirred up by the event as ants in an unroofed nest — and their activities were almost as frantic and purposeless.

Burak seemed to be despatching parties of pursuers at random in all directions. So angry was he, indeed, that all logical thinking had deserted him. Had he not lost two prisoners whose capture would have brought him reward and high honour? Was this not because he was afflicted by as incompetent, unreliable, untrustworthy and brainless a lot of so-called soldiers as ever a man could be cursed with? Soldiers? Stupid buffoons, rather! He was stamping, spluttering and hoarse, seeming in his rage like a great brown bear at a baiting.

Soon Avran was permitted to join me. He was finding it hard to conceal his glee at the news of his cousin's escape. For the moment, he also was attributing this to the sheer strength of the black-haired man. The ropes by that man's tree had been so much stretched and chafed that his bursting of his bonds seemed quite feasible. Nor, in a disorganized and chaotic morning, did I have a chance to tell Avran the truth. Instead I learned how Darolayn had been captured — by treachery and a trap.

'Do you recall seeing a rather sly-looking man yesterday, Simon? — the only one, other than the escaped prisoners and we, who was not in soldier's gear? He was riding over to our right, if you remember. You don't? Well, that man is a leader of the Lenavvars, by name Zeladh Lenavvar. Darolayn properly distrusted that family, but he was anxious nevertheless to secure their aid against the Abaletsens. In consequence, having quietly secured the promise of a substantial reward beforehand from the narat, Zeladh Lenavvar proceeded to play Judas, as his accursed family have done so often.'

As Avran paused, I asked: 'Yet Darolayn must have been watchful. How did they entrap him?'

'Yes, he was watchful, but they were too cunning for him. Darolayn was invited to a very private dinner, to explain to the Lenavvars his plans for the uprising. He was careful to take along his bodyguard, but that did him no good. They were both given drugged wine — no, not in the first, but in the second bottle. Very clever, Zeladh thought himself. Now he's not so sure! Darolayn, when he recovered consciousness, vowed swift vengeance. Well, that didn't concern our dear Zeladh Lenavvar, so long as Darolayn was safely in custody. When I saw Zeladh just now, though, his face had a distinctly greenish tinge!'

Breakfast was prepared and eaten at leisure amidst an uneasy hum of talk. The rain, which had slackened overnight, ceased altogether in mid-morning. The shelters were taken down and the hasedain loads prepared, but the fires were kept burning and the talk continued around them while the return of the search-parties was awaited.

Burak Ekonar, though he had fallen silent, seemed about as tranquil as a hive of bees newly overturned. He had put eight of the guards under arrest for incompetence and possible culpability in the escape; they were chained in a disconsolate ring about the tree from which the massive, dark-bearded man (no-one seemed to know his name) had been freed. Moreover, though the sun was soon shining and the air becoming warmer, the spirits of the other soldiers remained low. Unless the prisoners were recaptured, there would be trouble ahead for all, upon return to Doriolupata.

For some hours I was on tenterhooks, fearing I must surely be searched and my other throwing-knives discovered. However, this did not happen. Indeed, as I came slowly to realize, Avran and I were the only ones considered exempt from suspicion. Had we not been under the continuous surveillance of guards? If we had been associates of Darolayn, would we not have fled with him? So the soldiers reasoned; and even Burak Ekonar's suspicions of us diminished thenceforward.

By mid-afternoon the search-parties were back, all reporting failure. The grass was too wet and the wind had been too continuously strong overnight for tracks to persist; the fugitives' lead was too long and there were too many possible hiding-places. Such were the reasons given for unsuccess. Not having expected anything better from his men, Burak responded to their excuses with nothing worse than disgusted words of dismissal.

At last the fires were put out and we were on our way again. Under the twin pressures of their leaders' simmering anger and their own sense of failure, the soldiers rode faster and observed closer formation than they had done yesterday. Avran and I were kept too firmly apart to be able to talk.

However, on this journey I did identify Zeladh Lenavvar, a thin man in a yellow cloak, the colour of which seemed reflected in his countenance. So afraid was he of ambush that he was staying firmly in the centre of the wedge of soldiers and, even so, kept glancing about him uneasily.

The ride was not a lengthy one. An hour before sunset, camp was made on the lee slope of a hill ridge, the fires lit and a guard set. For the soldiers it proved a depressing evening of uneasy conversation and recurrent sulky silences; but Avran and I, no longer under serious suspicion, were allowed to walk about the camp and talk. When he learned that I was responsible for Darolayn's escape my friend's delight was unbounded and his praise unstinting. Together we wove the thread of the story of that escape, as follows:

My knife must have been quickly found and put immediately

105

to use. After freeing himself, Darolayn must have lain quiet till a soldier came by. That man had been seized, choked into unconsciousness and tied to the tree in Darolayn's stead. In the darkness and rain, this substitution had deceived the patrolling parties of guards until morning.

Meantime Darolayn had found and freed his colleague, thoughtfully fraying the ropes so as to suggest a quite different means for their escape and thus diverting attention from Avran and me. The second patrol had blundered upon the escaping men and been quietly silenced — no, not killed, just rendered unconscious by blows of the dark-bearded man's massive fists. Thus swiftly dealt with, those soldiers had not even glimpsed Darolayn. After that, the two escapees had located their own sevdreyen — no difficult task, given the mental guidance those animals could provide — and ridden away undetected into the night.

From what Avran had heard, the soldiers guarding the sevdreyen had been far from vigilant, not even noticing till daylight that two animals were missing. When he learned this, Burak Ekonar's comments had been especially vitriolic! Along with the guards charged with watching the prisoners, these men were under arrest. All were likely, at very least, to be dismissed from the Denniffeyen army.

Well, that was their problem. Ours was to escape northward, and we were given no chance to do so either during that night or during the rest of the journey to Doriolupata. The next day was cool, with flotillas of grey cloud passing overhead and rain seeming ever imminent. That last ride with Burak Ekonar's soldiers was much like the first; the brief coherence of the previous afternoon was lost and again they rode without enthusiasm. They were like truant children returning home because they knew they must, yet well aware that chastisement awaited them.

We followed a road between fields either cultivated or under grass, with barns at intervals. Occasionally we glimpsed a group of farmhouses, set on a mound surrounded by ditches. Always there was a round stone tower at the centre, much like an English castle keep. The farmhouses were also of stone, elongated structures arranged about the tower in cruciform or stellate pattern. Though there were many trees amid the fields, none was permitted to grow where it might impede a view from the tower or mask the approach of an enemy.

Strong structures, yes; and in as good a defensive design as Sandastrian farms. Yet they seemed relics of an earlier, more prosperous age. Grasses and weeds grew from crevices in their walls; stones were missing; doors were unpainted, ill-repaired or lacking. Sometimes only one or two of the farms in a group were inhabited, the roofs and even the walls of the others having been allowed to fall in. Yes, this had once been a prosperous countryside, but it was no longer so.

Moreover, the unpopularity of the soldiers was quickly apparent. Men working in the fields ignored our passing or turned away; children ran from us. When we neared a farm, its women would retreat inside, locking the door and dropping the bar; we knew that, because we could hear the falling of those bars. A man leading a group of sevdreyen along the road turned abruptly onto a side-path and sent them scattering — fearful, presumably, that his beasts might be seized. Not beloved and welcome heroes, these soldiers of Denniffey, but hated despoilers of the land.

When first we glimpsed Doriolupata, it was from above and from a couple of leagues' distance. Like a conical heap of grey stones it looked then, against a green background turned dark under the shadows of the clouds. However, as we rode steadily north and downhill, the city took on shape, seeming ever more massive and formidable.

Doriolupata must have been first settled, long ago, because it was so excellent a site for a fortress — a hill of limestone, detached from the main mass of the Heights of Denniffey, with steep slopes on all sides and marshland to north and west. On such a strong site, even a conventional motte and bailey would have been adequate to deter aggressors; but the designers of this fortress city had been much more imaginative. With infinite labour over the centuries, they had quarried, delved and built till they had produced a structure that was impregnable indeed.

As Avran and I rode toward the city, increasingly were we struck by the vastness and height of the walls that surrounded it. Not one curtain wall, surely, but two — no, three, with a castle within on the hilltop! So we thought, but we were

107

KEY
■ Fortifications
▨ Residences and commercial buildings
⬚ Ruins

N
W — E
S

Koirusdort

Bevnustegor

Naradsdort

Nostegor

Parade
Ground

Koirustegor

Bevnusdort

Agirustegor

Airusdort

Filsovensdort

Uldsovensdort

sovenstegor

Outer
Bailey

Osumlet
Marshes

DORIOLUPATA

wrong. After all, there was only one single, huge wall, eight poles high at least, climbing the hill in a great spiral from the city gate all the way to the castle at the top. If Sandarro had been designed on the plan of a flower, then surely Doriolupata had been designed on the plan of a snail-shell!

A linear mound had been constructed to carry the road easily from the hill-skirts to the south over to the main gate of the city. There was marsh on both sides of this mound. Deeper marsh, with many pools a-clamour with waterfowl, lay to our left. (Indeed, these were called the Osumlet — the wildfowl — Marshes.) To our right was a shallower marsh grading into meadowlands.

Two round towers guarded the outermost gates of the city, but their massive doors were standing open and the soldiers on the towers regarded us incuriously. Within was a bailey, overgrown with grass and weeds, and beyond, three great towers guarding twin gates; the Sovestegor, 'the gate of the strangers'. One of these, that at left, was closed. Weeds were growing high and untended against its great doors and the huge, elaborate hinges were rusting. In contrast, the doors at right were in good order and, like the outer gates, stood open. Through these we passed.

It was a depressing entry to a city. This ward, the Sovensdort or 'stranger's ward', was overshadowed not only by the great, spiralling curtain wall but also by a third, lower wall between its courses, separating the Sovensdort into an inner and an outer quarter. Built against, or out from, the three walls had been many fine houses of stone and wood, but these were now in sad decrepitude. All were neglected, many were ruinous and some had collapsed entirely, their foundations tumbled and their stones overgrown by tall weeds and tangling creepers. The ragged men and women who watched us go by, and even the few half-naked children, were dully apathetic — a reaction worse, or so it seemed to me, than even the hostility of the country folk.

The median wall ended before we came to a third double gateway, the Koirustegor, 'gate of the merchants'. Again, the gate at left was closed and neglected, that at right open and, this time, guarded; we were scrutinized carefully as we rode in. Intrigued by this disparity, I asked the soldier riding by me to explain it.

'The left-hand gate is the ceremonial gate,' he explained gravely. 'It is to be opened only when our beloved narat rides forth. As it chances, that is seldom, for His Highness feels — er — more at ease, shall we say, in the heart of his city. His — er — delicate constitution is ill-attuned to the rougher life outside.'

I glanced at him. His face was perfectly grave, yet we both knew what he was implying — that the narat felt safe only in the heart of his fortified city. It was a sad commentary on the condition of this land of Denniffey.

Things were better in the second ward of the city than in the first, for here lived the protected merchant class and the servants of Denniffey's regrettable ruler. To our left, below the inner coil of the great wall, were warehouses and inns which, if rather dirty and unpainted, were at least in vigorous use; to our right were lines of tall houses, with shops in their lowest storeys. There was a bustle of people in the street, most of them quite well-dressed. Though they made way for us quickly and paused to watch us ride by, they showed no particular apprehension of us. Indeed, from some doorways, painted ladies called out greetings or invitations as we passed.

All in all, it should have seemed much like an English town. Yet, here again, something felt wrong. An English crowd would have been noisier, more obviously cheerful; there would have been good-humoured gibes and catcalls as well as greetings, to which the soldiers would have responded in kind. These people were too quiet, too — what was the word? — obsequious.

The next gate was the Bevnustegor, 'gate of the beasts'; and beyond, we entered quietness and greenery. Here were trees and bushes, grass, flowers and pools; here, sevdreyen and hasedain were grazing. True, there were stables and a few houses; true, there were soldiers patrolling the walls and towers on either side; but this was a pleasant place, a place of tranquillity. I could feel a new enthusiasm in Yerezinth as he sniffed the clean freshness of this quarter, while Zembelen was tossing his horns joyously.

A fifth double gate was passed, the Agirustegor, 'gate of the noblemen'. The gate at left was, as usual, closed; but it was free of weeds and obviously in regular use — so the narat *did* ride out into the Bevnusdort, at least! Within, there were again trees and bushes. Set among them, however, were handsome houses, the city residences of the great families of Denniffey. The houses of such families as had retained the favour of the Abaletsens during their long rule exuded opulence, with fresh gilt or silver on the heraldic devices over the doorways, rich furnishings and tapestries visible through the leaded panes of great windows, and a swarm of servants. Others, in contrast, seemed neglected and several were shuttered or empty.

It chanced that, as we were passing one of these, Zeladh Lenavvar was riding just a little way in front of me. Since arrival in Doriolupata he had recovered his spirits. In a high voice, as unpleasant as the scratchings of an unrosined fiddle bow, he had been complaining of the soldiers' ineptitude in losing 'his' prisoners. Indeed, he was threatening that, if necessary, his reward money would be deducted from their pay.

Suddenly I heard an all-too-familiar whir above and behind me. I ducked, but was still looking forward when the sasial dart struck the betrayer of guests full in the back. He gave a cry, crumpled sideways and fell dead from his sevdru. Vengeance had indeed come swiftly!

Chapter Twelve

WITHIN THE WALLS

In automatic reaction, the soldiers broke and scattered; but there were no more darts. Already Burak Ekonar was howling with rage and pointing upwards. A lithe figure in brown tunic and hose was running swiftly along the roof of the house toward the wall; the assassin, surely! However, he was high above us; neither darts from the sasayins of the soldiers, nor even hurled javelins, could hope to hit him. (Some of the latter were thrown, but they fell amply short.) There was a rope awaiting him and, above, a second man in the uniform of a soldier to haul him up.

As he reached the top of the wall, the first man — could it really be Darolayn Estantesec? — turned and waved cheerily. Then he and the supposed 'soldier' disappeared beyond the wall.

Predictably, there was utter confusion for a time. Burak's men had broken into the house and were soon up on its roof, while the guards from farther along the wall came running to investigate. Long before the two men could be intercepted, however, they had swarmed down another rope, to vanish among the hovels and ruins of the Sovensdort.

The ambush had been carefully prepared. The skull of a sevdru, with a sasayin ribbon between the horns, was found affixed to a beam on a swivel, in such a fashion that it might despatch its dart downward at any required angle. (I had not heard of such a device before, but it was used regularly in street fighting in southern Rockall, where the only bows were not effective in man-killing.) The soldier patrolling that section of the wall had been somehow silenced — later he was found, bound and gagged, in an upper room of the empty house — and another man had taken his uniform and place. The time of our arrival in the Agirusdort had been gauged very

113

accurately, for a change of guards had happened only an hour earlier and the ambush set up in the ensuing short time.

If Burak Ekonar had been angry at the loss of the prisoners, he was even more furious now! Summoning most of his men, he rode at frantic speed back down the spiral roads of Doriolupata, to begin an intensive search of the Filsovensdort, the inner and closer part of the Sovensdort, and then of its outer part, the Uldsovensdort. However, though much time was spent on this search and many citizens grievously mis-handled, Darolayn Estantesec (if indeed it had been he) was not found. A search of the Koirusdort over the next two days, by a larger body of soldiers, was to arouse even more resentment but produce no different result.

Left behind with the residue of Burak's troop, Avran and I were ordered to dismount. Their sevdreyen and ours were led away to be groomed and taken to pasture, not in the Bevnusdort — that apparently, was reserved for the beasts of the narat and his cronies — but in the meadowlands beyond the city. At the time, this seemed a considerable setback for Avran and me, since it meant we must either escape afoot from the city or await some future expedition before attempting an escape; but it was to prove an advantage. For the moment, all we could do was mentally to instruct our sevdreyen to be ready for a call at any time.

The body of Zeladh Lenavvar had been wrapped in blankets and taken to the house of his family — not one of the most opulent — to await burial. For more than an hour the remaining soldiers and we, with nothing to do, simply waited around, the soldiers discussing the Lenavvar's death in awe-stricken dismay.

Eventually one of Burak's centenars arrived bearing orders. Avran and I fell obediently into line with the soldiers. With packs on back, pack-saddles under our arms and bowstaves in hand, we marched with them onward up the road, past the last of the great houses, across a parade ground and through the innermost city gate, the Nostegor or 'heart gate' — this time just a single arch between two great towers — into the city's innermost ward, the Naradsdort or 'ward of the republic', where the soldiers were quartered in great barracks below the castle.

114

There the adjutant dismissed the soldiers to their quarters. We were taken along to join them at dinner, in a small canteen just within the gate. That was again an uneasy evening, for the soldiers could talk of nothing but the killing of the Lenavvar, the escape of the prisoners and the likely consequences to themselves of both events. We were called fortunate, since we could not be held responsible for either happening, and we were treated well enough. However, when we were taken to sleep, it was in a large and guarded dormitory, on pallet beds some way apart and far from the doors. Escape from Doriolupata would not be simple.

Nor did it come to appear easier in the days that followed. The next morning, Avran and I were transferred away from Burak's troop, into another barracks where new recruits were accommodated. Quite a lot of them there were, some being mercenaries like Burak's men but most the scourings of the Denniffey countryside. Only a few of the latter had been willingly recruited to the Abaletsens' service; the majority had been entirely reluctant, yet forcibly impressed in view of the anticipated threat from rebellious Darrinett. The friendliest of all to us, strangely enough, were the mercenaries; the willing Denniffeyen recruits were a pretty noxious gathering of thieves and rogues, whilst the unwilling classed us with all other foreigners and hated us accordingly.

Because so many of the recruits were as eager as we to escape this service and were more obvious about their desire, we were all watched and guarded as if we had been prisoners. Though we were supposedly soldiers already, we were not trusted with weapons. Avran's sword and mine, my belt of knives and even our supposed 'quarter-staves' were taken away, with an assurance that all would be returned later. Instead, during the first week, we were permitted to drill and exercise only with sticks.

We were under the direct charge of a bitter-tongued serjeant and the indirect authority of a fat Denniffeyen centenar, who lolled on a stool and watched the proceedings languidly. All was done on foot, the sticks simulating swords, spears and javelins at different stages of the exercises. It was quite well managed — this was, after all, a highly professional army, whatever its moral quality — and, in a way, I enjoyed myself, hating only the recurrent bullying of the unwilling or incompetent. Though I saw Avran every day, I had no chance to talk privately with him, for indeed there was no privacy between our morning rising and our being locked into the dormitory at night.

However, at the end of the week, the selection of the better soldiers began. In particular, we were given a test in swordsmanship. In this, of course, Avran excelled; moreover, after the long hours of practice in Sandarro with Oled Orexin, my own performance — though not in the same class — was much better than that of most other recruits.

Twenty of us — almost all the others were mercenaries — were selected for advanced training. We were given surcoats of green with the cockatrice emblem, swords were issued to us (or, as in the case of Avran and me, returned to us, along with our other possessions), and we were transferred to another barracks, joining one of the hundred companies into which the Denniffeyen army was divided. The centenar to whom we were assigned was a long-moustached Fachnese mercenary, fierce and forceful enough during the day's training, but easy-going (and, by repute, hard-drinking) out of hours.

Whilst we had not yet been allowed to go beyond the Naradsdort, Avran and I were at least able to stroll about and talk together, watching the soldiers and courtiers come and go from the castle. On one occasion, we were ordered by a centenar to stand at attention while President Vizien Abaletsen himself, a surprisingly small man with a plump, pouchy face, rode by on a snow-white sevdru. As Avran commented sourly, the rider dishonoured the beast.

Though we discussed the question at length, we could see no immediate prospect of escape from Doriolupata. We were in the innermost coil of its high spiral of walls; we had not seen our sevdreyen since the day of our arrival, though assured we would do so 'when the proper time comes'; and, even if we escaped from the city and avoided the Osumlet Marshes, we had no idea how we might cross the River Werenthin — always a difficult task, as Senraidar had warned us.

These were serious problems, but we had certain advantages also. First of all, there were few Sandastrians in the barracks and Avran had not been recognized. Secondly, though wearing

116

the green surcoats, we were permitted our own clothes beneath. (Not until soldiers were finally admitted to the Denniffeyen army were they issued with full uniforms.) My hidden knives remained undetected and the true purpose of our bowstaves passed unperceived.

As a precaution, Avran and I simulated quarterstaff fights on some evenings, receiving encouragement and advice from the other soldiers. When asked why our staffs were notched, Avran responded calmly that the notches could be used to twitch the staff out of the hands of an opponent. Indeed, he bemoaned that he was not yet skilled enough to manage this!

All in all, that was not an unhappy time. Yet we could not be at ease — in part, because our quest for Lyonesse (and, for me, my return to Ilven my beloved) was being so much set back, in part because, for both of us, our future safety was a matter for question. Yes, Avran had not yet been recognized, but his eventual recognition seemed daily more likely; and my fears for my friend in that event were as great as his own fears for its effect on his father's realm.

Yet twelve more days passed by without untoward incident. On each Sunday we were lined up with the other soldiers and recruits for a religious service of the most perfunctory kind, a stout cleric intoning scriptures in so formulaic a fashion that none of us even understood him. Later in that day and on all other days, we either paraded or exercised with simulated or real weapons. With my usual ability at throwing things, I found I could excel at hurling the javelin, and there was none who could match Avran's swordsmanship.

However, in our urge to attain greater freedoms by doing well, suddenly we found a new problem pressing upon us. Along with eight other recruits — the Denniffeyens seemed only to think in groups of ten, for some strange reason that bemused my English mind — we were brought before the centenar and informed of an imminent promotion. In three days' time, he told us beamingly, we and other recruits who had excelled would be admitted to the Denniffeyen army. Furthermore, we would have the particular honour of swearing fealty to the narat himself!

In the meantime, we were each presented with a bagful of kals, the etched quartz spheres that serve as low-value coins in southern Rockall (higher values are garnets or zircons,

117

each facet bearing an inscription and the device of the realm). In addition, we were each given an engraved metal disc which, the centenar told us, would enable us to pass at will through the three inner city gates, though not through the two outer gates.

'Time to go and enjoy the Koirusdort!' he growled genially. 'Have a good time, but be back by sundown.' Waving dismissively at us, he turned to other concerns.

For almost three weeks we had seen nothing but the grey buildings and high walls of the Naradsdort and the stones of the parade ground by the Nostegor. It was a pleasure for me even to walk among the tall houses and trees of the Agirusdort — I noticed again, with wry amusement, the roof from which the Lenavvar had been slain — and a positive delight to wander down through the trees and flowers of the Bevnusdort. The month of Devbalet (February) was well advanced now and it was high spring in southern Rockall; more than ever, this was a beautiful place.

Seeing that Avran and I were disposed to linger there, the other eight recruits left us, hastening away to explore the delights of the Koirusdort, its inns, its shops and its women.

When they were out of earshot Avran, who had said little hitherto, burst out: 'Simon, we must leave this place — and quickly! Playing at soldiers is well enough, albeit a waste of time; but I refuse absolutely to take any oath of fealty to that greasy Vizien Abaletsen! You've seen, as I have, the evil that he's done to this land; can *you* take any oath to him? For my part, I'd rather die!'

I looked at him in startlement. 'You know, that question hadn't even occurred to my mind, I must confess. I suppose I was getting too used to our life among the soldiers to be thinking clearly. You're right, of course, Avran; we cannot do it. Yet, if we say we don't wish to join the Denniffeyen army, they won't merely let us go. Most of the other recruits are quite as unwilling. What may we do, though, to avoid taking that oath?'

Avran gave me a strained smile. 'Well, Simon, it was I who plunged us into this morass — as usual; much use I've been to you on your journey, so far! But I'm afraid it is you who must devise a means for our escape. You're the cunning one, not I!'

I looked at Avran bleakly, then at the high, guarded walls about us, and sighed. Saturday today; Sunday and Monday; then the oath-taking on Tuesday morning. Was it possible, in so short a time?

'Well,' I answered slowly, 'I'll try my best to think of something; but, at the moment, I'm quite without inspiration. We need to know more about this city. Let's go and look around the Koirusdort.'

When I had first glimpsed the merchants' quarter, its crowded, clamorous street and high, close-set buildings had reminded me of an English town. At second look, that impression persisted. Yet there were many differences — in the clothes of the people, of course, and their language; in the greater number of written signs, appropriate in a land where far more men and women were literate; but, most of all, in the behaviour of the people. I had felt this difference when we rode through; I felt it more strongly now — a submissiveness, an obsequiousness that surely sprang from unease, even from fear. It was apparent in the way that men looked at us in our soldier's garb, moved out of our path unnecessarily, smiled at us with nervous over-courtesy. It was apparent in the fashion that children's games were instantly stilled as we approached, only to be resumed when we had gone past. This might be a good city in which to have the privileges and money of a soldier, if one lacked sensitivity; however, it was not a happy city. I hated it.

Yet there *was* a street life, and some of it was amusing. We stopped to listen to a trio of goliards, one strumming on an embelin, the second blowing powerfully on a horn-tipped pipe much like a hautboy, the third tapping away with his fingertips on a skin-covered double drum suspended from his belt. Wild, exhilarating music it was, as unfamiliar to Avran as to me, for these musicians were Montrions. Then there was a prestidigitator, producing amazing objects from the sleeves of passers-by or even from the air; and a juggler, manipulating ever-increasing numbers of coloured balls till the air seemed a-dazzle with them.

It was as we were watching this that Avran felt a touch on his sleeve. A slim, dark-haired young woman stood beside and slightly behind him. Her lips were tinted scarlet and her eyelids powdered a bluish colour, yet she seemed somehow

119

different from the other painted beauties whose blandishments we had ignored.

'Come with me, young sir,' she whispered. 'Your cousin awaits you in the Inn of the Winged Fish. Follow me.' Instantly she turned away.

After a single, startled glance at me, Avran did indeed follow and I after him. She led us along the main highway for some distance, weaving a graceful way through the jostling crowds, and then turned right down one of the short side-streets under the shadow of the inner city wall. It was a street mostly of warehouses, but at its end there was a tiny inn with the hanging sign of a fish improbably endowed with a bird's feathered wings. The woman beckoned, then ducked inside the rather low inn doorway.

Avran paused and glanced at me; then, our hands on our sword hilts, we followed. It was gloomy inside for, though there was no sunlight in the deep shade of the walls, no candles or dips had been lit. We hesitated under the lintel till our eyes adjusted to this dimness.

There were just four people in the little room — the girl who had led us there, still now and smiling at us; a diminutive man in an apron, surely the innkeeper; and, at a little table with goblets of wine before them, two other men. I recognized the massive figure of the first quicker than I did the leaner shape of the man behind him, even though I had seen the latter more recently; and I marvelled. All over Doriolupata, these two fugitives were being energetically sought, high prices having been set on their heads. Yet here they were, sitting relaxedly in the heart of the city of their greatest enemy!

Chapter Thirteen

THE PASSAGE OF THE WALLS

The lean man rose to his feet and held out his clasped hands in greeting.

'Welcome indeed, Prince Avran,' said Darolayn Estantesec. 'We have been watching for you and hoping for your coming.' After his hands had been seized and shaken vigorously, he turned to me. 'And thrice welcome to you, Avran's friend. I know not your name, but I know you to be my deliverer and shall be eternally in your debt.'

I blushed, but clasped his hands with pleasure. This was the first time I had seen Darolayn at close quarters. I liked what I saw. He was only a little taller than I, with a bush of hair and a trim Castilian-style beard, both surely once as flaringly red as Avran's but now fading into greyness. His face was creased and weathered, redeemed from grimness by the puckerings of good humour about lips and eyes. Those eyes were of the same blue as the wings of the little butterflies I had seen so often on limestone uplands; they looked at you very directly and clearly missed little. I was pleased when I saw, by the broadening of his smile, that the liking was mutual.

Avran was smiling also. 'If you are in his debt, Darolayn, then so emphatically am I! Let me introduce you; this is Simon, from Hallamshire in England. Since his true surname is almost unpronounceable, we call him Simon Vasianavar.'

Again we solemnly shook our clasped hands; then Darolayn turned to introduce us to the others in the room. 'These three are my good friends and trusted colleagues. First of all, my beloved cousin Dorren Estantesec, who risks more in my service than I dare to contemplate.' The dark-haired girl blushed and gave a little curtsey. 'And Radim Perilumin, who puts his house perilously at our disposal.' The little

121

innkeeper bobbed at us and grinned. 'And finally, this minute scrap over here' — he indicated his craggy, black-haired companion — 'is Vaien Vaghat, also very much in your debt.'

Vaien's huge hands engulfed my clasped ones and his smile informed me that I had gained another formidable friend.

Three further stools were set about the table and goblets of wine brought; then the innkeeper went to keep watch in the doorway. However, no customers came, for the warehouses were quiet today and the inn too much off the main road to attract casual visitors. Soon, prompted by Avran's eager questioning, Darolayn was giving us an account of the situation in Denniffey.

As we were already aware, pretty lamentable it was. The Abaletsens had, it seemed, been at the outset reasonable governors of the republic, but that was seventy years or more ago. The last three generations had treated it as a personal fiefdom, to be plundered at will and to the fullest possible extent. Under their misgovernment, Denniffey was tottering ever closer to complete ruin, Vizien Abaletsen proving even greedier and more corrupt than his father and grandfather had been. Moreover, after an assassination attempt had failed six years ago, Vizien had ceased ever to venture forth from the walls of Doriolupata, taking his unpleasant pleasures within the castle and never riding beyond the Bevnusdort. Thus he saw nothing of the land that he ruled and cared nothing about it. The Ruling Council was a farce, being made up only of his close relatives and particular cronies, all of the Abaletsen or Elietin families. Complaints to the Council went unheard, injustice was rife and crimes left unpunished. Indeed, in their own view, the narat's party and the army that was their instrument were above the law and could do no wrong.

However, though the whole land was seething with discontent under this misrule, Darolayn and his colleagues were pessimistic about the prospects of its being ended.

'The army is our greatest problem,' Darolayn said sadly. 'With so many imported mercenaries, it is too strong and too skilled. If the power of the Abaletsens were broken, those men would gain nothing and lose much. My people hate the Abaletsens and would like to rise against them, but they are afraid.'

'Is there no hope, then?' Avran asked.

'Oh yes, there is hope; one can always hope! As you know, after their successful revolt against the Fachnese, the Darrinnettans are in high fettle. They claim some of our territories and might decide to invade Denniffey. If they do, who knows what might chance? And of course, were our cousins of Sandastre to choose to intercede . . .?' Darolayn looked questioningly at Avran.

'Small chance of that, I fear,' he responded. 'Our people have no desire for war, now or ever in the past, as you know well. Moreover, we've been coping with our own internal problems.'

Avran told the three something of recent happenings in Sandarro, making overmuch of my contributions, but saying nothing about the grey riders. He went on to recount how we had been captured and brought to Doriolupata and of our wish to escape from that city.

Darolayn smiled at this. 'If Vizien Abaletsen knew he had you under his hand, Avran my cousin, how he would crow! But he must never know. Even were I not indebted to you, I would wish to ensure your escape from Doriolupata. As matters are, I am entirely at your service. But why did you venture into Denniffey and with what aims?'

Briefly I explained, to see Darolayn's brow wrinkle in puzzlement. 'Of Lyonesse, I have never heard. Have you, Vaien, or you, Dorren my dear?'

Both shook their heads; and he went on: 'It may be in the great forests, as you say; we learn little from those lands. As for a crossing of the River Werenthin, that can be arranged, I am sure; but you will be fortunate indeed if you can traverse the yellow plains in safety. Yet if the hand of God be upon you, perhaps you may. Others have done it, though not often.'

He pondered for a while, then said: 'Excuse us a moment.' At the jerk of his head, the big man and the girl followed him out to the doorway, where all three were soon in earnest conversation with the innkeeper.

Avran looked at me smilingly, the shadow of strain quite banished from his face. 'It seems we are to be fortunate again, Simon. If Darolayn was so readily able to ease himself into this city, surely he can ease us out of it!'

I nodded relievedly. 'If so, that's as well, for I've not been visited by any inspirations. You relied on me in vain, I'm afraid.'

He laughed. 'Not at all! Was it not the knife you threw to Darolayn that made this encounter possible? Well, they're returning; let's hear what they propose.'

However, only Darolayn and the mighty Vaien Vaghat were coming back. The innkeeper was resuming his watch, while Dorren, with a farewell wave, had slipped out of the inn door. The two men sat down again at our table.

'We can do nothing for you today,' Darolayn said flatly. 'Not only will the arrangements take time, but also you have been seen with Dorren and I cannot put her in danger. She will be returning shortly with a friend. The two girls will escort you during the rest of this day, when you must visit the inns and appear to be carousing. Your lengthy stay in this inn will be attributed to quite other pursuits, of course, which is all to the good! By sundown, you must be back in the Naradsdort, like good little soldiers should. Tomorrow is Taltegis [Sunday], with its religious services and parades. You will not be allowed past the Nostegor before late afternoon, but, given even ordinary good fortune, you should be allowed free time then; it is usual. Now, pay close attention while I tell you what you must do.' He proceeded to give us detailed and careful instructions.

Twenty minutes later, we were walking and chattering among the stalls, Avran arm-in-arm with Dorren Estantesec and I with a curly-haired, brown-eyed girl whose name I do not recall and whom I never saw again. Even though our dalliance was entirely feigned, it provided a pleasant enough interlude. We dined and drank wine with the two girls in an inn so noisy with music and song that there was little need for conversation; we lingered with them to watch the street entertainers; and we bade them protracted and affectionate farewells under the indulgent eyes of the Bevnustegor guards, before hastening back to our barracks in the waning evening light.

The Sunday morning was one of gusty wind and shifting cloud. In alternating sunshine and shade we endured, along with the other soldiers, the bumbling intonations of the stout

124

cleric and performed elaborate military exercises under the uninterested eyes of a group of councillors, who hastened away as soon as they might. The afternoon brought further exercises under a sky that was ever more heavily clouded; hand-to-hand combat, sword-fighting, javelin-throwing. I was nervous that some trivial accident might occur which would upset our plans. Nevertheless I performed better than usual, gaining generous praise from the large-moustached centenar. Under the circumstances, this embarrassed rather than pleased me. He and some of the other mercenaries were worthy men, however unworthy the ruler they served, and it caused me no pleasure to know that I was deceiving them.

It was late afternoon before we were dismissed. Hastily we returned to our quarters. Obviously we dared not be seen leaving with our packs, nor yet with the quivers of arrows; these must be forfeited. However, we detached the arrowheads and secreted them in our money-purses. The bowstaves would be a more serious loss; it was worth taking a chance to preserve them.

Thus it was with each a bowstave in hand that we walked boldly toward the Nostegor. My heart jumped with dismay when the guards stopped us.

'Hola, you recruits; your passes, please!' And, after we had showed them, 'Why those great sticks, pray?'

'Well, sir, we've been invited to take part in a quarterstaff contest in the Koirusdort. For the honour of the army and — er — a small wager.' Avran coughed discreetly.

The guards laughed. 'Why then, we must not hold you back! And make a wager for us also, provided you're quite confident of winning — but we want no losses, mind!' We were waved through the gate.

Swiftly we walked down through the Bevnusdort, hastened on our way by a sprinkling of heavy rain. At the Bevnustegor we were stopped again and Avran told the same story. These guards were puzzled and suspicious.

'A quarterstaff contest? We've had no word of it. Where is it to be held?'

'Oh, it's quite a small affair,' I interjected hastily. 'Just for the wager. It'll be held in the yard of the Star and Crescent Inn, if the rain keeps off. But I fear' — I glanced at the sky with simulated disgust — 'that the contest may be cancelled and the wager with it, curses be on this weather!'

At this these guards laughed also. 'I don't fancy your chances!' said one. 'Well, get along with you!' And again we were waved through. As we walked out from the shadow of the gate, I found that my knees were trembling.

The streets of the Koirusdort had been almost as crowded as yesterday, but the crowds were dispersing, for the rain was coming on harder. The pedlars were putting their wares back into their packs and the goliards wiping and packing away their instruments. This was fortunate for, in such general movement, our own proceedings were likely to pass unperceived. Indeed, with the people about us hastily seeking shelter, our own haste appeared entirely reasonable.

As we went along, we counted the streets to our left, seeking the ninth as instructed. Before long we were running through a downpour that entirely emptied the streets and turned the colour of our surcoats to a darker green.

Ah! at last, the ninth street! A rather ramshackle one for this quarter, with sheds built against the houses and piles of planks, stones and sand, evidently intended for sale, in its middle. There were few signs of life, yet we were conscious of being watched as we walked along.

'The sixth house on the right-hand side,' Avran muttered. 'Four, five — this must be the one. My, but it looks a dingy place!'

So it did. The woodwork was chipped and discoloured, the windows closed with sacking instead of the usual fine cloth or horn, and the steps to the front door ill-set and cracked. The door stood open, but such was the gloom inside that it was not inviting. However, any shelter from such rain would be welcome; in we went.

I did not see the black-haired giant until he spoke. 'Greetings again!' said Vaien Vaghat. 'You are in good time — excellent! Follow me.'

The stairs were rickety and creaked under our weight as we ascended. Though the light was so poor, I could see how very filthy and ill-maintained this house was and I guessed correctly that no-one lived in it.

On the second flight, there came a surprise. Vaien turned

126

abruptly and pressed a panel with his palm. Immediately a section of the wall swung inward, revealing a narrow passage.

'These places were not built for such as I,' he grumbled. 'More for small folk like you, Simon! Don't follow me too closely; I may become wedged.'

However, having turned right side foremost, he edged along the passage successfully enough. Since, at his word, Avran had swung the panel shut behind us, it was a traverse in darkness and seemed to take a long time. Eventually I heard Vaien's grunt of satisfaction and was dazzled as another panel swung open, to reveal a brightly lit room beyond. Stumbling after him, I tripped on a board and was prevented from falling only by his massive arm.

As I recovered, I saw that we had come through into a very different house, if it could be judged by the room we entered. For here were tapestries on the walls, fresh rushes on the floor, a handsomely-wrought table laden with good food and drink, and two welcoming figures — Darolayn Estantesec and Dorren. Their lack of surprise indicated that they had been informed already of our arrival. Indeed, the eyes of which we had been conscious in the street had been those of Darolayn's watchers. Though, in both our encounters, he appeared to be unguarded, it was not so.

We were urged to remove our sodden surcoats and hose, fresh garments having been prepared. Someone — Dorren? — had a good eye for measurements, for they fitted perfectly. There were brown tunics of the length, though not of the cut, of a cotehardie and hose of a moss-green for each of us. Avran, with his love of bright colours, winced a little at the prospect of having to wear garments of such subdued hues. Our new surcoats, however, pleased him better. Though moss-green on the outer side, they proved to be reversible; the inner side was of as vivid a yellow as a wagtail's breast in springtime.

Dorren, after watching us change our clothes with a cool interest that I found embarrassing, told us that we must wear the surcoats green side outermost until we had crossed the Werenthin, yellow side outermost to evade notice in the grasslands beyond. *Yellow* grasslands? That was a startling prospect!

127

As for our military surcoats, they were folded carefully and taken away, doubtless to be used in future schemes against the narat and his minions.

After that, the four of us had a meal which surpassed any since leaving Peratenay. It included roast waterfowl, an array of salads and fruits, tarts made from sweet yellow berries and a golden wine that frothed from flasks into glasses and was strangely exhilarating to quaff.

Over the meal, we talked about many matters. I learned that we were in the last house of the row, that closest to the wall. It was owned ostensibly by a wealthy trader in builders' materials, but actually by Darolayn. This was only one of several centres for the rebels in the Koirusdort and Sovensdort, the old houses of which had many concealed doors, secret passages and hidden chambers.

Dorren railed against the spiritlessness of the Denniffeyens who, though so frustrated and unhappy under Abaletsen rule and quite willing to aid Darolayn and his associates covertly, were yet unwilling to take up arms and free themselves. Darolayn was more understanding.

'The problem is that, after more than a century under the Abaletsens, we Denniffeyens have become accustomed to misgovernment. We've been trampled down so often that we've forgotten what it is to stand upright and free.'

'Can you ever convince your people to rise?' I asked.

He looked at me rather sadly. 'I try, Simon, and I hope. Yet I do not know . . . I do not know!'

Darkness came early that wet night and, with darkness, action. Equipped with new packs containing spare clothing, food, and horn flasks of wine, Avran and I followed Darolayn, and were followed by Dorren and Vaien, down four flights of stairs into the cellars of the house. A barrel was rolled away to reveal an iron ring set flush with the floor. This was grasped and pulled upward without effort by the mighty Vaien. What appeared to be a stone flag, but was actually a wooden trap-door, rose with it, revealing a vertical shaft into whose dark abyss there descended a narrow-runged ladder.

Darolayn descended first, Avran and I following, with Vaien, grumbling again at the narrowness of such places, last. After giving us a farewell smile and wave, Dorren stayed behind to shut the trap-door and conceal it anew.

When the light above us was shut out, the descent became a matter of rhythm and endurance. Extend a left foot down; find the rung; put one's weight on it; reach down with the right foot. Again and again, endlessly, in pitch-black darkness, with the sounds of Avran and Darolayn moving below me and Vaien grunting bad-temperedly above. The bowstave in my hand was an ever-present nuisance and, at times, my sword-sheath caught tiresomely against ladder or walls, causing the hilt to press bruisingly into my stomach. Down, down, down, with no pause for breath, till my calves and knees were aching.

At last Darolayn called up: 'Easy now! Solid ground below.'

Twelve more downward steps and my foot found a stone flag instead of a ladder-rung. A hand — was it Darolayn's? — steadied me and guided me aside to make way for Vaien. Then we were walking along a narrow tunnel that sloped gently downward, its walls so close upon us that we seemed to be ever brushing against one side or the other. The ground became slippery with water, then muddy. Another pause, then a door was swung inward. I saw before us the greyer darkness of a cloudy night and smelt the fresher moistness of recent rain.

'Wait a moment,' came Darolayn's whisper. Then: 'All is well, but — quietly, now!'

We emerged into a dimple of the northern slope of the hill of Doriolupata; or rather, at the point where the steep earthwork below the great walls arose from the gentler natural slope. The door to the passage was shut carefully behind us; its handle was what appeared to be the stump of a dead bush, in the shade of a cluster of living bushes. When closed, the door was quite indistinguishable from the wet earth of the hillside, so carefully had it been concealed.

'Now we must summon our beasts,' Darolayn said quietly. 'No, Vaien and I are not returning by the same route; that ladder is too arduous a climb. We have business to attend to, up in the hills. Good; then let's go on down.'

The grasses and weeds of the hillside were slippery with moisture. For the first time I was grateful for the bowstave; I could use it to probe my path and as anchor when my boots slipped. Darolayn moved quite swiftly, but Vaien followed slowly. He had broken off a leafy branch from a bush and was employing it to obliterate the signs of our passage. Some way to our left below, I could see a gleam of waters and knew we must be close to the edge of the Osumlet Marshes. Immediately below us was a coppice and, to our right, parklands with many shrubs and small trees.

It was in the coppice that we awaited the coming of the sevdreyen. We knew they were coming, of course; clearly could I sense the responsive gladness of Yerezinth. Yet they must have been many miles distant, for it was almost a half-hour before we saw their graceful shapes moving through the trees toward us. By then, Darolayn and Vaien had long since greeted and fondled their own beasts.

It was a delight to be mounted again, and in open country, after so many days afoot and pent up in a city. As if in response to my pleasure, the moon sailed forth from the clouds, silvering the bushes and trees with its light. We rode contentedly through a long night into a bright dawn, and continued riding while trees and bushes became ever fewer and the green weeds and grasses of the parklands ever more densely flecked with the yellow of the coarser grasses of the Werenthin plains. Several times we passed barns or ruined padin, many times we saw groups of grazing hasedain. However, in this land forever threatened by Montariotan raids, no men ventured far from their homes before full daylight.

Soothed by the steady pace and entire trustworthiness of my mount, I was beginning to doze when, abruptly, Darolayn checked his mount and pointed. Ahead was a green line of bushes, wrapped in a billowing sheath of ground-mist.

'The Werenthin,' he said simply.

We rode on for another hour or more, till the sun had climbed high in the sky and the mist dispersed; first up to, and then eastward along, that green line of bushes, to attain a place where a cluster of small trees furnished shelter and concealment. While the sevdreyen browsed discreetly and Vaien Vaghat, seemingly tireless, kept watch, the other three of us wrapped ourselves in our cloaks and slept.

I awoke to find the afternoon well advanced and Darolayn deep in conversation with a little gnomelike man. He had a stiff fringe of a grey beard, a red, rather bad-tempered face and pale blue, rheumy eyes. He was clad in what looked like a collection of cloth rags attached together arbitrarily by

130

someone who knew the principles of sewing but entirely lacked skill in that art. Avran also was awake, Vaien Vaghat deeply asleep and snoring like an old hound on a hearth.

'This is your boatman, Simon,' said Darolayn. 'He is a shy man, and with good reason, so he prefers that you should not learn his name. He will convey the two of you across the Werenthin, which is presently too deep in flood to be forded. As for me, I must watch while my friend slumbers. I shall say farewell and Godspeed here.'

Avran took his clasped hands. 'We are profoundly grateful to you already, cousin. If you send to Sandarro the word that we have safely crossed the Werenthin, you will place us yet more deeply in your debt. Be sure I shall try, upon return, to repay it.'

'To speak thus of debts, Avran, is ridiculous. Have you and Simon not given me life itself?' He turned to me. 'Avran tells me that you have been accepted by his family as a new brother. That means you are an Estantesec in actuality, if not in name, and thus my cousin. I take great pleasure in that knowledge.'

I clasped his hands in my turn. 'Thank you, Darolayn; and, er, I hope all goes well — that you succeed in all your aims. Maybe we'll meet again someday?'

A smile flickered across his face, a strange, almost mystic smile. 'Oh yes, we'll meet again. The fates of the three of us are interwoven closely, of that I'm sure. I shall look forward to that next encounter. Before parting this time, though' — he delved into an inner pocket of his cloak — 'I must return this knife to you; I shall hope not to need it again! Good travelling.'

Pleasedly I placed the throwing-knife back in its sheath, shouldered my pack and picked up my bowstave, while Avran did similarly. Then, with a farewell wave, we followed the boatman out of the grove, to be followed in turn by our two sevdreyen. So dense was the foliage that, within seconds, the two Denniffeyens were lost to view.

There was no path from the grove to the riverside, but the boatman found his way through the bushes with the ease and speed of a weasel. Suddenly he stooped and pushed; and the boat he had concealed slid easily before him, down a short slope and into the water with never a splash. He leapt in lightly, stooped again and produced a length of rope, the middle portion of which he tied about the boat's sternpost.

'Step in, will ye? Gently, now; ye're not hasedain seeking a mud-wallow!'

Avran managed it well enough. However, when with trepidation I followed, the boat rocked violently and sent me tumbling into the old man's lap, causing him to splutter indignantly. Remembering Bristol, I wondered whether it would be always my fate to be clumsy in boats?

I was sent to sit in the bow, while the old man remained amidships. Avran, under his instruction, tied one end of the rope about the horn-bases of Zembelen, the other about those of Yerezinth. Both sevdreyen were made unhappy and nervous by this and, uncertain ourselves, we found it difficult to calm them.

The boatman mumbled disgustedly to himself, then unshipped two oars and, with a single powerful stroke, sent his craft skimming out into the river. As the ropes tightened, the sevdreyen perforce splashed out into the water. Soon they were swimming behind the boat.

The Thames at London was the biggest river I had seen hitherto, for one could not count the Severn's salt estuary. After the winter rains, the Werenthin was at least thrice as wide as the Thames and flowing much more swiftly. Moreover, we were crossing it obliquely with the current, making the traverse yet longer. The river waters were so clear that we could see waterplants waving beneath us and strange fishes swimming among them.

I was so engrossed in watching these that I did not see the other bank approaching. We struck it with a thump and, for a second time, I was sent tumbling against the boatman.

On that occasion he was rendered positively inarticulate with rage, his eyes popping and his whiskers seeming to bristle like a cat's. It was some minutes before I could distinguish his words: 'Get out, damn you, get out of my boat! Call yourself a waterman? Why, I'd sooner have a galikhu in my boat! Get out, get out!'

Hastily I did so. Meantime, Avran was unfastening the sevdreyen's horns. They had swum well; however, but for the pull of the boat, they would surely have been carried away by the river's strong current. Then Avran leapt up onto the

132

bank neatly. As he turned, the old boatman drove in his oars and shot away from the bank, too swiftly to be offered any reward. If he heard our cries of thanks, he did not respond to them.

As we watched him out of sight, I realized that Avran was quivering with laughter. 'Oh Simon, that was hilarious! You should be a tumbler — or rather, you *are* one! Poor old man, he'll not forget you in a hurry!'

I smiled sheepishly. 'Well, anyway, Avran, we're across the Werenthin.'

He sobered instantly. 'Yes indeed; and henceforward we must take even greater care. On this side of the river, there are no friends to be found.'

Chapter Fourteen

THE YELLOW GRASSLANDS

Back in Sandarro, Enar Servessil had told us a little about the Montariotans, and Senraidar Estantesec, who had fought against them, had told us more. Yet, in sum, Avran and I knew far less than we would have wished about these people of the plains.

There were seven principal tribes, each with its own ruler, customs and territory. Though the boundaries of these seven territories shifted somewhat according to the fortunes of war, we knew their position with fair accuracy. Matruvak was the westernmost tribe, its lands close to where the Werenthin debouched into the sea. Mestei came next, north of the former Baroddan realm of Aldagard. Sedlaviss occupied the grasslands north of Darrinnett; and the easternmost Montariotan realm was Brantava, at perpetual war with neighbouring Volendar.

Unless we missed our way on the plains, we should be in no danger of encountering any of those four tribes; nor did we expect to be in danger from the riders of Ayanessei, whose lands lay north of Mestei. Instead, our path lay through the territory of the two remaining tribes. Our passage of the Werenthin had brought us into the plains where roamed the turbulent Amatomarr, the particular enemies of Denniffey; and, if we succeeded in safely crossing their territory, we must traverse also that of the Eldernet.

While the Volendarans had ceased to roam and had accepted Christianity, the other Montariotans — some called them Montrions — remained wanderers and heathens, worshipping gods of the sky and wind. They wore grass-yellow robes, carried bright, strangely shaped banners and were armed with broad-bladed spears as long as lances. They lived in tent-cities, moving with the seasons or at the whim of their rulers. Mostly they rode the heavier, slower hasedu rather than the lighter, fleeter

135

sevdru. Hasedain are close grazers and can find food enough
to survive in the grasslands even in summer, when aridity kills
off the taller plants and sevdreyen would die. However, so early
in the spring, there should be fodder enough for our sevdreyen
and, with luck, our swifter mounts would enable us to outride
any pursuing Montariotans. So, at least, we trusted.

We spent the rest of that day in concealment among the
bushes on the Werenthin's banks, but not in idleness. I was
eager that our long-bows be restored to usefulness. Having
found a straight-branched shrub much like a withy, though
with broader leaves, I proceeded to cut for us some new
steles, using the newly-returned throwing-knife as whittle. To
these steles Avran affixed the arrowheads we had salvaged.

The fletching was more of a problem, for it had not been
possible to detach and bring with us any of the stiff leaves
with which the Sandastrian arrows had been fletched. However,
after I had finished cutting the steles, I ventured prospectingly
along the bank and chanced upon a dead waterfowl caught
up in some grasses by the water's edge. Its pinions served,
when trimmed, as perfectly adequate fletchings. Our arrows
would not carry quite so far as usual, perhaps, but they
would nevertheless serve to surprise any assailants!

The making of quivers proved easy. We found needles and
coarse thread in our packs, placed there no doubt by the
thoughtful Dorren. The inner bark of the withy-like bushes
— no, Avran could not name them — was flexible enough
to be shaped and sewn into a satisfactory form. Since we
had no saddles, the quivers thus fabricated were fixed to our
belts; they fulfilled their purpose admirably.

By the time all this had been done, the evening was already
well advanced. We ate sparingly of the bread and dried meat
stored in the packs and then, worming our way into deeper
shelter, went quickly to sleep. We knew that our sevdreyen,
who had rested since their swimming of the river, would
guard us adequately and waken us at dawn.

I was roused by the gentle pressure of Yerezinth's soft muzzle.
It was dark still under the bushes but, when I stretched and
rose, I could see the first pale light of a new day edging
the Werenthin's waters upstream with brightness.

136

Zembelen was striving to awaken Avran, but having much less success. In the end, to my amusement, he prodded my friend's cheeks quite sharply with his two nasal horns. At this Avran awoke with a startled cry, rubbing his face indignantly.

Zembelen stepped back quickly, tossing his head in fright. However, when I told Avran what had transpired, he smiled ruefully and gave his sevdru the caress that was deserved.

Hastily we ate hunks of bread and meat and took swigs from our wine flasks. We turned our cloaks yellow side outermost and then, followed by our beasts, made our way cautiously up through the tangle of bushes, across a broad berm that paralleled the river's course and, through diminishing cover, out into the grasslands. In the pale morning light, the grasses seemed the colour of cream atop a butter-churn. Their colour and their stillness, for there was no wind yet, gave our venturing forth a strangely dreamlike quality.

The view was not considerable, for we were on a low step of land with two higher steps beyond. We mounted our sevdreyen quickly and, alert for danger, rode upward until we had ascended both those steps. As we did so, the light brightened and a little breeze began to stir the grass-heads into a motion reminiscent of the rippling surface of a gently flowing stream.

Neither on those three valley terraces nor in the much broader view now opening before us could we detect any sign of human life. Far away to the west a few black dots were moving away from us, wild creatures of some kind, though we could not tell what. Some wading birds were flying toward the river, in the random manner of cloth shreds blown by a gusty wind. Otherwise, the landscape seemed quite empty.

So it continued to seem, throughout a long day's riding. Never hitherto had I traversed grasslands so vast and so open. The view changed so little that I felt almost that Yerezinth and I were not moving, but that the ground was flowing slowly past us.

As the sun rose higher, the grasses changed in hue from cream through a pale yellow to the rich colour of wheat at harvest-time. Just as such wheat is flecked by the scarlet of poppies and the blue of cornflowers, so also these grasslands were flecked by the blues, violets and reds of spring flowers whose names we did not know. The buzzing of the insects that haunted them was lost in the continuous susurration of the wind-stirred grass. Only our own voices and, occasionally, the calls of birds overhead rose above that steady murmur.

By late afternoon, our sevdreyen were tiring and we knew our ride must be brought to an end; yet, in this monotonous landscape, where were shelter and concealment to be found? Only our cloaks could furnish either. Arbitrarily we decided to stop for the night. While our two beasts cropped the coarse herbage with evident reluctance and distaste, we ate a sparing supper. Then Avran wrapped himself like a caterpillar into the cocoon of his cloak and went swiftly to sleep, while I kept watch.

The sun went down in a splendour of colour that would have delighted any herald. For a brief while, I could see an irregular purple line on the southern horizon that must be the Heights of Denniffey. The night sky was clear and the waning moon washed the landscape with a pale light, making me feel as lonely and as conspicuous as a black beetle on a flaxen sheet. I shivered and huddled deeper into my cloak.

The wind had dropped with the rising of the moon and I was aware of much movement about me. Furry-winged moths blundered buzzingly from flower to flower. A cricket-like creature made a high humming sound, like the whir of a metal ring rotated rapidly at the end of a string, while another shrilled like an indignant starling. There were night-jar-like birds pursuing insects overhead, diving again and again with a flurry of wings and a soft, moaning cry; and several times I glimpsed a nighthawk hastening above me on silent wings. Small animals rustled and chittered among the grass-roots and, quite close by, a subdued gnawing sound told me that one of them was feeding. Twice I saw the black shapes of deer-like creatures running by and once a badger-sized creature trundled gruntingly past, heeding me not at all. Though the grasslands might seem empty under the bright sun, they teemed with nocturnal life.

As the hours crawled by toward the time at which I should rouse Avran, I found it ever harder to avoid falling asleep. I stretched and shifted at intervals but was reluctant to rise and move about, for fear of disturbing him prematurely. The sevdreyen had stayed close to us but they were asleep also, trusting in me as I had trusted in them.

Abruptly I became fully awake. There was a strange new sound, almost a rumbling, distant yet but coming closer. Some large creatures, surely, and running quite fast; I could hear heavy hooves and a curiously unattractive bubbling grunt that made the hairs rise on my neck.

Yerezinth and Zembelen were awake also and on their feet, gazing tensely, alternately at me and toward that sound. Like me, they were unsure of its meaning but sensed danger.

With sudden decision, I bent over my friend and shouted into his ear. 'Avran, rouse yourself! Something is coming toward us; some animals, I mean! They may not be dangerous, but I believe we'd be wise to be ready.'

My friend shook himself into wakefulness, like a dog shaking off water after a swim, and sat up, listening. The pounding hooves were coming ever closer, the bubbling grunts sounding ever louder and more unpleasant. Suddenly I found I could see the creatures, a tumbling mass of them, approaching us at a rapid rate.

Avran stood up. 'I don't like this. I'm going to mount.' In a moment, he was a-straddle Zembelen.

He had been unwise, for the creatures sighted him instantly. There was a horrid cachinnation and they were racing toward us. For a moment I stood frozen, then I leapt onto Yerezinth's back. He needed no urging; immediately, he and Zembelen were in full flight from the pursuing creatures.

It was a mad ride across grasslands that seemed palely gold in the moonlight, with Yerezinth and Zembelen galloping at the limit of their speed. Yet, fast though a sevdru can travel, the creatures were gaining on us steadily.

Huge they were, quite as long-legged and high-bodied as horses, but bigger than the largest horse I had seen and moving more as would running pigs. As they closed upon us, I glimpsed them in the moonlight and recognized them. The short, gleaming tushes, the squared-off snout, the distorted warty cheeks and swollen-tipped, hairy ears — why, these were the nightmare, hoglike creatures I had seen depicted on that wall-painting in Sandarro Castle and had believed could not be real. Well, nightmare had turned into reality with a vengeance!

139

One of the creatures had outdistanced the rest and was almost upon me, the sound of its drumming hooves and its obscene, gurgling cry loud in my ears. There was no hope of using my bow against it and I did not think of my sword. Instead, I seized a throwing-knife from my belt and half-turned.

It was almost alongside me already, its yellow teeth champing, its nostrils flaring redly and its eyes a baleful, bloodshot yellow. Ugh! I could even smell the creature, a whiff of ordure and decay, horrible! As it reached to seize me, I rammed the knife straight down into that gaping throat, snatching my hand away barely in time before its jaws closed.

The creature gave a choking, gurgling groan and lurched against Yerezinth's flank, causing him to gasp in frightened pain, stagger and almost fall. My heart skipped wildly in fear; but then we were past and the beast was falling away from us, to tangle with its pursuing fellows and bring some of them down.

I heard an unpleasant tearing sound, as if they were savaging it; but some of them, at least, were surging past to continue pursuing us.

Our headlong flight went on for almost an hour longer. However, the creatures never again came so close, their stamina fortunately not matching their speed. There came a final, braying cacchination that had a note of frustration, then the pounding sound of their pursuit slackened and ceased altogether. Nevertheless, we rode on at undiminished speed for fifteen more minutes before we felt safe enough to slacken pace.

'My, what an unpleasant awakening!' Avran gasped. 'What vile beasts! Our legends tell of them, but no Sandastrian has seen one for centuries. Ukhuren they are called, ghost-hogs, for they hunt and scavenge only at night. Phew! I'm glad we got clear of them — they'd have finished us pretty swiftly!'

'I remember a picture of them, in the castle. Are all the creatures in those pictures real? I thought those, at least, must be legendary.'

'I'm not sure. Some of the pictures are of creatures long gone from our lands, like the ukhur and the ramora — the big, blue creature with the massive horns. Others have never lived in Sandastre, to my knowledge, though travellers' tales tell of them. The xalihu, which you'd call a unicorn, is one.

140

Does it live in England? Never did I see one there, though I heard strange stories of how it was hunted — if I recall aright, that it could be lured only by maidens.'

'There are no unicorns in England nowadays,' I answered pensively. 'Once though, at a fair, I saw a twisted, ivory horn they said was a unicorn's horn; I believe it was ground up afterward to make love-potions. People say the unicorn lives far away in the east, in the lands of the infidels where the Crusaders fought.'

'Well, after tonight, I'm prepared to believe that *all* those creatures exist somewhere, but I trust that none of them will disturb my future nights' slumberings! You must dismount and rest now, Simon. I'll watch for what remains of this night.'

Glad was I to do so. Sleep took me swiftly and was undisturbed by any further visitations, of animals real or unreal.

Chapter Fifteen

THE MONTARIOTAN CAMP

Dawn was amply past when I awoke and the shadows of the sevdreyen were long on the yellow grass. For a while, the events of the night seemed to me too dream-like to be real; but I groped for my belt and, yes, one throwing-knife was missing. Avran was still on guard. On glancing up at him, I was disturbed to see that he was looking somewhat worried.

'We came closer to disaster with those ukhuren last night than I realized,' he said. 'Did you know that Yerezinth has been injured?'

I sat up hastily, remembering my realization of my sevdru's pain and chiding myself for not examining him. 'No, I didn't. Is it serious?'

'I hope not; I did my best to treat it; but summon him and look.'

Yerezinth's movements, as he obeyed the summons, were decidedly stiff. He was limping a little on his left hind leg and along his left flank was a gaping, zigzag gash cut by one of the sharp tushes of the falling ukhur. Concernedly I examined this wound. I was relieved to see that, though deep, it was clean and appeared already to be showing signs of healing.

'I noticed the cut at first light,' Avran said. 'There was quite a heavy dewfall; I used a damp cloth to wash the wound, then washed it again with a little of the wine. I think it will close up quickly, though it will leave a scar. The problem is that, to allow it to heal, we'll have to ride slowly today.'

Grieved at my own inattention to my sevdru, I was caressing his head and horns. 'Thank you anyway, Avran. Well, if we can only travel slowly, so be it.'

'However, we face another problem, Simon. Where exactly are we? Those ukhuren chased us for a considerable way; was it to east, west, north or south? I wasn't thinking about that while they were pursuing us and now I'm not sure.'

'Let me consider. Oh yes, when I first heard them they were over to the east of us. I'm not sure either, Avran, but I believe we must be considerably to the west of our original course.'

Avran sighed. 'Well, that accounts for it. We must be in the western reaches of Amatomarr, where its territories march with those of Eldernet and Mestei — disputed terrain, I gather. That might prove good for us, or it might prove ill. Such lands are likely to be empty of permanent settlement, but we'll be in considerable peril from raiding parties. *Not* the place to be slowed by an injury to one's mount, I'm afraid.'

I stroked Yerezinth's soft nose and he snuffled affectionately at me. 'Well, I'm only grateful that I killed the beast in time.'

Avran was clearly startled. 'Was it so close as that? Whatever transpired?'

So I told him how the ukhur's attack had been foiled, ending lightly: 'I suppose we ought to ride back and seek for my knife, but I'm inclined to let the creature lie.'

He smiled quirkily in response. 'No, Simon. It would be easy enough, I'm sure, to backtrack our course; but we've been fortunate once and I thank God for your quick thought and quick hand. To risk another encounter with the ukhuren, especially with a lame sevdru, would be the sheerest folly. No, in whatever direction we ride today, it must not be eastward.'

We breakfasted quickly, then set off again northward across the grasslands. At first I walked alongside Yerezinth, to give him chance to rest that injured leg. However, I could sense his feeling of inadequacy and his wish that I were again on his back. As soon as I was confident that he was walking more easily, therefore, I mounted him. Nevertheless, we went along at a pace no faster than a horse's walk.

Avran preferred to prospect ahead for hidden dangers. He was riding about ten poles in front of us when, suddenly, he and his mount stopped. Waving me to be still, Avran

144

dismounted and continued on foot. I looked past him. In my concern for Yerezinth and my general dazzlement by the bright colour of the grasses in the morning sunlight, I had not realized that the land, flat for so long, was beginning to dip downwards. Avran was on his knees now, gazing ahead intently.

'Simon!' His call was low-toned, but urgent. 'Dismount, then come and take a look — quietly, now!'

I obeyed and was soon beside him. Before us, the slope at first steepened and then slackened, forming the southeastern flank of a broad valley through which a small, shallow river meandered. About it was a whole town of tents, most of them basically dyed yellow but all of them splashed with other bright colours in crude, barbaric patterns. One tent, set midmost, was especially large and was tinted as red as a robin's breast. Beside it was a high pole from which a tongue-shaped banner of the same hue was stirring idly in the breeze.

'A red banner,' Avran muttered, 'and the device in black . . . Three chevrons . . . No, I have it! Three spearheads, the middle one the largest. The emblem of Mestei! We have ridden far west indeed, or they have moved further east. But the river . . . Let's see now. No, I cannot give it a name, though it must be tributary to the Werenthin.'

There were many hasedain grazing about the camp and, though their yellow robes made them hard to see against the grass, many men and women moving among the tents. If guards were set, it was not obvious; yet I knew the Montariotans were ready always for attack, for battle.

'Well, we cannot go that way,' Avran said quietly. 'We must divert to the northeast and be gone from here quickly, ere their warriors ride forth. Come now, Simon.'

Soon we were mounted and on the move again, as rapidly as Yerezinth's condition allowed. Even when we were an hour's ride away from the camp, we were reluctant to descend into the valley, where bushes grew thick about the river and ambush was a danger. Instead we kept to the high ground. However, the course of the river was swinging steadily toward the east; this meant we were riding, not northward as we wished but back eastward, to our increasing unease.

At length Avran stopped Zembelen and, having waited for me to catch him up, said: 'This won't do. We cannot chance meeting the ukhuren again; we'll simply have to cross the valley.'

I concurred without enthusiasm.

'Very well then,' Avran responded decisively. 'I'll ride ahead down the slope. You follow, but stay at least twenty strides behind me.'

The slope was open and shallow enough; no peril was apparent. As they descended, Zembelen was kept to a steady walk. Avran had strung his bow and was holding it loosely in his left hand, his right fingering the arrows in the quiver, while he gazed watchfully about him.

As he neared the bushes, there was a sudden flurry of movement and he started back, setting arrow hastily to bow. However, it was only four deer-like creatures, two fully grown, two mere fawns, racing frantically away. I noticed the short, stout, three-branched horns of the adults, in shape like a caltrap set upside-down; their yellow pelts with brown dapple patterns on their flanks; and even the tufts of coarse hair about their flying hooves as they fled away upslope.

Avran had been greatly startled, but now he was laughing merrily. 'Come on down, Simon! There can be no Monta-riotans in these bushes.'

Relievedly I did so and soon we were splashing across the river. As we were thrusting a way through the denser bushes on the further slope, Avran stopped again.

'Fool that I am!' he exclaimed. 'Why, we are about to ride up from this admirable valley out into the grasslands; and yet, this is the only cover we've found in two days! I realize that it's only mid-afternoon, but your beast has been injured and needs rest, while both sevdreyen deserve a feed on something better than grass. Simon, we must hide up here for the remainder of today. After all, it'll mean we can start earlier and ride farther tomorrow.'

And so we did, taking our ease and refreshment by the quiet stream. For a second time we trusted to the sevdreyen to stand guard. Wrapped in cloaks that had been again turned green side outermost and hidden deep within the bushes, we slept well and long, never dreaming what perils the next day might bring.

At its beginning, indeed, everything about that day seemed auspicious. First of all, the long rest had benefitted Yerezinth considerably. The stiffness was gone from his hind limbs and a jagged, whitish scar had formed over the gash left by the ukhur's tusk. Secondly, though the morning was fine, a fresh wind was driving a procession of woolpack clouds before it from the southwest, producing a patchwork of brightness and shadow which, we trusted, might make us less conspicuous even in so open a landscape. Thirdly, Avran had risen before me and had caught four trout-like fishes, by the tickling method used by English poachers and hungry Sandastrians. He lit a tiny fire and cooked the fishes on a spit, furnishing us with our first good meal since fleeing Doriolupata.

Dawn was three hours past ere the ashes of the fire had been scattered and we were mounted. However, with Yerezinth better, we could hope to cover a much greater distance today. Avran was uncertain how far the grasslands extended — two more days' journey, at least, he estimated — but he hoped that by late evening, we might reach parklands where there would be better shelter. With luck and swift travelling, we might even attain the deeper shade and greater safety of the forest itself! Thus we were in good heart as we left the undergrowth by the river and rode up out of its valley.

As we ascended its highest and steepest declivity, we did so cautiously. There were hasedain grazing in the grasslands beyond; were there any herdsmen nearby? If so, we did not see them; and the feeding beasts, though certainly domesticated and probably part of the Mestei herds, took no particular notice of us. Clad as we were in our yellow cloaks, we must have seemed familiar enough to them, even though we were riding sevdreyen, to occasion no alarm.

There were a number of fawns, some so newly born that they could not raise themselves onto twig-slender legs even to totter from our path. We saw also one dead male hasedu, the overnight kill of some predator and partially devoured. However, by the relaxed behaviour of the hasedain grazing nearby, we knew the killer must be gone far away. Soon we were beyond the herd and relievedly riding away northward into grasslands whose emptiness was, by comparison, welcome.

The wind had become intermittent, rippling the grasses into waves that faded quickly into stillness, only to be recreated by the next gust. Its cool freshness was exhilarating and raised our spirits further. A large flock of starling-sized birds with azure-blue plumage — isitelnen, Avran called them — flew over around noon, eddying briefly about us in the fashion of gnats in a rising air current, then flying on. A while later we saw grazing hasedain far to the east, but were not tempted to view them more closely. Otherwise it was a steady ride, as fast as a horse's trot, for hour upon hour across golden grass flecked with bright flowers, with cloud shadows gathering above us and passing to yield sunlight again.

We paused for a while early in the afternoon, to snatch a bite of bread and sip of wine while Yerezinth and Zembelen munched grassheads unenthusiastically. Then on we rode again for two more hours over unchanging grasslands.

By that time, the pleasant monotony of riding was dulling our watchfulness. It was, I think, Yerezinth who first perceived the men behind us. I sensed his awareness of them and turned about. Yes, I could just glimpse a group of riders, so far to the south of us that only their motion enabled me to distinguish them. Which way were they moving? Why, toward us, and quite rapidly!

Zembelen and, through him, Avran, by then had been brought to attentiveness. 'Better ride faster,' Avran said briefly. 'Mayhap they haven't noticed us, but we can't chance it.'

Our sevdreyen needed no other urging than the thought. Soon we were riding at a gallop, a gentler, more fluid motion than that of a horse and quite as speedy, yet below the fastest pace of a sevdru. That faster speed was reserved for a more immediate emergency.

Were the riders pursuing us, or were they merely headed the same way? At our more rapid pace, they were not gaining on us, nor yet were they falling behind. Had they, then, speeded up? Since we had not gauged their earlier pace, we could not be sure; but our tension mounted.

Looking ahead, I became aware that at last the landscape was changing. Not dramatically at first; just a beginning of undulations, as a water surface begins to stir before one becomes aware of the breeze that is urging it into motion. The grasses became sparser and I glimpsed sandy soil; these, then, had been sand-dunes before the vegetation stabilized them.

Just as waves become ampler as a wind freshens, so did the height of these dunes increase as we galloped onward, their lateral spread diminishing so that their slopes were steepening. Our pursuers, if indeed we were being pursued, were soon lost to view. Surely we might evade them among these hillocks?

Yet what was that to the westward? Another rider, high on a ridge-crest; he had seen us and was setting a horn to his lips. Its sound was like the bark of a red deer at rut. Now there were other riders mounting that crest, pouring over it and surging down in pursuit of us. Worse still, the horn call had alerted a third party of riders, to the east and much closer; more yellow cloaks, more bright spears coming after us!

As they descended into the hollows between dunes, the two groups of riders were lost to our view. However, the Montariotans must know this terrain better than we; they would be soon upon our heels. We must hasten indeed!

Unfortunately, the dunes to the north were rising ever higher and we dared not turn southward. To make matters worse, the sun had slipped behind a cloud. Without its guidance, a correct direction was not easy to maintain in such confusing terrain.

Avran glanced at me tight-lipped, then set Zembelen to ride straight up a high dune directly in our path. He was right; we must gain a view ahead and behind, at whatever cost in effort. It was not an easy ride, over tussocky grass in mats no bigger than a man's head, with sand between. Again and again hooves slipped, then gripped with an effort. Yerezinth was trembling; after such a long ride, the effects of yesterday's injury were telling.

Ah! good, we were at the top! We stopped momentarily and looked back. No, we could not see the pursuing riders, nor could we hear them; but that meant little, for sand absorbs sound. Yet they could not be far away. No time to waste; over the dune crest and down the other side, through a belt of dense brush growing in its lee and up onto the flank of another grass-grown sand mound. Down into a second hollow and into closer-set, shoulder-high vegetation; the sevdreyen could scarce thrust their way through it, for there seemed no paths.

What was that, behind? Horns sounding, surely; a rider, high on a dune crest to our left, had sighted us. Were our pursuers so close already? Frantically we forced our way through the dense shrubs and, free of them, rode up onto and over the shoulder of a third, broader dune. Beyond it was a wider hollow, even more closely grown with shrubs and low trees, but beyond, again, there were gentler dunes and open grassland. If we could gain that, then surely they would not catch us!

Yet how to penetrate the dense brush that lay immediately ahead? We could not linger, for there were horns braying behind us already. Down we went. Ah! there was a path; a broad game-path, leading through the brush toward an open pool where many creatures must drink nightly. At full pace we rode along that path, splashing through mud on the pool's verge and then racing on toward the north and the lower dunes.

There were yellow-cloaked riders spilling down the slope behind us, but our lead was good. Into the second belt of trees we headed, almost abreast now. Yerezinth's chest was heaving, but I could sense there was yet enough stamina in him to keep us going for an hour or more. In open country, hasedain could not match sevdreyen for speed. Surely all would be well?

Avran was optimistic also and turned to smile at me as Yerezinth drew alongside Zembelen. But almost at that moment, the triumph we looked for turned into disaster. Both our mounts stumbled; the ground crumbled away beneath us and we plunged forward into a deep pit trap.

Down we tumbled, into the meshes of a great rope net which closed about us. In a trice we were hanging in the darkness, as furious, frightened and helpless as flies in the web of a hungry spider.

Chapter Sixteen

THE PURPLE TENT

Often the unfortunate fly caught in a spider's web is left long dangling in its meshes. In the Montariotan trap, we suffered no such fate. Within minutes we heard men's voices and laughter above us. The net began further to tighten about us, causing Yerezinth and Zembelen, Avran and I to fall against one another in a helpless jumble. Avran had the wit to lean forward and grasp Zembelen's brow-horn bases, to give himself some stability and protect himself from them. I did not react so intelligently and fell against Avran, my right leg caught and compressed between the sevdreyens' heaving flanks and my arms seizing my friend's shoulders in frantic alarm.

As we were drawn up to the surface, the back of the net was brought forward above us, so that we were pulled head foremost out of the pit. My bowstave, carried so carefully for so many miles without discernible benefit, was again a nuisance: it had twisted about in the net and was pressing painfully into my back. My sword-hilt was driving up into my stomach, my right leg was numb, and altogether I was a bruised, miserable element in the writhing, kicking bundle that emerged.

We found ourselves in the midst of a crowd of yellow-cloaked men and the focus of a ring of spear-points. Had we been capable of resistance, it would have been wholly vain; but we were not. Though Avran was less bruised than I, he was much more thoroughly enwrapped in the meshes; even after I had been extracted from the net, seized and disarmed, he was still entangled.

After Avran in turn had been loosed and deprived of his weapons, the sevdreyen were lifted free of the net, quite tenderly, for these were valuable animals to the plains-dwellers.

151

I was surprised and relieved to see that neither Zembelen nor Yerezinth had been hurt by their fall. I understood this better when I learned later that such traps were designed to capture even the heavier hasedain without injuring them.

There was much talk among the yellow-robed men — for, indeed, not only their cloaks but also their tunics and cloth-topped boots were as yellow as spring primroses — as we were drawn forth. However, though their language must surely be close to the Sandastrian tongue, I understood it not at all. They spoke in spurts, their voices rising and then dying away as if, like the grass, wind-rippled. It made quite an attractive sound but was no more comprehensible to me than a jay's call. Nevertheless, I did perceive their surprise when first they noticed the jagged scar on Yerezinth's flank. Indeed, inexplicably, they seemed disconcerted by it.

Ropes were fastened about the horn-bases of our sevdreyen, tying each to the saddles of two riders whose heavier mounts would be able readily to control even big Yerezinth. As for Avran and me, our wrists were bound tightly together behind our backs, then we were lifted and set astride two other hasedain.

From this position we watched while the pit-trap was reset. After the net had been lowered back into place, a cross-weave of frail leafy branches was made. Then sand and clay were mixed and wetted with water fetched from the pool in leather buckets. This mixture was spread over the woven branches and smoothed, making a lid to be set over the trap. When this lid was in place, its edges were concealed by clay and leaves, after which dust was cast in handfuls over the whole. All was done with such quick skill that, within no more than thirty minutes, the game-trail looked as solid and inviting as ever. What unfortunate creature would be the next to blunder into the trap, I wondered bitterly?

By that time a third group of yellow-cloaked warriors, presumably those who had been following us from the south, had ridden up to join our captors. They eyed us with such evident surprise that I became convinced they had not been pursuing us, after all. However, puzzlingly, when their attention was drawn to Yerezinth's scar, they seemed quite as disturbed.

Among them was a tall man whose hood and yellow robe were embroidered in purple thread, evidently a leader. As he rode up to examine Avran and me, I saw that he had a grey beard trimmed like that of a Castilian and bright brown eyes under brooding brows. He addressed to me what was evidently a series of questions, but I could not understand them and he did not comprehend the Sandastrian phrases with which I tried to respond. Nor did Avran and he have any greater success in communicating.

Disgustedly the tall newcomer turned away. The other Montariotans were sped to their mounts by a sweeping gesture and, within seconds, the whole party was riding northward along the game path.

I had Montariotans riding before, behind and on either side of me; Avran was further to the rear and the sevdreyen, trotting between the riders to whose mounts they were roped, were yet further back. All four of us, beasts and men, were under the close scrutiny of fierce eyes. Sword, bowstave, arrows and belt of knives had been taken from me and, though I had still the other knives concealed in my clothing, my arms were tied too tightly for me to reach them, even had this scrutiny relaxed.

The hasedu on which I was riding, a slender doe, moved in a placid forward lurch like the gait of an ass, with none of the fluidity and grace of a sevdru. I could make no mental contact with her and suspected she was incapable of such contact. Probably, indeed, she had been given me as mount because of her slowness and stupidity. I saw no least hope of escape and, with my bruised body resenting every jolt, felt utterly disheartened and miserable.

Once clear of the undergrowth-choked hollow, the Montariotans bore left, westward, following an irregular course that found the easiest route through the tussocky dunes to the grasslands beyond. Westward . . . Who were these riders, then? The lands of the Mestei had been left behind; were these men of Eldernet or were they a marauding band of Ayanessei? I had no means of telling, but at least the question furnished something for my mind to work on during the uncomfortable monotony of that journey.

Abruptly our course veered northward, across a shallow dip and about the skirts of a marsh whose greenness gave brief relief from the monotonous yellow of the grass. As we rode up out of the dip, the riders checked and there were exclamations of surprise. Ahead of us, still a considerable distance away but clearly to be seen in so featureless a landscape, was a tent.

And such a tent! As we approached it, I saw that it was huge, much bigger than any in the Montariotan camp Avran and I had seen yesterday, bigger even than any I had seen at a tournament. Beside it stood a high pole, topped by a cross, each of whose four symmetrical limbs had crutch-shaped ends. It was termed in heraldry, I recalled, a 'cross potent' and served as emblem for the crusader kings of Jerusalem, being often depicted in the coloured scrolls sold at fairs. What did it signify, I wondered? About pole and tent were grazing some animals much like sevdreyen, but furred in dappled brown, not grey, and with horns differently shaped.

The Montariotans rode toward the tent, not in any disciplined order but in a series of surges and eddies that suggested excitement and unease. As we drew closer, I could see that the fabric of the tent was elaborately embroidered in gold, silver, green and red, with stick-like figures of men and animals and with numerous cabalistic signs, some familiar to me but most unfamiliar. Three armed men were sitting about the tent's closed entrance-flap, as if on guard. As we approached, they rose to stand at attention. Each was clad in purple and armed with a sword and a mighty, crescentic-bladed axe.

At a word from their tall leader, the Montariotans stopped and raised their long spears to the position of salute. One of them rode forward a little before raising his weapon. As he did so, I saw that it bore a fishtail-shaped green pennant with the device of a jagged lightning-bolt and, remembering Senraidar Estantesec's words, knew what tribe had captured us — Ayanessei.

Whoever was the inhabitant of the tent, it was clear that the Montariotans respected — maybe even feared — him. Their leader rode forward, then dismounted and stood with arms apart in what was surely a gesture of welcome. A purple guard came forward to stand before him, making the same gesture and then offering the clasped hands of friendship. As the leader grasped them, both men inclined their heads respectfully and a few quick words were exchanged. Then the guard returned to the tent and went inside it, while the Montariotan leader waited.

154

The other Montariotans sat relaxedly yet attentively on their mounts, Avran and I uncomfortably but equally attentively on ours. Somewhere behind us, the sevdreyen were moving uneasily and I could sense Yerezinth's unhappiness.

How many minutes we waited, I do not know: in my discomfort, it seemed a long time. Eventually, however, the guard emerged and walked briskly over to speak to the tall leader. There was a mutual, gracious inclination of heads and the encounter ended. The Montariotan directed a brief flurry of sentences at his men that caused a ripple of excitement — gratified excitement, if I judged correctly — and we were once again under way. We rode past the tent in a respectfully wide sweep and, watched incuriously by its guards, headed westward once more.

The rest of our ride was not long. Though the grassland ahead had seemed to me to continue unbroken into infinity, we were in fact quite close to another valley. This one was cut deep into the plain like a plough-slot into tilth and had flanks nearly as vertical as those of such a slot. However, hasedain, like sevdreyen, are unworried by steep descents; the riders and we continued over and down with as little hesitation as water flowing over a fall. Below us stretched quite a wide space, with a shallow shrunken stream at its centre and, about the stream, many yellow tents, a whole town of them.

As we came closer, women emerged to watch our approach and children — boys clad like riders in miniature, barefooted girls in dresses as long as those of English country children — ran noisily and excitedly to meet us. Avran and I evoked much interest, our sevdreyen even more. Yerezinth, indeed, seemed again to amaze and disconcert these people, though I could not comprehend why.

The majority of the riders dispersed among the tents, but a dozen escorted the sevdreyen, Avran and me to the very heart of this tent city. Close by the edge of the stream stood the biggest of the tents and, before it, a tall pole from which a much larger green fishtail banner fluttered in the wind. The leader dismounted, inclined his head to the banner with the grave respect of a soldier to his warlord, and walked over to the tent. At its opening he was welcomed by an elderly woman, in a dress thickly broidered with silver thread. He followed her within.

Two of the riders of our guard also dismounted. A pile of stakes was lying at one edge of a space of open ground, before the tent and beside the stream. One of the Montariotans seized a stake and held it upright, to be driven deep into the earth by blows of a stone wielded by the other. A second stake was driven in close alongside the first and two others, at a greater distance apart, by the stream banks. Yerezinth was tethered to one of the latter, Zembelen to the second; both animals were close enough to the stream to be able to drink at will from its waters.

Then Avran and I were lifted from our mounts and set down by the first two stakes, each to be tied to one stake by a rope attached to our already-bound wrists. The two dismounted Montariotans squatted down to guard us, keeping their spears at hand; the others rode away.

A knot of women and children gathered to look at us. All had darkly tanned faces and black hair; some were brown-eyed but many had eyes as blue as the petals of a speedwell. They evinced no hostility to us and, indeed, seemed much more interested in the sevdreyen. After a while, the women went about their business and even the children drifted away.

At that point, Avran spoke to me for the first time and, to my surprise, in English. 'I think we can talk, Simon; but we should use your tongue, for our guards may understand Sandastrian. Well, yet again we are in trouble, friend. It seems we have tumbled — how do you phrase it? — out of the cauldron into the flames.'

'These people are the Ayanessei, aren't they? Well, they've not harmed us yet — not truly harmed us.'

'Not yet, Simon. Not yet. However, think to yourself that no travellers — *no* travellers, Simon — have been captured by these people and survived to report it.'

'Perhaps we'll be the first, then!' I replied, simulating a cheerfulness I did not feel. 'I wonder why they're so interested in Yerezinth?'

'I do not know, Simon. He is a fine sevdru, of course, and very big — bigger, perhaps, than they have seen. Yet he is no bigger than a large hasedu . . . No, I do not understand it.'

'Can you comprehend their language? I can't.'

'It is difficult, certainly. I can pick out a few words, odd

156

phrases, little more. The tall man is their leader, their eslef; they style him *akhled*, but it means the same. They did not call him by his own name, only by that word of respect. This place is the *akhledet*, the leader's town; but only a part of the tribe live here. They have several, perhaps many, other settlements.'

'And who lives in that splendid purple tent?'

'Ah, that is interesting. I am not sure, but some important personage — a great doctor, a prophet perhaps, or a wizard. Of whoever dwells there, they seem both respectful and afraid. Indeed he must have power, to travel safely on these battle-torn plains with so small a guard.'

The evening was well advanced by then and the light fading fast, shadows reaching out ever farther from the valley sides. Cooking fires were being lit among the tents, their smoke spiralling upward in the relatively still air of the valley until caught and torn into grey shreds by the wind from the plains above. A group of women brought sticks and dry grass sods into the clearing, arranging them into piles before, and somewhat to the right and left of, the big tent. A tripod of iron rods was erected over one, a turnspit built over the other, and a burning taper brought to set each fire alight. Soon a cauldron of stew was cooking over the first and a joint of hasedu meat was being roasted over the other.

The stew, in particular, smelled delightful. I licked my lips hungrily. Even if these Montariotans intended to kill us, it would be an appreciated courtesy if they fed us beforehand!

In this, at least, we were to be fortunate. The akhled and his wife the akhledan emerged from their tent, to accept food proffered to them with solemn deference on trenchers and in dishes of polished metal. Rather to my surprise, they ate standing upright; was this a Montariotan custom, I wondered? When they had eaten, they astonished me — and, indeed, impressed me — by proceeding to serve food to those who had served them.

I was even more pleasantly surprised at what followed; for, after serving the two guards and receiving brief instructions from the akhled, two of the women brought food for Avran and me. Mouthfuls of deliciously flavourful stew were given to us in horn spoons and hunks of meat presented to us on skewers. We ate well.

157

The akhled and akhledan meantime were drinking wine poured from elegant glass flagons into metal cups. Of this also we were given our share, though in beakers of earthenware. Afterwards our lips and cheeks were wiped with coarse, moist cloths. When Avran endeavoured to express our gratitude, the women may not have understood his words but certainly grasped his intent, for they gave us pleasant smiles before hastening away.

Night was coming on now. Tripod and spit were removed and the two fires built up to a much larger size, so that the whole open space was lit by their brightness. The children were gone long since and the women — the akhledan among them — leaving. In contrast, men were assembling, singly or in groups, to squat down in rows about us. Soon there was a whole crowd of them, in a great arc extending from the stream bank to beyond the further fire.

'I feel better for that good meal,' Avran said quietly, 'but oh, Simon, my arms are numb — as yours must be, I'm sure. And this gathering — what does it mean? I doubt that it bodes well for us.'

Chapter Seventeen

RIDERS INTO THE FIRELIGHT

By then the whole valley was in black shadow; thus late in the month, there was only a rind of a moon and it was not within sight. If any stars shone overhead, they were masked from view by the more local brightness of the fires.

Two wooden stools were set between those fires, one closer to us, one further away. When this had been done, a group of musicians assembled and began to play — a strange tune, with a sustained trembling beat on oddly-shaped double drums and a windily wailing overlay from horn-tipped pipes. It was an uneasy sound, disturbingly like the irregular heartbeat and gasping breath of someone very sick, and it increased my own feeling of tension. The crowd of men fell silent, as if charmed or drugged by the music. Belatedly I noticed that the akhled had emerged unheralded from his tent and was sitting on the further stool, waiting. Yes, waiting; we were all waiting.

Suddenly there came a whooping of horns from beyond the camp. The music ceased and everyone jerked to attention. There was a pause, then the horns sounded again, louder and brassier.

All of us looked in their direction, straining our ears. Yet we did not hear or see the riders until, suddenly, they were coming out from between the tents into the firelight glow. Two black shapes on black mounts, they seemed at first, each bearing aloft a flaming torch; then two more following, each with a long golden trumpet in hand.

As they entered the firelight I saw them better. They were not clad in black after all, but in purple. Indeed, these were the three guards who had stood before the purple tent, plus another similarly attired. Their mounts were the same dapple-

159

brown animals that had grazed by that tent, but wrapped now in purple saddle-cloths. I perceived that their horns were quite different from those of hasedain or sevdreyen — a single, blunt nasal horn and two brow-horns that reached forward. Each brow-horn had five tines, clustered together like five fingers and making the horns seem like hands reaching out to seize.

The four riders stopped, forming a lesser arc between the fires and before the akhled, the torchbearers outermost. The two trumpeters raised horns to lips and blew a final, peremptory blast, then lowered their instruments and sat at ease. Again we waited.

Then, from the shadows, there emerged a fifth and yet more splendid rider. In the firelight he seemed a shining vision of silver, for he wore shirt, cloak and hose of that colour, a strange tricorn cap that seemed made of scintillant metal and long boots of palest grey leather. His mount was caparisoned from head to rump in cloth of silver patterned with blue stars: its hooves were sheathed and its horns tipped with silver. He rode forward till his mount stood midmost among the four purple-clad riders. Though I had seen King Henry among his noblemen at tournament and court, I had never seen any group so magnificent.

Yet, within moments, the scene had ceased to be simply splendid and had become almost eerie. The newcomer reached out a gloved hand for the torch of the outermost rider to his right, was handed it and flung it immediately into the fire nearby. As it engulfed the torch, the fire changed in colour, its leaping flames turning from orange-yellow to a strange, unnatural green.

As I, and those about me, watched in wonderment, the second torch was taken and flung into the other fire. Its flames also changed colour, not to green but to a bright magenta, causing the Montariotans to gasp in awe and fear. I heard the alarmed snorts of Zembelen and Yerezinth as they strove vainly to pull free from the ropes that bound them, and I sensed their fright. Indeed, their emotions matched my own.

The two trumpets whooped again, in a strange double wail. The akhled was on his feet now, head bowed and arms outstretched in deferential welcome. In the interplay of colour

160

from the two fires, his robe and those of his followers seemed to shift in hue from orange through brown and green to almost white. Their brown skins were turned sickly pale and the purple robes of the four riders changed to brown. Only the silver garb of the fifth rider was unaltered in hue. Indeed, it seemed to shine brighter, so that he became gigantic, radiant, superhuman.

Then the colour in the flames began to fade. The fifth rider dismounted and accepted the clasped hands of the akhled; and I saw that he was but a man clothed in silver fur. Indeed, he was considerably shorter than the Montariotan leader, for the topmost tip of his tricorn hat barely reached to the level of the yellow coif.

After an exchange of courtesy, the akhled resumed his stool and the newcomer sat down facing him. The watching Montariotans seemed to sigh and relax, and the scene became normal again. Nevertheless, that magical transformation of the flames had left its shadow of awe upon us and our tension did not ease.

The akhled clapped his hands. Instantly two women appeared from his tent, one bearing two splendid goblets of ruby-red glass, the other a flagon of wine. One goblet was filled and handed to the akhled; he drank from it, swallowed and then, after a moment's pause, handed the goblet to his guest. (This action, I presumed, was to demonstrate that the wine was not poisoned or drugged.) The second goblet was filled and handed to the akhled; then he and his guest drank deeply, completing what was evidently a ritual signification of honour and friendship.

There followed an interchange of sentences, the akhled speaking in eddying gusts of words, his guest responding with slow, sonorous cadences equally incomprehensible to me. However, it was soon to be made clear that we captives were the subject of their talk. At a call of command from the akhled, our two guards scrambled to their feet and bent to free Avran and me from the ropes holding us to the posts. We were assisted up, steadied (for our legs were cramped after sitting so long) and then conducted over to stand between the two stools.

We stood there for fully three minutes, under the steady scrutiny of the akhled and his guest. During that time not a word was addressed to us, nor did we speak. The face of the fur-clad man was partly shadowed, but I saw dark brows and bright, brooding eyes.

Eventually he made a dismissive gesture and said: '*Khadrash-lesar iga khafeslar atim.*'

This was the first phrase whose meaning I could guess. If the Montariotan *kha-* prefix was equivalent to the Sandastrian *ksa-*, it must mean: 'Unbind them and keep them near to hand.' That I had guessed right was swiftly demonstrated, for our guards freed our wrists from their ropes and then led us to stand beside the akhled's great tent.

In response to another brief order, Yerezinth and Zembelen were brought for inspection. Zembelen attracted only cursory attention, but at the sight of Yerezinth the fur-clad man rose to his feet. He walked forward and stopped to make a close, careful inspection of the jagged scar that disfigured my sevdru's flank.

As he did so, there came a sudden gust of wind that drove the smoke from the fires across into our eyes. I grimaced at this, blinking and throwing back my head. When the smoke cleared, it so chanced that I looked upward and saw the fishtail banner streaming against the sky. Then I looked again at Yerezinth and, for the first time, understood the surprise and awe of the Montariotans. Why, my sevdru's healing wound had exactly the shape of the lightning-bolt emblem of Ayanessei!

The fur-clad man turned and spoke again to the akhled. This time I did not catch his words, but their import was made apparent when the two beasts were led away, to stand just beyond the fire almost at the centre of the arc of watching men.

The shadows were lengthening anew, for the fires were dying down; yet no attempt was made to replenish them. The four mounted riders were becoming again creatures of darkness and the watching Montariotans reduced to a rim of smoke-yellow from which gleamed many eyes. In contrast, the yellow robe of the akhled seemed golden-bright and the silver furs of his guest shone in the fire-glow like an unsheathed sword.

Of a sudden, the latter turned about and, raising his hands in a gesture of invocation, cried, '*Khasadin! Tsoned khasenast!*'

162

Again I understood him: 'Come to me!' he had called. 'Grant strength to me!' As if in response, the two fires crackled and flared up into great pillars of yellow light, causing Yerezinth and Zembelen to buck and ululate in terror and the watching men to gasp and tumble backward. As for me, I was very sure in that moment that the silver-shining man was more than mortal, a prophet, a wizard.

He stood with arms outstretched to the dark sky for a long moment, then turned away. As he did so, the fires dwindled.

With mutterings of awe and amazement, the tribesmen crawled back to their positions about us. Two of the riders — those at the centre — dismounted and came forward, to place before their leader a tall, narrow stand and set on it a bowl that seemed wrought of shimmering, scintillant silver. Each bowed, then both returned to their mounts.

The wizard, if such indeed he was, bowed in turn. Then, with a flick of his fingers, he set the bowl spinning, touching it again and again so that it rotated faster and faster. He passed his hands over it and lo! there was a column of smoke rising from the bowl, turning quickly into a little leaping point of red fire. He was nodding and crooning now, his fingers flickering about the flame as if caressing it.

As the bigger fires subsided into dullness, their fuel almost consumed, this little flame glowed ever brighter, a red eye looking out between the scintillant tricorn covering the bowed head of the wizard and the sharp coruscations from the spinning bowl. Then the wizard straightened his head and stepped back.

Now the wizard began addressing the Montariotans in measured, doomful cadences, his voice like the roar of a gale in a gully and no more comprehensible to me. The silver of his robes was reflecting the last red fire-gleam, but ever more dully, like a horseshoe cooling on an anvil. The flame dissolved into smoke, dwindled and expired; the spinning of the bowl slowed and stopped.

As the bowl stopped spinning, the wizard ceased speaking. The two trumpets blared as he walked back to his mount. Within moments the five riders, their leader midmost, were hastening away. There was a last bray of horns, then they were gone into the night.

163

After their going, the Montariotans stayed silent awhile, then stirred into movement and noise. Yerezinth and Zembelen, still trembling, were led away. Though I could feel my sevdru's mental turmoil, I could transmit no calming thoughts to steady him, for my own mind was too uneasy and confused to be of aid. I sensed an enhanced respect in the very fashion in which the two beasts were being led away, but it gave me little comfort. Were they destined for continued good treatment or for sacrifice? I could not tell.

The treatment of Avran and me allowed an equal ambiguity of interpretation. We were conducted to a tent not far from that of the akhled. Our own clothes were taken from us — to my bitter regret since, though my remaining knives seemingly had not been discovered, they were removed beyond my reach — and we were provided with clean robes and new hide blankets in which to sleep. Well and good; but we were kept under close guard and so firmly apart that we could not even converse.

I was unable, therefore, to know Avran's interpretation of this change of behaviour. For my own part, I had sufficient knowledge of the practices of the heathen cults still surviving in England to be set uneasily wondering. Yes, we were being treated well; but future sacrificial victims were treated exactly thus, during their last hours on earth.

Despite my unease, I fell into sleep with the speed of a stone settling in a deep pool and slumbered without ill dreams.

Chapter Eighteen

THE CREATURES OF THE NIGHT

A wandering beam of sunshine, probing in through the open tent-flap onto my face, awakened me. I stretched, blinked, and realized sluggishly that it must be mid-morning already; I had been suffered to sleep long.

When she saw that I was awake, an old woman who had been waiting patiently nearby came over to tend me. With dampened cloths and a coarse towel, she laved and dried my face and hands as tenderly as if I had been her infant. This done, she brought me a wooden platter laden with slices of cold cooked meat and different breads. These, with an earthenware beaker of hasedu milk, furnished an excellent and welcome breakfast. As I ate and drank, two squatting guards, each with spear in hand, watched impassively.

I can have been only semi-awake until then, for I did not notice that Avran was missing until he returned to the tent. He was dressed in the yellow robes of a Montariotan and seemed remarkably cheerful.

'Awake at last, then, Simon?' He was speaking in English, as he had done last night. 'You were snoring as loudly as a timber-saw and I thought you would sleep the day through. For my part, I am not such a sloth; I have been up and about for two hours or more. We're still prisoners, of course, but these Montariotans do not seem likely to kill us out of hand. Indeed, they've allowed me to wander around quite freely. They barred my way, though, when I tried to walk beyond the camp and they wouldn't let me approach our sevdreyen. Nevertheless, there's plenty to see. Come, robe yourself and let's sally forth!'

I found that, like Avran, I had been furnished with cream-white underwear and a yellow tunic and cloak in the Montariotan style, garments unfamiliar enough for me to welcome the old woman's help in dressing. Short boots of tawny-yellow leather completed the outfit. In warm weather, such a garb is admirable, for it is light and cool; presumably cloaks of fur would be substituted in chillier conditions. Out into the sunshine we went and, followed but not impeded by the guards, walked about the camp city for the rest of the morning.

There was indeed much to be seen. Some of the women were weaving cloth from long strands of vegetable fibre, using strange looms that rotated horizontally, not vertically like those I had seen in England. Lengths of the cloth thus produced were being dipped by other women into odoriferous vats, afterwards either to be bleached or dowsed in shallow troughs full of a yellow dye. This dye was made, we discovered by further watching, from decoctations of the crushed bodies of grassland grasshoppers. We saw the white cloth being made into undergarments, the yellow into over-garments for men, women or children; while, by the stream banks, clothes were being washed or draped on stones to dry. Other women were preparing food, cutting up sun-dried meat, scraping or chopping root vegetables with little stone adzes, or crushing grain with rollers on shallow saddle-querns.

Some elderly men were moulding leather in troughs of steaming water or decorating it with sharp graving tools. Others were shaping pots with quick skill on treadle-turned wheels or fashioning vessels from thin silver, by means of swift blows from tiny hammers or merely by use of their strong fingers. Two brawny individuals, stripped to the waist, were shaping arrow- and spear-heads in bright flames, then passing them to younger assistants who sharpened them on rough stones. Among and between their busy elders skipped and ran many children, while others either played with toy hasedain or competed in elaborate games, among patterns of lines graven by sticks into the streamside muds.

All in all, it was a busy and cheerful place. Though many of the women and children paused to watch with interest as we passed by, we suffered neither insult nor any abuse. Again and again I heard the word *drahaklen* and knew it must apply to us; I wished heartily that I knew its meaning. Nor did Avran comprehend it.

'I presume it must mean "stranger" or "foreigner",' he

166

hazarded cheerfully. 'These people are so friendly that, surely, they cannot mean us harm.'

Twice we walked across the open space where, the previous night, those strange fires had burned. The scars from that burning were still to be seen in the turf, but the ashes had been cleared away and the stakes to which the sevdreyen and we had been tied had been drawn out of the ground and restacked. The flaps of the akhled's tent were closed; we presumed he must have gone hunting or raiding, along with most of the younger men.

I had hoped Avran might have comprehended more of the wizard's pronouncements than did I. Unfortunately, he had not. Yet he was inclined to be grateful to that gentleman, believing it was his words that had caused us to be freed and treated well. I was less confident but, in that bright morning, my dark anxieties of last night seemed too ridiculous to mention.

At about an hour past noon, one of our four guards seized Avran by the sleeve, made a pantomime of eating, and gestured to us to follow him. Back we went to the tent in which we had slept, to find the old woman engaged in cooking scraps of meat on a spit over a little fire. Soon the guards and we were eating these, from platters on which there were also hunks of bread and slices of a green vegetable tasting much like onion. One of the guards then served the old woman with grave courtesy, after which we all sat together drinking wine poured from a tall earthenware flask into crimson glass beakers. These, Avran told me, were made in faraway Fachane and must have been acquired by trade or theft.

Scarcely was our meal ended when we saw a group of riders approaching the tent. Evidently our guards had been expecting this, for they leapt immediately to their feet and gestured to us to rise also.

The riders — there were twelve of them — halted in a half-circle about us. One, evidently a leader from the elaborate green embroidery on his hood, uttered brief orders. Two hasedain, each saddled for riding, were brought forward and we were urged quite courteously to mount.

Our former guards raised their spears in what was evidently a salute of farewell. Then, with green-hood in the lead, we turned about and threaded our way out through the woven paths of the tent city.

All whom we passed, men, women and children alike, stood still and watched us with a quiet intensity that I found disturbingly different from their casual attitude of the morning. I noticed also that two laden pack-hasedain were following. Did this mean we were going on a long journey? If so, surely that fact must forebode well for us. But why were all the Montariotans so very silent?

The tents left behind, we splashed across the river downstream from the camp, a ford used regularly and positioned so as to keep the tribe's waters clean. Steeply up the slope beyond we went and regained the general level of the plains; but now we were to the north of the valley. Two guards saluted with their spears as we passed.

Thereafter we headed steadily northward throughout the rest of that afternoon. Two riders had hastened ahead, two had dropped behind to serve as afterguard, and the other eight were bunched about Avran and me. The Ayanessei rode in a disciplined fashion and silence that contrasted sharply with their irregular order and gusty talk of yesterday. With our hands free, Avran and I could ride much more comfortably than we had done then. Since two of the Montariotans, one of them green-hood, separated us, we had no chance to converse. I could not gauge Avran's mood; for my part, I was in no better spirits than after our rescue from the trap.

It was a ride of few incidents. Once my hasedu bucked in fright when a long-tailed bird flew up whirringly from beneath his hooves, twice we passed herds of hasedain grazing under the guard of armed Montariotans who responded gravely to our salutes, and several times, fleet-footed wild creatures, perhaps wild hasedain, were glimpsed running from our path. The yellow grasslands seemed endless, yet we did not pause for rest or refreshment. Even when the sun began to set behind a phalanx of little clouds, the ride went on.

The light seemed to seep away southward while, before us, there loomed a long, dark cloud on the northern horizon. I began to notice low green bushes studding the yellow grass, whilst ahead — could that be a tree? Yes indeed; quite a small one, but the first I had seen since the dune country was left behind. Surely that was another tree; and another;

and now a whole grove of them. And that dark line ahead . . . in the fading light, it was hard to be sure; might it be, not cloud, but forest?

Abruptly green-hood raised his right hand, then gave a sweeping gesture to the left. If indeed that had been the forest, we rode toward it no longer but headed westward instead.

South of us, the sun was dipping below the horizon. The clouds were grey now and edged with red, whilst the sky above shaded from gold through turquoise to deep blue, a gradation of colour that would have astonished and defeated the most skilled heraldic artist. Steadily the light drained from the sky until we were riding under an arch of deep blue, from which the first stars glimmered brighter than the pale rind of moon; yet still that long ride did not end.

What was that dark shape ahead, that hump against the western horizon; a hill, surely? Yes indeed; and a hill, moreover, that was flanked on all sides by a dense wood of trees.

Was that hill natural or was it some artificial creation, a motte built to elevate some fortification? We were no longer riding on grass, but on some sort of road; even in the darkness, the changed sound of the hasedain's feet and their different manner of movement told me that. Yet, if this was indeed a man-made mound, it must be very old. Soon we were passing among those trees. Though they were not tall, the thickness of their trunks showed them to be exceedingly ancient.

The road sloped ever more steeply till we were riding upward at an angle no horse could have managed. The riders had closed tighter about Avran and me, thinking perhaps that we might try to break away into the woods. Up and up we went; I seemed to glimpse stone courses to left and right about us and wondered if this might be the wreck of an ancient sun-temple, like that Avran and I had seen in Menavedravard.

Then the slope eased and we found ourselves atop the great mound, in an open, flat area rimmed by trees on all sides. Underfoot were flagstones covered with mosses and lichens, with tall grasses and weeds thrusting up through cracks. At the exact centre of the clear area was one immense old tree, with great branches spreading widely; a tree that was nearly dead, for it retained few leaves and its trunk had been repeatedly cloven by lightning-bolts.

Green-hood spread out his arms palm-backward, so that the other riders and we stopped. He rode forward, dismounted and walked on a few paces before dropping to his knees. With arms spread again, but this time in the attitude of respectful greeting, he began to chant what sounded like a hymn to the ancient tree. The other Ayanessei dismounted and stood beside their hasedain with bowed heads. Puzzled and disturbed, but still uncomprehending, Avran and I watched and listened.

Suddenly green-hood turned about and clapped his hands. Instantly, four of the riders flung themselves upon each of us. Tumbling us from our mounts, they proceeded to strip us of our clothing. Naked, we were taken over till we were standing beneath two great branches reaching outward in a broad V-shape, like two arms raised in invocation. Our arms were forced over our heads, spread widely apart and bound by short lengths of rope to those branches. Avran cried out in angry protest but, if he was understood, he was ignored; I, though very much afraid, remained silent.

Green-hood waved his men back to their mounts and then, standing between us but looking toward the tree, uttered some wordy incantation that we comprehended not at all. While he did so, the two pack-hasedain were brought forward into the clearing and unloaded. Though the light of the shrunken crescent moon was dim indeed, I could perceive what was being brought forth. Unbeknown to us, one hasedu had been bearing Avran's clothes and possessions and the other, mine. These were set down in two heaps, too far away from us, alas!, to be reached even by our feet.

The garments stripped from us having been rolled and put into their packs, the two hasedain were sent away. Green-hood began a new incantation, in which the other Montariotans joined. Then, backing from the tree in the fashion of a courtier respectfully leaving the presence of his monarch, green-hood returned to his hasedu. He was still singing when, having mounted, he and the other Ayanessei retreated from the clearing. Their hasedain backed until their dark shapes blended into the trees. Then, at last, the chant ended. There was the sound of their descent of the steep road, then silence.

170

Allowing for the divergence of the branches to which we were bound, Avran and I were almost facing one another, though fully three poles apart. I saw him leap from the ground and hang from his bonds, pulling with all his might. All that resulted was a chafing of his wrists; the branch did not even bend, nor did the rope stretch. He repeated the action, with as little effect, then tried swinging from the branch, feet off the ground, in an attempt, I presumed, to cause the rope to fray. However, there was too great a distance between Avran and the branch for this to happen and he did not keep up his attempt for long.

Half-heartedly, for I knew Avran to be much stronger and heavier than me, I attempted the same manoeuvres, but I gained only sore wrists. The rope was too strong for us, the knots unassailable.

Avran had relaxed and was looking across at me with a sort of wry amusement. He spoke in Sandastrian again, now there were no listeners. 'Time for you to be thinking, Simon my friend! Nothing I can achieve will free us. Well, on this occasion I can be blamed only for over-optimism this morning. For the first time — and, I fear, for the last time — I can truly claim it was not I that led us into trouble!'

'A great consolation, no doubt,' I responded lightly; though, in truth, my spirits were very low. 'It would seem that we are some sort of sacrifice to this hunk of vegetation,' pointing with my right toes at the tree-trunk. 'Well, men still make sacrifices to venerable oaks back in my own land. What a waste of effort it has been, crossing all those seas and mountains, merely to become an offering to an even more ancient and accursed plant!'

Avran laughed, then shivered. 'I wonder what is intended to be our mode of demise? Starvation, or just sheer cold? I could wish they'd left us some clothes to wear.'

'I could wish they'd left me my knives! Yet I do not think our end will be so slow, nor will we be the first to meet it here. Look down at your feet, Avran. Can you not see the bones scattered around? Pieces of bone, rather; they seem all to have been split or bitten by strong teeth.'

Avran gazed around him as I had done, then shivered again; yet his jaw had set grimly. 'Well, whatever is to be our fate, we must await it with due patience. *Not* the ukhuren,

171

I trust; I have no desire to encounter those creatures again, however briefly!'

He paused, then said seriously: 'No, not the ukhuren. Look over yonder, Simon.'

My eyes followed his gaze. On the western side of the clearing, two animal shapes were moving among the long shadows of the trees. At first I was reminded of the wolves so recently eliminated from England and still surviving, men said, in Ireland. However, wolves move much like dogs, whereas these moved in a curious, pouncing sort of lope. Moreover, wolves are brown, whereas the colour of these creatures was hard to determine, an uncertain wavering between light and shadow, as if they were formless. It was my turn to shiver now, and not from cold.

Clearly the creatures had perceived us, yet they were not approaching directly. Instead they were edging toward us in an oblique, weaving fashion, as if half eager, half afraid. Taller than any wolves they seemed, and gaunter, with long, flat-topped skulls that appeared earless and with forelimbs longer than hindlimbs, their bodies sloping backward to a sinuous, never-still tail.

Two of them, were there? The moonlight was so pale that it was hard to see . . . No, three; and was that a fourth, over there where the road came up onto the mound?

One of the creatures emerged fully into the light and was still for a moment. Ah, now I saw why they seemed of such changeable colour! Striped they were, but with stripes running, not down their flanks as in the tyger of heraldry, but along their bodies in broad slashes of — what colours? Hard to tell; dark grey and a dirty white, perhaps?

The creature looked toward me and snickered, revealing ugly, pointed teeth. Its bleak yellow eyes, like grave-lamps, met mine; but only for a moment. Then, as if in sudden alarm, all four animals — if indeed there were four of them — fled back into the trees.

I sighed in relief. 'They're gone, praise be to Our Lord. Excellent! For a while, I was fearing we were going to provide dinner for a pack of spectral hounds!'

Avran was looking past me. 'No, Simon, they're not gone,' he said quietly. 'Two of them, or two others, are behind you now. I do not fancy our chances, friend.'

I tried to look back but could not turn enough to see them, a fact that gave me no comfort. Moreover, within seconds I could see another sidling out from the trees near the clearing's rim, behind Avran; and, after that, two more.

'They're behind you too, I'm afraid. What are they, Avran? Can you give them a name?' Somehow it appeared to me important, to be able at least to name them.

'Yes, I think so,' he said slowly. 'Our travellers' tales tell of a creature called the selth. It roams the plains at night, feeding on carrion, the injured and the helpless. It is said to be hard to see, a ghost creature, yet having jaws strong enough to rend flesh and crush bone. None of our paintings depicts one; our savants have argued whether selths exist, even. Well, we can reassure them on *that* point, if ever we are given opportunity; but, Simon, I fear we will not. A strange prospect, my friend, to be eaten by a legend!'

Even now he was striving to be cheerful. For my own part, I was rigid with fear. The selths, if such they were, seemed reluctant to face our eyes, yet hungry for our blood; they were edging toward us with a deviousness that was more nerve-straining than any direct attack. Moreover, it was so hard to keep them in view in the faint moonlight. They would fade into a patch of shadow, only to reappear in some lighter place, yet never quite where one anticipated. I shuddered.

'Avran, do you remember anything about them — anything that might help us?'

'So little is known of them, Simon . . . That they are cowardly, of course; but that is evident, I do not need to remember it. And yet . . . Yes, it might help us. When they attack, if we should both shout with all our might — not in fright, you understand, but as if in ferocity. If we do, perhaps they might flee. Yet we must try it only when they attack.'

It seemed to me a faint hope, yet I could think of nothing better. Indeed, I was becoming so paralysed with fear, with those dreadful creatures weaving ever closer, that I could scarcely think at all. 'Very well. Let's — let's attempt it.'

There were eight of the creatures, at least, in the clearing now. Some were still hugging its verges, but two were approaching ever closer to Avran. Moreover, two others, as fearful glimpses over my shoulders told me, were closing upon me. Abruptly, one of them opened its slab-like jaws and wailed, a shuddering, throaty sound that sounded like the mad laughter of ancient evil. Another echoed it, then a third. The sound stopped and, in sudden decisiveness, they were running upon us.

'Now, Simon! Shout with all your might!'

And we did so, bellowing like bulls at a baiting. The effect was immediate. All four of those attacking halted in their tracks, turned and fled back to the bushes, the other selths preceding them. In a trice, the clearing was empty of them.

'It worked, Avran. It worked! Splendid — splendid!' Overjoyed and relaxing, I found myself weak from the prolonged tension.

'For a while, Simon; for a while. Yet I fear they will return soon enough. If only we might free ourselves!' He wrenched at his bonds, but with no effect; those ropes were just too strong, those knots too well tied.

His words brought me up with a jolt. Avran was right, of course; the selths would surely return. *Could* we get free? I pulled frantically at my own ropes, but they would not yield.

The respite was indeed brief. All too soon, I glimpsed a sinister shape in a patch of light far over on my left; then saw another behind Avran. Yes, they were returning. For minute upon excruciating minute, they circled the clearing, approaching ever closer to us. When we shouted, again they fled; but they fled less far and resumed that circuitous approach more immediately.

Avran's chest was heaving; he looked across at me gravely. 'That shouting — it worked for a while, friend, but it won't serve us much longer. Think, Simon, think — what else can we try?'

But I could think of nothing — I could scarcely think at all, so terrified was I.

They attacked a third time. Again we shouted as loudly as we might; and again they retreated. This time, however, they went back only a few yards, breaking into an ululation of mocking wails as if informing us that our strategem had been exposed.

All eight of the creatures were soon circling us. Sickly, I knew that their next charge must mean our deaths.

Closer they came, ever closer. I could see now that they were striped in dark brown and a pale, nauseous yellow. I could see large, divided claws on their feet — strange claws; and, as their jaws opened to howl, I could see great triangular teeth. Their evil earless heads, their yellow lamp-like eyes that seemed windows into nothingness — the horror of them was pressing ever harder upon me. So close they were, so close — they must attack soon, surely, surely?

Ah! they were attacking! I tensed, readying myself for a last frantic shout. One was leaping at me, two others at Avran; our time was come!

However, as it leapt at me, the selth was transfixed by a thrown spear and fell sideways, howling in death. Another flung spear had struck down one of those attacking Avran; and, in a moment, the remaining selths were in panic flight.

With the very fangs of those dread beasts about to close upon us, with the sacrifice about to be consummated, we had been preserved from death; but by whose grace?

Chapter Nineteen

THE BURNING OF THE TREE

That question was to remain, for a while, unanswered. The two men who came to my side were each hooded and cloaked in dark brown, so that their faces and forms were hidden. Nor, at first, did they speak. While the Montariotans had been taller than me, both these men were shorter and found the knots out of their reach. One held me, therefore, while the other chopped awkwardly with his sword at one of the ropes binding my hands so high. Tiresomely, the rope resisted such treatment and he tried sawing at it instead. Meanwhile, a third cloaked figure was standing watchfully by Avran, a throwing spear in hand ready for use and two others held slackly by his side.

Several minutes passed before my right hand was free, and several more before the strands of the second rope were cut through. I collapsed forward, to be supported by one of the men — his bright brown eyes, glimpsed under the hood, were kind — and guided over to the heap of my clothes. I was shivering with cold and reaction and was so helpless that I needed to be dressed. After that, my rescuer rubbed and pummelled my wrists and arms till they were warm and pulsing with returning blood. Meantime his companion was trying to chop Avran free, with little effect until the third man set down his spears and went to aid him by holding the ropes taut.

However, this meant that, for a while, none of the three was on watch. Suddenly, over the shoulder of the man who was tending me, I glimpsed anew the shadowy shape of a selth, edging toward him.

Hastily I thrust a hand into the pocket of my tunic and drew out my bowstring, then pushed my rescuer gently aside in order to pick up my bowstave. In my weakened condition, to bend the bow was more than I could achieve; but he perceived my purpose and aided me.

By then, the whole pack of selths was again ringing us. The deaths of two of them had not been the deterrent one might have expected, considering their evident cowardice; perhaps such swift slaying was outside their comprehension. There were more of them than I had thought; ten still living, at least.

Avran had only one hand free and could not be of aid; the swordsman was still striving to cut the other rope. The spearman was attempting unsuccessfully to loosen a fourth throwing-spear from the body of the selth it had transfixed. Certainly, three spears — or even four — would not be enough to defend us long from so many potential attackers; my long-bow would be needed. Yet, with wrists so weak, could I use it effectively? Well, at least I must try!

Normally, archery was a pleasure for me. On that night, it was an ordeal. As swiftly as I might, I set arrow to bow; but to draw the bow was almost beyond my powers. At first attempt I could not manage it and had to relax in failure. The selths were closing in upon us; I must try again! . . . No, I could not do it.

The brown-eyed man had obtained a spear from his companion and held it ready for throwing, yet in a fashion that suggested neither skill nor confidence. The spearman was standing on guard beyond Avran, while the third man sawed frantically at the single rope by which my friend was even yet bound. The selths were howling again, a dreadful, mocking sound that surely served to inculcate despair in their victims. Soon they would attack once more.

For a third time I strove with my bow, gasping in effort. Pull, Simon, pull! Ah! At last the arrow was at its notch; and barely in time, for the selths were upon us.

My brown-eyed friend had thrown his spear, but missed. Already a selth was leaping at him, ugly jaws open and fangs bared. I loosed my arrow.

At such close range, I could not miss. My shaft drove deep into the creature's flank, throwing it backward against a second selth, which rolled over and promptly fled. Hastily I seized a second arrow and, by some freak of strength, drew back the string at first attempt. A third selth leapt at us; my loosing was over-hasty, yet the creature was sent tumbling over with an arrow through its forelimb and, after regaining its feet, fled limping away.

Avran was free now and had fallen forward, with the sword-wielder standing over him. A thrown spear had slain a fourth selth, but the spearman had cast his remaining spear in vain and was reaching frantically for his sword. Four selths were closing upon Avran and he, while two others hesitated in the shadows.

I stepped forward to pick up another arrow but, in my feeble condition, stumbled to my knees. The brown-eyed man leapt to my assistance, steadying me and helping me to fit arrow to bow. With his aid, I managed again, tremblingly, to draw back the string, and strove to sight my arrow upon one of the selths that were closing in upon my fallen friend. How hard it was to see the creatures! Why, they seemed to fade from one spot and grow again in another . . .

Ah! One had paused, to throw back its head and howl. I hesitated, then for a third time I shot. A fortunate shaft, indeed; it transfixed the creature's ugly head, silencing that dreadful voice forever.

Almost at the same moment, the spearman hurled his sword at another selth that was about to leap upon him. His weapon hit the beast on its shoulder and glanced away, but the blow was enough to send that selth and the two others into retreat. By running forward to retrieve his spear, my brown-eyed rescuer turned that retreat into panic flight.

This time, I was sure, the selths would not return. It was well, for my strength had gone utterly and I could not again have drawn my bowstring.

Avran was helped into his clothes and we were both escorted — or, rather, supported — away from the tree. We were settled against a bank, with our weapons by us, and allowed to rest while the spearman kept watch.

By then, he and his colleagues had thrown back their hoods to reveal dark, curling hair and beards. They tried to speak to us, in Montariotan and in some other language even more unfamiliar, but we could comprehend their words no more than they could understand our replies in Sandastrian.

While we rested, our two other rescuers were busy. The thrown sword and spears were gathered up or withdrawn effortfully from the corpses of slain selths, as was my third arrow. My second arrow had gone with the selth it had injured, while the first was so deeply buried that it would have needed to be cut out, an effort not worth while.

The subsequent activities of brown-eyes and his companion perplexed me considerably. With laborious effort they were dragging the dead selths up to the trunk of the ancient tree, arranging them about it, and stacking branches over them. Was this some sort of ceremony of tribute? Soon they were piling up twigs and leaves, until the dead creatures were covered completely — to hide them from Montariotan view, perhaps? I was sure that these men were not themselves Montariotans.

What was happening now? It was hard to see in the difficult light, but brown-eyes seemed to be sprinkling something among the heaped twigs and leaves.

By that stage I was entirely puzzled; and, in a moment, I was startled also. They had set fire to the heap and were hurrying back toward us. The flames spread with amazing swiftness. To my astonishment they were green flames, like those the wizard's spell had produced. I gasped in awe and leapt to my feet, to find Avran on his feet also.

'Avran, these men that rescued us — they must be the wizard's soldiers, the guards from the purple tent!'

In my startlement, I had spoken in English. My surprise was enhanced when our spearman guard replied in the same language. He was smiling.

'Excellent, so we can converse after all!' he said. 'You're quite correct, my friend; we are indeed the servants of he whom you call the wizard. But let us hasten away, now. The fire is growing bright and other eyes may be watching.'

Indeed, the flames were leaping up about the old tree and engulfing it. One great dead branch was suddenly aflame, then another. The smoke was reaching a steadily thickening arm up toward the bright stars.

With friendly hands grasping and steadying us, we hastened over the rim of the great stone platform and down into the dark tunnel of trees. Suddenly I was aware that there were animals ahead of us, approaching us — not selths, thank goodness, but horned, deer-like creatures. Yet, by their manner of movement, they could not be hasedain or sevdreyen. Of

180

course, these must be animals of the sort we'd seen grazing by the wizard's tent and ridden into the twilight by the purple guards! I was helped onto one, Avran onto another. Brown-eyes climbed up behind me, the sword-wielder behind Avran, while the spearman mounted a third beast and led us away downslope into the darkness.

As we rode into the morning, I was aware of a billowing pillar of smoke and red flames, at first close and then ever further behind us, until I dropped into an abyss of sleep in which there was no awareness of anything.

My eventual emergence from that sleep was reluctant and painful. My eyelids felt as weighty and sticky as if they were coated with resin; my arms — the right one, in particular — were throbbing and felt as ponderous and weak as if they had been filleted; and my mind seemed reluctant to function, as if shuddering away from any recollection of that terrifying last night.

Yet all must be well now, for I was wrapped up warmly and there was a sound of soft voices nearby. It was daytime again; even with eyes closed, I could tell that. However, this was not the harsh sunlight of the grasslands, nor was there any wind. Some pleasant place; we were in some pleasant place . . . Soothed, I relapsed into a drowse.

Many more minutes passed before, slowly, I climbed back to wakefulness and opened my eyes. I was indeed well wrapped in blankets and with a bed of cut boughs beneath me. A pillow, made from my rolled cloak, had been placed beneath my head. The light was filtering though branches clothed in the first green leaves of spring. The tree was of a kind I had never seen, with twigs arching upward and outward from its branches like ribs from a fish's backbone. Bright orange catkins hung down between the pale leaflets.

Two little green birds were nibbling with long, curved beaks at the catkins. They were swinging upside-down and performing quite unnecessary acrobatics, as if from sheer delight in living; I watched them with amusement for many minutes. Only when they flew away did I turn onto my side and look about me.

So we were in the forest at last! Not gigantic trees, these, like the ones about Lake Vanadha, but trees of a reasonable size, like the oaks and sycamores of Ecclesall Woods close to my Hallamshire home, and with many sunny patches between them. Yet all the trees were of unfamiliar sorts. Some had trunks as dark and smooth as the smoke-blackened beams of an old manor house; others had scaly trunks, as russet-red as a squirrel's fur; yet others had brown trunks, corded like great, rigid ropes. In the patches of sunlight between their reaching roots, there grew many flowers. Some were of the same innocent blue as English bluebells in spring, others scarlet as pimpernels or yellow as campions, but all were of unfamiliar shape and leaf. Everything was beautiful, yet everything was strange to me.

Avran was lying under the tree nearby me, still fast asleep among his blankets, and one of our rescuers of last night — the spearman, surely? — was equally deeply asleep close by him. At a little distance away, a fire burned in a hearth of rough stones. Over it was an iron tripod from which hung a pot, bubbling merrily. Squatting by the fire were our two other rescuers; it was their quiet voices that I had heard. Beyond, under other trees, the three horned beasts we had ridden were browsing quietly — and, no doubt, serving as guards. The tranquillity of the scene, after so many days of strain, was a delight.

I slipped out from my blankets, sat up and, with an effort, got to my feet. Ow, how my poor arms ached! One of the two men by the fire rose and came over to greet me. It was brown-eyes.

'Greetings, friend!' He spoke in English, though a strangeness in intonation told me it was not his native tongue. 'I trust that you slumbered well?'

'Well indeed, thank you — and lengthily, I imagine. What hour is it?' Under these trees, I could not read the time from the sun.

He laughed. 'Long past noon! All of us slept late; and small wonder, after such a night. You are no mean bowman, friend. Even so weak as you were, your arrows saved us from those accursed selths. We owe you much.'

'Not so much as we owe you! Had you not come to our aid, by now we'd be merely a litter of chewed bone fragments under that terrible tree.'

182

He grimaced. 'It should not have been so close a call. We had been ordered to be there an hour earlier, but we had presumed the Ayanessei would return immediately to their town. They did not; and indeed, it was a foolish presumption, for we should have guessed they would stay to learn what transpired. Instead, they camped out on the grassland only a little way from Nekhalések — the temple of the sun tree. We had to skirt them in order to reach you. It was a tricky passage, for the ground was open and they are wary people; consequently it took us over-long. Even so, we never guessed that the selths would gather so swiftly.'

I shuddered. 'Speak not of them! Whether you were late or not, we are deeply grateful to you. Yet why did you burn their bodies, and the tree?'

'The tree deserved to be burned; it was ancient and evil.' He was speaking solemnly now. 'Yet we did it, not for that reason, but to serve as a sign.'

'A sign? I don't understand.'

'Aye, of course, you speak not the Montariotan tongue, so you will not have comprehended what transpired in the town of the Ayanessei. Well, your beast — or was it your friend's beast? — bears the lightning-bolt emblem of that tribe. The Ayanessei believed that you must be harbingers of good or of evil, yet could not decide which. So they appealed to our master for his judgement. They had come east to attack the Eldernet, their ancient enemies. Did your coming mean that they should ride to triumphant battle or did it mean that they should avoid defeat by returning west to their own territory?'

He paused, and smiled at me. His eyes were brown as polished walnut wood and his hair and beard almost of that colour; I liked him very much. The other man was watching from the fireside and listening.

'So the magician provided the sign?' I was eager to learn more.

He chuckled. 'Aye, you might say so! Our master, he has a kind heart. He knows that the Ayanessei slay all travellers from the south. They admit few enough from the north, at that! Strange it is, for they're not evil folk, these plains peoples; yet it's their custom. So our master contrived a way to save you and your friend. He urged them to expose you, in the old fashion, under the sacrifice tree. If the sacrifice was accepted and you were devoured by the selths which they consider sacred, well and good; the Ayanessei might attack the Eldernet and be sure of victory. If aught went amiss, though, they must hop off back to their own lands. After last night, I reckon they'll be hopping away briskish!'

I laughed also; and he went on more seriously. 'And so you'll see our master's contrivance. Yes, the two of you have lived to see another day; but also quite a few other folk, who might have been slain, have been granted longer lives upon this earth. Our master's both wise and kind.'

'He must be so, indeed. But what about our beasts — our sevdreyen?'

'Is that how you name them? Well, they're not so unlike our own beasts in looks and not so unlike in name either, for ours are styled rafneyen . . . Aye, but I'm straying away from your question. Well, I doubt that you'll ever see your beasts again, but they'll not fare badly. Was the marked beast yours, or your friend's?'

'Mine. His name is Yerezinth and he means much to me.'

He nodded. 'I comprehend well your feeling; indeed, I have a like affection for my own rafenu. Well, Yerezinth is destined to be the mount of the akhled himself, so you may be certain he'll be well looked after. Since the other beast is to be ridden by the crown prince, the indrakhled, it will fare well also, be sure of that. The Montariotans depend much on their animals and so treat them well, even ordinarily; but royal beasts are treated royally.'

It was gratifying to know that my sevdru's future was assured. 'Thank you for that,' I said. 'All your tidings are good. But please, will you tell me your name?'

He chuckled again. 'Why, imagine me talking so long, and us not introduced! I'm Rahir Ravatseng, and yon hulk by the fire is my own brother Delhir. Both of us at your service.' He bowed in the English fashion, then beamed at me.

'Well, men name me Simon Vasianavar in this land, but truly I'm Simon Branthwaite, from England and very much at *your* service. My sleeping friend is Avran Estantesec, prince of Sandastre.'

Rahir looked puzzled. 'Of England I've heard, of course. There's plenty of folk from your land, settled in these forests.

184

Good men, some of them, and some bad. Yet, Sandastre; no, I've heard of no such realm. But then, few folk of these woodlands have ever heard of *our* native land of Reschora. It lies north of here, on the flank of the mountains — no great distance after all, but not many folk travel so far. Yet enough of chatter; you'll be wanting your dinner. We can talk while we eat, or afterwards. Is your friend stirring yet? He's a grand sleeper.'

I chuckled to myself, remembering Avran's strictures of — my goodness, it was only yesterday, yet it seemed so long ago! However, Avran was indeed awakening. Gratifyingly soon, we were both dipping hunks of bread into stew hot from the pot. Before eating, I had introduced Avran to the two Reschorese and, between mouthfuls, I told him all that Rahir had told me.

Ere we were done, the spearman had awakened also and had yawningly joined us. His name, we learned, was Felun Daretseng and he appeared to be the leader of the three, if they had a leader. He was much like the brothers in appearance, but quicker in thought and graver in mood.

'You have a good opportunity to rest and relax,' he told us. 'Our master is travelling to join us, but he will not be here before the morrow's noon. Meantime there is naught for us to do but wait.'

After we had eaten, Rahir took us to a place where a little stream wound its way through the trees. We drank, then bathed. The water was crisply cold, but it served to take the aches from our limbs and we returned to the fire much refreshed.

Delhir Ravatseng, who seemed a tranquil soul and less able in English than his brother, was playing sweetly on a little double pipe. After a while Felun Daretseng began to sing softly. He sang in a language strange to us, yet with echoes of familiar words that made it seem not so very different from Sandastrian. Then Avran and I were persuaded to sing also. Avran's song of his homeland meant much to me, but little to them. In contrast, my own two ballads, the old song of the cruel sister and the newer one of the combat in Chevy Chase, were understood well enough.

Thus pleasantly did afternoon pass into evening. Since all five of us were still very weary, we retired early to our blankets, leaving the fire to dwindle to ashes. Under the placid guard of the rafneyen, we slept our weariness away and rose refreshed to a new day.

Chapter Twenty

IN THE TENT OF THE WIZARD

The next morning brought an earlier and more relaxed awakening, for my weariness was gone and the ache in my arms had eased greatly. It brought also a breeze to rustle the new green leaves on the forest trees, with puffy white clouds that presaged showers rather than any considerable change in the weather.

Avran and I woke almost together, to find that Felun Daretseng was gone hunting and the Ravatseng brothers were busy preparing breakfast. Thin pieces of dried meat were cooked to crispness over a little fire, then folded between slices of dark bread and served to us. We each drank draughts of sweet berry wine from a skin-covered flask. During this repast, we talked; or rather, Rahir questioned Avran about the peoples and realms of the southern hills. I interposed only an occasional comment, while Delhir sat smiling and silent.

'Well, that's a power of news, and no mistake,' Rahir said eventually. 'I'd heard tell of Denniffey and of the Fachnese; but all these other kings and princes, 'tis strange enough and wonderful to me. Mind you, I've little need to be surprised. How *can* tidings travel north, when the Montariotans slay all who try to traverse their lands?'

'They're a barrier indeed,' Avran responded. 'Yet we of Sandastre have heard a little about these forest realms. Word comes sometimes from the Montariotans, sometimes from Antomalata or Sapandella. Not that we trade often with those two kingdoms, for they seem forever to be at war.'

'Aye, well, maybe we'll venture into those lands some day; but the master and we, we don't often travel so far south. Mostly we stay among these forest earldoms or roam the northern plains.'

'Are there more plains, then, beyond the forests?'

'Yes indeed, and some fine country too. There's deserts that will match anything the Knights Templar tell of in their yarns of the Crusades and there's grasslands richer than any that the Montariotans have for pasture. Beyond the plains, in the north, there are the mountains that are our home; and in the east, other mountains. And beyond those mountains and ours, the great sea itself; or so they say. My brother and I, we've never gone far to the north or to the east, nor yet has our master.'

'It seems that, even though Sandastre is so ancient a realm, we know little enough about our own island of Rockall,' Avran sighed. 'Why, even of the realms in the forest, our learned men can name only a few. Let's see, there are Dellorain and Orelney — somewhere in the west, I think — and Atelone, and, oh . . .'

'Dakalet and Seretta,' I prompted, for I had those names by heart.

Rahir laughed. 'Well, that's a few of them! Yet you're wrong in part. The realm of Seretta is not in these forests, but in grasslands by a great inlet of the sea. It lies north of Sapandella and northwest of that strange closed land, Dedesta. However, the others you mention are indeed forest realms. Dakalet lies far northeast of here; we travel there often, for its earl is a fine man and the friend of our master. Atelone is directly north of us, beyond the Bransworth River, and Orelney is over to the west, by the Mentonese sea. But Dellorain; why, at this very minute you're in Dellorain!'

It was strange to have a land of rumour transformed into a reality about us; I gazed around at the trees with a new interest. Then, remembering my quest, I asked eagerly: 'And Lyonesse? It is for Lyonesse that we seek. Surely it must be somewhere in these forests?'

To my deep disappointment, this name merely caused Rahir to look puzzled. 'Lyonesse? No, I can't say as ever I've heard of it. Would that be a realm or an earldom? Or is it just a town or fortress?'

'A realm, I think; and peopled by Englishmen.'

'Well, there's English folk a-plenty; aye, and Welshmen and Gascons too, and even a few Frenchmen, all of them

188

settling in these forests during the last three hundred years. Whenever there's a big war over in your countries, there are folk fleeing from it and settling here in Rockall. But Lyonesse; no, I've never heard tell of any such place. Have you, Delhir?'

His brother shook his head. 'Our master might know, mayhap,' he ventured. Then, evidently tired of all this talk, Delhir produced his little double pipe and began to blow on it, quietly but sweetly.

The rest of the morning was passed tranquilly. We went to wash in the little stream, then exercised with our swords and bows. The brothers watched us interestedly. When in swordplay Avran adroitly disarmed me, they applauded vigorously.

It chanced that Felun Daretseng returned just then. He was bearing a small deerlike creature slain by a fortunate spear-cast; a danatel he called it. This was passed to Delhir, to be skinned and cooked; then, smilingly, Felun invited Avran to a contest in swordsmanship.

I was made proud by the ease with which Avran disarmed him also. To Felun's credit, he was more admiring than disconcerted.

'Well, friend,' he said a little ruefully, 'they rank me a good swordsman in my own land, yet I am not of your quality. How do you fare with the throwing-spear?'

This was a weapon with which Avran and I had been made to practise in Doriolupata; and, indeed, hunting with spears was a familiar Sandastrian art. Yet it was one at which my friend had little skill and he was soon outmatched. I fared better, making casts that almost equalled, in accuracy and distance, those of Delhir, the Reschorese spearman. His praise was quite ungrudging.

'It is not only with the long-bow that you have skill, Simon! Should the two of you travel with us, your ability at arms may benefit us greatly. Though there are good men enough in these forests, there are evil men also.'

It was long past noon ere the rafneyen and, through them, our friends became aware of the approach of those for whom we were waiting. First came two purple-clad riders, each with lance in hand, great axes slung over shoulders, and horns strapped to saddles; I recognized them, for I had seen them as guards by the purple tent and riders into the firelight. Next came four rafneyen, harnessed in twos side-by-side. One pair carried a huge roll that must surely be the tent itself, the other pair its great supporting poles in a rope-secured bundle. Two more riders followed, armed like the vanguard but not bearing horns; it was they who had carried the torches into the Montariotan camp. Then came six more rafneyen, each bearing packs; and lastly, another rider in purple. Remembering as I did a glorious figure in silver, it was only at second look that I realized this was the wizard himself.

The other riders and the pack-rafneyen had already come to a halt in the clearing. The Ravatseng brothers and Felun greeted their comrades with cheery waves, then fell respectfully silent as the wizard approached. He had perceived Avran and me, but it was Felun whom he addressed. He spoke in swift sentences in a language I took to be Reschorese, for it was incomprehensible to me and yet had none of the gusty cadences of Montariotan.

While the two conversed, the other riders dismounted and, setting down their weapons, began unloading the pack-animals. Rahir and Delhir hastened to their assistance. Heavy hammers and a narrow-bladed spade were produced from one of the packs and the great poles were extracted from their bundle. There were six of these. One was slotted into another and fastened to it with leather bindings, to make a tall centre-post; this was planted in the exact middle of the little clearing. The other four poles were set around it at uniform distances from each other, then the fabric of the great tent was wrapped about and over them all. This was done with a swift skill that argued long practice. Avran and I stood by uneasily, feeling we should help but fearing we might merely hinder.

I was surprised not to see the pole bearing the potent-cross emblem, that had stood so tall by the purple tent out in the grasslands. Later I learned that this had significance only to the Montariotans: consequently it had been left in concealment near the forest's edge, ready for use next time the wizard visited the grasslands.

Felun, having completed what was evidently a detailed report of the doings of his comrades, assisted his master to dismount. The wizard caressed his rafenu's head briefly and dismissed the animal. Only then did he glance our way, for the first time since his arrival. At his word, Felun beckoned us over.

I had noticed before that the wizard was quite a small man, but the tricorn hat had enhanced his apparent size. I perceived now that, though burlier, he was shorter even than me. Yet I found him again impressive, for he had a quality of forcefulness and authority that made one forget his height. His hair, his bushy eyebrows and short beard were all of a dark brown unflecked with grey, even though he must be past middle age. His skin had been tanned deeply by wind and weather. From that dark face, there shone forth eyes of quite exceptional brightness, so bright indeed that they seemed illuminated from within by an errant shaft of sunlight.

What colour were they? I was never to be quite sure. Sometimes they seemed brown, sometimes honey-coloured, sometimes — especially at night — as yellow as a cat's. Strange eyes, indeed; but this was a strange man.

Remembering that the wizard's orders had saved our lives, I knelt before him and Avran did likewise without hesitation. Immediately, however, he gestured to us to rise and spoke to us peremptorily in English.

'Stand, gentlemen; you are not servants, of myself or any other. Nor do I hold such high rank as to merit your reverence. I am a mere traveller, as you are; Vedlen Obiran, physician and alchemist of Reschora. I trust that my men have treated you well?'

'More than well,' Avran responded. 'We owe our lives to them, and to you; and for that, you do indeed merit our reverence. Avran Estantesec, at your service.'

'And Simon Branthwaite, at your service and deeply in your debt.'

A smile flickered across that dark face. 'Yet I think the debt is cancelled already, if matters be as my lieutenant tells. My men were tardy and they owe their own lives, in turn, to you. The board is clear; we may converse this evening as equals. I shall look forward to that conversation.'

Without more ado he turned away, to vanish within the newly-erected tent.

After the unloading of the rafneyen was done, there was

191

leisure for other introductions. Three of the men were also Reschorese. Drakht Belineg, a big, broad-faced man with the down-pursed lips of one forever striving to conceal an urge to laughter, was one of the trumpeters and Narel Evateng, a lean man with a deeply lined face, the other. The third Reschorese had the same brown, curling hair and brown eyes as the Ravatseng brothers and was much like them, though bigger. When he proved to be their cousin, Hebehir Ravatseng, I was no whit surprised.

However, I *was* surprised when I was introduced to the fourth of the wizard's soldiers, for he was an Englishman — or rather, a man of English descent. He was broad and short, round-faced, red-cheeked and beaming, his name Amos Sloly.

'Pleased am I to meet you, sor,' he said to me. 'And your friend likewise.' His voice had that deep, rich burr that I remembered from Bristol. 'Simon, is it? And from England. Well, 'tis from England that my grandfather travelled, seventy years back. From north Devon he came. Moses Sloly, his name was, and as foine and handsome a man as you could wish to meet. All of us Slolys be foine men!'

The gleam in his eye told me that this self-praise was humorously intended. Indeed, such phrases were often in his mouth, and hugely did he enjoy them! 'Whoy, let a real man carry it,' he would say, taking a pack from a burdened colleague; or 'That needs proper skill. I'll show you how 'tis done,' as he seized a hammer to drive in a pole. Rarely have I encountered a man who enjoyed life more, or found it so continuously amusing. And yet, as I was to discover, there were depths in Amos Sloly that were not readily plumbed.

We were shortly to be grateful for the tent. Scarcely had we eaten our evening repast when there came a heavy shower. It did not persist long, but the grass was left wet and the trees dripping. By then, however, we were sitting dry beneath a high, thin roof of hide that let in no moisture, yet permitted some light to penetrate. The tent interior was almost square. One quarter of it was partitioned off by screens of purple cloth, to serve as private quarters for the wizard, who had indeed eaten within. The rest made a sort of messroom for his seven guards and we.

No watch was necessary when fourteen rafneyen were

grazing in the forest about, so all nine of us could relax and talk. Avran and I learned that the soldiers' master, Vedlen Obiran, was a man of renown in forests and plains alike, famed for his skills as physician and magician (for his men, like we, thought him more than a mere alchemist), his wisdom and his ability to read men's thoughts. The purple robes worn by the men and, when he did not choose more impressive attire, by their master served, as it were, as a proclamation that they were not mere travellers, but wonder-workers and healers. And indeed, the seven served as assistants to the wizard, as well as guards. In such garb, a man might travel freely across frontiers and through any of the realms of what they styled 'the middle lands' — the lands between the mountains of north and east and the highlands of the south. However, encounters with wild beasts and wilder men happened often enough to make the martial skills of the wizard's guards needful.

On the day of our departure from the camp of the Ayanessei, their akhled had sent the sick and the maimed of the tribe to be cared for by the wizard and those four of his men whom we had seen in the firelight. (Indeed, as I realized belatedly, we had encountered no ill or injured people in our walk about the Montariotan camp.) The wizard's other three men had been off hunting when the Montariotans chanced upon his tent. After learning of our captivity and being asked to judge us, their swift-thinking master had kept those three from the view of the suspicious nomads and had sent them to our rescue. Of their existence, fortunately for Avran and me, the Ayanessei had never become aware.

Their work of healing done, the wizard and his four assistants had dismantled the tent and ridden away during the night. It was a departure that, by design, was mysterious enough to enhance their prestige in any future visit to the plains. They had slept in a sheltered place during much of the next day and thereafter had made an easy journey to join us.

'Can't say I'm sorry, usually, to leave those plains behind,' growled Drakht Belineg, 'but this time, I have my regrets. I'd have liked to be in that camp, to see the faces of those Ayanessei when they heard you two folk were gone and that horrible old tree — yes, we saw it once — burned to a cinder, as surely it was.'

Narel Evateng's trouble-creased face was lit by a smile. 'Aye, indeed!' he chortled. 'They'd be packing up and running like ants from a broken anthill. And my! but they'll consider our master a mighty magician!'

Felun Daretseng smiled at Avran and me. 'Better not cross the western plains again. If you do, they'll believe you're gods returning! No doubt they'd construct for you a temple that would be all your own!'

Avran shivered. 'Speak not of their temples!' he implored. 'I cannot think of such matters without seeing again those prowling selths. I fear it will be long ere they fade from my nightmares.' And I concurred with my friend most heartily.

Almost at that moment, the sweet sound of a bell was heard. Instantly Felun sprang to his feet and hastened into the wizard's sanctum. In a moment, he came out again to inform Avran and me that his master wished to speak with us. We rose and followed Felun within.

The small space that formed the wizard's retreat was lighter than the rest of the tent, for a tall white candle, set in a silver holder, was burning with a bright flame of palest blue. (I was reminded of the Bristol quaymaster's yarnings and guessed the candle must have been traded from Mentone.) By it sat Vedlen Obiran on a purple cushion tasselled with gold. His own garb echoed those colours, for he wore a purple tunic embroidered so elaborately with gold thread that it seemed to shimmer in the flickering light. His hands were tucked within the tunic's sleeves and he seemed as still as a tree-stump. In the candle-glow his eyes shone palely, like glow-worms in a hedge.

Felun gestured to us to sit on two other cushions that had been set before his master. We did so, while Felun stood deferentially behind us.

For what seemed many minutes, the wizard scrutinized us silently. Under his gaze I found myself shifting uncomfortably, like a child before a priest at first catechism. Avran bore it rather better. It was to Avran that the first words were addressed, albeit obliquely.

'Red hair; yes, the Montariotans say it is common among

you southerners: I've seen too few of you to form my own opinion. Some Englishmen are redheaded also, and many of the folk of Mionia, over in the eastern mountains. Such hair is rare in the north; you would be noticed and remembered, should you venture there. But you, Simon Branthwaite' — he pronounced my name perfectly, his eyes bent upon me — 'would cause little remark. There are many among us that are much like you. You would not attract notice; and I think that is your special skill, not to attract notice.'

These remarks did not invite a response; nor did he seem to expect one. He went on speaking pensively. 'Yet you have other skills also, Simon: a skill with the bow and, I think, with the thrown knife.' At this I started in surprise. His men must have seen my weapons, of course, but their use would not be comprehended, even in England. 'Your other skill is with beasts; you watch, and understand, and they feel your sympathy. The animal you lost to the Ayanessei will be well treated, but he will remember you long and, as I foresee, to your great benefit some day. Yet there will be other beasts with whom you will forge an understanding, and always to your advantage.'

The evening was drawing on and drops of rain again rattled on the hide roof. Under the darkening sky, the light of the candle seemed ever brighter, the shadows about us ever darker. The wizard's attention was again upon Avran.

'And you, prince of the realm beside the southern sea, have a skill with beasts also, although learned and not innate. Yet you have only a small patience and you cannot stay quiet in the shadows; you must be ever out in the sunshine and acting with vigour — often, indeed, with too much vigour and too little thought. Yet defeat will come to you only rarely, nor will you allow it to deter you overmuch. You are the stuff of travellers, for you are ever eager for fresh scenes and new contests. But you, Simon' — his eyes turned again to me — 'why do you travel so far, when your heart lies behind you?'

At this thrust I blushed, started to speak, then hesitated. How had my love for Ilven, and my reluctance in leaving Sandastre, been so readily perceived? I had not talked of Ilven in many days, even to Avran; and, though she was often in my thoughts, I had striven to put behind me all

195

my doubts, concentrating my attention wholly upon the finding of Lyonesse.

The wizard spoke again, with a kindness in his voice I had not heard hitherto. 'Only your strong sense of duty, your commitment to your cause, can have torn you away from she whom you love. Tell me, Simon, why *do* you seek that land of Lyonesse?'

Stumblingly I tried to explain; and he nodded in understanding — an unexpectedly English gesture, for the Rockalese use it not. 'So you reason that, since so many of your countrymen have settled in these forests, that realm must be in the forests also. Yet most Englishmen that come here travel, not from Bristol, but from your city of London to the free port of Warringtown, far away in the east beyond the plains of Herador. True, some French or Gascon ships do sail to Saint Lorraine on the great bay; but your countrymen do not voyage on such vessels. I have not heard that any Englishmen have come to the forests from Bristol, nor that any others have voyaged to Rockall, as you did, with those heathen Mentonese.'

He paused and, when he resumed speaking, he seemed to be talking more to himself than to us. 'Yet Lyonesse . . . Lyonesse . . . No, not in the forests, but where in this great island? Is it a new realm in the dry plains or an old one in the eastern mountains? Of those mountains, I know little. Or is it somewhere in the far north; some valley in the Wainlands or the Delven Hills, or somewhere beyond the mountains? I do not know; perhaps I shall never know. And these young men, will they discover it?'

It had become so dark now that no light penetrated the tent roof. The candle flame had flickered down; its dimmer radiance picked out only the tracery of gold on the wizard's tunic and his eyes, making them shine brighter and yellower. Abruptly, and through no apparent cause, the flame flared up and burned brightly, seeming to awaken the wizard from his reverie.

'Simon and Avran, you must travel with me for a while. We have rafneyen that you can ride; our beasts are laden lightly and two can be spared. Felun my good servant, not only must you find tunics of purple that will fit these new friends, but also you must teach them our Reschorese tongue.

You will not find that difficult, for it is not much different from the language of the south that Avran has known from birth and Simon can now speak so freely.'

He paused, then went on: 'As we travel, we will ask questions. If the whereabouts of the land of Lyonesse can be learned, then somehow we will learn it. Be sure of that, Simon, and take heart.'

Chapter Twenty-one

DOUBTS IN DELLORAIN

It was a night of tempestuous winds and swift, brief showers. Each approaching gust rippled the trees into progressively more violent motion, beginning like a distant tide and culminating in a soughing sound, like waves breaking on a sandy shore. The first light drops of rain in each shower sounded like fingertips pattering on the taut tent fabric. As the raindrops fell harder and heavier, the noise would swell, like kettledrums played during a joust in some tournament. Then, as the shower slackened, the rattle would die away into a muttering, like the hubbub of a distant, angry crowd, before ceasing altogether. After a pause, a breathy sound of rising wind would betoken the approach of the next squall.

Avran and the soldiers fell quickly asleep, the massive Drakht Belineg snoring like a blunt saw cutting beechwood; but I lay long awake. My thoughts were sombre. So many leagues traversed, so many perils survived! I remembered our tense ascent of the tower and the snarls of the thassak, my fearful night ride with the grey warriors, our tumbling into the Montariotan pit-trap and, worst of all, those dreadful prowling selths. Yet, having endured all this, still we did not even know where Lyonesse was!

Might it be in the forests, as we had guessed back in Sandastre? Surely not, when these much-travelled men — even the wizard himself — had never heard even its name! After all, Lyonesse was not such a new settlement; more than sixteen years must have gone by since the ship of Sir Arthur Thurlstone and Sir John Warren had first set sail from Bristol.

If not in the forests, might Lyonesse be in the open lands beyond them to north or east? For the same reason, this seemed equally unlikely. It could not be hidden among desert

sands, for it had been reached by ship; it must be close to
a coast. In the mountains to the east, perhaps? Ships might
find harbour there, unbeknown to the wizard. Or in the
mountains of the north, maybe? Yet these Reschorese were
men of the northern mountains, but knew it not.

That Lyonesse was somewhere in Rockall, I remained sure;
but I was becoming sure also that it was still far away. Would
Avran and I ever discover it? And if we *did* find Lyonesse,
could we hope safely to re-traverse all the long leagues back
to Sandarro, where my heart lay?

There had been an interval of silence, but now there was
a new murmuring of wind among the trees. It was an uneasy
sound that matched my uneasy thoughts. Should we go on?
I remembered my father and brother, who loved me. They
would be overjoyed to see me again, and my father proud
that I had proved to him my worth; but, truly, could we
ever hope to find them? Was not the attempt a mere
casting-away of the lives of Avran and me, to no purpose?
Oh, how I longed to see Ilven again, to embrace her, to
know that all this strife-full wandering was over and she and
I safe again, to live and love together!

The moan of the rising gale seemed an expression of the
pain in my heart. Vedlen Obiran was right; I was not by
nature a wanderer, but one who longed for home and
tranquillity, for a simple life and small pleasures. What was
I doing, straying so far from she whom I adored? Avran and
I must abandon this stupid search for a lost land forthwith;
we must return to Sandastre, and swiftly!

Yet how could we return, admitting that we had merely
given up our quest? How could I explain without shame its
abandonment to Prince Vindicon, to Ilven? How could I
explain my faintheartedness to Avran the brave; Avran, who
had nothing to gain even from a successful outcome to the
search, who was taking all these risks simply because it was
my quest and I was his friend? No, I could not let them
down by scurrying south to Sandarro. I had embarked upon
a path which allowed no turning back; I must follow it to
its end, even if that end were death.

Though that thought was chilling, it was also strangely
calming. Outside the sound of the gale reached crescendo,
then dropped in register and was lost in the steadier beat

of a more continuous downpour. I must go on; I had no other choice.

The new rhythm of the raindrops on the tent roof seemed to repeat those words to me. You must go on; you have no choice. You must go on; you have no choice. You must go on . . . And I slid into sleep at last.

We woke to bright sunshine and the sound of the steady drip of water from the trees. Breakfast was good, but the dismantling of the wet tent, its folding and rolling, the drying and grooming of the rafneyen and their loading were tiresome tasks. Clad in the purple tunics Felun had found for us, Avran and I felt ourselves now to be numbered among the wizard's men and, naturally, aided our new comrades in these endeavours. If we did not enjoy the work, we were gratified at least by their immediate acceptance of us and their approval of our attempts to be helpful.

After that, Avran and I were introduced to our new mounts. Rafneyen are forest creatures and about as different from sevdreyen as roedeer are from red deer. Their whole build is slimmer, for one thing. Their nasal horn is not directed upward, but forward and outward, like the point of a spear. Their brow horns divide above a broad base into five un-branched tines, the three foremost longest, the two hindmost shortest. Since the central three tines curve whereas the two outermost are straight, the clustered tines are curiously like the spread fingers of a hand.

Rafneyen are softer-muzzled and larger-eyed than sevdreyen. Instead of being silver-grey, their pelage is as brown as polished walnut wood, but dappled or flecked with spots of cream-colour that make them hard to see among trees, whether in sunlight or in shade.

The mounts found for us were both rather small animals, which suited me well enough but made Avran look oversized, like a grown man on a child's pony. Yet he liked his new beast and I mine. Both were bucks. Avran's was named Lanenot, 'small-spot' in Reschorese speech; mine was Gahelad, 'streaked-fur'. Amused by the similarity of their names to those of two of King Arthur's knights, I suggested we restyle them 'Lancelot' and 'Galahad'.

201

This renaming did not upset the rafneyen, since they identified our thoughts rather than the sound of our words. Since my idea amused Avran, we adopted these new names definitively.

Galahad was an animal as noble as his name, or so it seemed to me. I was quick to forge a mental link with him and, though he never supplanted Whitebrow and Yerezinth in my affections, I became very fond of him. Rafneyen are longer-legged than sevdreyen and move differently; the motion of riding him was at first strange, but soon came to seem just as familiar and pleasant. On flat ground a rafenu is quite as swift as a sevdru, and it is swifter in finding a path through woodland. However, as we were to discover later, rafneyen are much less agile than sevdreyen in rocky terrains and on steep slopes.

Our ride that morning was rendered less enjoyable by the perpetual drip, drip, drip from the tree-branches overhead; and I was reminded of that last wet ride to Doriolupata. However, this ride was much happier. Many small birds were singing on the branches about us; there was the occasional flash of bright butterfly wings; and the trees and flowers wove an ever-changing fabric of beauty that delighted our eyes.

We saw no people and no dwellings. Indeed, the first indication to us that Dellorain was inhabited came when we emerged onto a bridle track. Initially this was little broader than a field path, a brown slash through the green grass. However, its beaten surface was pitted by the waterlogged hoofmarks of rafneyen and the rain-filled furrows of cartwheels, showing that, if not used heavily, it was used by a varied traffic. Many of the marks were fresh; men had been travelling that road today, and in the same direction as we.

After a mile or so, a track joined ours from the left and two more from the right, so that the bridle path broadened into a road. Soon there were many tracks and the road was becoming ever muddier. As we splashed along its slippery surface, I remembered wistfully the good roads of Sandastre. There were no stones or setts to make *this* road firm and no drains to make it dry; nor, indeed, were we to encounter any made roads anywhere in the forestlands.

We rode that day in an order that was to change little

on later days. The two trumpeters, lean Narel Evateng and huge Drakht Belineg, led the way — their habitual position, for they served as foreguards as well as heralds. Narel's watchfulness was reflected by a continual swing of his head from side to side. In contrast, Drakht's massive head remained still, but his eyes were ever roving. Felun Daretseng rode just behind them, seemingly relaxed but ever ready to respond to an alarm. Avran and I followed at his rafenu's heels, and behind us came the pack-rafneyen that bore the tent and its poles. The Ravatseng brothers came next, then the four remaining pack-rafneyen, each now more heavily laden than yesterday. The burly Hebehir Ravatseng followed, with Amos Sloly alongside him.

Last of all rode the wizard (for so I was always to think of him). It was a vulnerable position perhaps, but one that allowed him to hasten or dawdle at whim. Sometimes, indeed, he would fall so far behind that Felun would stop our progress and go in concern to seek his master. Either they would return together, or Felun would ride back to assure us all was well, after which we would await the wizard's tardy coming with patience or impatience, according to our temperament. Sometimes, after delaying us for a few or many minutes, Vedlen Obiran would arrive bearing a plant, berries or a frond from a shrub, to be handed to Hebehir for storage in one of the packs. More often he bore nothing and the delay remained forever unexplained.

The trees arched over our road, their branches forming, against the blue sky, a green network among whose meshes swam white clouds like amiable, puffy fishes. When we set forth there had been a ground-mist, but this had long since lifted and, since the sun was behind us, our shadows rode before us down the path.

After so many days during which talking had been dangerous or difficult, it was a pleasure for Avran and me to be able to converse relaxedly. Indeed, with the strains and doubts of the night behind me, I was rather inclined to babble, Avran contributing only an occasional smiling word. From time to time, Felun glanced back at us amusedly or threw at us a comment that splashed like a pebble into the merry flow of my chatter and sank beneath it.

Suddenly we became aware of the sound of voices and

movement ahead. Our two leaders checked, then went forward more slowly. The wizard, who had dropped behind, caught up and rode past us, his rafenu falling into step with Felun's.

As we rounded a shallow bend of the road, the trees opened out ahead of us to reveal a broad river. On its banks was a cluster of high pavilions, such as one sees at a tournament. About them were stalls, many beasts and many people. Beyond, a broad wooden bridge without rails stretched across to a further bank similarly set with pavilions and a-swarm with people.

However, it was the figure in the middle of the bridge that caught my eye — a knight in the full splendour of plate armour. He was wearing a jousting helmet, its visor open, and his iron-gloved hand held a lance, upright and at rest. From its tip a narrow green pennon floated in the breeze and at his arm was a shield of similar hue, each bearing a device in gold which, later, I was to discover was a waterbird in flight.

The knight's mount was a massive animal, armoured in plate about head and flanks. Curiously, I could see no horns. Only when we drew closer did I realize, to my surprise, that it was a horse — the first I had seen in Rockall. Horse and rider gleamed in the sunshine, reflecting and reflected in the bright water.

The crowd on our bank, though noisy enough, seemed far from happy. The men were chattering in that busy, yet slightly furtive, fashion that the transmission of ill news seems to generate, while the children, instead of running around, listened open-mouthed or formed subdued groups at the tent skirts. As we came into view and our purple cloaks were perceived, all stood back and fell silent.

One pavilion was larger than the others and tinted chevron-pattern in scarlet and silver. To it our heralds made their way, their master and the rest of us following. As we approached the pavilion, an elderly man, whose silver-broidered scarlet tunic showed him to be of high rank, emerged. He paused surprisedly, then ran to us.

'Your coming is timely, Messer Obiran,' he cried. 'We have a knight here who is badly injured. On my lord's behalf, may I implore your assistance?' He spoke in English.

'My small skills are at your command,' the wizard responded

gravely. He and Felun dismounted and went within the pavilion, while the rest of us waited.

The crowd had gathered all about us now. For a while the awed silence continued, but soon the murmur of conversation began anew. At first I could make little sense of their talk. Fortunately a late-arriving woman pushed through the crowd to join a man who was standing close to me. When she demanded to be told what was happening, I was just as interested as she in his response. Indeed, I listened intently for many minutes, while Avran sat silent and uncomprehending by me. Eventually his impatience became too much for him.

'Simon, what's going on here? I don't understand.' Avran was addressing me in Sandastrian.

I answered in the same language. 'From what I can gather, there's been a long-standing dispute between the Lord of Dellorain and the Earl of Brantwood, about fishing rights in this river; the Antoman, it seems to be called. The river marks the frontier between their two territories. Well, you'd imagine they'd be content to agree that half the river belonged to each; and so they do. However, there are islands just upstream, in the shallows about which many fish spawn. Those islands are claimed by both realms. And so they'd settled on a contest to decide the question; but now things have gone wrong.'

'What sort of contest, and what has gone wrong?'

'A contest of champions; a joust on the bridge. The knight in armour is Sir Brian Beauchamp, son of the Earl of Brantwood. He was to be matched against the champion of the Lord of Dellorain, a French knight called — oh, Sir Guy de Guisdard, or some such name; I could not make it out. Well, the French knight appears to have stayed up too late last night, celebrating his victory in advance. He rode here fast this morning, too fast; his horse's hooves slid in the mud and the horse fell sideways against a tree. The horse's leg is broken and so, I gather, is the French knight's. The consequence is that they want Vedlen Obiran to set matters right for them — to perform a miracle, if possible.'

'Cannot the Lord of Dellorain find another champion, or take up the challenge himself?'

'It seems not. The Lord is an experienced knight, but he

205

is old, too old for jousting. He has many daughters, but only one son and he a cripple. Moreover, there are no other horses in Dellorain, believe it or not. The French knight was a traveller from some land called Rockaine; it was only his presence that caused the Lord of Dellorain to agree to a contest of this kind.'

'A problem indeed! Perhaps the French knight might be mended well enough to be set in his saddle. However, I cannot conceive how even our friend the wizard can have the horse back into good enough shape for any jousting this day!'

'It's worse even than that, Avran. The champion of Dellorain must accept the challenge before noon. If he does not, the contest is lost and the islands are forfeit to Brantwood. Only two hours remain.'

We both fell silent, for there seemed nothing more to say. Behind us, Amos Sloly was explaining the position to the Reschorese. Soon after, Felun Daretseng emerged from the pavilion and spoke quickly to the Ravatseng brothers. They dismounted and, having extracted two bundles from the packs, followed him into the pavilion.

At a word from Drakht Belineg, the rest of us dismounted also and the rafneyen were sent away to browse among the trees by the river bank. Narel Evateng went with them to guard the packs. We others stood and waited, the crowd eddying about us.

After a while, the Ravatseng brothers emerged from the pavilion. As always it was Rahir who spoke, at first in Reschorese to his fellows and then in English to Avran and me. 'Our master's set yon Frenchman's leg for him, and done it well; he'll be hobbling for a while, but he'll ride again soon enough. However, there'll be no jousting for him, today or for many days to come. As for the horse, 'tis in worse condition. Aye, the break will heal, but the beast will be too long pasture-bound to carry his master back to Rockaine, even by the year's end.'

Avran pulled a wry face. 'A sad disappointment for these folk of Dellorain.'

'Aye, 'tis so; but that being how matters stand, there's no sense in repining.'

At that point, Felun emerged for a second time and

206

beckoned to Avran and me. Rather surprisedly we followed him into the pavilion.

It was very high and brightly lit by candles. On one of the several couches, a man lay wrapped in blankets; the injured knight, presumably. Beside him stood a group of richly dressed men and women, among them the wizard, the elderly man in red and a taller, much older nobleman whose rich accoutrements surely proclaimed him to be the Lord of Dellorain. I bowed to him respectfully and Avran followed suit. As we straightened, Vedlen Obiran spoke urgently.

'My new friends, I know that you have many martial skills. Does it chance that either of you has any familiarity with the lance — any knowledge of jousting?'

We looked at one another. 'Not I,' answered Avran sadly. 'I have witnessed tournaments, but I have never ridden in one.' Dearly would he have loved to respond otherwise, that I could see.

I hesitated, remembering my exercisings with the old ashpole in that high field in Hallamshire. 'Well, I have a little knowledge of the art,' I stammered, 'but . . . but I cannot claim any great skill — any skill at all.'

The Lord of Dellorain's face looked worn and old and his eyes were anxious, but he managed to smile at me. It was a gentle smile that made my heart warm to him.

'Are you willing to ride for me, then, as my champion?' he asked. 'I do not expect you to win, but it were better that my champion appear and be defeated than that Dellorain default on this contest.'

The red-robed man swelled indignantly. 'But this is ridiculous!' he spluttered. 'How can this unknown young man be our champion? He is too small to wear Sir Guy's armour; he would rattle about in it like a pea in a pot. And what will he ride? The horse is lamed beyond mending — certainly beyond mending within two hours! The idea is absurd beyond comprehension.'

The Lord of Dellorain gazed at him reprovingly. 'This decision is mine and mine alone. Please remember that.'

At this reprimand, red-cloak swallowed and fell silent; and the Lord went on: 'As to the armour, why, there is the suit that was worn when young by the Prince my son. It will

207

serve; it can be fetched readily enough. And as to the mount . . .' He paused uncertainly.

'As to the mount, that is easily settled.' Vedlen Obiran was speaking now. 'The rules of the contest surely do not require that it be a horse? No, I thought not. My servant Drakht Belineg is a big man; his rafenu is amply strong enough to bear Simon in armour — if Simon proves willing to ride, that is. What is your decision, Simon? Will you serve as champion for the Lord of Dellorain?'

I hesitated anew. For many years I had desired passionately to ride in a tourney, but I had not expected either to be thrown so suddenly into a contest or to fight when so wholly out of practice. Nor had I even dreamed of riding in borrowed armour, on an unfamiliar mount, against a knight whose skill was undoubted. That was much to attempt! However, I remembered also the great debt owed by Avran and me to the wizard and his men. That decided me. I faced the Lord of Dellorain.

'I am at your service, my lord.' The words sounded loud and resolute, infinitely more resolute than I felt.

The Lord nodded gravely. 'And I am in your debt,' he said solemnly. Then he turned to the others. 'The armour must be fetched swiftly, and Simon's mount also. We have little time.' In a moment, the pavilion was all a-bustle.

The wizard's bright eyes were upon me. 'Good, Simon, good,' he said quietly; then he chuckled. 'A joust of rafenu against horse! That will be something to remember. Consider your rafenu, Simon; think how best to employ his special abilities. For my part, I am by no means convinced that you need experience defeat!'

Chapter Twenty-two

THE JOUST ON THE BRIDGE

With less than two hours remaining before noon, when the challenge from Brantwood must be either accepted or ignominiously declined, I had so much to do that there was little chance for pondering — or even for anxiety.

First of all, Drakht Belineg had to introduce me to his rafenu. This was a heavily striped male called Gahewen, 'broad-streak'. Remembering King Arthur's turbulent follower, I rechristened him 'Gawain'. He was doubtful of me at first, but we became friends quickly enough.

Watched uncomprehendingly by a crowd yet unaware of my appointed role, I rode Gawain off into the forest and tried his paces. I was pleased to find him, not merely obedient, but also quick and intelligent. Moreover, I knew that Drakht had ridden him in many fights; Gawain could be assumed to have an awareness of weapons that rafneyen without combat experience would lack.

When we returned, it was to find that the armour had been fetched; not only for me but also for Gawain, since a rafenu could not wear a horse's accoutrements. The war armour of rafneyen is much like that worn by Sandastrian sevdreyen for battle. It comprises a cap of hammered steel, notched near the front to accommodate the nasal horn and closing about the bases of the brow horns. To protect the rafenu's breast and back, a coat of chain mail is provided, padded within and bearing a high metal saddle from which stirrups hang.

Gawain had never worn armour and it took all of Drakht's cajoling before he would permit himself to be so accoutred. Even then he was most unhappy. He tossed his head, swayed his back, heaved his flanks so that the stirrups jangled against the chain mail, and came close to bucking.

Wisely, Drakht decided to take Gawain off for a brief exercise before the poor rafenu faced the added unfamiliarity of an armoured Simon as rider. Their emergence from the shadows of the pavilion provoked astonished comment from the watching people.

While they were gone, it was my turn to be fitted. I put on a heavily padded gambeson which, when fastened, fitted snugly enough about my body; then a padded hood was placed over my head. Next the hauberk of mail was placed about me and the heaume set upon my head, to be fastened to the hauberk at front and back. Tournament gauntlets — the left, bridle gauntlet heavy and stiff, the right one lighter and more flexible — were placed upon my hands, while greaves and sabatons, all of steel, were put on my legs and feet.

I felt almost overwhelmed by the weight of it all and wondered how I might manage ever to move, let alone ride. Moreover, although my vision was ample with the visor open, I was disconcerted by the narrowness of the slit through which I must look when the visor was closed. How might I watch an opponent properly, with such a restricted view?

I had been sitting while the greaves and sabatons were fitted. Urged to stand up, I did so effortfully; yet, having done so, I discovered that walking about was remarkably easy. The joints of the armour at elbows and knees were unexpectedly flexible, though I could not, of course, turn my head. Moreover, though the skirts of the hauberk were divided at front and back to permit sitting on a horse, I could not possibly mount unaided. What would I do if I were unseated?

However, when Avran showed me my reflection in a hand mirror, I was curiously comforted. How splendid I looked! This was, indeed, a dream of my youth come true.

Though most of the armour was unadorned, the body of the hauberk had been lacquered scarlet and the front of the heaume was adorned with a tiny shield, displaying the scarlet field with silver chevrons of Dellorain. The jousting shield I would soon be carrying was almost square in shape, but it curved inward at the base to be lodged on a horse's back and was notched at upper right to accommodate a lance. It bore the device of the French knight, a crowing scarlet cockerel that matched well with the colours of Dellorain.

When Avran handed the shield to me, I beamed with gratification at my own martial image. Certainly I looked impressive enough to disconcert any opponent unaware of my lack of skill!

Unfortunately, when Drakht returned, his mount found my appearance even more alarming! Poor Gawain shied away, snorting with fear; and my soothing voice, issuing from so disconcerting a source, failed entirely to comfort him. Only after much persuasion would he stand still, permitting me to be laboriously heaved up by four sweating servants and set in the saddle.

After that, matters improved quickly. Gawain could sense my calming reassurances without being upset by the sight of my scarlet and silver self and, for my own part, I had to sustain the weight of the armour no longer. I took the shield and set it in place, then was handed the jousting lance. This I found hard to grasp in my metal-gauntleted hand, but it was less heavy than I had feared. Experimentally I raised and lowered it, then flourished it — and promptly embedded it in the fabric of the pavilion, so that it was twitched from my hands and fell among the watching servants.

This accident amused them greatly, but they were courteous enough not to laugh aloud. One of them handed the lance back to me and, holding it loosely before me, I emerged from the shadows of the pavilion into the sunlight.

By then, most people had wandered away to gaze over the river, examine stalls or continue talking dispiritedly. My unexpected appearance caused at first startlement, then cheers and much excitement.

Since it was not yet quite noon, there was time for another brief ride into the forest. The wizard had been right; Gawain was so strong that, even with the weight of the armour added to that of my small self, the burden was not overwhelming for him. As I rode along I exercised with the lance, raising or lowering it, couching it or setting it upright, until the feel of it was more familiar. Then I tried a few mock charges at trees before, reluctantly, turning and riding back to the riverside.

By then the people were crowding about the skirts of the bridge, chattering like starlings on a cottage roof. At my reappearance, they raised a renewed cheer. They sounded so pleased and confident that, knowing how inadequate a champion they had, I felt quite embarrassed.

A platform had been raised by the bank, on which were sitting the Lord of Dellorain and his Lady, with Vedlen Obiran and the man in red, their chancellor. I rode over to this platform and raised my lance in salute, to receive smiles from three of them and a still-disapproving frown from the chancellor. Then I turned away and, with heart pounding, rode up onto the bridge.

The champion of Brantwood had, of course, seen an armoured figure riding on the riverside; but was he aware that he had a different opponent? Though he must have seen the injured horse being brought back, he might well not know that the French knight himself was injured; he might well presume that his challenger had merely changed mounts. The fame of the French knight had been spread abroad, whereas I was a mere tyro, deservedly without renown. Clearly it would help if Sir Brian were kept unaware that any substitution had taken place.

'Who are you that blocks zis bridge?' I asked, striving to imitate the accent proper to a Frenchman.

'I am Sir Brian Beauchamp,' he responded sturdily. 'I defend the right of my father, Earl of Brantwood and Lord of the Leafy Dales, to the proprietorship of all islands in this river between Brantwood and Dellorain. He who denies that proprietorship must contend with me.'

'Zat proprietorship I deny and zat right I challenge. Zose islands belong to ze Lord of Dellorain.' Was I overdoing the accent, I wondered? It sounded pretty spurious.

'Zen . . . I mean, then' — he corrected himself in so embarrassed a fashion that I was convinced he must be blushing — 'you must joust with me. May he who wins claim those rights for his Lord, henceforth and for ever.' Slipping off his right gauntlet, he flung it down on the bridge before me.

I knew I must take up that gauntlet, but I dared not dismount. What could I do? Fortunately, the problem had been anticipated. A soldier of Dellorain had followed me onto the bridge; he ran past me, picked up the gauntlet and handed it to me.

'Ze challenge, it is accepted,' I said loudly; and there was cheering on both banks. I passed back the gauntlet to the soldier, who handed it to Sir Brian. Rather awkwardly he slipped it back on — a feat I could not have managed unaided! — and, turning his horse about, rode back to the Brantwood end of the bridge. Following his example I turned back toward Dellorain, noting anew the lack of rails on the bridge and gloomily expecting I might soon be plunging into the waters beneath.

But such thoughts would never do! I must be confident and must give Gawain confidence. Instead, I strove determinedly to think out manoeuvres in the joust and to instruct him in his rôle. Ah! the end of the bridge; we must turn. What was the signal for the beginning of the joust? Oh yes, the sound of a bell, to be rung from Brantwood. Sir Brian was couching his lance and I must do likewise.

The bell rang, faint in the distance. In a moment my opponent was riding swiftly toward me. At my mere thought, Gawain also was in full motion, moving even more swiftly, so that we had crossed the centre of the bridge before the coming-together.

Knight and horse seemed to be hurtling at us, massive and implacable as a rock rolling down a hillside. Sir Brian was trying for the point stroke. Indeed, as I peered out from the slit in my helmet, his lance seemed to be coming right at my face with terrible swiftness.

As for me, what was I trying for? I did not know; indeed, I had never decided properly. By now I had time only to attempt a sweep of the lance. Yet would I have chance to make *any* stroke?

I crouched behind my shield and tried to sway away from that dreadful point — quite needlessly, for Gawain danced aside just at the right moment, swift as my thought. The lance-tip swung by me in an arc of brightness; my own lance, aimed so hastily, missed amply; and we were past one another.

Sir Brian's impetus had carried him over the crown of the bridge. I could hear the sound of his horse's hooves scrabbling as he pulled on the reins and strove to turn about. For a moment, I could see through my helmet-slit the bright tents and crowding people on the Brantwood bank. No doubt they were shouting or cheering, but I did not hear them. Gawain had slowed and was already turning, as easily as if on a broad road; the small space presented no problem to him!

Again I couched my lance and again my mount and I were past the bridge centre before we met our opponent. Neither of us was moving so swiftly this time and, with one encounter safely past, I was gaining confidence.

It was my turn to attempt the point stroke, but Sir Brian used his shield to divert my thrust. Despite Gawain's nimble sidestepping, the Brantwood knight's swinging lance came so perilously close to my helmet that I felt the wind of its passing on my hot cheeks.

Down the bridge we went and turned about again, the Dellorain contingent cheering us wildly. Sir Brian had turned his mount more quickly this time and we met right on the bridge crown. On this occasion I was wiser; I held my lance fairly loosely till the last moment, then clamped it tight and swung it at him. By then, his own lance-tip had skidded off my shield as Gawain danced agilely aside. My swinging stroke cleared Sir Brian's shield, hit him in the middle of the chest, skidded up the plate armour and . . . lodged under the gorget protecting his neck!

He was toppling backward off his horse into the river, but I was in no better condition. Since my lance was still clamped to my body, I was thrown sideways and off balance. My feet were trapped firmly in the stirrups; I could not fall clear of Gawain, but was carrying him sideways with me!

My slit of a world view spun round. Frantically I leaned forward, somehow managing to clasp with my gauntlets his horn-bases and clinging with my knees as best I might to the high saddle. The rafenu's hooves scrabbled for, and lost, their grip on the wooden planks. Then Gawain and I fell helplessly, and with an enormous splash, down into the deepest channel of the bright-flowing Antoman.

It was, indeed, the very depth of the water that saved us. In a shallower river Gawain might well have broken a limb, and I been seriously injured, by impact with the bottom. As it was we plunged deep down, followed by a trail of bubbles, Gawain's legs flailing and myself gasping as water flowed into my helmet.

Somehow, in the plunge, Gawain righted himself. Up to the surface we bobbed, he snorting and I spluttering. Then Gawain shook the water from his horns and, transmitting confidently calming thoughts to me, swam back to the Dellorain bank where the crowd was cheering in welcome.

' 'Tis a question to try the abilities of Solomon himself,' the Earl of Brantwood grumbled. He was a massive man, with fading blue eyes under knotted brows and a beard with the texture and colour of a Pennine sheep's fleece. 'Setting aside the question of the propriety of riding a rafenu in a tournament — a question that should have been argued ere the joust was begun and which, as you say, my Lord of Dellorain, was settled when our champions couched lances — I perceive no means for deciding who was victor. It may be true, as you claim, that your champion's lance upset my son from his mount; but then *his* mount, at least, remained on the bridge, while your champion and his — ahem — rafenu were both thrown into the river.'

'But then, Simon stayed in the saddle of *his* mount and rode it to the bank,' the Lord of Dellorain countered mildly. 'Your son had to be hauled out from the river mud and rescued by boat and then, er, dried out ashore.'

'As to that, your champion's lance was broken, whereas my son's was not.'

'Broken or not, your son lost it, for he dropped it on the bridge. And he lost his shield also, whereas Simon retained his.'

The Earl was purpling. 'But it was not your champion's skill that caused my son to drop his shield! He did so, sensibly, when he found himself in the water. And we recovered it without trouble.'

Sir Brian Beauchamp spoke up at this point. Having shed the concealment of his jousting helmet, he proved not nearly so formidable as I had imagined. He was a merry-eyed man of some twenty summers, with curling blond hair and a beard which, compared with that of his doughty father, seemed quite sparse.

'For my part, I consider myself defeated. My lance wrought no harm to Simon; it was his lance that sent us both into the river.'

His father would not yield to this argument. 'Yet was he an acceptable champion? He is not of Dellorain, but of the

215

following of Messer Obiran here. Could he properly represent Dellorain, anyway?'

The Lord of Dellorain was becoming annoyed. 'You put forward no objection when you thought a knight of Rockaine would represent me! And, had your son emerged as winner of the joust, you would not now be crying "Unfair! Unfair!"'

We had crossed the river and were sitting about a table on the raised mound from which the Earl had watched the contest. A silent crowd of men and women from Dellorain and Brantwood stood about and below us, Avran and the wizard's men among them. The Dellorainian chancellor (more amicable now), Felun Daretseng, Sir Brian and I sat on one side — the north side — of the table. Facing us, their backs to the river, were the Earl and the Lord, with Vedlen Obiran seated between them. The wizard seemed smaller than ever when flanked by the burliness of one and the tallness of the other. His ever-bright eyes were amused.

'Peace, peace!' he intoned. 'No-one has won and no-one lost. The tourney showed your champions to be of equal ability and thus, that your claims are of equal strength.'

'Then who owns the river islands henceforward?' demanded the Earl. 'Or must we bicker over them for yet more years?'

'Not at all. Since your claims to them are of equivalent merit, quite evidently the islands belong both to Brantwood and to Dellorain. They must be conserved or fished at your joint will, by both your peoples. You must each nominate three men of wisdom to a council. That council must decide how the fishery should be administered and who should have rights in it; and those rights must be exactly equal. Do you both agree?'

The angry flush had faded from the cheeks of the Lord of Dellorain. 'That is acceptable to me. This quarrel has divided us for too many years.'

The Earl drummed his fingers on the table and glanced at his son. Then he rumbled: 'So be it. As you say, we have disputed long enough.'

At these words, there was frantic cheering from the listening crowd. The Earl waited till it had subsided, then went on: 'As for me' — a slow smile gave unexpected lightness to his heavy features — 'I never did care much for fish, anyway!'

There was laughter at this. The Earl slumped backward

in his chair, his eyes roving about our faces. Again he smiled. 'And this night ye shall all dine with my son and me at our castle of Brantley — Dellorainians, Messer Obiran's men and all.'

At this, the cheering was even more resounding since, as we learned later, the Earl was renowned for the lavishness of his hospitality. So it was amidst a joyful crowd of men and women that, after retrieving our rafneyen from the Dellorain bank, we made our way north through the forest to Brantley.

It was, to my eyes, rather an old-fashioned fortress, a simple motte-and-bailey encircled by a moat formed by the diverting of a tributary of the Antoman. Within the bailey were many small houses and, in the shadow of the keep, a spacious banqueting hall. There we dined, while musicians played on cittern, rebec, psaltery and pommer from a gallery above. Predictably, no fish was served!

Avran, Sir Brian and I fast became friends, for the merry spirits of the Earl's son made him a most agreeable companion. At one point in our cheerful talk, Sir Brian eyed me curiously: 'Simon, why did you speak so strangely when you challenged me? Was the helmet distorting your voice?'

I blushed, then admitted: 'I was striving to sound like a Frenchman. I thought you might mistake me for the knight of Rockaine and perhaps fear me more!'

He laughed heartily. 'It was a vain device, Simon! I have seen that knight fighting in tournaments in the Deerlands. He is a much bigger man than you, and burlier. Moreover, he speaks not at all in that fashion!'

Avran was laughing also. 'Well, it was a brave try, Simon my friend; and you rode bravely also. Indeed, when I remember that this was your first tournament, I marvel.'

Sir Brian had raised his ale to his lips, but at this he set it down so suddenly that the froth splashed out. 'Say not so! His first tourney? Why, from those skilled evasions of my lance, I had thought him a veteran of many contests!'

I was blushing again. 'It was my rafenu that was skilled, not I. Without him, I would have been unseated at the first joust.'

'Well, well!' Sir Brian was marvelling. 'Though I accept not your renouncing of all credit for your victory — and you *did* gain the victory, whatever my father and Messer Obiran might claim — I must believe also that your rafenu aided you. We ride rafneyen when hunting, of course, but never at tournaments. Yet horses are few here and they're costly to buy and keep. It is time that we altered our ideas.'

He paused reflectively, then went on: 'Mayhap you have done more than fight in a tournament, Simon. Mayhap you have given a fresh twist to our games of war!'

Chapter Twenty-three

THE ROLLING-UP OF A CHART

Choleric though he had seemed at our first meeting, the Earl of Brantwood proved a large-hearted and generous host. So pressing was his hospitality that the wizard, his men and we stayed at the castle of Brantley, not just for one night but for a whole sennight.

For Avran and me, it was a time of relaxation and recuperation, physical and emotional, from the strains of a journey that — great Heavens! — had only taken two months. Hard to conceive that so much incident and so many perils had been packed into so short a time! I remembered my tranquil years in Hallamshire, not with real regret but rather with a dim nostalgia, as one recalls a peaceful dream upon awakening to a bright day of hard work.

The Lord of Dellorain and his Lady departed on the first morning, on the last day of Devbalet, the month we call February. They had wished to reward me handsomely for acting as champion of Dellorain. However, I would accept nothing from them since I had fought in the tourney, not from any desire to serve Dellorain, but to pay off in part the debt owed to Vedlen Obiran by Avran and me. Though I strove to explain this, the Lord continued so to protest his indebtedness to me that I was relieved by their departure.

Indeed, even had I been willing to accept some gift, there was nothing they could have given me that I wanted. My only desires were to complete my quest swiftly and return to Sandarro and Ilven.

During those days in Brantwood, Avran and I learned much about the strange world of the forests and the plains about them. It was more than three hundred years, we gathered, since men fleeing from the wars or the laws of Europe had begun to arrive in Rockall. They had found the mountains of the north and east and the plains and hills of the south to be already quite densely inhabited and divided into many republics and princedoms. In contrast, the central lands of Rockall were almost empty. Yes, there had been a handful of people living in the grasslands east and north of the great forests, most of them fugitives from neighbouring realms, but these people had either welcomed, or else failed successfully to resist, the newcomers.

New realms had arisen amid those grasslands, often with Rockalese names but always with European rulers. Predominantly these were men of English birth or descent, like the self-styled Kings of Herador, Devoria, Tarnevost and Merania and the Earls of Felessett, Bayansavar and Odunseth; England had been torn with fratricidal strife during those centuries and many men had found it easier to leave their homeland than to disentangle the knots of conflicting loyalties.

However, numerous Frenchmen and Gascons had likewise come to Rockall, for their lands had been war-torn also. Most of the Gascons had found new homes among the English settlers; yet they had also set up two independent realms, Rockaine and Haviland, in the foothills northwest of the plains. The Frenchmen had founded two realms. One of these, Delisle, lay in hills southwest of the forests. The other lay on the shores of the great bight north of Dedesta; it was centred upon the port of Saint Lorraine and named Bayard, after the great hero of chivalric legend.

In the winter of 1307 to 1308 a great party of Knights Templar had arrived, fleeing with their retinues and such wealth as they had saved from greedy, murderous betrayal by King Philip IV of France and his tame Pope at Avignon. Received sympathetically by the earlier settlers, the Templars had been permitted to settle in the last unoccupied area of grassland remaining between the forests and the northern mountains. The Gascon knights of Rockaine and Haviland were their neighbours to the south and the Reschorese to the north.

The lands allotted to the Templars were not very good, for by the early fourteenth century all the better areas, whether for grazing or the planting of crops, had been taken. Though new arrivals continued to be welcomed in some of the grassland realms, they were received less enthusiastically in others. Men come soon to regard a new land as theirs by right and become jealous of any who they think might try to claim it. Moreover, among the descendants of earlier settlers there were many men of small fortune but high ambition, eager to set up fiefdoms of their own. If the grasslands were filling, might there not be room to be found among the great forests?

About these, the native Rockalese seemed to know little but told uneasy stories — of haunted groves and poisoned rivers; of fell beasts and fearful ailments; of fairies and giants, goblins and green men. So solemnly recounted were the tales that the Frenchmen and Gascons had been wholly unwilling, and even the rasher Englishmen long reluctant, to venture into those endless-seeming forests.

However, when men did begin to do so, they discovered that the stories had as little substance as those told around English firesides in winter. There were fell beasts, certainly, but none worse than might be encountered among the grasslands — no dragons, no cockatrices. Yes, some venturers did disappear forever among the trees, but many more returned without having encountered excessive perils. And so, at first slowly but then more swiftly, men began setting up homesteads and carving out new demesnes among the forest glades.

At the outset they followed the practices of England, practices that had worked well enough in the plains except where the land was too dry. They had cut down trees and cleared fields for their crops or had sought streamside meadows where their cattle might graze. However, such procedures were quickly abandoned. It was easier to harvest the forests than to plant and tend corn, oats or barley, in a land where serfs were unknown and freemen reluctant to labour in the unremitting fashion that their ancestors had done. It was easier to keep hasedain, which would browse happily among the trees and underbrush, than to tend cows that, however luxuriant the meadow grasses, seemed always to remain lean and sickly. Horses bred poorly and, if they were to stay healthy, needed more attention here than in England; moreover, they were hard to train. It was better to keep them for tournaments and, for day-to-day activities of work or hunting, easier to ride instead the forest-loving, quicker-witted rafneyen.

Yet, however their mode of working their demesnes might alter, the social practices of the settlers changed little. The tiny realms of the forestlands were mirrors in miniature of the greater realms of England and France. The little courts of the forest earls strove to emulate the greater courts of King Henry and King Charles. However, ships from France and England were not frequent and their crews not likely to be well-informed concerning current court fashions and attitudes. Moreover, such tidings as they *did* bring were altered or delayed as they passed from mouth to mouth, from the ports of Saint Lorraine or Warringtown, through the forest realms to these farthest and southernmost reaches of settlement.

In consequence, everything here was, in European terms, somewhat outdated. The houppelande, hennin and pourpoint were unknown. Ladies wore the sleeveless surcoats and the crespines or pork-pie coifs fashionable in English courts of earlier times, while men still wore parti-coloured cote-hardies and hoods with long liripipes. The suits of mail worn by Sir Brian and me had seemed impressive enough to the watching crowds, for plate armour was rarely seen here in Rockall; but an English armourer would have scoffed at our mail, pointing out a number of faults in construction. (That my lance had caught under the gorget protecting Sir Brian's neck was condemnation enough; in any decently constructed suit of armour, such a mishap would be impossible!) Falconry was as popular here as in England, but the very hoods and jesses for the hawks were of an ancient style. All in all, to anyone from England, travelling in the great forests was like walking backward through the years.

However, I was not inclined either to criticize or to strive to inculcate new ideas among the gentlemen and ladies of the court of the Earl of Brantwood. This was in part because it would not have been good manners, but largely because I found it curiously restful to be in such a tranquil backwater of the stream of Time. Sandastre had been an utterly different realm, in which all things were new and there had been so much to learn every day. Here, all was familiar, if a little antique. I enjoyed my stay at Brantley very much.

A factor in my enjoyment was the cheerful company of young Sir Brian, in whom both Avran and I found a companion very much to our liking. He was greatly taken by this new idea of riding rafneyen in tournaments. We were cajoled into exercising with him each day, riding mounts swathed in padded cloth and using light wooden lances. The greater intelligence of a rafenu, in comprehending the wishes of his rider and evading the onslaught of an opponent, was patent.

Sir Brian marvelled in retrospect that our encounter had been the first of its kind. 'Quite a historic joust!' he would beam. 'A privilege for me to take part in it. My word, how I'll run rings round my opponents in the Deerlands tournament this summer! Well, let's try it again; I think I'll have you this time, Simon.'

Neither buffets nor falls deterred him; and he suffered many during those early contests. If an unexpected flick of his lance set me swaying in my saddle, he would crow with delight. However, in contests with Avran, a skilled rider but quite without knowledge of jousting, Sir Brian would be always charmingly apologetic in victory; and always he remained merry in defeat.

With this game and other martial pastimes, we passed our mornings and enhanced our skills. There were rides in the forest also, and races along narrow streamside meadows in which Galahad outmatched Lancelot and Sir Brian's mounts. Sometimes we went out with falcons at wrist, though the sport was poor so early in the year. I was able also, in a little chapel in the shadows of the castle walls, to express my thanks to God for bringing Avran and me safely through so many perils and to pray for a swift completion of my quest. Yes, that was a cheerful time.

The wizard we saw only rarely. Here in the castle, the duties of his men were few. Though Vedlen Obiran made himself daily available to treat the sick and injured of the Brantwood forest glades, this did not occupy many of his hours, for the people of the Earldom were few and healthy. The Ravatseng brothers were his chosen assistants in giving medical treatment and Felun Daretseng his preferred companion at other times. The remaining Reschorese found friends and occupation among the castle servants. Amos Sloly's 'Here, let a *real* man tackle that!', as he lent aid in some task with an aim of displaying his own superior prowess, was heard often in the yards and kitchens.

On the fourth day, the wizard requested that Avran and I be brought to his room. This was a comfortable chamber above the banqueting hall to which little sound penetrated, with a large window through whose thin parchment panes the day-to-day activities of the castle could be watched unaware. We found him seated at a table and, at his gesture, sat down on the bench at its further side.

He unrolled a parchment and spread it before us. At first glance, it seemed only to depict a massive and elaborate letter U, such as one might see beginning a chapter in some monastery bible. However, when he turned the parchment onto its side so that the U opened toward the right, I perceived it was a chart. The hills were drawn in brown ink, the trees in green, and also in green was a vein-like pattern that I realized must represent rivers and coasts. Upon this chart had been written in black many words, in an angular alphabet unfamiliar to me; nor did Avran comprehend it. Nevertheless both of us realized, even before Vedlen Obiran told us so, that we were looking at a map of the forestlands and the realms about them.

'I have not attempted this before,' he went on, 'and I know that my attempt is both crude and inaccurate. However, if indeed we are to find Lyonesse for you, such a chart may aid us a little. Now, the lands of the Montariotans are here' — he indicated the lower side of the U — 'and Brantwood and Dellorain are here,' pointing at a spot in the forests near the lowest curve of its base. 'Just east of us is Alberbrend' — he pointed again — 'and beyond again is a large area of dense forest which I believe to be still unsettled — here, between Alberbrend and Antomalata. Yes, just so. If indeed Lyonesse *is* to be found in the forests, then it must be in this region, for it is certainly in no other.'

'How may we ascertain whether Lyonesse be there?' I asked politely. I did not think the prospect at all hopeful; the area he had indicated was much too far from the sea.

As happened so often, the wizard seemed to catch my thought. 'No, I do not believe it probable either, Simon. That region has a strange reputation and only exceptionally brave men would venture into it. Of course, your father and his predecessors in Rockall may have been valiant enough to do so, but I believe I would have heard tell of any such adventurings. However, we shall ride soon to the castle of Skarngrove in Alberbrend, so that we may settle the question beyond doubt.'

He paused and considered the map anew, before going on: 'If that ascertaining proves profitless, as we anticipate, then we must travel on northward. Even I do not choose to venture needlessly into those forest heartlands. Now, there are little-inhabited highlands just beyond the forests and above the Great Marshes that surround the mouth of the Aramassa.' He pointed this time to the upper left curve of the U. 'There, a new realm may have arisen; we can try that chance. Here to the north and east of the forests,' — he indicated the centre of the upper stroke of the U — 'realms rise and fade like storms in summer. However, those realms are products of quarrels over old boundaries, not new settlements. I doubt that prospect, although it should also be enquired into.'

He paused again, then said pensively: 'If those chances fail, then you must seek either in the eastern mountains, where the folk are fierce and strange' — he placed his finger on the furthest upper right of the U — 'or in the mountains of the north. Concerning those eastern mountains, I have learned a little during my travels — enough to think them an improbable, though not an impossible, location for Lyonesse. After all, they have long coasts.'

'Yet you believe those highlands above the Aramassa marshes to be more likely?' Avran was asking.

'It is a possibility to be explored; yet not, I think, a strong one. However, that can be checked by only a small detour from our northward path.'

'But what of the northern mountains?'

'What indeed? Those mountains also have long coasts. My own land of Reschora lies here.' He set his finger at a position above the curve of the U. 'As you see, my chart depicts only a small part — the southernmost edge — of the northern mountains, for I have not travelled further. Yet at least I can assure you that Lyonesse is not to be found among the southern ridges and valleys. Those realms and territories are all familiar to me, by name at least, and all are ancient. If Lyonesse be among those mountains, then it must lie much further to the north.'

THE WIZARD'S MAP

He fell silent and, for many minutes, Avran and I contemplated the chart equally silently, striving to memorize its shape and to decipher its strange glyphs.

Abruptly the wizard sat back. In the thin light of the parchment window his eyes seemed yellow. They were glinting with wry amusement.

'Hard to read, is it not? Well, both of you must strive to learn Reschorese speech and characters.'

With a quick twist, he rolled up the chart. 'We will ask in Alberbrend, but I expect little from that asking. Whatever your night hopes, Simon, I fear your journeyings are far from their end.'

Then the wizard paused, eyeing us gravely. 'Yet I find other foreshadowings in my thoughts. I believe that our meeting happened not by mere hazard, but by design, and that our journeyings together were predestined, so as to achieve some end yet unknown to us. Moreover, these present journeyings will prove only a small part of that design, a weaving-in of only a detail of the tapestry. In that tapestry, Simon and Avran, you are to prove important threads — perhaps even crucial in shaping its pattern. Well, we shall see, we shall see.'

He waved us away and slipped again into his reverie. As we left the chamber, its brightness was dimmed as clouds spread across the sun — clouds that seemed to me symbolic of troubles to come.

Though Avran the traveller remained cheerful, I came away feeling quite daunted. The prospect of playing some large rôle in future events did not cheer me, for I was without large ambitions. So there would be no quick end to my quests; so our travels were but begun . . . In Vedlen Obiran's words, indeed, there was for me small comfort to be found.

Chapter Twenty-four

THE CASTLE OF CHANCELET

Of our visit to Alberbrend there is little to tell. It was brief and, as predicted, quite profitless. The Earl was away in his southern castle of Everbrend and the castellan of Skarngrove as reluctant to receive us as the Earl of Brantwood had been hospitable. The castellan was a thin and nervous, elderly knight, of the clerkly sort that executes decisions effectively enough but is almost incapable of making them. After the magician and we had consumed a meagre repast grudgingly offered, he was persuaded to answer our question only by Vedlen Obiran's persistence.

'No, of course not; there have been no venturings into the deep forests. Why should men go there? Ridiculous idea; much too dangerous. Trees too dense to pass; all sorts of evil beings — dragons, giants, witches, wizards —' He paused, paled, then corrected himself embarrassedly: 'Evil wizards, I mean; present company excepted, of course! Absurd idea. Waste of time your seeking further; and, er, no need to stay and await my Lord's return. The Earl would tell you only the same as I. There are no settlements, new or old, in those lands.'

And so we turned north, passing from Alberbrend into the Deerlands. This was the largest of the forest earldoms and a very pleasant place. There were light sandy soils underhoof and many sunny spaces amid the trees, in which farms and little settlements seemed scattered as randomly as if they had grown from seeds blown from a dandelion clock.

We were not heading directly northward. Instead, we were following a meandering route that took in as many of these farms and hamlets as possible. Wherever we encountered people, we were welcomed and treated generously. However, there were several nights when we pitched tent in a glade far from any habitation.

As we travelled, Avran and I learned much. The Reschorese tongue proved little different from Sandastrian in essentials, though there were bewildering shifts of meaning — *ushaz*, for example, means in Sandastrian 'to condemn' and in Reschorese 'to praise' — and a whole range of unfamiliar words, for some of which we could not even find equivalents. The northern alphabet proved easy; once we realized that the circles and curves of Sandastrian letters became squares and angles in the northern script, the letters were readily understood and mastered. Our progress was so rapid that, within a fortnight, both of us could read the place-names on the wizard's chart and take part, albeit haltingly, in the conversations of our companions.

We learned that, whereas the names of Sandastrian vardai are so ancient that they have no known meaning, the surnames of Reschorese families can be readily interpreted. The suffix *-eng* means simply 'man of'; thus the Ravatsengs were men from Ravatar and Felun was from Dareten, both being valleys amid the southern hills of Reschora. Similarly, Narel Evateng was named from Evatel, a valley somewhere in its northern mountains, though it was long since his family had moved southward. *Belineg* meant 'blacksmith', while *obiran* was the title given to the governor of a fortress. ('Seneschal' or 'castellan' are its nearest English equivalents, but they are not exact.)

We learned also something of the arts of the physician and chirurgeon. Even in the smallest and remotest habitations, there seemed always to be someone requiring Vedlen Obiran's skills. As I have mentioned, the two Ravatseng brothers were his principal assistants, Delhir having a special delicacy of touch in bone setting. Narel Evateng was responsible for the drying of herbs and the mixing of potions. The strange eyes and brusque manner of the wizard himself aroused awe and fear among those whom he treated, especially the women and children; Amos Sloly was principally of value because his cheerfulness and robust self-confidence were calming and reassuring. As for Avran and me, we looked on or rendered aid only when required, but we observed and we remembered.

Vedlen Obiran seemed never to expect recompense for the medicaments and treatments he provided, save in food, wine or the small services of hospitality. Remembering the high charges extorted by quacksalvers at English fairgrounds, I was both surprised and impressed by this. In genuine puzzlement, I asked Felun Daretseng how his master could contrive to live and maintain his men upon such meagre profits. He hesitated before responding.

'Well, it's not easy to explain. There is a special caste of . . . oh, alchemists, magicians, physicians, call them what you will, in Reschora. The Trident Mountains in the south of our land, and the valleys in their shadow, are a strange region, with strange earths from which one can prepare potions for healing or enchantment. The people living there are strange also, with abilities and skills quite out of the common. It is said that all the men are warlocks and all the women witches. Though I do not truly believe that, the saying is near enough right to be hard to dismiss. Many men from those mountains become travellers; it is their tradition that they must serve all people under God, whether barbarian nomads in tents or Christian kings in palaces. From the poor, no payment is exacted for services of healing. Indeed, even the rich are treated without any fees being demanded, though payment is accepted, gladly enough, if offered.'

'It sounds very noble and admirable,' I responded consideringly. 'Yet it must be an exhausting life, with no guarantee of adequate recompense. Such men must truly be saints.'

Felun smiled at this. 'Well, some of them are and some aren't. It is true that some of the Trident physicians travel far and undergo much hardship, in order to serve the needy. Our master is one; much though he may enjoy his small luxuries, most certainly he earns them!'

'Yes, indeed,' I put in sincerely.

Felun smiled again at my earnestness, then went on consideringly: 'Unfortunately, there are others who journey only as far as the nearest mansion of a rich noble who fancies a personal physician or enchanter. For them, the risks are few and the comforts and rewards are many. When the rich require services in astromancy, necromancy or any form of divination, in the breaking of seals or the setting of spells, a sizeable payment is always exacted. Even our master charges considerably for such tasks, but he performs them only rarely

231

and reluctantly. Some of his fellow wizards are much less scrupulous, I fear.'

'I do not think I would like to encounter an unscrupulous magician,' I commented reflectively. Then, as my thoughts veered, I asked: 'Does our master return often to Reschora? Does he have a home there, and children perhaps?'

Felun's brow darkened. 'He had a wife whom he loved and a son who was precious to him, but they were murdered and his home burned. Even though we Reschorese had no hand in that crime, the memory of it prevents him from returning to our land. Ask me no more; it is a story not for my telling.'

It was on the third day after leaving Alberbrend that we met with our next adventure. We were emerging from an area of thick forest into a clearing, with the wizard trailing behind as usual, when a cry of warning from Narel Evateng and a thrill of alarm from Galahad jolted me out of a daydream of Ilven. I glanced ahead and saw a huge brown creature, charging obliquely toward us at the ferocious pace of an angry bull.

At first I perceived only its size and its speed, but then I noticed other details. It was much bigger than any bull and had only a single, huge Y-shaped horn on the front of its nose, lowered now to impale any unfortunate victim. I could see its ears, flattened against its short neck, and the red gleam of fury from little piggy eyes.

'A kalvak!' I heard Felun say in surprise; then 'Ware kalvak!' he shouted as his rafenu leapt from its path.

Fortunately, Galahad jumped aside equally nimbly. As the creature thundered by, I saw the massiveness of its shoulders and haunches, noticed its absurd little tail, held stiffly like an angry bull's, and heard the 'huh, huh' of its heavy breathing.

The pack-rafneyen were scattering, but one of the two bearing the tent-poles could not move fast enough. It screamed as a prong of that great horn slashed its haunches, then fell sideways, bringing its fellow down also.

Swift running by the rafneyen of the three Ravatsengs carried them well clear of the charging beast, but Amos Sloly was less fortunate. He had barely emerged into the glade and, taken unaware when his rafenu jumped aside, he was swept from its back by a low tree-branch. He yelped in fright and began burrowing into the foliage of a dense thorn bush, with the determined celerity of a mole.

My heart pounded in alarm, for I thought the creature must surely turn upon Amos; but it did not. Its attention was elsewhere. Just at that dangerous moment, the rafenu of Vedlen Obiran had emerged from the thicket.

It was evident that the wizard had neither heard Felun's shout nor seen the kalvak; nor, more astonishingly, did his rafenu seem conscious of danger. The great beast was almost upon them before either rafenu or rider appeared to notice it. Even then, instead of leaping aside, the wizard's rafenu stood stock still.

My heart was thumping with a renewed and greater apprehension: I had acquired a deep respect for Vedlen Obiran and now, it seemed, was to witness his obliteration. Yet no such thing happened. The wizard reached down to his saddle, quite casually. There was a flick of his fingers, then of his wrists; and suddenly a ball of fiery green flame was hurtling at the kalvak.

The creature gave a mighty snort of astonishment and fear. It threw back its head and stopped, dropping its hindquarters and driving its great hooves so deeply into the turf that, afterward, one could see deep gouge-marks. As the ball of bright flame hit and burned its shoulders, the kalvak gave a convulsive leap and a bray of pain. Then, with tail down, it thundered away into the forest.

Its path took the kalvak past the unfortunate Amos. Convinced that his last moment had come, he yelled in renewed fright and dived deeper among the thorns.

When the beast had gone and we gathered about him, Amos had to be pulled backward out of his uncomfortable refuge. The poor man's clothes, hair and skin — his hands in particular — were so thrust through with prickles that we had all to set to and pull them out.

Amos endured this passively, while Rahir's rubbing of his skin with soothing lotion earned gratitude. Yet when Drakht Belineg rumbled, in tones very like Amos's, 'Why, let a *real* man tackle that thornbush!', the look he received was not one of affection! However, the imitation set the rest of us laughing.

233

The injured pack-rafenu had suffered less severely than we had feared, nothing worse than a gouge across its hind-quarters and the straining of the muscles of its left hind leg in its fall. However, its load had to be removed, those of the other pack-rafeneyen being so adjusted as to free one of them to share the burden of the poles. The injured animal's leg and wound were then bound up by Hebehir, under careful instruction from the wizard. Soon it was limping along cheerfully enough.

All in all, more than two hours went by before our journey was resumed. As we rode I reflected that the wizard, though he might trail behind us, was not quite so vulnerable as he might appear!

It was on the eighth afternoon that we reached Chancelet, a little town huddled about the banks of a narrow, swift-flowing river. The cottages, with their whitewashed walls and thatched roofs, looked very English and the castle keep, on the great grass-covered motte behind and above them, was as tall, and with the same six buttresses, as that of Conisborough, a castle close to my Hallamshire home. Furthermore, like Conisborough Castle, it was built of white limestone. Yet it was not of Conisborough that I thought as we rode into Chancelet, but of the great white castle of Sandarro where I longed to be.

As we rode over an arching bridge into the town, I noticed something that astonished me. 'Why, this river is flowing east, not west!'

'So it is!' said Avran in equal surprise. 'And flowing fast, at that.'

Felun turned in his saddle and smiled at us. 'Indeed, that is so. These are the headwaters of the Dainflete. If you were to follow its course, you would traverse the forest earldoms of Marcanlon and Dakalet and enter tidal waters where the river divides Seretta from Bayard. However, it would be a journey of many days.'

The little town proved quite as friendly a place as it had looked to me. The arrival of the wizard aroused pleasure and excitement, for he was a familiar and welcome visitor. It was only after many greetings and much merry chatter that we were allowed to pass up into the castle. The soldiers guarding its gate admitted us without hesitation.

Noting their surcoats — scarlet above, green below, and bearing the device of a running rafenu in brown — I winced a little and reflected that, in their crossing from England, the rules of heraldry must have suffered a sea-change. Colour on colour; why, no English herald or king of arms would permit such an abomination!

There was no separate banqueting hall here, only a high hall within the keep; but, bright with banners, that was a cheerful place, for the Earl of the March of the Deerlands — thus he styled himself — was as merry and benign as his people. He was a little, roly-poly man with short grey curls and a bristling fringe of beard, putting me in mind somehow of the tales of Old King Cole; I was gratified when I learned that his family name was Colefax! His countess, in contrast, was quite tall and thin, graver than her busband but with a twinkle of affection in her eye whenever she regarded him. There were six sons and three daughters, all of whom had avoided — thankfully, I do not doubt! — the physical extremes of their parents.

Though Avran and I made no friends so close as Sir Brian had been, our stay in Chancelet was to be almost as pleasant, and quite as long, as that at Brantley. Pleasant for us, at least; but it was a demanding time for Vedlen Obiran. An elderly family retainer was in great pain after a fall from one of the keep's stone staircases. Even after Delhir Ravatseng had reset the woman's bones with care and skill, several days, many potions and much attention were necessary before she was on the road to recovery.

The services of Avran and me were not required, nor was Felun Daretseng much engaged, so we received many further lessons from him in the Reschorese language, letters and customs. In between times, I would sit under a tree by the lowest slopes of the castle motte, strumming a cittern borrowed from a friendly court musician. Meanwhile, Avran did his best to master the fingering of a pommer bought in Chancelet market. The early squeaks and breathy sounds progressively gave place to more pleasing notes as the days passed.

I felt no impatience to be on the road, for I had quite lost confidence that we would ever find Lyonesse and had

235

no eagerness for further perilous adventure. Even Avran was happy to relax for a while, taking pleasure in his growing mastery of Reschorese and of his new instrument. Moreover, two of the Earl's daughters were casting upon him amorous eyes and seemed ever finding occasion for seeking his company. However, although enjoying their attentions and always courteous in his responses, Avran showed no sign of succumbing to their blandishments.

The Countess of the Deerlands was, it seemed, a fervent believer in Vedlen Obiran's abilities in divination. Repeatedly she implored him to predict for her the future of her family, her court and herself; but, concerned with their servant's condition, he would not do so at first. Only on the sixth evening did he yield to her importunings; and then he insisted that his services must be available also to anyone else in Chancelet who sought them.

After an early and hasty dinner, the courtiers and servants were sent out and the Earl's family persuaded to retreat to their quarters. Within the great hall of the keep, a pavilion of purple cloth, open at one end, was set up and other careful preparations made by his men and us.

When the people were invited to return, all had been arranged so as to impress, even to awe, them. The torches in the hall had been dimmed, save only those above the gallery where the court musicians sat, and the fire had been put out. All attention was thus focused, as it should be, upon Vedlen Obiran.

About the pavilion there had been ranged four of the tall Mentonese candles, each contained in a slim lantern of crimson grass that altered their blue flames to bright purple. Within the pavilion was seated the wizard, clad in his gold-embroidered tunic; he seemed still and yet shimmering, like some strange ornament from the Saracen lands. Before him, upon a little platform, was a broad, shallow copper dish, arched over by a sort of cupola of glass that was patterned and supported by a tracery of silver wires. The dish was filled to the very brim with water. In that water, there floated seven candles, each of a different hue and each burning with a flame of that hue; all the colours of the rainbow were there — red, saffron, yellow, green, blue, indigo and violet. The flicker of those flames spilled many-coloured shadows upon the stone flags.

236

Though Vedlen Obiran would never foretell the futures of any of his men — a refusal loudly bemoaned by Amos Sloly — we were all permitted to join the throng in the great hall and witness the proceedings. On the gallery above, the musicians played. Their music was solemn and slow, adding to our tension; moreover, it kept from our ears both the words of those who sought the magician's prognostications and his responses. However, we found it sufficiently entertaining to watch the approach of each petitioner and to guess, from his or her expression, whether the forecast had been good or ill.

Indeed, it was mostly the ladies of Chancelet who were anxious to know their future. Three of the male courtiers and a handful of tradesmen also ventured up to the purple pavilion; but the other men, knowing all too well the hazards of a life of contest and combat, had no desire to learn how brief their span on earth might be.

Usually, then, it would be a woman who approached. She would hand to Hebehir Ravatseng, who served as treasurer, the coins of gold or silver exacted for the augury. Then she would walk falteringly toward the wizard's seat, excitement and trepidation in her eyes.

There was a low bench placed just beyond the great copper dish. The woman would sit on that bench, her back to the hall and her eyes looking into the wizard's across the flames. He would ask her name and invite specific questions, then gaze silently at her for a while. Under the purple shade of the pavilion and in the flicker of the flames, his own eyes seemed sometimes black, sometimes golden, always as unhuman as a lizard's.

Abruptly he would reach into a coffer beside him and pick out a little coloured ball of some light material — a bubble of wax, perhaps? I could not be sure. With a strangely casual gesture, he would toss the ball among the bright flames of the floating candles. Sometimes it would fall into the water between them, shining in their glow. This, it seemed, was a good omen, a promise of long life at least, though the woman's fortune would depend upon the colour of the candles to which it floated closest. Long life does not always bring other blessings.

More often, the ball would be caught in the updraught

over the flames and would bob up and down under the glass cupola for a longer or a shorter time until eventually, in a puff of flame, it would vanish. The duration of its bobbing up and down reflected, we gathered, the likely length of life of the petitioner, its position among the flames her fortune during that life. More than that, none of us could determine.

One of the Earl's daughters, before approaching the wizard, threw so bold a glance at Avran that I guessed what her petition would be. The ball cast for her settled safely into the water close to the blue candle. However, by her look of annoyance on returning, I knew that her hope of wedlock to my friend had been pronounced vain!

When the Countess herself went forward, the little ball did not persist long above the flames; yet she returned so composedly that the predictions must have been gratifying in other ways. The fortunes of other petitioners were variable, by their expressions. However, on one occasion a ball went right into the green flame and vanished instantly. At this, the wizard covered his eyes and his suppliant, the town carpenter, staggered strickenly away. Just before we left Chancelet, we learned he had been killed by the collapse of the roof-arch of a house he was helping to build.

As the evening wore on and the line of petitioners dwindled, the number of watching people became fewer also. Husbands departed with wives who were requiring congratulation or consolation, while the elderly sought, and children were taken to, their beds.

It was as the divinations were nearing their end that I noticed a stranger entering the hall. He stayed so much in the shadows that I could not see him clearly. Only when the last petitioner had tremblingly departed and the musicians had ceased playing did the stranger emerge into view. He was a lean man of middle height, clad in brown leather and with a curl of grey beard, but with eyes as blue as Avran's. He tossed a gold coin to Hebehir, walked briskly up to the bench and sat down upon it.

'Prophesy for me, wizard,' he demanded, in ringing tones that carried clearly across the quiet hall. 'Is it to be in sack or in malmsey that we drink to celebrate our reunion?'

Vedlen Obiran leapt to his feet, put out the candle-flames

with a sweep of his arm and seized the stranger in a delighted embrace.

'Robin Randwulf, my old companion!' he cried. 'Met again, after so many years! This is indeed a cause for celebration. My Lord of the Deerlands, may I crave the boon of your hospitality for my friend?'

Chapter Twenty-five

OUT OF THE FORESTS

Amid the bustle that followed the granting of Vedlen Obiran's request, I wondered amusedly how reliable the wizard's predictions were, when he could himself be so much surprised by a friend's coming. While the wine was being fetched, I voiced this thought to Rahir Ravatseng. I did so jokingly, yet there was no responsive humour in Rahir's voice when he answered.

'Do not doubt our master! It is true that he will not prefigure his own future, any more than he will ours; but the cause is different. For us, I think it is because he feels foreknowledge of our fate might either destroy our confidence or so increase it that we became arrogant. For himself, it is because he believes that a foreknowledge of his fate might reduce his concern for the particular problems that each day brings. I know that to be his reason, for he has told us so. Be sure that whatever our master *does* predict comes always to happen!'

At the time his words did not convince me — perhaps because I did not wish to be convinced, in view of the wizard's predictions for Avran and me. However, when I heard of the carpenter's death, I began to believe Rahir's words. Yet, even while questioning Vedlen Obiran's necromantic powers, my liking and respect increased for one who could welcome a friend with such unaffected pleasure.

The health was drunk in malmsey. This is a wine rare in Rockall since it has to be imported, at great cost, from Castile by way of London and Warringtown. I learned next day that the Earl had but one bottle in his cellars. Yet, with typical generosity, he fetched it out without hesitation for Vedlen Obiran's guest. At the Earl's invitation, it was Vedlen who proposed the toast.

'My Lord and Lady of the Deerlands, gentlemen and companions, I present to you a friend lost for many years but now found again — Sir Robert Randwulf of Jarmswayle, great traveller and soldier, the rightful Earl of Odunseth!'

As we drank to him, the newcomer smiled at the wizard and spoke in amiable reproach. 'Now, now, Vedlen my friend, that's an old story and better forgotten. Let us drink instead to our coming adventures!'

And so we did, in a lesser but still palatable wine. Shortly afterward the courtiers were discreetly dismissed and the Earl and his lady departed. We of the wizard's following dismantled the canopy and took away the accoutrements, then were conducted away to our beds by Felun Daretseng. Sir Robert and Vedlen retired to the latter's chamber, no doubt to reminisce into the early hours.

Felun had told us that departure from Chancelet was planned for the seventh morning after our coming. However, my guess on awakening was that the coming of the knight of Odunseth would cause our stay to be prolonged. So it was, but only by one day. Nor did our departure mean an ending to the reunion of the friends, for Sir Robert travelled with us.

I had expected him to be accompanied by a retinue of servants or at least by a squire; but no, he had arrived in Chancelet quite alone, with only a pack-rafenu to carry his armour and other possessions. Consequently Amos Sloly decided to appoint himself factotum to the knight, a proceeding tolerated by the wizard and received with good-humoured resignation (or so I felt) by Sir Robert.

During the onward journey, the pattern of our progress changed. The wizard, instead of lagging, rode with his friend in the van, just behind the two heralds and ahead of Felun, Avran and me. Though we did not deliberately eavesdrop on their conversations, the snatches of their talk that we heard convinced us that Sir Robert was indeed a great traveller. Not only had he roamed the whole middle lands of Rockall but also he had carried his sword in campaigns in many other countries. He had been to England and to the various realms of Lower and Higher Germanie; he had visited the heart of the Church of God on Earth in Rome; he had

242

voyaged even to the Holy Land itself, venturing dangerously among the Saracens to visit its holiest places. Then he had voyaged back westward to Navarre, Aragon and Castile, wearing the Cross again in battle against the Moors. In part he had fought for conscience, in part for gold but largely, we became sure, because of a sheer love of adventure.

Most recently Sir Robert had been in Merania, engaged to fight in its monarch's service against the neighbouring Kingdom of Marrafecca. He had left in disgust.

'That young king will never go to war. To be sure, he loves to design uniforms for his soldiers — I've never seen an army so elegant. Why, every least soldier has a surcoat of fine green cloth to wear, with the crown and the crossed sword and sceptre of Merania broidered on it in gold, silver and purple — and woe betide any soldier whose surcoat is dirty or ragged or whose weapons do not shine! The King's own guards bear swords and halberds chased with gold and silver. For a while I was content enough in his service, for I was encouraged to drill my men to a perfection of discipline that would have made them a formidable fighting force.

'But did they have the chance to fight? No, not they!' There was deep disgust in his voice. 'Our beloved King loves to watch their marches and countermarches and to see the mock charges and formation rides of his cavalry — oh yes, we officers all rode horses, and a pretty penny they cost to keep — but he has no stomach for a real war. When the King of Marrafecca, on a trumped-up excuse, invades Merania and trims off its whole southeastern part to make a puppet realm for one of his favourites, what does our brave young monarch do? Nothing; nothing at all. Just makes a few querulous noises and sends off to Saint Lorraine for some new material for the court ladies' dresses!'

At this I broke in: 'Your pardon, sir, but could you tell me what that new land was called? Not Lyonesse, by any chance?'

He turned in his saddle and looked back at me surprisedly: 'No, it is named Feyensinn and its chief town is Wratney. Lyonesse? That name is familiar, somehow . . . Oh yes, I recollect. Surely that was the name of the sunken land from which came Tristan, to find adventure with King Mark of Cornwall and suffer an ill-fated love with his queen, Yseult?

243

My mother taught me that tale. But I had thought Lyonesse to be a realm of faery, not of the real world.'

'Yet Simon here, and Avran, seek that realm,' said Vedlen Obiran quietly. 'Simon's father and brother travelled to it. Simon is sure it is to be found somewhere on this island of Rockall.'

'To discover a lost land, that is a quest indeed!' Sir Robert was evidently impressed. 'Well, I've roved widely enough and I've heard the tales of many other travellers, yet never till now have I heard of any voyages to Lyonesse. Come, Simon my lad, tell me more! Expound to me the reasons why you're so sure Lyonesse is to be found in Rockall.'

To be truthful, I was wondering by then whether Lyonesse was to be found anywhere! However, as we rode along, I told the story of the settling of Lyonesse by Sir Arthur Thurlstone and Sir John Warren, recounted some stories of their doings that had drifted back to Hallamshire, and explained when and why my father and brother had fled to Lyonesse. When I was done, Sir Robert spoke again, consideringly.

'Well, I have never visited Rockall's southern realms and would have surmised Lyonesse must be among them; but you know those lands, Avran, and you say that it is not. Certes, 'tis not among these great woodlands, for I have travelled them all! Nor is it in the east. I know the grassland realms well — too well! — and, though I know the eastern mountains only by report, I am sure Lyonesse cannot be found among their ridges or valleys. The Mionians occupy the northern heights and the Sifatela peoples occupy the rest of those mountains. They are fierce fighters. If any Englishmen had settled there, they would have had to battle hard for their lands; and whilst in Merania, I would surely have heard of such adventurings. You need spend no time in eastward questing, for it would be wholly wasted.'

'There are new realms in the hills north of these Deerlands, or so men say,' Felun put in tentatively.

'Aye, so there be; but they are small and too far from the sea. Your English knights would have had to evade the Mentonese and cross the Great Marshes to reach them; yet the stories you heard echo no such adventures as would have befallen in that crossing. No, Simon; if Lyonesse is to be found in Rockall, then it must be far in the north, beyond the barren uplands and the great peaks. I have heard rumours of lands beyond — tales of black, burning mountains, of men with winged helmets and of trees that are alive, of evil gods and strange sacrifices. Such stories would accord well enough with those you heard in Hallamshire, Simon. Yet, for my own part, I place little credence in them.'

Sir Robert fell silent and we rode along quietly for a while. Then he spoke pensively: 'Yours will be a mighty journey and a dangerous one.'

He was sounding a note of warning to us; yet, strangely enough, he seemed almost envious.

In this northern reach of the Deerlands forests, the trees were less varied and even stranger; but they were very beautiful. The dominant trees were of a sort we had seen first around Skarngrove and, indeed, that place was named after them, for they are rare and remarkable in the southern forests. Here they were common enough. Skarns are massive trees, with a pitted, honey-brown bark whose layers overlap in a series of chevron patterns. In shape, their leaves are much like those of an oak, though yet more deeply scalloped; in colour, however, they are very different — a much paler green and flecked with yellow. This was a useful tree to the settlers in the forests. The bark, soaked in baths of hot water, yielded a solution for the tanning of leather; the wood, when polished, made fine furniture, for it had a grain of broken spiral patterns that was very beautiful; and the branches, though too inflexible to be used for bows, furnished excellent arrow-wood.

These northern woods were even more open, with many flowers crowding between the tree roots and grasses springing luxuriantly in the glades. The birds were singing less now, for they were busy building nests and feeding nestlings. Every tree seemed a-flutter, except when the swift passing of a hawk caused a brief freezing into stillness.

That night we reach Dunfield, the northernmost of the settlements acknowledging the sway of the Earl of the March of the Deerlands. It straddled the Dun River, a little tributary of the Dainflete, and was girded about by stone walls and deep ditches. The ditches were dry then, but separated from the river waters only by narrow dikes. They could be readily filled by the diversion of its waters and would serve as moats in times of peril.

One of the Earl's sons had just been appointed governor of Dunfield. He had ridden with us to take up his duties and to ensure we were made welcome — a needless precaution, for the townspeople were as cheerful and friendly as those of Chancelet. Indeed, the Deerlands seemed to me altogether a happy place. I regret that the chances of my life have never taken me back there.

Three nights and two days were spent in Dunfield castle while Vedlen Obiran treated the sick, and did his best to mend the maimed, of the little town — not a great company, but enough to keep our master busy. During our hours of leisure Sir Robert, who had heard from Felun Daretseng of Avran's skill with the sword, tried him out in contests with blunted weapons. These were exhilarating to watch, for Sir Robert and Avran were very well matched. Each knew tricks that the other did not. However, since Sir Robert was more experienced in battle, Avran was repeatedly deceived into error and either caught by a swordthrust or disarmed.

I was concerned at first as to how Avran would respond to his defeats, for my friend was quick-tempered and not accustomed to being bested, even in such mock-battles. Fortunately Sir Robert was so cheery, and so willing to teach Avran how to emulate or to counter his own tricks of swordsmanship, that my friend could not be angry with him.

Felun adventured his sword in a few contests and acquitted himself honourably. We others — yes, even Amos Sloly — knew ourselves to be amply outmatched and were content to watch and learn. Indeed, Sir Robert was prepared to provide lessons in swordsmanship to any who requested them. Most of us benefitted from these to some degree, but such feats were beyond Amos.

'You use your sword like a spade, man!' Sir Robert told him. 'Better stick to your axe; you're strong and can wield that well enough! You'll never make a swordsman.'

Yet Amos, redfaced with frustration, remained sure that this was a skill he *could* master even though, again and again, his weapon would be deftly flicked from his hands. Nor did Sir Robert's patience with Amos, or Amos's respect for his teacher, seem ever to diminish.

It was on the third afternoon following our departure from Dunfield that we came to the end of the forests. There had been morning rain and a heavy haze was still hanging over the trees, so that I did not see the hills until we were almost at their foot. Then, suddenly I was conscious of what seemed a great wall rising before us, grey in the haze.

'Ah! the Ferekar Naur — the Stoney Mountains,' said Felun with satisfaction. 'Though we are yet many weeks' ride from Reschora, the sight of them always cheers me, for it means we are heading north toward home. However, these are lands where troubles can come unlooked for. I am yet happier when I know they are behind us.'

Just as a sheepskin rug ruckles up when feet have pushed it against a wooden chest, so did the forest seem to swell up against the wall of the hills and end abruptly. Where the trees ended two bridle paths diverged, one climbing steeply upslope, the other following the forest edge eastward. We took the latter, ascending slowly and easily until the tree-tops were below us, a narrow shore of green with a sea of grey haze beyond. To our right was a steep rise of grass through which great crags protruded. They were formed of a rock I supposed to be granite — a mass of square pink shapes in a greyish ground, from which tiny glasslike crystals sparkled in the sunlight. As the path wound its gentle way ever higher up the hillside, the slope to our left became ever more precipitous and the grass sparser, while the trees below us became hidden altogether from view.

During that upward ride we saw no other travellers, though we had seen many on the forest roads. Nor did we see any wild creatures, save for a single hovering falcon. The slow ascent was not arduous, but it seemed endless. I felt somehow that we were diminished, that we had become mere beetles obliquely climbing a stone field wall. We had all fallen silent and it was as if to assert my humanity that I spoke to Felun.

'Surely we have left the Marches of the Deerlands behind us? What realm are we in now?'

'Yes, we have left Earl Hubert's lands. As to whose realm we are in, that is a difficult question. These are disputed lands. Yet I suppose we must be now in the feofdom of the Lord of Owlsgard, who we hope will be our host this night.'

'Owlsgard? I did not think there were any owls in Rockall, though we have plenty back in England.'

He laughed. 'Oh, indeed? I have seen that bird depicted

on the arms of Sir Samuel Saville, but I thought it to be a fabulous creature, like the wyverns and cockatrices on the arms of other knights from England and Gascony!'

I laughed in my turn. However, I remembered the device of the Savilles, for did they not hold lands around Leeds, not so very far north from Hallamshire? I looked forward to a meeting with a nobleman who, if not a north-country Englishman himself, at least must have had ancestors who came from the lands near my home.

However, I was to be disappointed. It was late evening when we reached Owlsgard, yet there were no lights. When we rode up onto the ridge upon which Owlsgard stood, we knew why. The keep stood out against the sky, hollow-windowed and smoke-blackened. Of the cottages that had relied so vainly upon it for protection, only charred ruins remained.

Chapter Twenty-six

THE TRAIL OF THE MARAUDERS

In the shock of this discovery we all stopped. The night wind brought to us the acrid reek of wet burnt wood. Somewhere nearby, we could hear a dog howling; it was long since I had heard that sound and it did not cheer me. Then, without orders, our rafneyen bunched together about that of the wizard, for all felt the need of his wisdom.

Sir Robert sniffed the wind. 'That fire was recent; there is an odour of fresh charring. Yet it must have been before this morning's rain — last night, I would trow.'

Vedlen Obiran sighed. 'Many unhappy chances have befallen those who settled in these hills, but I had not anticipated this! Sir Samuel was a worthy man and honest, but too trusting perhaps. I sense it was his very trustfulness that brought disaster upon him. Rahir and Delhir, the torches, please! Mayhap someone yet lives amid these sad ruins. We must search carefully, but we must be swift also.'

The torches were brought forth and kindled. We divided into pairs, each pair taking one torch; Felun was my partner, while Avran went with Narel Evateng. It was I that found the dog, a poor pathetic creature, its hindquarters so smashed by a fallen beam that I wondered it were still alive. At least I was able to provide a swifter end to its misery. The discoveries of Narel and Avran were even more depressing; an elderly woman impaled by a thrown spear and a child dead amid the charred rafters of its home.

Other searchers found more dead men and women, yet not nearly so many as to account for the settlement's whole population and no other dead children. There was little sign of any armed resistance to the attackers and much to suggest treachery. The stone keep would have been hard to assault, yet the dead men within it were few; they wore neither armour nor even jupons and seemed not to have borne weapons. The body of Sir Samuel was not found, though members of his household were recognized among the dead.

At least Avran and I had this fortune, that these slain people were not known to us. Our comrades, in contrast, gave many cries of grief as they recognized murdered friends.

When the search was completed, we gathered again about Vedlen Obiran. By then it was quite dark, for the moon was at its rind and the stars masked by high, thin cloud. Our flaring torches formed a bright ring, in whose light his eyes shone as yellow as an owl's. His voice was curiously calm.

'You are angry, my friends, and you are right to be angry. I know that you wish, as do I, to pursue those who have committed this vile crime; that you hope, as do I, to release those who have been taken captive and to avenge friends who have been slain.'

He paused and surveyed us sombrely, perceiving that, like hounds in leash, we were straining to be away. Nevertheless, he went on: 'Yet we must not permit our anger to betray us into foolishness. In so dark a night as this, it would only be feasible to find and read tracks if we sought them by torchlight. We cannot do that, for the torchlight would proclaim our pursuit, leading us perhaps into ambush unaware. Moreover, we must remember that the marauders greatly outnumber us. We must rest till the sun rises and, when we pursue, we must be as careful and thoughtful as we are swift.'

That night, though the rafneyen were freed from their loads, the tent was not erected. We ate and drank hastily and lightly, for our sombre mood and the reek of burning had stifled our appetites. Afterwards we rolled ourselves in our blankets and, guarded by our beasts, did our best to find sleep.

I was shaken into wakefulness in the soft grey of a misty morning. The haze from the forests seemed to have risen like a tide and washed over the hill ridges.

It was Rahir Ravatseng who had roused me. 'Our master says we must dress today, not for show as hitherto, but for combat. I have put out for you the surcoat and hose you wore when first in the forests. I have found a padded jupon also that you must wear beneath your surcoat, and a strong leather hood. They'll make you hot later on, no doubt, but you'll maybe need their protection. Look lively, now!'

He went on to awaken Avran and give him a like message. I rolled over, shivered in the cool air and rose. Quickly I took off my purple tunic and put on this other clothing, while Avran did likewise. Neither of us guessed then that we would never again wear the wizard's livery.

The jupon fitted well enough beneath my surcoat, though it made me feel fat. The hood, however, was so uncomfortably large that, after fastening it about my neck, I allowed it to hang loose behind my shoulders. I put on my belt of knives over the surcoat and attached my scabbard and sword to it. Then I went to lend assistance in the loading of the rafneyen. Poor beasts, they were all most unhappy, for they had not been able to feed upon the smoke-spoiled vegetation and had found nothing to drink.

By then, Felun and Sir Robert had gone off to discover the trail of the marauders. Though they were back within minutes, they found us already loaded up, mounted and eager to depart.

'They are striking away northward,' Sir Robert said rather breathlessly. 'After two dewfalls and the rain of yesterday, their tracks are not easy to read. However, if we have understood them aright, the situation is a strange one. The robbers must have brought only their own horses and rafneyen and must have captured few or none in their assault — I cannot think why. Instead, they appear to be using their captives as beasts of burden for carrying away their loot. Well, that will slow them all down and gives us better hope of catching them; but it is puzzling.'

'How many are they?' asked Vedlen Obiran.

'Reivers, or captives? Well, it hardly matters, since my answer must be the same. I do not know. A good number, certainly.'

'Well, Robin, for a task such as confronts us, it is best that you should take command. You are a warrior; I am not, though perhaps my advice may prove of aid at times. What do you propose?'

The knight's answer was prompt. 'As you stated last night,

my friend, we must be swift yet careful. We cannot afford to be encumbered by the pack-rafneyen.'

'It is true that the heavily laden beasts would slow us down,' the wizard responded thoughtfully. 'Yet I think at least two should accompany us. In particular we should take with us our supply of herbs and other medicaments, which will surely be needed to treat wounds and other injuries before this pursuit is over. Moreover, I can visualize other needs. If you concur, Robin, we shall take two with us, their loads adjusted for lightness.'

'Very well,' responded Sir Robert. 'As for the remaining pack-rafneyen, I suggest that they be placed in the charge of Amos Sloly, who — er — understands them best. There is no cause for making such heavily laden beasts hasten. Amos can bring them along behind us, at a more leisurely pace than that which we must adopt.'

Knowing Amos's perpetual desire to be at the heart of things, I was sure he would protest. Indeed, he did begin to frame a complaint but, under the cold eye of the wizard, fell quickly silent.

I looked away while I listened to Sir Robert's other orders. Then, happening to glance back at Amos, I was surprised to see him smiling to himself. What compensation for being left behind had he recognized, I wondered? However, other matters took my attention and I thought no more about Amos.

The rest of us were to separate into two groups. In the van would be Sir Robert, Felun Daretseng, Avran and I; Sir Robert and Felun because of their knowledge of the terrain, Avran and I because of our skill in archery. The others — the wizard himself, the three Ravatsengs, lean Narel Evateng and massive Drakht Belineg, with the two lightly laden pack-animals — would follow far enough behind to serve as reserve if we were ambushed, yet close enough to keep in contact. Avran and Narel would serve as go-betweens whenever necessary. Amos, with the remaining pack-rafneyen (including Sir Robert's), would wait an hour or so before following and would not hasten.

We four rode off abreast, down into the dip between the Owlsgard ridge and the main southern shoulder of the mountains. The morning mist veiled the burned ruins from view, but the sour smell of that burning assailed our nostrils anew. Soon, however, the ruins were behind us and their unpleasant odour diminishing.

The long slope beyond was gentle but monotonous, its curve as smoothly convex as the front of a bulging grain sack. The soil cover was meagre. The hooves and boots of those we were pursuing had scuffed and scarred the thin turf, but it was indeed hard to make sense of such meagre records of their passage. Nevertheless, I became sure that the captives were being led by men mounted on shod horses, while other men on rafneyen herded them from behind and rode on either flank. I remarked on this to Sir Robert and he seemed pleased.

'You have good eyes for a trail, Simon; better than mine. Keep watchful. Should you notice any new details — any parting of ways, in particular — you must tell me immediately.'

For almost two hours we rode steadily northward, up onto and along the crest of land. The mist was lifting only slowly, the slopes about us seeming to fall gradually away into nothingness. When the ridge and the trail we were following began to swing eastward, I did not perceive the change until Sir Robert remarked upon it.

'Heading east, then? Where can they be going, Felun? Not to Blackhill, for sure. I would not trust Sir Gabriel Jacklyn very far, but it seems he will not prove to be the villain in this particular play.'

'Well, there's a ford across the Marolane River about three leagues upstream from Blackhill Castle. They may strike down to that crossing. That would take them to Becketsward or, by the high paths, to Rewlenscrag.'

'True enough. Yet I cannot conceive that the Lord of Ralphsland would resort to such treacherous raiding, nor even Sir Cuthbert Reddlestone for that matter, stiff-necked and vile-tempered though he can be. No, some other hand than theirs has wrought this infamous crime.'

Felun uttered no response and we rode in silence for a while. Then Avran asked: 'I have seen no map of these mountains: can you chart them for me in words?'

Felun thought carefully, then answered slowly: 'Have you seen from above a duck flying swiftly, with its wings held close to its body? Well, if one ignores their most easterly

253

MENTONE

R.Mentone Valdevil

HAVILAND

TEM

ROCKAINE

WILDERWAR

Wildfell

MERLIN

Merlinward

R.Aramassa

THE GREAT MARSHES

Rewlenscrag

POCHARDSVALE

Pochard R.

DISP

(Cat)
Crags

Becketsward

Belden Br.

Swilling

RALPHSLAND

LAN

Marolane R.

Blackhill

BLACKHILL

Marolane R.

OWLSWATC

THE

Owlsgard

THE DEERLANDS

Dunfield

ATELONE

Ateloner R.

MAR

0   10   20   30   40   50   60   70   80
statute miles

0   10 20 30 40 50 60 70 80 90 100 120
kilometres

Chancelet Squillet R.

Sheneflete R.

THE FEREKAR NAUR
IN THE YEAR OF OUR LORD 1404

ridges beyond the River Edflow, the Stoney Mountains are much of that shape. Conceive that your duck is flying from the west to a little north of east. Its tail would be defined by the valleys of the Pochard River on the north side and the Marolane on the south side. Its beak would be pointed to Takrallen, the easternmost stronghold of the Templars. Owlsgard would be on the outer pinions of its right wing, Becketsward on its back just above the base of the tail, and Rewlenscrag on the innermost pinions of its left wing.'

'Yes, I can visualize that readily enough,' responded Avran. 'Are those the only holds in these mountains?'

'By no means; those are merely the western holds. Close to the tip of our duck's left wing is the castle of Wildfell and, at the very tip of its right wing, that of Falconward. And then there is the hold of that Welsh knight. Some strange name he has, harder even to remember than your difficult English names.'

'Sir Hugh ap Llewellyn, do you mean?' Sir Robert was amused. 'His hold is called Merlinsward. It is in the valley separating the left wing from the neck of your flying duck. Yet surely there is some other castle, closer to hand than Merlinsward? What is it called, now? I seem to have heard dark rumours concerning it.'

Felun stopped his rafenu, so suddenly that we were all startled. 'Cat Crags!' he said excitedly. 'That filthy nest of carrion birds! Yes, of course; Casimir of Chattaine, whom they call the Wild Cat, has ever gathered evil men about him. I would wager it is from thence that this dastardly blow was struck.'

'You may be right,' responded Sir Robert, 'but we cannot yet be sure. There may be quarrels of which we have not learned, or other knaves of whom we have no knowledge. I propose that we make no assumptions, but continue following the trail and ascertain where it leads.'

Yet Felun's suspicions were to be confirmed within the hour, and in most unexpected fashion.

Before that happened, however, we made some other discoveries. We were riding along quite swiftly for, though those whom we were pursuing must be travelling slowly, they had a lead of a whole day of marching time. The ground underhoof was covered with grass, little thicker than a coarse linen sheet laid out to dry in the sunshine and of almost the same hue, for it had died off and bleached to a creamy yellow colour in which there were yet a few touches of spring green. On this monotonous surface, the footprints were even harder to see; but suddenly I perceived, as Sir Robert and Felun had not, that the tracks were swinging away to our left.

'Hold hard!' I cried. 'We're over-riding the trail!'

The others stopped and gazed at the ground more intently. 'So we are!' said Sir Robert. 'I am obliged to you, Simon; your eyes are indeed sharper than mine.'

Over to our left was a tor made up of huge granite blocks that seemed stacked atop one another, like cheeses outside a cheesewright's door. The trail led toward these. When we came closer, we saw on the ground a litter of food fragments not yet found by birds and some broken earthenware flasks, plus many indentations and scrapings. Evidently the reivers and their captives had rested here during the day after the burning of Owlsgard. Discarded wine-flasks and a forgotten dagger indicated that the marauders themselves had sat up on the tor, doubtless so that they might oversee their captives. Felun examined the dagger carefully, but it told him nothing.

The onward trail was soon found. It led, not back to the hill-crest, but along the northern flank of the ridge, as if the marauders had not wished to risk being seen on the skyline. Below us, the valley of the Marolane was still hidden from view in haze. Hollows in its nearer slope contained stands of shrubs that had found enough soil to root in, and enough shelter from winds, to permit a ragged growth.

Where one patch of shrubs reached upward to the ridge we found the body of an elderly man. He had pitched forward on his face and seemed to have died from simple weariness, for he showed no wounds. This discovery caused us each a lurch at the heart and a tightening of lips, but our haste did not permit any last attentions. Instead, we must ride on and try to save the living.

As we prepared to do so, however, we heard a frantic call from the trees below. Looking down surprisedly, we saw a boy scrambling up the slope.

'Help, Messer Daretseng — help me!' he cried out breathlessly.

Felun dismounted and ran down to gather him up in his

arms. As Felun walked back toward us, we saw that the boy was holding on to him frantically and sobbing into his shoulder. The boy could only have been about seven years old. He was slim and dark-haired, his clothes torn by the branches but of good quality.

By that time, the second party had caught us up and ranged themselves about us. However, Felun waved us away and sat down on the slope, speaking soothingly to the boy until his sobs ceased. We dismounted and waited.

Quite soon, Felun beckoned the wizard over and the two of them talked for a while with the boy. After a longer while, Vedlen Obiran returned to us.

'The child is the son of a servant who was slain in the castle; his mother, I am afraid, must have been slain also. When the marauders had plundered the castle, all who were still living were rounded up and made to shoulder burdens — yes, even he, small though he is. He attached himself to the old man — his grandfather, I think. When the old fellow collapsed from exhaustion, the boy threw down his burden and ran off into the bushes. Though his flight was noticed, he was not pursued.'

'Whatever happened at Owlsgard, then?' Sir Robert asked eagerly. 'Was it treachery?'

'Yes, treachery brought about by greed; but' — and a wintry smile passed over the wizard's usually impassive features — 'treachery that failed of its main object. The boy's father was a trusted servant of Sir Samuel Saville and the boy himself is quite sharp; he has the story clear in mind. Gold is at the root of it, as it is so often at the root of quarrels and fights. It seems there is a dry stream-bed just above Owlsgard keep, dug into by chance when a ditch was being extended. In a pocket in that old stream-bed they found many little pebbles of gold. By careful washing, they obtained also much gold dust — enough, in all, to fill a small coffer, or so the boy claims.'

Seeing how we all stirred at this tiding, Vedlen Obiran gave a somewhat wryer smile; then he continued: 'Well, Sir Samuel had no thought of hoarding the gold — he is no miser — but much interest in what it might buy for his people; weapons, tools, small comforts. He decided to take the gold to Thraincross in Herador, whence merchants travel regularly to Warringtown, and he was to have departed today.'

The wizard paused; and, when he resumed speaking, there was anger in his voice. 'As I guessed, though, Sir Samuel had been too trusting. A while back, his seneschal died in an accident and there was no obvious successor. So, when a wandering Gascon man-at-arms turned up at the castle and proved intelligent and amusing, that man was appointed to be the new seneschal.'

'What was his name?' Sir Robert demanded abruptly, his moustache bristling like the whiskers of a cat that has smelled a mouse.

'Pierre Paradis, he called himself,' responded the wizard. 'A lean fellow, the boy tells me, with greying hair that formed a widow's peak over his brow. Ah, I see that you know him, Robin.'

'I have not encountered him, but I've heard tell of him — a wily fox of a man, they say; but, like a fox, he leaves a trail of ill odour behind. He does not always use that name, though.' Sir Robert seemed disinclined to say more.

'Well, it seems this unworthy seneschal was overcome with lust for the gold. And so he plotted to gain it — or some share of it. He arranged the raid on Owlsgard and, when the raiders came by night, he opened the gates to them. But they came too late. Sir Samuel had learned by chance that a party of Mentonese merchants was at Trayad-in-Riotte — you know the Mentonese have a trading station there? So, seeking to save himself a longer journey, Sir Samuel loaded his rafneyen with the gold and other goods for sale and hastened off to Trayad, two days before his announced date of departure. The seneschal sought desperately to delay Sir Samuel's leaving, I gather — the boy's father seems to have remarked on this and wondered why — but he could not persuade his master to linger. So off went Sir Samuel, with his lady and their two sons, many of his men and most of the rafneyen. When the raiders came, the gold was gone already.'

We laughed at this, but the wizard said: 'Yes, it is pleasant to think of evil men discomfited; but it was not good for the people of Owlsgard that remained behind — Sir Samuel's daughter among them. In their frustration and wrath, the raiders sacked and burned both castle and village, slaying any that stood in their path. And now they are driving away the people of Owlsgard like laden hasedain, but with less mercy than such beasts receive. They have said they will free their captives — or most of them, though not the younger women — when they reach Cat Crags. For my part, I would place no trust in that promise.'

'Cat Crags!' Sir Robert, Avran and I spoke almost with one voice.

Vedlen Obiran nodded gently. 'Yes, indeed. Felun guessed right. Along with the evil Gascon, the other prime culprit in this crime is he whom men call the Wild Cat — Casimir of Chattaine. Well, maybe we shall bell that cat.'

He paused, then went on thoughtfully: 'Cats and owls are both night creatures, I understand. Yet men tell me that, if a cat should ever attack an owl, bitterly it rues having done so. I believe that Casimir and his kindle of vile kittens will come soon to wish they had never marched on Owlsgard.'

Chapter Twenty-seven

THE PEN ON THE HILLSIDE

Already we had been a small party to be pursuing so large a band of reivers. In the next few minutes, our numbers were further reduced. After only the briefest of discussions with the wizard, Sir Robert gave us new orders. The Lord of Ralphsland and Sir Cuthbert Reddlestone, though they might not much love one another, were known to have even less liking for the Wild Cat of the Crags. Consequently Felun Daretseng and Hebehir Ravatseng were sent off to seek their aid against him. Felun, carrying the little boy before him on his saddle, was to ride to Becketsward and rally Ralphsland. Hebehir would take the longer road to Rewlenscrag and seek to rouse the people of Pochardsvale.

Narel Evateng, who had much endurance and whose rafenu was reckoned the swiftest, was sent off on the still longer trail after Sir Samuel Saville and his company. They had been gone two days and more, but they would not be travelling speedily. It was hoped that, as yet, they might only have crossed the Edflow to Amsetch, an isolated stronghold north of Dakalet whose lord was known to be friendly to the men of Owlsgard. If that were the case, then Narel might catch up with Sir Samuel within a long day's hard riding. However, since Narel could not hope to bring Sir Samuel's company back in less than three days, they could be of little service in freeing the Owlsgard captives.

When we rode onward, then, there were only three in the advance party — Sir Robert, Avran and me — and only four in the second group — Drakht Belineg, the Ravatseng brothers and Vedlen Obiran himself. A small number, indeed; yet I comforted myself that, with the wizard amongst us, we were much more formidable than we seemed.

Narel had ridden away swiftly. Soon Felun, with the little

boy sitting before him and chattering away happily and with Hebehir riding beside him, rode away back along the slopes to seek a path down to the Marolane crossing.

As they departed a light wind rose, rippling the grassheads and shredding the haze into cobwebs that faded swiftly in the emergent sunshine. Below us, I could now perceive a broad valley down which a river threaded its way through patches of trees, green beads on a sparklingly blue string. Beyond was a line of greater hills that looked much more rugged than the cow's-back ridge on whose flanks we were standing. Gazing down river, I could see a cluster of turrets that must be the castle of Blackhill, that stronghold whose castellan was so much distrusted that his help was not even being sought. Looking up river, I could see only more trees and a confusion of rocky hilltops. The lair of the Wild Cat, I presumed, must be hidden among those crags.

Before we moved onward, there was a brief conference between Sir Robert and the wizard. Sir Robert was sure that the marauders would continue to herd their captives along the ridge top. At the head of the Marolane, it seemed, there were many streams, bogs and patches of woodland. Among these, so large a party could not be kept together, especially when it included captives eager to escape. Thus, though a crossing of the valley might have shortened their journey to Cat Crags, it would be considered too hazardous to be attempted.

The question was: need we continue to follow the trail along the exposed hill ridge, risking being seen by those we were pursuing before we could come close to them, when we knew their destination already? Or might it be wiser to take another route that would allow for more concealment, along the southern shoulder of the hill or among the trees of the Marolane valley?

Two arguments of Vedlen Obiran seemed to decide the question. First of all, he pointed out that the Marolane valley was more populated than the southern hill slopes. The marauders would be apprehensive of chance encounters on that flank and especially watchful in that direction. In contrast, the raid on Owlsgard had destroyed the principal settlement on the southern side of the hills; that flank would not be watched so closely. Moreover, with the sun so bright, the raiders would be reluctant to gaze long into its glare.

So it was that we three of the advance party crossed the ridge at speed and headed down its southern side, till the out-arch of the slope concealed us from view from above. Then we found our way, as best we might, along that steep flank of the Stoney Mountains. Stoney indeed they were; we had to thread our way across or about curving outbulges of granite — their angle was too shallow for them to deserve the name 'cliff' — and across devexities of turf so thin that it tore away under the hooves of our mounts, causing them to slip again and again.

How I longed to be riding a sevdru, those masters of rock and steep slope! Our poor, forest-bred rafneyen had no skill in pathfinding on such hillsides. Indeed they were so unhappy and insecure, and dropped to so slow a pace, that we found it easier to dismount and lead them along.

Chancing upon a spring from which a little waterfall cascaded in a deep slot down the hillside, we took the opportunity to allow our thirsty beasts to drink their fill, then drank ourselves. While we were doing so, the wizard's party caught up with us. Vedlen Obiran looked hot and annoyed.

'We cannot go on with this absurd scrabbling across rocks and steep hillsides,' he announced firmly. 'The idea was mine, but it has proved a stupid one. What do you suggest, Robin?'

Sir Robert grinned at him. 'Now, now, Vedlen, it wasn't so very bad a concept; just a mite too difficult in execution, maybe! You were right, in that we couldn't all go traipsing along that ridge, as obvious as coals on a snowbank; and I reckon this flank of the hills is indeed the safer. Yet it's a tiresome traverse, that I'll agree. I suggest, Vedlen, that the three of you and the pack-rafneyen should go down to the foot of the slope and ride along just inside the trees. We'll send Simon up onto the ridge top; he can read signs and he's watchful. Avran and I, we'll follow along far enough behind him that he's only in distant sight for us, and we quite out of sight of any other watchers. If Simon *is* spotted, why then, he's only a single rider. He won't alarm them, for they'll consider him just a wandering hunter. That suit you, Simon?'

'Well enough,' I answered promptly; though, to be truthful,

I was a little dismayed at being given prime responsibility in the pursuit.

'Good; then we'd best have a quick bite before you take those pack-beasts and the food away, Vedlen. We'll all be the better for it.'

The meal was welcome indeed. While we ate, our beasts took the opportunity to browse on the plants that fringed the streamlet.

Twenty minutes later — a *vekruan*, or 'hour-third', the Sandastrians would say — I was leading Galahad awkwardly and apprehensively back up the steep hill shoulder. Below me, Avran and Sir Robert waited on their beasts; and further below, our four other companions were relievedly descending with their rafneyen to seek that simpler path along the forest edge.

When I reached the hill crest again, I looked about me very carefully before daring to mount. The ridge top stretched empty away to the eastward, but the tracks of those we were pursuing were again to be observed before me. They were still following the ridge, then; good!

Though I could not relax my vigilance even for a moment, I found it pleasant to be riding at speed along a flat surface again, after the ordeal of the slopes. Galahad was very much happier and more confident, tossing his horns gaily and making that strange sniffing sound which, in a rafenu, signifies contentment.

As I rode along, I strove to reason out for myself how far the marauders and their captives might yet have travelled. They must have set forth, I presumed, some time in the morning after the burning of Owlsgard. Though the plundering of castle and village would have preceded that burning, the binding and loading of reluctant captives would have occupied some hours; I did not think they could have set forth until well after first light. From Owlsgard to the tor where they had rested was, say, five leagues. How long they had paused, we could not tell; an hour at least, I guessed. Could those poor prisoners have been made to march a further six leagues before darkness fell and another halt was enforced? Well, perhaps as much as seven; but not more, certainly. That overnight resting-place must be close now. Ah! there it was; a churning of tracks, scrapes and hollows in the grass where people had lain, more empty flasks, the rubble of a meal and the rag of a torn garment.

So, all in all, they had travelled about eleven leagues in that first day — a long, hard day's march for those poor captives when some were children, some old and all heavily laden. Assuming they had set forth at first light on this second day, how much further might they have gone before stopping again? Six leagues at most, I thought; probably less, for the captives would be even more exhausted. After that third stop, the reivers would certainly make their captives march as far as they could; yet another six leagues seemed the absolute limit. So they must be not much more than nine leagues ahead of Galahad and me, probably less.

While we were eating, Sir Robert had told me a little about the terrain. This hill ridge would end soon. Then there was a broad, lower saddle of land to cross before the central mass of the Stoney Mountains was attained and, after that, a difficult path through rocky country to the castle of Cat Crags. Those laden prisoners could not go all that way before nightfall; they would be too weary and the path too arduous. I thought it likely they would cross the saddle and then rest for the night.

If so, should we seek to attack the marauders before they stopped and put themselves on guard? That might be effective but I doubted it, for how might so few of us successfully attack so many? By now I knew, from the tracks, that there were at least fifty of the reivers, with nigh on a hundred captives — some of them men, certainly, but most of them women and children.

Another problem was that the weather was changing. Long fingers of cloud were reaching up across the forests from the southwest: the sun seemed to be skipping across them like a child across stepping-stones, sometimes shining brightly, sometimes hidden. I was riding across moving lines of shadow, my view ahead at times brightly lit, at other times shaded.

A line of deer-like animals traversed the ridge ahead in an irregular straggle until, sighting me, they plunged downslope to disappear amid the dense shades of the narrowing Marolane valley. Narrowing — and ending, for the land below me was rising to meet my ridge and the inner heights were looming closer now.

Turning in the saddle, I could just discern Avran, far behind me and hugging the hill slope. Of Sir Robert I could see no sign.

While I rode onward, the cloud fingers reached ever farther north, till they were above me and more massive clouds darkening the southern horizon. My ridge was tilting northward and slots had been cut into its flanks by several small streams, among which the Marolane could no longer be distinguished. The path of those we were pursuing still followed the ridge crest, but the ridge must end soon. Why did they not head downslope?

I saw the reason, in a last gleam of sunlight before the great hand of cloud closed over and hid its rays. Much of the saddle was occupied by marshes; that hummocky surface, with its tufts of rushes and coarse grasses, was unmistakable. The marauders would follow the ridge until they could not, then take a northward path across the higher, drier land beyond those marshes. Well, since I was riding much more rapidly than the captives could walk, the distance between us must be closing.

Slowly the trail I was following began to swing away from the ridge crest and down hill. I had a brief view of the great granite bulwarks that ended the ridge on its southern side, then they and the forests passed from my sight.

I followed the trail obliquely downward across the much gentler slope linking the ridge with the bridge of land to the central mass of the Stoney Mountains. The higher marshes were dotted with bushes; these became ever more numerous as the ground became drier until they formed an irregular pattern of thickets. In this grey light, it would be hard for me to see the marchers among those thickets; but, of course, it would be hard also for them to see me!

Ah! they had taken another rest here. More debris of a meal, the shards of some broken flasks, the trodden husk of a loaf of bread and — what was that, lying over there? Why, it was the body of an old woman, dead from exhaustion seemingly, for she showed no obvious injury. Someone had regarded her with affection, for her poor limbs had been straightened and her face covered with a silken cloth. As I gazed upon her, the tide of anger against the marauders so rose within me that I could have shouted my fury to the skies.

A movement beside me caused me to start; but it was only Avran. 'Another victim,' he remarked grimly. 'Indeed, these reivers have a debt to discharge for their brutality.'

'Ought you to have caught up with me?' I asked concernedly. 'Surely the idea was that you should stay well behind me?'

'Sir Robert instructed me to join you. He crossed the ridge to speak to me, and now he is gone to summon our comrades. He thinks the marauders cannot be far ahead now and believes they may have left a rearguard hidden amongst these thickets. He suggests we ride together, keeping our bows strung and our arrows ready. He says: "Take heed! Watchfulness remains more important than haste." '

I was reckoning again to myself. 'Nearly seven more leagues since their overnight camp; why, they must have driven these poor souls, unresting, for six full hours.'

'They would have been here around noon, then, and stayed for an hour, at least.'

'Aye; and since then, how far can they have marched? Two leagues; three; maybe four. That would be their limit, I trow. It would take them across this bridge of land to the hills beyond. There, surely, they must camp. Indeed, they cannot reach Cat Crags this night, if the distance be as far as Sir Robert estimates.'

'So they will be keeping guard and looking back. When they commence to climb again, they will be well situated to spot us. We must be especially watchful now, so that we see them before we are seen.'

Our crossing of that saddle was made with all the care we could contrive. We would ride only when we knew that a thicket shielded us from view from ahead, and then never together. Usually I led while Avran watched, and watched while he followed. Where the screen of bushes was minimal, I would dismount and run or walk forward at a crouch, while Galahad came after me in so wide a circle that we would not be viewed together. Then Avran would come on more swiftly, while Lancelot came circling after him.

At the centre of the saddle there was no cover at all, just an open expanse of tussocky grass. I had to drop onto all fours and crawl, like a hunter stalking a stag, with Avran behind me and the rafneyen waiting. Only when we had safely found shelter in a little thicket beyond this open space did we summon our beasts to us.

If the Wild Cat's men had thought to leave an afterguard at that point, we would surely have been seen and slain; but they were too confident and did not. Perhaps the darkening skies urged them to haste and carelessness, for indeed the clouds seemed ever more lowering and the air had that throat-catching dryness that precedes a storm. It was already late afternoon; on such a day, night would fall early.

On the northern slope of the saddle, the bushes were low and scattered, affording no concealment for a rider.

'Avran,' I asked, 'will you wait here with Galahad and Lancelot? Sir Robert and the others cannot be far behind us and, as you see, there's no good cover ahead. I'll go forward on foot and try to spy out their camp. Look after my bow, would you? It'll be too awkward to carry.'

He was visibly anxious. 'Must you take this risk, Simon? Remember, there are many evil men ahead of you, and they will be at their most watchful. Let me go instead; or at least permit me to come with you. We can leave our rafneyen here, with a message.'

I had slipped off the unwelcome leather hood and the heavy jupon; they would be more hindrance than help henceforward. As I buckled the belt about my waist again, I responded: 'No, Avran. Should we both go, it would more than double the chance of our being detected. Moreover, friend, you're less able a tracker than am I, just as I am the less able swordsman. I shall not be weaponless, remember, for I have my knives. Please wait here. Honestly, Avran, I shall be both swifter and safer alone.'

My friend threw up his hands in exasperation. 'So be it! I shall pray for your return.'

'Do so,' I responded cheerfully, before setting off up the slope.

Were it not for my anxiety about those whom we were hoping to rescue, I would have been enjoying myself thoroughly. This shallow hillside, with its tufty bushes, was much like a Pennine slope dotted with broom and gorse; indeed, some of the bushes were quite as prickly. Yet I had been able, on such slopes, to approach a watchful fox at the mouth of its lair, provided the wind were with me. I was confident that I could approach any average human guard undetected. However, it was an effortful climb. I was glad not to be encumbered by the jupon and my bow.

There was now no need to follow the tracks closely, for they were easy to see, even from a distance. The captives must be very weary; they must have almost crawled up the hill, for they had displaced grass-sods and broken down small bushes as they heaved and sweated their way upward. Criss-crossing tracks of horses and rafneyen showed how the marauders had been driving those poor men and women onward. I pictured the cursing and the cracking of whips, the stumbles, the whimperings of tired children and the agonized cries of the elderly; and I felt a renewal of my anger.

Where the slope slackened, a guard was sitting astride a big brown horse. He was a heavy-set man, in a brown leather jupon and armed with sword and long-bow. On his head was a mail cap adorned with the device of a leaping, clawing cat. After following the marauders for so long, it was almost a shock to have my imaginings transformed into reality. The guard seemed more bored than watchful and I contrived to pass him unperceived.

Beyond, the hill widened out into a broad, shallow hollow, like the lap in the apron of a sitting ale-wife. At some past time, a great pen for beasts had been built there, hemmed closely on all sides by high bushes. It had a containing wall solidly made from blocks of slate, wide enough for a man to walk along. Indeed, half a dozen armed men were on watch upon it — not walking, though, but sitting at ease.

I made my careful way forward till I was in the welcome screen of the bushes and, finding a strong stump, clambered onto it so that I could peer over the wall. The pen was clear of vegetation and had a single entrance on its further, upslope side, closed by a heavy gate. Within the pen, additional guards stood on watch while other armed men walked about distributing food to a concourse of captives sitting or lying on the short grass. I could hear the wail of a hungry baby and saw children lying asleep, too tired even to eat. On the far side of the enclosure were stacked bundles, packages and kegs, the plunder of Owlsgard.

But where were the rest of the Wild Cat's men? They

must be higher up the hill, surely? It steepened again sharply beyond the pen and, against the grey sky, I could perceive another, taller wall of slates. Beyond that second wall was some sort of a tower and, yes, a thread of smoke that showed a fire to be burning within.

It was not hard to evade the attention of the guards on the wall, for they were looking, not outward, but inward. Passing silently through the bushes round about was much harder, for they were densely intergrown and there were many brittle fallen branches to be avoided.

Fortunately I chanced upon an animal trackway, made by some creature of roebuck size. Crouching low, I was able to make my way along this track quietly and with speed. I found that it did not join, but ran closely parallel to, the broader path up from the pen entrance to the old tower above. The path had been overgrown until some recent time, when men with swords — the cuts were too clumsy for scythes or axes — had opened it up by trimming back the bushes. The trimmed-off twigs and branchlets, though trampled underfoot, still showed the fresh green of newly-opened buds.

As the slope steepened, the animal track swung away from the main path and headed westward. Fortunately the foliage was becoming less dense so that, without joining the path, I was able to find my way upward, slowly, carefully, above all quietly. When the slope became steeper still, I was forced to haul myself up from one root or strong stem to the next, blessing my good fortune that the bushes were not spiny here. Then the slope slackened again and the brush grew thicker. I could hear movements and voices. With infinite care I edged toward their source.

Yes, this had been a castle of sorts, a wall of stone surrounding a small bailey, in the midst of which was a tall, square tower. It was a typical hall-keep of the sort once built by the Normans in England but now long out of favour. Whether it had become ruined, or had simply never been finished, was not clear. The uppermost part of the keep had so jagged an outline that I presumed hall and chamber must now be open to the sky. However, there was a spire of chimney protruding up beyond one corner, from which smoke was spiralling skyward. There were men within, for I could hear the intermittent sound of voices; yet it was the men nearer at hand that commanded my attention.

Eight of them there were, five on horseback and three standing by on foot. Four of the five horsemen and two of the men on foot wore chain-mail tunics, with yellow surcoats bearing a rather clumsily drawn device that I read as a cat salient sable — a leaping black cat. However, these men had chain-mail hoods, presently thrown back, instead of steel caps. Each was armed with sword and axe and each bore a round shield of coppered iron, with a boss at centre. They were solid, rather squat men, with low foreheads, black curling hair and black beards, surely Gascons.

It was the foremost horseman who took my attention. His surcoat was of yellow silk and the leaping cat had been embroidered upon it with much more care, its claws done in silver and its tongue in red. He was armed like the others, but his sword-hilt and scabbard were chased with gold. His face was strangely shaped, broad and yet flat at front and back. When he turned toward me, I saw that he had a little, hooked nose between two unusually large eyes — strange eyes, with yellowish-brown irises and black pinpoint pupils. He had a way of suddenly smiling, twitching his cheeks so that the ends of his moustache stuck out like feelers and drawing back his upper lip to reveal irregular, discoloured teeth. Yes, he was very like a cat, a fighting cat of town alleys.

That this was Casimir of Chattaine, I never doubted. It was important to know what he was saying: screened by a low bush, I crawled as close as I dared.

He was addressing the third of the men on foot, a thinnish man with greying hair and clad in a plain brown surcoat over mail. His back was to me. He and Casimir were speaking in French and I blessed Lord Furnival's chaplain who had taught me that language so well, for I understood them easily. Casimir's voice was unpleasant, harsh and throbbing like the growl of an angry tom-cat before battle.

'No, Pierre, I shall not wait longer. I am bored by this endless slow driving of these stupid villagers. After a night of storm such as comes upon us now, they will be drenched and dismal and even slower. Edmond,' — he turned to one of the other men standing by — 'make sure all our loot is

271

covered and kept dry. Little enough we have gained by this expedition; we must not lose that little.'

'It was not my fault that Sir Samuel was gone with the gold,' the man called Pierre protested; why, he must be the traitorous seneschal, Pierre Paradis! 'How could I anticipate that he would depart so early? I did my best to delay him and the pack animals; you know that.'

'Not a very good best, though, was it, Pierre?' Casimir's smile was not attractive. 'And your reward will not be very great either, will it, dear friend? Indeed, I am not sure whether you deserve to be given the woman you desire so much. We shall see . . . tomorrow.'

The man Paradis had stepped backward as if struck, but now he spoke up bravely enough. 'At what hour must we expect you, cousin Casimir? And what shall we do with all those villagers — drive them away, or just keep them here?'

'Why, keep them here, of course!' Casimir's voice was almost caressing. 'For tonight, that is. Tomorrow — why, we'll take along the few girls and wenches that we fancy, and perhaps some of the young boys. As for the rest, we don't need them. So what shall we do with them, eh, Edmond?'

'Slay them, of course, just like we do always!' The other man had contemptuous amusement in his coarse voice. 'No cause for leaving tale-bearers behind, is there, eh?'

The lean Pierre appeared as horrified as was I by the brutality of this proposal, but the other soldiers were expressionless and Casimir positively purring.

'Always you're *so* sensible, Edmond; I leave matters in your charge with complete confidence. Not in yours, dear *cousin* Pierre' — he twitched another smile at the lean man, his teeth gleaming unpleasantly — 'for, after all, you're not always quite trustworthy, are you? I should not wish you to be tempted again. Adieu, then, till morning.'

Without more ado, Casimir drove his spurs into his horse's flanks with such vicious force that the poor beast neighed in pain and leapt into motion. Off westward he went, the other riders following without a word and swiftly passing from my view.

Chapter Twenty-eight

THE END OF PIERRE PARADIS

As Pierre Paradis turned to watch them go, I saw for the first time his narrow face, close-trimmed beard and greying hair, with its widow's peak almost reaching down to the base of his nose. There was concern, even a sort of guilt, in his expression. The burly Edmond perceived this, for he nudged the lean man and laughed.

'Shaken you a bit, has he? Aye, he's a tough one, our Casimir; no room for weaklings in *his* following! Better have your wench tonight, if you want her. No sense waiting for tomorrow, for then you might never get her!'

Laughing heartily, he walked away through an arch and into the castle bailey. The third man, though, seemed reluctant to follow. He was almost as broad as the others, but was younger and seemed of a more imaginative, nervous type. His next words underlined my impression.

'I like it not, Messer Paradis.' He spoke so quietly that I almost missed his words. 'I like it not. This expedition has been misfortunate from the very outset. No gold; no rafneyen; that woman screaming her curses at us, till Edmond slew her in the doorway of her home; and now, this talk of a greater slaying tomorrow. The thought of it makes me sick at heart. Evil fortune will follow such a deed, surely. I would that I had never left Takrallen; I fear I shall never see it again.'

Paradis looked at him sharply and seemed briefly to mirror his fear. Then, with an effort, he drew himself together and assumed a very different guise. He cocked his head and his face wrinkled into a smile. As for his voice, why, it was positively caressing!

'Do not let our lack of luck dishearten you, Gilles! Mayhap we'll gain that gold yet, who knows? And we have food and

273

wine a-plenty among our plunder; and women, too! No cause for being so downcast, man! Why, 'tis merely the imminence of the storm that is affecting your spirits.'

Since it was now his desire, Pierre Paradis exuded an astonishing warmth and charm. Spurious though I knew this to be, I could comprehend now how he had bemused poor Sir Samuel Saville. How could one dream for a moment that such a man, with such a smile, could be anything other than trustworthy? Why, the very thought seemed absurd!

The simple Gascon soldier responded immediately to this encouragement. 'Aye, you're right of course, Messer Paradis! Just as you say, it must be the storm as has upset me. Well, doubtless I'll be cheerful enough when 'tis past. I'd best go down and make sure our loot is well covered against the rain, else we'll all rue the day!'

He hastened away down the hill, but Pierre Paradis did not follow. I saw his lips twitch in what, I am sure, was wry amusement at the simplicity of the other man; but then he became grave, stroking his cheek pensively. He was speaking to himself now, so quietly that I was barely able to hear him.

'Well enough; but I think Gilles is right. This adventure *is* ill-fated . . . And Edmond Arsenac spoke sense also. If I delay till tomorrow, I may indeed never enjoy she for whom I have risked so much. It grieves me to have to take her tonight, in such rough surroundings; but I must, I cannot risk waiting . . .' His voice trailed off altogether and he stood silent.

Perhaps I made some slight sound, for he glanced suddenly toward me. Fortunately I was lying quite still and he did not perceive me. Instead, in sudden decision, he strode away — not into the castle bailey, but down the path. So the woman about whom he had been speaking must be one of the prisoners? I pitied her.

It was time for me to move also, for I must acquaint Sir Robert and the others of the situation and of the dreadful fate menacing the other captives. Yet I dared not hasten. There were many men close by; there would be other reivers on the path; and there were the guards about the beast-pen to be passed. To fall into Edmond Arsenac's bloody hands would put at risk much more than my own life.

It had been hard enough to ascend that steep slope silently, but it was very much harder to descend quietly and I was much slower. Careful though I was, at one point both my feet slipped in the leaf-litter. To save myself from falling, I seized the stout stem of a bush. Unfortunately, its root tore free from the shallow soil and I found myself hanging by one hand over a declivity.

Just as I was about to loose my hold and drop, I heard voices on the path close by. I froze for an uncomfortable minute, while eight of the Wild Cat's men walked leisurely by unperceiving. Then, my wrist aching, I made the drop.

It should have been easy enough. Unfortunately, an old log was concealed beneath the leaf-mould. My feet slipped on it and I sprawled sideways, my left leg twisting under me. As I fell, some dry branches broke under my weight and the log, displaced, rolled away downslope.

The amount of noise I caused seemed to me immense. Again I froze, my heart pounding madly. I was quite sure that I would either receive an arrow in my back or be hauled away by investigating soldiers.

However, all remained quiet. Carefully I sat up and probed my knee anxiously. I winced at the touch, but nothing seemed to be broken. There came again the sound of voices on the path; I froze a third time, but the men were passing by uphill, not coming my way.

They must have been some of those who had been serving the prisoners, for I heard one grumble: 'All that good bread wasted, eh? Senseless to feed 'em first, ere we've had chance to eat. Senseless to feed 'em at all, come to that!'

An affirmative was growled in another voice; then they passed from my hearing.

I stretched my leg carefully, massaging the knee with hands and palm. Ah! I had eased it a little; that felt better! I flexed my leg again, stretching the ankle prospectingly, then got carefully to my feet, standing as upright as the slope allowed. Good! The pain was easing. Slowly and carefully I descended to the level where the slope slackened and found the animal path again.

My knee had behaved well enough for that brief time of walking upright. However, now that I must crouch, it began again to throb uncomfortably. Painfully I moved forward,

275

yard by yard, as quietly as I might manage, for I was still dangerously close to the path from the beast-pen.

I crawled perhaps seventy yards, then sat for a while, stretching and relaxing that knee to try to ease it. I felt safe enough, for I was well concealed; but, as it chanced, a gap in the branches enabled me to see some way along the path toward the pen.

Thus it was that I saw Pierre Paradis for a second time. As I might have expected, he was not alone. Before him was walking a girl, slim, with a tangle of dark hair and wearing a dark red surcoat that was obviously of good quality, though its hem was torn and streaked with mud. Her feet and arms were bare and scratched. She was walking stumblingly, with a sort of forward stoop and her arms thrust out behind her. As the two came closer, I saw that her arms were roped together and that Paradis had so twisted the rope as to force her wrists upward. No, she was not accompanying him voluntarily.

He was speaking to her, and in English, not in French. 'Well, my dear Lauretta, the decision is yours. You may become mine willingly or unwillingly, yet you *shall* be mine, and on this night. You are entirely at my mercy, you know. Whatever happens, there will be no-one to help you!' His voice was so triumphant, so gloating, that it sickened me.

Though she was so helpless, there was yet a fire of anger in her. 'I shall never be yours willingly, be sure of that! You, the devil who has betrayed us, robbed us, caused our people to be killed — why, I'd rather be had by the meanest scullion than by you!'

There was such disgusted contempt in her voice that Pierre Paradis responded furiously. He hauled viciously on the rope, so that she was pulled backward and fell sideways. As she fell, he struck her twice about the face, causing her to cry out in pain.

I was angry already and that was altogether too much for me. I do not remember rising and stepping forward; I do not even remember drawing the knife from my belt, but there it was in my hand. As Paradis stepped back — I think he was intending to kick the girl, for he had slackened the rope — I threw. The knife caught him full in the throat. He gasped and, spouting blood, collapsed backward onto the path as he died.

My painful knee altogether forgotten, in a moment I had thrust my way through the bushes and was kneeling by the fallen girl. She was breathing gaspingly, her breasts heaving. She looked at me searchingly with large, dark eyes, then wordlessly suffered me to turn her about and undo the rope from her arms. I raised her to her feet and she stood tremblingly. Only then did she speak.

'I was praying to God for vengeance on that monster and vengeance came. Are you some sort of angel?'

The incongruity of the question made me laugh aloud. 'Not really,' I said, 'though I may have usurped the role of an angel on this occasion. However, we must be swift and careful; we can talk later. Into the bushes, quickly. There's a path just a few yards in. I'll follow you, but first I must retrieve my knife and try to hide the traces of our going. Haste, now!'

Obediently, if shakily, she scurried away out of view. I withdrew my knife and cleaned it by driving it deep into the earth. Then I dragged Paradis's body a few yards up the path, so that it would be less evident from whence his assailant had come.

The effort reminded me again of my twisted knee; I was limping as I returned. As I followed Lauretta into the bushes, I did my best to smooth away our tracks and so to interlace the branches that our passage would be concealed.

Lauretta had not gone far along the path; she was kneeling and awaiting me. As I came up to her, I saw that she was smiling.

'No, not an angel, perhaps. Angels are supposed to be tall and blond and handsome, are they not? And you are so slight and so dark; yet you do very well for me. Pray tell me, what is your name? I cannot go on without knowing that, at least.'

'I'm Simon Branthwaite and you, I presume, must be Lauretta Saville. I am sorry to be so informal, but we are in much danger. Listen! Already someone comes. Be silent!'

We were out of sight of the path now, but still perilously close to it. Two men at least were coming along it, from the direction of the pen. I heard one call out in French: 'Why, what's that? Someone fallen?'

There was a sound of heavy feet running a few paces,

then the same voice cried out: 'Why, 'tis Messer Paradis —
and dead! Whatever has happened?'

The next voice I recognized; it was that of Gilles. He
sounded frightened.

'His throat has been torn out, by some beast or some
devil! Was I not saying to him, not even an hour since, that
this expedition was accursed? Yet he would not have it. And
now the curse has fallen on him, as you see!'

The first speaker seemed equally alarmed now. 'Aye, happen
you're right. Well, we'd best tell Messer Edmond. Haste,
now!' And they fled away uphill.

As they went, I beckoned to Lauretta and led the way
through the bushes. However, it was becoming increasingly
difficult for me to move fast. After a while she whispered;
'You're limping: what is the matter?'

'Oh, I had a fall, that's all. I was stupidly careless. Come
on; we can't waste time.'

All too soon, though, the pain became too much for me
and I had to rest. Lauretta stopped beside me.

'You must go on!' I whispered. 'I'm too slow. You'll
remember the wizard, Vedlen Obiran? Well, he is below,
with some of his men. Go to him and tell him about the
old castle where the Wild Cat's men are, and the pen. Tell
him also that the Wild Cat intends, tomorrow, to kill all
your people — save, maybe, the young women and boys.
You must not wait for me; you must hasten! Be careful and
quiet, though; and beware of the mounted guard, at the place
where the slope steepens.'

She was evidently shocked by my words, but she said: 'Let
me examine your knee, please. I have some skill at healing
but little, I fear, at moving swiftly in woodland. I shall need
your help, Simon.'

I groaned. 'Oh, very well.'

Soon I felt her fingers probing about the bones of my
knee, then winced as she found and manipulated some tendon
or muscle. There was a flare of pain, which made me groan
a second time and for a different reason. Then Lauretta said:
'You must try to move it. Now, is that not better? Good;
then please lead the way again. It is so dark in here.'

And thus, again, I set off along the animal track. It was
indeed much darker now, in the deep shade of the bushes

278

and with the storm-clouds massing overhead. We passed the beast-pen without seeing it, for the path led downhill by a different route than that I had followed when ascending; nor, this time, did I glimpse the guard on the horse.

My knee *was* easier since Lauretta's manipulation of it, but I found the descent painful and difficult, suffering many jolting stumbles. At long last, the slope began to slacken and the bushes to thin out. We were some way to the west of where I had left Avran, but not too far.

We paused in the shadow of a high bush at the foot of the slope. For the first time, I was able to straighten. Suddenly I realized that Lauretta had come very close to me. She put her arms about me.

'Thank you, Simon,' she said. 'Even though an injured angel, I think you're a very effective one.'

She kissed me full on the lips, then loosed away; and, moving carefully and crouchingly from bush to bush, we made our way to where Avran and the others were waiting.

Chapter Twenty-nine

THE TAKING OF ALUNSWARD

'So Casimir of Chattaine is gone to his hold and Pierre Paradis is dead,' said Vedlen Obiran musingly.

We were all sitting in the deep shade of a thicket, a ring of browsing but watchful rafneyen about us serving as guards. Lauretta and I had recounted our adventures and had told all else that we knew, I of the old castle, the beast-pen and its guards, she of the condition and present spirits of the captives.

'Aye, it's good to know that villain is finished with,' growled Drakht Belineg. 'Though I could wish I had been privileged to set my hands on him. He'd have died, but much more slowly. He did not merit a swift end.'

'He died fittingly.' To my surprise, it was the normally silent Delhir Ravatseng who was speaking now. 'He wrought much evil and he died while striving to commit further evil. Be sure he has gone straight to Hell.'

Seemingly exhausted by this rush of words, he began playing quietly on his little double pipe.

'The important point is that he is dead,' Sir Robert was speaking now. 'This land is cleaner for his going. Soon, I trust, we will be despatching that dastardly Casimir after him to Hell. Simon has done well, better even than I anticipated.'

At those words Lauretta, who was keeping very close to me, seized and pressed my hand. Even in the greyness, I could see that her eyes were shining.

The wizard gave one of his rare chuckles. 'Simon *has* done very well, better even than any of you yet conceive! Consider, now. Their most intelligent leader, Casimir, is gone to Cat Crags. Pierre Paradis, the only other man among them capable of any perception, is dead — and dead in a fashion which, as we know, seems to them strange and inexplicable. We can

281

be sure that the man Gilles is busy spreading alarming rumour among them. Edmond Arsenac may not be at all afraid himself and will surely try to pacify them. However, he can do it only by force, not by persuasion, for he is no sort of reasoner. If they are left in tranquillity, their fears will die down; but they are not going to be left in tranquillity! We shall see to that.'

There was a mutter of thunder in the far distance and Vedlen Obiran laughed again. 'Why, even the weather is coming to our service! An approaching storm ever induces disquiet and unease in men's minds, especially when they have no immediate occupation. That castle will be a brew of tension already; we shall cause it to spill over! Look, now — already their fear is becoming manifest. See there, up the hillside?'

All of us looked from our concealment up towards the reivers' camp. There were gleams of brightness among the trees.

'I can tell you what they have done,' said the wizard quietly. 'They have ringed the beast-pen with torches. The guards are fearful, not of men, but of the fierce creature which, they believe, ripped out the throat of Pierre Paradis. So, by lighting torches, they think they are protecting them-selves. Wise fools! For they will be looking from light into darkness and we can be so much surer of approaching them unseen. Remind me, Simon; how many men were on watch?'

'I counted six,' I answered.

'Well, mayhap the number has been increased, but it cannot be by many. Edmond Arsenac will be finding it hard even to maintain that guard, let alone to augment it. His men will be most reluctant to go down to the beast-pen when, as they believe, some monster is on the prowl. Robin my friend, I'm going to take back from you the command, just for this evening. You are the better warrior, but this will be a time when we employ the devices of wizardry.'

Sir Robert laughed. 'Well, Vedlen, you're the one for devious doings in darkness, not I. I relinquish my command to you gladly!'

'My thanks to you, Robin. We cannot commence operations until complete darkness has fallen and we must trust that the storm does not arrive too swiftly. Even so, I shall begin

282

issuing my instructions. Delhir, will you serve out food and
drink to us? While he is doing so, would you unload the
pack-sevdreyen, Avran and Drakht? Rahir, I shall need your
assistance. We must set Simon's knee altogether to rights if
we can, for we shall require his skills again this night.'

Within the hour, we ventured forth up the hill. My knee
had undergone further examination and manipulation. It had
then been bound in flexible fibre made from some sort of
tree-bark, the bindings being stitched into place by the
neat-fingered Rahir. This extra support enabled me to walk
freely and even to crawl, though I could not have run far.

We had all received careful instructions from Vedlen Obiran
and some of us had been furnished with special supplies from
the rafenu-packs. All of us were travelling on foot, the
rafneyen awaiting our summons below.

We were moving, not in a single group, but in four smaller
parties. Rahir and Delhir had left early and gone off eastward,
to discover some new route up the hill; though Rahir was
no woodsman, Delhir was skilled enough to find them a way.
Sir Robert and Drakht Belineg were cautiously climbing the
main path, to deal silently with the horseman-guard if he
were still on watch. (This was a precaution only, for the
wizard believed the guard must have been withdrawn; and
so it proved.) My partner was Lauretta, our task to find
again and follow the animal trackway. Just a little way behind
us were the wizard and Avran, neither of them good woodsmen,
though Vedlen Obiran could see as well as a badger in the
darkness.

It had indeed been the wizard's intention that Avran, not
Lauretta, should be my immediate companion; but she would
not leave my side. The reason she presented was that she
felt she might assist me, should my leg prove troublesome
again. Vedlen Obiran had appeared to accept this. For my
part, however, I suspected strongly that Lauretta had some
other motivation. A residual distrust of my companions,
perhaps? Or . . . I declined to speculate further.

The trackway was found without difficulty and up it we
went. I had my bow over my shoulder this time and my
quiver at my hip, so this second crouching ascent was more

283

awkward than the first had been. However, my knee, though throbbing a little, behaved well enough.

I speculated what might happen if we encountered one of the animals that had made the track; and maybe we did, for we heard a grunt and a scrambling sound as something, up ahead, fled before us. The noise caused Lauretta to seize my arm in alarm. She pressed herself against me for a long moment before we resumed our slow climb.

When we were over the first rise and at the level of the beast-pen, we began to glimpse, through the dense mass of leaves, the firefly-light of the torches. As the animal track converged with the main path, the lights shone brighter and larger.

Eventually, knowing we must be beyond the further end of the pen, I found a place where the branches seemed less dense, gave my bow to Lauretta and wormed my way cautiously through the underbrush to the path. Having made the passage, I enlarged it by breaking off or bending back branches and twigs; then I fetched my bow. As I crawled again to the path, Avran was following close behind. For a while Lauretta stayed within the screen of bushes, then she in turn came out onto the path. As for the wizard, he had gone on up the hill.

Cautiously, with bows at the ready and arrows at string, Avran and I made our way along that path. For some distance, it continued as a narrow slot through the thicket; but then it swung to the left and widened, approaching the pen gate.

Hugging the shade as best we might, we looked past the bend. Yes, there were the high slate wall and the entrance to the beast-pen, flanked by crudely shaped sandstone pillars and closed by a heavy wooden gate. A torch flared and smoked on each pillar, forming a patch of brightness and causing the shadows to dance about it.

On the nearer side of the wall, a guard was standing. He was clad in mail and quite still; I could see the bow slung over his shoulder, the scabbard hanging from his belt at left and the quiver at right. Since he was facing toward us, we could perceive also that upon his breast there hung a horn. Beyond the gate was a second guard, similarly equipped but seeming much more nervous, for he was pacing up and down on the wall and glancing uneasily to left and right.

'You must deal with that nearer guard when the time comes, Avran, my friend,' I whispered. 'Then you must go forward to the gate and see whether any of our friends need aid. As for me, I must try to edge closer to that other guard.'

Avran gave a rueful smile. 'Today it seems my part to remain still while you adventure, Simon. Well, so be it; but again I ask you, take care! That last waiting aged me by many years.'

I smiled at him, for it was good to know I had such a friend. We clasped hands and then, dropping to my knees, I crawled round the bend in the deep shade of the bushes.

Though the first guard was still looking toward me, I knew he could not see me; but, with the bow burdening me, could I pass him without being observed? No, it was impossible; the torch-flames lit the area about the gate too brightly. Moreover, the bushes by my side were so dense that I was not sure I could force my way into them. Certainly I could not do so without causing noise.

I approached the gateway as closely as I dared, then waited in the last patch of deep shade before the lit area. I could see now that there were seven guards on the wall, the two about the gate and five at further stations, some of them pacing up and down, some still. Between each two guards a torch burned. Cautiously I sat back on my heels and then straightened, wincing as the effort caused a brief flare of pain in my knee. Slipping the bow from my shoulder, I raised it and, taking from my quiver an arrow, set it to string. By now, our other comrades must be in position. When would the signal come?

Ah! That was it — a curiously eerie, wailing whistle from somewhere up on the hill, close to the tower. Even though I was expecting it, the sound startled me. It must have caused the guards much greater startlement. All of them became still, gazing upward toward the source of the whistle. I could hear uneasy sounds from the captives within the beast-pen, some of whom seemed not to be asleep.

This was the moment. Quickly I drew back the string and loosed, aiming at the further guard; the nearer one was Avran's concern.

Had my target been moving, I do not think I should have

285

hit him; the flickering light was too uncertain. As it was, he dropped without a sound, falling backward beyond the wall. Almost at that moment, the guard close by me grunted and crumpled. Before he fell from view, I glimpsed the feathered end of Avran's arrow protruding from his chest.

As Avran ran out from the shadow, I straightened effortfully and walked toward the gate, scanning the wall anxiously as I did so. Good! All the guards were gone from it, and this had been achieved without a horn being sounded. I wondered how it had been managed. Each of our comrades must have been ready to act, of course, but one of them must have dealt with two guards. Later I was to learn that had been Delhir, whose sling had proved quite as deadly as any long-bow. Rahir and Sir Robert had employed flung nooses, binding their victims afterward and leaving them under the wall's shade, while mighty Drakht Belineg had simply leapt at a guard and dragged him from the wall.

As Avran and I slipped back the catch of the heavy gate and swung it outward, we realized that Lauretta had joined us.

'Bravely done! Oh, bravely done!' There was a sob in her voice and tears in her eyes; yet, in the torchlight, I could see that her face was almost radiant with joy.

'Now it becomes your task!' Avran said urgently. 'Speak swiftly to your people, before they become alarmed.' Indeed, I could see that many more of the captives were awake and some leaping to their feet.

She ran quickly into the pen and then stopped. 'It is I, Lauretta,' she called out. 'All is well; your release is at hand, but' — as a hubbub of sound began to rise — 'please, please be quiet, for you are still in peril! Now, is anyone so unwell as to be unable to walk? If so, tell me quickly. And the children; you must awaken them, if they sleep still, and ready them for departure — but you must not allow them to be noisy. John Stanton, Bevis, Alban, Bernard, come to me quickly, please; I shall need your help. You must uncover the pile of the reivers' loot and distribute the bundles, such as can be carried. This time, remember, you'll be taking your own possessions homeward, not serving as beasts of burden for brigands!'

There was a ragged cheer at this. Indeed, Lauretta's words and vigour had lit a flame of hope in their breasts, quite as bright as the torches. She silenced them, then spoke again. There was a reminiscent anger in her tone.

'You will wish to know also, I think, that our betrayer is dead. Pierre Paradis was slain earlier today by our principal saviour, Simon Branthwaite.'

She set her arm upon mine, beaming at me. This time, the shout of joy was so loud that it alarmed me.

'Keep them quiet, Lauretta,' I said urgently. 'There are still nearly forty of the reivers in the castle above; we few cannot deal with them.'

'I'm sorry, Simon,' she said contritely. 'Quietly, good people, please — and quickly. We must be away from here, ere we are discovered or the storm breaks.'

Indeed, there was a growing turbulence in the air, a gusty wind ruffling the women's dresses and causing the wrappings of the bundles to flap. The two Ravatsengs and Drakht Belineg had clambered over the wall by then. Soon they were treating the injured as speedily as they might or speaking words of comfort to the bereaved.

Ere long Sir Robert was riding into the pen, on the foremost of a line of nine rafneyen. Two of the women and one elderly man were ill enough to require carrying; each was placed upon the back of a rafenu, the soothing thoughts of whose owner reconciled it to the unfamiliar rider. The other beasts were laden with the bundles carried hitherto by the children and by such men as were determined to participate in our harassing of the marauders. Then, in a surprisingly orderly procession, the freed captives went out from their place of confinement. Led by one of the Owlsgard men who knew the Marolane valley well enough to find his way even by night, they set off to seek the road to Becketsward.

Lauretta was to go with them also. Briefly she returned to my side, watching while the last of them were going out of the gate. Then she embarrassed me deeply by flinging her arms about me and, in the full view of my colleagues, kissing me again upon the lips. After that, without a word, she hastened off to follow her people down the path and out of view.

Avran grinned at me. 'Careful now, Simon my friend! Remember, you're betrothed to my sister; none of these wayside romances, please!'

I blushed. Fortunately I was spared from responding by another gust of wind, which set the torches guttering and sent smoke across the beast-pen.

'Come, we must be moving,' Sir Robert urged. 'Drakht, would you swing back the gate? But do not quite close it until Rahir has joined you; he has a last task to perform. You men of Owlsgard, follow me, please! The rest of you know your next tasks. Waste no time, for the storm must come upon us soon!'

As Avran and I hurried off along the path, we became aware of some strange change in the light behind us and looked back. Why, the torches were still flaring, but they were no longer burning white! Instead they had become palely, eerily green, like the strange corpse-lights one sees sometimes over marshes at night. I presumed that this must have been contrived by Rahir, during his last hasty circuit of the beast-pen, but I could not guess what he had done.

As we rounded the bend of the path and the torches vanished from view, we heard another wailing whistle. This time, though, the sound was more sustained and throbbing. The Owlsgard men, who were ahead of us and following Sir Robert, hesitated and seemed inclined to turn tail; however, when he beckoned them, they hastened on uphill. The Ravatseng brothers and Drakht Belineg had vanished from view. As for Avran and me, we found the tunnel I had made through the brush and, by it, returned to the beast-track.

We followed that track to the point where it swung westward; then, for the second time that day, I faced the prospect of clambering up the steep slope toward the castle. In the darkness, carrying a bow and with my unreliable knee, this was an even more difficult task. Fortunately, this time I had less need to move silently and could rely on the sturdy support of Avran.

However, the gustiness of the wind was a hindrance. At one moment, it would be blowing so hard that one had to lean against it, with branches whipping one's face; at the next, it would drop and one would find oneself off balance. There was a strange throbbing, ululating note in that wind, like derisive spectral laughter. I had heard no such sound in any storm before. Was it merely that the wind was wailing about the stones of the castle or was it a contrivance of the wizard's, a device to try further the nerves of Casimir's men?

At last the effortful ascent was done and we were again on the ridge top, close to the castle. The wizard had told us that it was called Alunsward and that it had never been completed, its people being slain or driven away in some raid. He thought that crime might also have been committed by the Wild Cat's men, but was not sure. As, with extreme care, we crawled closer to its gate, we could see the bright fire in the keep and the torches burning about the bailey.

There was a considerable commotion within. Soon six horsemen were riding out from the gate, the guards swinging it open to allow them to pass.

The riders stopped at the top of the hill beside us, at that last level point before the path plunged steeply. They were talking urgently together in French and were manifestly uneasy.

'Green lights,' one said. ' "Go and find out what's wrong," says Messer Arsenac. But does he come with us? No, not he. Stays snug in the castle, *he* does. And the rafneyen all gone, too. Whatever became of *them*, I wonder?'

'Stop snivelling,' said another, evidently the leader. 'Come on, now! The guards'll still be on duty, you may be sure. Those lights, they're just some queer effect of the storm; nothing to worry about. Haste, now! Soonest gone, soonest back.' And, spurring their beasts, they all set off down the hill.

'What were they saying?' asked Avran eagerly; and, when I told him, he chuckled. 'Well, they're in for a surprise!'

Indeed they were. Amid the wail of the wind, we heard a sudden outburst of shouts from below us and the brief sound of a horn, so quickly silenced that its note could not have carried to the guards at the castle gate. We knew well what had happened; the riders had been ambushed by Sir Robert and the Owlsgard men. Hastily we set arrows to our bows and waited by the path, in case any rider should escape back up the hill. None came. Six more men accounted for; thirty or so still to go.

According to instructions, I left Avran in hiding by the gate and, after making a cautious way westward far enough to be quite out of view of the guards on the castle gate,

289

traversed the rough road. Somewhere near, I knew, Vedlen Obiran must be awaiting me.

There came a wailing, chuckling voice in the air beyond the castle, seeming to ask amused, demonic questions; then another and louder voice, quite as sinister-sounding, seemed to answer from close by. This so startled me that I stopped short; but then I heard a much more human chuckle. Yes, it was the wizard. Good though I believed my night sight to be, he had seen me long before I was aware of him. The wailing ebbed away on our side, though the spectral voice to the east still continued chuckling to itself.

'Welcome, Simon,' the wizard said cheerily. 'Delhir tells me that the captives are safely away — excellent news!'

'Why, has Delhir met up with you already?' I asked, astonished.

'Oh, yes. He moves swiftly in the darkness, that one! I believe we are stirring up those rats in the castle to no small extent. They appear not to be enjoying the singing of my thunderstick very much.'

'Oh, is *that* what the sound is?' I said, enlightened; for I had made them for myself often enough when young.

'Would you like to try it?' he answered; and handed it to me. Soon I was happily whirling over my head the wooden slat on the end of its string. The sound would have been startling on a bright day, in a light wind. On such a night, in such a gusty gale, it was truly devastating.

A third 'spectral voice' had joined in now, on another side of the castle; I wondered which two of our comrades were whirling the other thundersticks. To add to the effect, real thunder was rumbling away in the distance, with brief flashes of lightning.

'Hand me the thunderstick now, Simon, and take this device instead. Whenever the sound of my thunderstick subsides, set it to your lips and speak into it loudly but throbbingly. This is what you must say — but in French. Since I cannot speak French, you must translate for yourself.'

He gave me brief instructions, then said: 'Let's try it now.'

This second device was a sort of long conical tube, with thin leaves of wood slotted into its sides within. Even when I spoke into the open tip of the cone, my voice was amplified and strangely distorted. When I shouted — or rather, wailed —

into it, my voice sounded so wholly inhuman as to be truly eerie.

'The curse is falling upon the evil followers of the Wild Cat!' I shouted as the ululating note of the thunderstick subsided. Then it throbbed louder for a while. I waited till the sound dwindled, then: 'Flee!' I wailed, 'Flee, ere it is too late! Flee, for God's wrath is upon you!'

After that first trial, we moved closer to the castle, repeating the performance several times as we did so. There would be silence for a while, then the thunderstick would wail and, as its sound diminished, I would shout: 'Flee, ere it is too late! Flee! Flee!'

The massive gate had been left open, presumably to permit the re-entry of the six riders when they returned. Its two guards had huddled together and were gazing outward in silence; nor was there any sound within the castle, save the crackling of the torches.

Suddenly a green flame was to be seen among the bushes close to the castle wall; and another, burning in a second position; and another; and another, till the whole castle wall seemed ringed in a virescent glow. Immediately and with frantic haste, the guards slammed the gate shut. Again the thundersticks screamed their mocking laughter, while the real thunder rolled closer and lightning flashed in the southern sky. Again I wailed into the cone: 'The curse . . . The wrath . . . Flee, flee!'

Then: 'Now for the next act,' said the wizard amusedly. He ceased whirling the thunderstick and, instead, raised a little wooden pipe to his lips. This was the third time I had heard that strange high whistle.

At that moment, from all sides it seemed, balls of bright magenta fire were hurled over the stone wall into the castle bailey, so that its whole interior was bathed in a weird purplish light.

Once more I shouted into the cone: 'Flee, ere doom falls on you! The curse is come!'

Then, strangest sight of all on that eventful evening, a wavering white shape rose high into the air above the wall of the castle over to our left. It appeared to have two great eyes of green fire and a curving, red-lipped mouth. There was a wail of fear and someone shot an arrow at the strange thing; but the arrow passed through it without doing it harm.

One last time did I wail through the cone: 'Doom is coming upon you. Flee! Flee!'

At that, the nerves of the reivers finally cracked. There was a surging rush for the castle gateway, in which the two guards were bowled over. Out came a terrified crowd of men, fifteen of them at least.

As they scurried past us, another magenta fire-ball — this one flung by the wizard himself — fell among them. Never till then had I heard men whinny like horses in terror, but I heard the sound now; and away they fled into the night.

Only a few had stayed behind in the castle. They strove to close its gates, but too late. Before they could do so, Sir Robert, Avran and the men of Owlsgard, armed with weapons taken from the slain horsemen, were within.

There was a brief, frantic fight. Edmond Arsenac was one of those who had kept his nerve and it was Avran who slew him, after a short but fierce duel. When the wizard and I entered its gate, all of Casimir's men remaining in the castle either had surrendered or were dead.

Gilles must have been one of those who had fled into the night, for he was not among those slain or taken. I was glad of that. Inadvertently, he had served us well. Moreover I believed that, after such a fright, there was every chance he would turn away forever from evil-doing.

Chapter Thirty

THE RETURN OF CASIMIR

I was roused from deep sleep by a gentle shaking. In the moment of awakening, I gazed about me bewilderedly. What was this place, with its broken stone arch casting its shade over me, and on whose silken-sheeted couch was I lying? I stretched, groaning at the pain of a knee that had stiffened overnight. Only then did I become aware that Rahir Ravatseng was bending over me.

'Is all well with you, Simon?' he enquired anxiously. 'Last night — or this morning, rather, for 'twas amply past midnight — either you fainted or else you fell asleep on your feet. Friend Avran caught you and 'twas our master himself that put you to bed here, on Edmond Arsenac's own couch. Not that *he'll* be needing it any more . . . 'Tis a shame to be rousing you so early, before your slumber is properly done; but we must be moving soon. Will you be able to manage it, think you?'

I blinked at him and then contrived a smile. 'Oh, I'm well enough, I'm sure. I needed that sleep, though. Are we still in Alunsward, then?'

'Aye, but we must be shifting out shortly. Now then, how's that leg of yours?'

I tried to flex it and winced. 'Stiffish, I'm afraid.'

'Well then, I'll just take that wrapping off and give you a massage.'

He drew back the sheets. Then, using a little knife, he cut the stitches in the bandage and peeled it off. I winced anew as his firm fingers probed the muscles of my knee, but soon he had it feeling easier and was stitching a new tree-bark wrapping about it. While he was doing this, he talked amicably and steadily.

'While you were dreaming, Simon me lad, we had a real

old storm. The thunder was something to hear; I'd have thought it would have awakened anyone, but no, you slept sweetly right through! And the rain, it came down positively in pailfuls. Funny, though; it was just around here. Those folk from Owlsgard — the old folk, the women and children, and your friend Lauretta — they would be far enough down the track not to have felt it at all, I reckon; a few drops, at worst. It's like as if the very heavens arranged to lave this place clean of all the foulness of the Wild Cat's doings — the dirt, the blood, the very tracks, all washed away.'

'How strange! Yet certainly Alunsward needed to be cleansed.'

'That it did. And, you know, those fellows that ran out from here, none of 'em headed for Cat Crags. Sir Robert followed them some way, ere the storm really set in. They were all fleeing off east, headed toward Falconward and Lukeyne. We put a proper scare into 'em; I doubt not that they're running yet!'

I laughed. 'It was a good performance, right enough! I understand how the wailing was managed and, as for the talking, I did it myself, though I don't really comprehend how that hailer device works. But those fire-balls, and especially that shape in the sky; however were those contrived?'

'The fire-balls I don't rightly understand, either. They're made up in the Trident Mountains; we brought them along with us from Reschora. As you throw, you pull out a sort of roughened rod and that sets 'em burning.'

Rahir paused reflectively, then went on: 'Come to think of it, those wands our master carries inside his cloak must work the same way. He has a piece of coarse stone fixed to his belt. When he's in danger, he pulls out one of the wands and strokes it briskly across that stone before throwing it. By then, the wand's blazing. You saw how he scared off that kalvak, back in the forests? Many's the time I've seen him use those wands to frighten off men who tried to rob or kill him. But as to what causes the burning, I've no idea. Some sort of magical element, I suppose.'

'And the shape in the sky?'

He chuckled. 'Why, I fashioned *that* myself and brother Delhir touched it up! 'Tis composed of gossamer-thin cloth, woven from plant fibres. Delhir drew the eyes and mouth, using tinctures that our master prepared. They're made of some stuff that shines in moonlight. The cloth rolls up small, so you can carry it easily, and there are four thin bladders of skin fixed to the top edge, which you blow up and tie so that the breath won't leak out. Then you let 'em go, and up she floats. En-Dor I call her, after that witch in the Bible. She's frightened plenty of other folk before this!'

I laughed in response. 'She's quite a sight! Not beautiful, maybe, but striking! But didn't the arrow damage her?'

'No, it went straight through; I'll just have to stitch up the hole sometime. Now if that archer had shot higher and punctured one of the bladders, we might have been in trouble . . . There, that's done. You'll find your knee a sight easier today and, given a couple more days, it'll be as right as ever it was. Time to rise, lad. The sun's shining and there's an ample breakfast, courtesy of Casimir the Cat.'

Indeed, when I emerged from the shade of the arch, I found that the sun was already quite high in the sky; the morning must be half over already. The darker colour of the soil of the paths and the brighter greenness of the turf within the bailey gave evidence of the overnight rain, but the puddles were already shrinking.

A cloth had been spread on a fallen stone; on it were placed platters of bread and meats, with slices of dried apple and a flask of wine set about by horn goblets. Sir Robert, Drakht Belineg and Avran were sitting on other stones nearby; they had just finished eating. Avran greeted me cheerily.

'Ah, the sleeper awakes, now that the worst of the work is done! I'm blithe to see you looking so well, though, Simon. Your knee must be much better, by the easy fashion in which you're walking.' Indeed, after the first hesitant paces, I was finding that I could step out freely. 'Here, have something to eat and drink.'

As I provided myself with food, I asked: 'Why, what *have* you been doing this morning?'

'Tidying up this place, mostly,' he replied. 'Taking away the bodies of the slain, first of all. Eight of Casimir's men died here in our little fracas last night, and three more surrendered. Then there were the six riders who were ambushed on the path; none of them survived.'

'They were given no opportunity to surrender, I fear,' Sir

Robert commented grimly. 'The men of Owlsgard were not in forgiving mood. Had you not slain Edmond Arsenac, Avran, he would surely have been torn to pieces, for he had earned much hatred. I was hard put to it to protect the other three, even though they were lesser villains. Those who fled were wise in their terror.'

Avran gave a wry smile. 'Curious, isn't it, how often it is the brave who die and the cowards who survive? Yet if they'd not fled, we wouldn't have taken the castle.'

'Nay, Avran, you're wrong there,' Drakht Belineg rumbled. 'Our master would have seized this keep somehow. He does not fail.' With an air of finality he seized the flagon of wine, refilled his goblet and took a long swig.

'And those seven guards down by the beast-pen; were all of them slain?'

Rahir chuckled. 'No, three live yet, but they had a sorry night of it. We tied 'em up, you see, but then had so much else to do that we forgot all about 'em! When we went down there this morning, we found them sodden with rain and stiff with cold and fright. Serve 'em right, of course. The trouble was, it meant that Delhir and I had not only to massage their limbs to life but also to calm them down. Not that we carried *that* too far! Truly I believe that they've had such a scare, one way and another, as to make honest men of 'em.'

'Where are they now?'

'On their way to Becketsward, all six of 'em, in the charge of three of the Owlsgard men. This time the Owlsgard men are doing the riding, upon rafneyen captured last night, while it's the reivers who are walking. And what's more, they're chained together and carrying the rest of the food and loot that we recovered from this place. The Owlsgard men are enjoying *that* turnabout, you may be sure!'

'So what must we do next and how much time have we?'

It was Sir Robert who answered. 'Difficult questions, Simon. We're assuming that Casimir and his villains will not have started out early from Cat Crags, yet we cannot be certain. The storm did not extend even that far, so they will not have been delayed by it. Nor can we know how many men will accompany Casimir when he *does* return. More than the

296

four he took with him, assuredly, and with many more beasts, for he plans to be carrying away both loot and women.'

I started up in alarm. 'But that means they may be arriving any time, and in force!'

He smiled at me. 'Now, Simon, think you that I'd be sitting here so calmly if that were the case? No, no. There's a guard on the gate and watchers on the ridge. We've arranged our signals and we'll be given ample warning of Casimir's approach.'

I relaxed again and took a sip of wine. 'What are we to do, then? Ambush them on the road or here in the castle? That should be easy enough.'

'Oh, Simon, come now! You're capable of being more astute than that; I don't think you're properly awake yet! If they were riding horses, of course we might ambush them; if not on the ridge, then certainly here in this castle or in the coppice below. But they'll be bringing rafneyen, many rafneyen. Would rafneyen advance into such danger, or allow their riders to do so? Certainly not; they'd sense the ambush, half a league away! No; what we must do is to puzzle Casimir so thoroughly that he wastes time and rides too far away from his hold. By then, I hope, we'll have the men of Becketsward and Rewlenscrag to aid us. Delhir and my good friend Vedlen rode away early to arrange the setting of the trap which, we trust, may today catch the Cat!'

He rose to his feet. 'Are you done then, gentlemen? Good; then we must complete our preparations, the first of which is the final vacating of this castle.'

Indeed, the ruin of Alunsward looked already as if it had long stood desolate. Rising early and working energetically while yet I slept, the wizard's men and those of Owlsgard had removed, not only the bodies of the slain but also all traces of occupancy, save only the food and vessels from which we had breakfasted and the bedding in which I had slept. These latter were now packed up into a satchel which Rahir slung over his shoulder, while Drakht used a thorny branch broken from a bush to obscure our footmarks.

Having seen this done, Rahir and Sir Robert left us and walked out of the castle bailey, each towing a thorny branch behind him to conceal his own footprints. The big wooden gates were not only standing widely open, but held so by huge blocks of stone. As they approached the gates, Sir Robert whistled and a lean, sandy-haired man carrying a bow — the Owlsgard man who had been guarding the gate — scrambled down from the wall to join them.

Before the three were gone from view, Avran turned to me. 'So, friend, we are to be among the custodians of this place. We both have our bows; good! We may be needing them. I'm afraid you face a bit of a climb, though, Simon. I trust your leg won't prove troublesome.'

However, it was not my knee, but my nerve that came close to failing me. We went inside the square shell of the keep and ascended a broad stone stairway that led up to an uncompleted first floor high above the hall. Stepping cautiously across its widely spaced beams, we reached a much narrower second stairway. This zigzagged parapet-less upward past the levels of two higher floors, both marked by lines of protruding stones but neither yet constructed. The stairs ended about thirty cloth-yards above the framework of beams and about twenty more below the irregular upper rim of the keep. The wall inside was poorly built and crumbling. Nevertheless, someone had climbed it, for a strong rope was dangling down to us.

'The last stretch is a little more difficult,' announced Avran cheerfully. 'Just do what I do, though, and you won't have any problems.'

Taking the rope in both hands he placed a foot against the wall, leaned backward and just *walked* up that vertical face of stone. Upon reaching the top, he slung a leg over and pulled himself up out of my view.

'Easy enough, Simon, isn't it?' he called down. 'Your turn now!'

How could Avran have climbed so calmly and easily? The very thought of emulating him appalled me. My heart was pounding already, and not because of my ascent of the stairs. Unwisely I gazed down, from this highest stone step to the grid of beams far below. A long way to fall, already; and if I slipped . . . Then I looked up at the dangling rope and felt sick. I took a deep, apprehensive breath. No, I could not make the climb; I would have to turn back.

'What's the matter, Simon?' Avran called down impatiently. 'Recovering your breath? Don't waste time, now!'

298

Courage works in strange ways. In that moment, it seemed to me preferable to attempt the climb, even though I might fall and break my neck, than to be shamed in Avran's eyes by showing fright. I took two deep, shuddering breaths, closed my eyes and grasped the rope with shaking hands. Then, setting my right foot against the wall and leaning outward so that my body was at the proper angle, I took my first step.

Well, that was all right, even though my legs were shaking. Another step, and another; no, this wasn't so difficult, after all! I dared to open my eyes, then wished I hadn't, for I was at a dizzying angle to the stones. My sweat-moist palms slipped a little on the rope; I tightened my grip frantically and half-closed my eyes again. Another step; another; another . . . Then Avran's strong hands were seizing me by the shoulders and hauling me up onto the top.

As I lay there panting and with eyes again closed for fear of looking down, my friend spoke remorsefully.

'Oh, Simon, I do apologize for hurrying you; I'd quite forgotten your injured knee. Take your ease for a while; you'll recover soon enough, I'm sure.'

Lying there with heart beating away frantically, I was too dishonest or too craven to admit that I was suffering, not from physical pain, but from sheer fright.

Then, far away, I heard a sweet, high trill, much like the call of a whimbrel. The sound was repeated closer by and I raised my head. The keep of the castle stood high above its walls and we were perched atop its westernmost corner. In front and over to our left, the land fell away shallowly into the marshy upper reaches of the Marolane valley. Exactly to our left was the saddle we had crossed yesterday. I found I could see down into the more distant half-circle of the beast-pen, though its nearer end was hidden from view. Almost in front of us was the open bailey gate and beyond, the rough track leading away northwestward into the hills, fringed by a bristle of bushes like the hairs on the chin of a man who had remained for a week unshaven. (At that thought, I felt my own upper lip and chin, still so hairless and unmasculine — appropriately so, I thought, for a coward like me!)

Hearing a sound of scrambling below us, I looked back

299

for the first time into the hollow shell of the keep. There was that dreadful rope dangling; and there, further below, was Drakht Belineg, satchel on back and bow over shoulder. He was running — yes, running! — up that parapet-less stone staircase. He reached the top and then, in the most confident and rapid fashion imaginable, grasped the rope and walked up the wall. Soon he hauled himself up and turned about to pull up the rope, coiling it neatly beside us.

'Casimir's lot are on their way here,' he announced briefly. He seemed only slightly out of breath, big and heavy though he was; and I felt ashamed. 'Can't say how many of 'em yet, though. We should see 'em soon. Keep down; they mustn't spot us.'

'Won't their rafneyen detect us, though?'

'Nay, they won't sense us — or not as a danger, for they'll know we're intending them no immediate harm. Aye, we might make 'em uneasy, but I don't mind that. Nor will Casimir's men look so high; why should they? Ah! There they be.'

As a drifting cloud took away its shadow from the grey, irregular hills ahead and to our right, I perceived the approaching reivers. At first I could distinguish only their movement; then I began to descry the riders themselves and, as they came closer, the character of their mounts. Only five — no, six men were on horseback, one of them surely Casimir himself. Eighteen other men were riding rafneyen and there were — how many? — oh, around fifteen other rafneyen bearing empty pack-saddles.

As they came closer, one of the leading riders hollered a formless cry, presumably a prearranged signal of greeting. Of course, there was no response. The reivers rode a little closer and then halted in evident puzzlement. After they had conferred briefly, five riders on rafneyen were sent out in front, the rest following them at a slower pace.

When it was realized that the gates of Alunsward Castle were standing open there were startled exclamations, another halt and a second hasty conference. On this occasion, only the advance guard of five riders proceeded closer, so very slowly and with such caution that it was evident an ambush was expected, even though the rafneyen could be giving no warning of one. At long arrow shot, the five halted and conferred once more before timorously approaching the castle gateway.

At last one, bolder than the rest, urged his mount in through the open gates. His cry of astonishment caused the four others hastily to follow him. Soon the main party of reivers came up. I could distinguish Casimir of Chattaine now; he and the other horsemen rode just inside the gates and halted there, the remainder of the rafenu-men staying outside with the pack-rafneyen. I whispered Casimir's name to Avran and Drakht, pointing him out to them.

'So that is he!' murmured Avran. 'One well-placed arrow, Simon, and Rockall would be a sweeter place.'

'Aye, and those other brigands would be pulling this keep down stone by stone to get at us,' Drakht rebuked him in a rumbling undertone. 'Don't thee be so daft, Avran.'

It was evident that the reivers were not just surprised, but very much disconcerted. On an order from Casimir, the five rafenu-men and two of the horsemen dismounted and, while the other horsemen remained on watch, began a careful exploration of the bailey. Eventually some of them ventured into the keep. Voices below us told us of their entry; then we heard feet on the stone steps.

However, the reivers did not climb much higher than that skeletal first floor. Why should they, when the stairs beyond were so evidently empty and the rope no longer within view?

We heard the dwindling sound of their footsteps and, a minute later, saw that they were remounting, to gather with the other horsemen about Casimir. I could hear their voices, but they were talking too rapidly, and in tones too low, for me to distinguish any words, try though I might. However, their gestures indicated dismay and uncertainty.

Casimir's anger was evident from the peremptory fashion in which he waved his men out of the castle; yet he must surely be as puzzled as they. However, he did not hesitate any longer. Soon the whole party of the reivers was cascading down the path and out from our view.

Drakht Belineg straightened and gave a sigh of satisfaction. 'They're gone to discover whether their captives are still safely penned, I'd suppose. Well, that'll give 'em no joy. Indeed I doubt, now, if they expect anything joyful. I reckon we've got yon Casimir properly rattled. Well, he doesn't know it yet, but his troubles are just beginning!'

Chapter Thirty-one

THE SPRINGING OF THE TRAP

Avran sat up, stretched and then stood upright, a piece of hardihood that did nothing to sooth my still-plangent nerves, for the stonework crowning the keep was not broad. 'Well, Drakht, do we go down now?'

'Best wait a while longer,' the big man rumbled. 'I'd like to be sure what those reivers will do when they've reached the beast-pen. If all goes as our master guesses, they'll be off along the track of the Owlsgard folk.' He rose to his feet also. 'Aye, we can see down well enough. They'll be back in view shortly; and, meanwhile, 'tis good to have a stretch. Don't you want one too, Simon, after all that crouching?'

'No — er, I'm all right lying here, thanks.' The thought of standing on that narrow edge of stone quite horrified me.

'Simon's injured knee made the climb difficult for him,' Avran said in sympathetic — and inaccurate — explanation.

'Aye, of course it would,' responded the big man understandingly. 'If I'd borne that in mind, Simon could have gone off with Sir Robert instead.'

All this undeserved sympathy was embarrassing me, so I spoke hastily to change the subject. 'Actually, I'm not quite clear why we *did* come up here. Yes, I know we were able to watch the coming of Casimir and his brigands; but surely we might all have done that from outside, from a distance, along with Sir Robert? Since we were much too high to hear what they were saying, we've not learned anything, have we?'

Drakht Belineg rubbed his cheek. 'Aye, but suppose yon Casimir had split his party and left some of his men as garrison here? He'd have been able to use this place as a refuge at need; and last night's tricks wouldn't serve to scare *him* out. But three stout fellows like us, right in their midst, unbeknown to 'em and armed with these good bows — why, we'd have accounted speedily enough for any guards he'd left! As it chances, though, Casimir didn't leave any and we weren't needed.'

And my enduring of that dreadful climb was all in vain, I thought bitterly to myself. However, an exclamation from Avran diverted my thoughts: 'Ah, there they are!'

The greater height gained by standing brought Casimir's men more quickly into my comrades' sight than mine, but soon I could see them also — or some of them, at least. Yes, men on rafneyen were circling within the beast-pen, no doubt questing for evidences that might explain how their prisoners had escaped and what had happened to their vanished comrades. Soon, however, the riders withdrew from our view.

'Time to go down,' Drakht said. 'They'll not miss the tracks toward Becketsward, we may be sure. However, there's a chance — a small chance — that yon Casimir might decide not to follow 'em. Just in case, we'd best close the gates against him.'

He picked up the rope, checked its anchorage, then uncoiled it and threw it down again within the keep. 'I'll go down first. Then, Simon, you'd better follow — I can catch you if that wobbly leg of yours causes you to slip.'

In a moment, he had swung himself over and was clambering down, as fast as a dormouse running down a plant-stem.

'All right, then, Simon,' he called up. 'I'll hold the rope away from the wall, to make it easier for you.'

I gulped in apprehension and then, grasping the rope, swung myself off the wall, with about the degree of willingness of a condemned man mounting a scaffold.

In my fear and haste, my feet failed to find position. As they slipped, I rotated dizzily, clasping my knees frantically about the rope and hugging it with thumping heart. Then, taking a deep breath, I began to lower myself hand over hand, inch by inch down the rope, keeping my eyes firmly shut. The descent seemed to take hours. Eventually, feeling Drakht's big hands steadying me, I opened my eyes again and saw that I had just about reached the stairhead.

'Well, that was a funny way of doing it,' Drakht commented puzzledly. Then, as my legs gave way under me and I collapsed backward against the welcome solidity of the wall, he went on more sympathetically: 'Your leg's hurting again, then? Be easy for a bit, lad. Me and Avran, we can see to the gate.'

Avran was already on his way, walking backward down the wall with the rope gripped in confident hands. Within moments, he was again beside me. Evidently he had heard Drakht's words, for he echoed them: 'Yes, do rest awhile, Simon. You can follow us whenever you're ready.'

What, be left to descend that parapet-less stairway alone? The thought made me shudder. Hastily I rose to my feet. 'No, I'll come down with you,' I said decisively.

'Good for you! But take my arm; it'll steady you.'

When I had climbed the stairs, they had not worried me unduly. Now, however, after my experiences on the rope, any least height held terrors. Clutching Avran's arm was truly a comfort. I was grateful also to be able to keep close to the wall, with his solid body between me and the drop. Thus we descended, past the gridwork of beams and down to the very welcome firmness of the floor within the keep. There I released Avran's arm.

'Thank you, Avran,' I said. 'I shall be all right now.'

He looked at me steadily and gave a half-smile. 'Your knee wasn't truly the problem, though, was it, Simon? Oh, don't look so shamefaced, friend! There are many otherwise courageous people who find heights frightening. Yet, when climbing the narrow stair on that tower in the Trantevrin Hills, you showed no fear.'

It was a relief to know that my friend had both perceived my weakness and forgiven it. 'Well, that ascent was made in darkness; I had no view of what was below,' I answered. 'Yet I might have managed here well enough, but for that — that *awful* rope . . . I'd never climbed a rope, anyway, and to watch it swinging . . .'

Avran's smile had broadened, but it remained an understanding smile, not one of mockery. 'Yet, after all, you did very well, Simon. However afraid you felt, you *did* manage the climb and, when you were told to go down, you didn't hesitate. I was quite anxious for a moment, though, when your feet slipped!'

'Not nearly so anxious as I was, I'm sure — I believed my last hour was come! I can only be grateful to God that we're down safely. Most sincerely I thank you, for being so understanding — and for concealing my weakness from Drakht.'

Avran laughed and, putting his arm about my shoulders, gave me the briefest of hugs. 'Come on, then. We mustn't leave all the hard labour to Drakht!'

However, by the time we emerged from the keep, our powerful friend had rolled the great stones away from the gates already and was swinging one of them shut. We helped him with the other and dropped into its socket the massive bar that secured both gates.

'Avran, will you go up on the wall and keep watch?' Drakht asked. 'If Casimir and his pack of cutthroats do come back this way, we'd best be ready. If not, no doubt Sir Robert'll be sending his orders to us shortly. Sit down for a while, Simon lad, and rest that leg. We'll be needing your assistance soon enough, I don't doubt.'

I caught Avran's wink as he turned away and I blushed. Fortunately, Drakht did not notice. Yet I was glad enough to sit down on one of the stones. The ascent *had* put some strain on my knee and I was suffering also from the reaction that so often follows a thorough fright. Drakht sat down beside me and, producing some hunks of bread and cheese from his satchel, shared them with me.

We munched in silence until Avran called down: 'Here comes that Owlsgard archer. Would you open the gates for him?'

It was the lean, sandy-haired man who had been on watch earlier. Seeing him again and more closely, I recalled that, last night, Lauretta had addressed him as Bernard. As he stepped inside the gateway, his freckled face was beaming.

'All proceeds well, masters,' he said. 'Sir Robert said to tell you that the robbers have ridden off westward and that the trap will soon begin to close about them. You can be easy for an hour at least, and maybe more. Some of my friends are on watch outside; they'll give us warning if there's trouble.'

So Avran came down from the wall and, while we shared the bread and cheese and drank from a flask from Drakht's pack, we talked. Bernard knew this area of the Stoney

Mountains intimately. Not only was he able to explain Sir Robert's plan, but also to tell us how it depended on the character of the landscape.

'Cat Crags is easy enough to approach from the north, but it's difficult to reach from south or east. It's wild country indeed. There's two roads — this bad one up the hill from Alunsward and another, better road from Blackhill, up through the Marolane meadows and the valley of the Swiftling Brook. Once the robbers have followed my people down from Alunsward into the upper Marolane valley, there's no way they can turn, either southward or back into the hills, between here and the Swiftling. There's marshes in the valley bottom and there's dense, spiny scrub on the slopes, with cliffs above. Since they can't gain the Swiftling road, they'll have to come back toward Alunsward.'

'And why can't they use the Swiftling road?' Avran asked.

'Because they won't be allowed to, that's why! Our Owlsgard folk mostly crossed the Swiftling last night; there's a stone bridge, just above where it joins the Marolane. Even our three friends that went off with the prisoners this morning should be safely across by now. Well, according to the messages we've had from Felun Daretseng, the men of Ralphsland were really angry when they learned that Casimir had pillaged Owlsgard and burned our homes — they're good neighbours, the Ralphsland folk. They were already on the march last night, hoping to rescue us — though I fear that, but for you and your friends, they'd have been too late.'

He leaned forward to take another hunk of the bread and cheese, then continued: 'Anyhow, they met our people this morning. Half of 'em turned back to render aid; the others, under the Lord of Ralphsland, came on. But not too far, for they'd had word from Sir Robert what to do. There's a coppice, just where the Swiftling flows into the Marolane. When Casimir gets to it, he's going to find the men of Ralphsland waiting for him in ambush. He won't pass through that way, you may be sure.'

Bernard paused to take a large bite of his bread and cheese, then resumed speaking, his mouth full and voice a little muffled. 'But, if he *did* get past, he'd find no joy. Pochardsvale has been roused also, thanks to your friend Hebehir. Sir

307

Cuthbert Reddlestone and his men are marching upon Cat Crags.'

'Excellent!' said Avran. 'Will they attack it, then?'

Bernard swallowed, then continued more clearly: 'No, they can't hope to take the castle, for it's well-nigh impregnable. However, they'll prevent Casimir from bolting back to his lair, or his other men from riding out to his aid — supposing Casimir could get word to them, which I doubt. So, since the robbers won't be allowed to reach the Swiftling road and can't find a path either westward or southward, they'll need to come back this way if they're to regain their roost — or so they'll think. And, since the Ralphsland men will be on their tails, they'll be riding fast and frantic!'

'That'll be pleasant,' rumbled Drakht. 'I was fearing we might not be seeing 'em again.' He took a swig from the flask and beamed at us benignly.

'So what then?' Avran asked eagerly.

'Sir Robert believes they'll pass this castle and try to take the ridge road back toward Cat Crags. Well, we're not going to let 'em! There'll not be another ambush on that road, but there'll be a real scare for 'em! Your master the wizard has plenty of tricks up his sleeve. He'll be there, with Rahir and Delhir; he says he won't need anyone else.'

Bernard paused again, took another huge bite and masticated it between bulging cheeks.

'But what then?' asked Avran impatiently.

'Why, Casimir'll turn back into Alunsward!' Bernard responded, with a sort of muffled glee. 'The gates will be standing open; it'll be looking as deserted as ever it was. But this time, the rest of us'll all be waiting inside to welcome him.'

Drakht laughed uproariously and gave Bernard so hearty a thump on his back as to cause the poor man to choke. 'That'll be a welcome indeed! How long must we wait for that pleasure?'

Bernard was coughing and spluttering; it was a few seconds before he could speak. 'An hour,' he gasped at last. 'About an hour, Sir Robert estimates. It depends how fast the robbers ride. Yet our men are on watch and you may be sure they'll warn us before then. My, but you've got a heavy hand,' he said half-resentfully, half-admiringly to Drakht. 'I'd sooner be your friend than your enemy — but it's painful enough to be your friend!' And Drakht's rumbling chuckle was heard again.

So, for a second time, the gates to Alunsward bailey were propped open, Drakht taking care to place the great stones back as exactly as possible into their original positions. Then there was nothing for us to do but wait. Drakht leaned back against one of the doorstones and drowsed. Avran, Bernard and I were too excited to follow his example and, instead, continued to talk.

On prompting from Avran, Bernard gave us a brief and reluctant account of the robbers' taking of Owlsgard — an assault that came, of course, wholly without warning, since the gates were opened to them while most folk were sleeping. He would say even less about the hardships of that forced march — the whips, the blows, the jeers — but enough for us to glimpse the bleak fire of anger that burned beneath his placid exterior.

'Aye, and you killed that accursed traitor Paradis, Simon, while you finished off that hard-handed rogue Arsenac, Avran. We folk of Owlsgard, we'll be forever indebted to you both. Yet I could envy you the pleasure, for all that. I'm looking forward to this next encounter, you may be sure.'

The bright weather of the morning had proved insubstantial. When we had been up the tower the sun, though still it shone bravely, was already hemmed in by phalanxes of clouds marching from the southwest. By now, they had overwhelmed it. The sky had become uniformly grey and the light was fading, whilst intermittent wind gusts set the grasses rippling.

As one gust found its chill way in through the open gates, Drakht shivered and woke up. Stretching and yawning, he rose to his feet and inspected the sky.

'This'll suit our master fine,' he observed cheerfully. 'Just so long as the rain doesn't come before the reivers do, that is.'

His comment puzzled me, though I was to understand it later.

Almost at that moment we heard sounds from outside. In through the gate, in cheerful if undisciplined array, came the twenty other Owlsgard men, each now armed with a sword or an axe, a bow or a spear, obtained during or after last night's fighting. Though we were given smiles, they spoke no word but scattered about the bailey to find concealment. That was not a difficult task, for there were numerous crumbling walls and stone-heaps, the roofless ruins of houses and storeplaces that had once hugged the inner side of the bailey wall. Sir Robert, who had followed the men in, stopped to speak to us.

'All goes well enough, though not quite so well as I would have wished. Casimir and his brigands are in flight back up the valley, but they — or, more likely, their rafneyen — detected the ambush too soon. None were slain or taken; nor, though the Ralphsland men are in pursuit, are they so close on Casimir's heels as I'd hoped.'

He paused consideringly, then ordered: 'Bernard, you'd best conceal yourself inside the keep; I won't have it used as a refuge by our enemies. Avran and Drakht, I want you to make sure that no-one is readily visible and no tracks obvious. When you've done that, you must both hide also. Simon, you're the best archer; please come with me.'

Just to the right of the gates on the inner side, a flight of steps wound up to the top of the wall. Since anyone up there would be seen easily from outside, that would not have been a good position for keeping watch. Fortunately for us, however, there was a place three-quarters of the way up where some stones had fallen out, leaving a gap in the masonry through which one might peer without much likelihood of being spotted.

When we had taken up position, I strung my bow and placed a line of arrows to hand on the step beside me; then I crouched beside Sir Robert to look out. I found that, though we could not see any distance down the hill, we could see quite some way along the road toward Cat Crags. The light was indeed poor by now and, though I thought I could see the figures of men concealed among the roadside bushes, I was not sure.

'Hark! Here they come,' Sir Robert whispered. 'Be very still, now.'

Up the road from the cattle-pen came the reivers, in an irregular straggle. In front was an advance guard of five rafenu-riders; then seven or eight of the pack-rafneyen; then the six horsemen in a tight group, a grim-faced Casimir midmost; and, after that, the remaining thirteen rafenu-riders, with the other pack-rafneyen among them. The flanks of the horses and rafneyen were heaving, after so steep an ascent at speed.

The advance guard checked outside Alunsward, as if considering taking immediate refuge, but Casimir bellowed in French: 'Back to Cat Crags, idiots!' At that, they hastened onward.

But not far. Suddenly there were creeping lines of greenish fire crossing the rough track before them, beyond which could be glimpsed what seemed to be the shapes of many men. Strange, stiff figures they were, in the eerie green glow. After brief puzzlement, I realized that these must be the bodies of the reivers that had fallen last night, propped up in gruesome rows.

Whether Casimir's men recognized dead comrades and were appalled, or whether they merely thought they faced another ambush, I cannot say. Anyway, the leading rafneyen reared up in fright, one rider being thrown, and the others halted.

At that moment, two fire-balls were hurled among them. A second rider fell from his mount, slain, as I learned later, by a stone from Delhir's sling. By then, the other reivers and rafneyen were milling about in confusion.

As two more fire-balls dropped in their midst, the confusion turned to panic. Back they all streamed toward Alunsward. The pack-rafneyen fled away downhill, but the riders poured in through the gateway.

'Quick! Quick! Shut the gates!' came a call in French from someone. Immediately four of the rafenu-riders leapt down from their saddles to obey.

At that moment, prematurely, the trap was sprung. Whether some Owlsgard man was seen too soon by one of Casimir's men or whether one reacted too quickly in excitement, I am not sure; but suddenly, there were shouts and the reivers were being attacked from all sides.

In terms of numbers, the fight was pretty even. However, the reivers were already demoralized and our people had the advantage of surprise. I saw Drakht Belineg leap at a rafenu-rider and pluck him from his saddle; I saw Avran hurling himself, sword in hand, upon another rider; and I saw the

311

reivers who had dismounted striving, too late, to remount their beasts before the men of Owlsgard caught up with them. Then, remembering my duty, I seized my bow and set arrow to string.

Amid the confusion, the six horsemen — Casimir and his particular guard — had kept together. Moreover, they had not ventured far within the gates before the attack was launched. Now they were turning in flight — and the gates were still open!

Hastily I loosed an arrow and had the satisfaction of seeing one chain-mail-clad figure tumble from his horse. Sir Robert had run some way down the steps; as the others rode by, he leapt down upon one of them, he and the rider struggling briefly before the horse threw them both off and fled. I loosed a second time, but missed; and it was an arrow of Bernard's that emptied a third saddle. However, Casimir and his two remaining cohorts rode down two Owlsgard men that tried to oppose them and passed out of the gate, four rafenu-riders following.

I seized my arrows, stuffed them back into the quiver and, forgetful of my injured knee, scurried down the stone steps. As I reached their foot, Sir Robert, who had finished his opponent, came up to me.

'Quickly! Out of the gate!' he cried. 'I hope and believe we'll find Rahir outside with our rafneyen. Hasten, now!'

Swiftly he ran before me, while I hobbled after as best I might. Yes indeed, the wizard, Rahir and Delhir were already approaching on rafenu-back, followed by six other beasts, Galahad and Lancelot among them.

Our three friends did not pause, but set off immediately down the hill in pursuit of the fleeing brigands. However, Sir Robert and I were soon mounted and following. Down the hill we cascaded, Galahad making me very aware how he hated such a rapid descent — and into another turmoil of action, for the reivers had ridden straight into their pursuers of Ralphsland.

In that brief affray, the brigands did not seek quarter. Soon all were slain — all save one. Casimir cut down two of the men of Ralphsland and, spurring his horse viciously, rode through the press of men, out past the beast-pen and away.

312

Immediately Sir Robert, who had already slain another of the horsemen, rallied the rest of us in pursuit. We were joined by six of the Ralphsland men, the rest continuing up the hill toward Alunsward.

It proved a long chase. We could see Casimir far in front of us, well out of arrow-shot, but we could not catch up with him. His horse was a splendid beast and, even after so long a ride and so much mishandling, possessed such remarkable endurance that it had not tired.

Back across the saddle below Alunsward we rode, at a speed vastly greater than during our careful crossing of yesterday, and up onto the ridge along which the Owlsgard folk had been driven.

Quite why Casimir took that route I do not know, though I puzzled over the question as we rode along. He cannot have been hoping to find refuge with Sir Gabriel Jacklyn for, if doing so, he would surely have sought the Marolane valley. Was he aiming to ride down from the ridge, as soon as he was able, and to seek refuge in the forests? Yet neither the Earl of the Deerlands nor the Earl of Marcanlon would knowingly have given him sanctuary.

Whatever his reasons, Casimir chose to follow the ridge crest, under ever-darkening skies and amid the mutter of distant thunder. He could be glimpsed whenever lightning flashed to the south, as a dark shape fleeing along the skyline.

His lead was at first quite long. However, when we had gained the ridge crest also, we approached closer to him minute by minute. I believe, indeed, that we would have caught him eventually; in a straight race on level ground, rafneyen are faster than horses and our mounts were much less tired than his. Yet a different fate awaited Casimir.

Suddenly, he and we became aware that other riders were coming eastward along the ridge toward us. Caught between his pursuers and the approaching party, Casimir reined up and gazed about him wildly. Then, desperately, he urged his horse directly down that steep southern flank of the granite ridge.

We raced onward to the point where he had halted. Indeed, some of us might well have ridden down after him, despite the dangers of the descent. Wisely, however, Sir Robert held up his gloved hand to arrest us from doing so.

313

Casimir was riding downward at great speed and, for a while, was going well, keeping to the turf and avoiding those dangerously smooth outswells of granite. Yet, as we had learned yesterday, that turf was extremely thin.

Abruptly a whole sheet of it peeled away from the granite, crumpling and shredding under his horse's hooves. With a neigh of terror, the horse lost its footing and fell sideways, tumbling down the hill.

Casimir's foot was caught in the stirrup; he was dragged, screaming, after and then under his horse. A flash of lightning gave us a brief glimpse of man and beast rolling down in a mass together. Then they were hidden by the slope of the hill, gone into darkness and silence.

Since there seemed no point in risking the lives of others to try to aid one so evil, Casimir was not sought until next morning. The unfortunate horse was broken-backed and dead; the body of Casimir, bruised and battered almost into shapelessness, lay beneath it. Curiously enough, though, his head was little damaged. On his dead face was an expression, not of pain, but of such stark fear that men said he must have seen the gates of Hell opening to receive him.

Delhir Ravatseng was quite sure that he had.

Chapter Thirty-two

The Cleansing of Cat Crags

As we gazed down the hill slope, the other party had joined us. However, it was only when the rolling horse and rider had vanished from view that I became truly aware of them. Their leader spoke first.

'Well now, who was that, Messer Obiran? One of those accursed robbers, I presume, since you were pursuing him?' He was a slight but forceful-seeming person, with thinning hair and a forwardly-thrusting beard that had been dark but was now flecked with white.

'Their leader himself,' answered the wizard. 'You knew him, I think, Sir Samuel — Casimir of Chattaine. He has done you grave injury, but he can never do so again.'

'Grave injury indeed! When your man Narel Evateng came up with us, I could scarce believe his terrible tidings. Yet, when I saw the burnt-out ruins of our castle and village, I was forced to do so. Tell me quickly; what has become of the rest of my people? And my daughter?'

'Some few of your people have died, I regret to say, but most live yet and are well enough. The women and children, and the older men, are safe in Becketsward, with all the property that Casimir had made them bear away for him. As for your daughter, she is with them and safe also.'

Sir Samuel Saville drew in his breath and released it in a long sigh. 'I thank God to hear it. After seeing the ruin of our little settlement, I came close to losing hope. But what has been the fate of the rest of those robbers? And that vile creature Pierre Paradis, whom I trusted so foolishly? Most bitterly do I rue the day that ever I allowed him within my gates!'

'Some of Casimir's men are fled and some taken; some remain to be smoked out from their retreat in Cat Crags;

315

but the greater part of those who raided Owlsgard are slain, Paradis among them. Here is the rain at last; let us be moving. I will recount to you the story as we go.'

So the two parties became one and, as we rode back along the granite ridge, the events of the last two days were told and told again. Not only was Sir Samuel eager to hear the tale, but also Narel Evateng and the other men of Owlsgard who had ridden with Sir Samuel. Among them was his elder son Dominic, a darker-haired replica of his father; his lady and younger son had remained for safety in Amsetch, where Narel had found them all.

Narel Evateng himself, after two such long rides at so great a pace, was soon nodding in his saddle. I felt almost as tired and left it to Sir Robert and Rahir to repeat the story of our doings to those who were out of earshot of Vedlen Obiran's recounting. It seemed to me an even longer ride back; nor was it an enjoyable one, for the rain fell steadily. Yet our spirits remained high, for had we not achieved all that we set out to do?

It was late in the evening when, looking up toward Alunsward from the saddle of the ridge, I saw again the bright spark of flames, though this time the beast-pen was unlit. When, at long last, we rode up to the gates of Alunsward, we found them still standing widely open. Now, however, there were torches burning all about the bailey and a bright fire before the keep. The men of Owlsgard and Ralphsland were singing and making merry in the fire-glow. Though the rain was still falling steadily, such was their mood that no-one seemed to mind.

They were on watch for us, however, and surrounded us with greetings and eager questions. Sir Samuel's return was welcomed with joy by his people. Among the crowd were Bernard and Avran; Avran's eyes were only for me.

'You're back, friend — excellent!' Then, in quick concern: 'Yet you seem very weary. Is all well with you, Simon?'

'Oh yes, I'm tired; it was a long ride. But otherwise I'm well and glad to see that you're safe. Were many killed in the fight?'

'Four of Owlsgard died and three were injured; Felun has been tending them. Three men of Ralphsland were slain also, alas. But, of the reivers, none remains alive; the Owlsgard men were not inclined to be merciful. As for me, I'm fine and flourishing — and most thankful to know you're uninjured. What happened to that foul creature Casimir?'

'He must be dead also, I'm sure,' and I told Avran what had happened. Then, at long last, I dismounted and, after giving Galahad the caresses he merited, sent him off to browse. Many other rafneyen were feeding about and within the bailey and I noted several horses tethered in sheltered places among the long grasses.

Avran conducted me over to the fire and found for me bread, meat and wine of a strange, aromatic sort. Before I had eaten, however, I was beckoned over to be introduced to Sir Henry Harbayne, Lord of Ralphsland — grey-haired, grey-bearded and as lean and keen as a gaze-hound — and a second time, more formally, to Sir Samuel Saville. The latter seized me by the hand.

'Vedlen has told me how you rescued my daughter, how you slew that dastardly seneschal of mine, and of your part in the saving of my people. I cannot hope to repay you for your services and courtesies, but I shall not forget them.'

For my part, I shall never forget the note in his voice and his smile, as he spoke to me thus. It gave me an ampler reward than ever I deserved.

Soon I was seeking my blankets and a sheltered place in the lee of a ruined wall. As I fell away into sleep, the men were still singing and carousing round the fire, their joy at the day's victories undampened by the rain.

Maybe some men woke with the dawn next morning, but I was not one of them. Indeed, I suspect that the only ones who were about early were those few hardy souls who had continued celebrating right through the night. When I was awakened, it was to find the sun shining and the sky blue and clear; the sun's height told me that the time was almost noon.

It was again Rahir who had awakened me. His brown face was beaming. 'There was no cause to rouse you so soon today, Simon. Indeed, I was not about early myself! Yet I thought that, having slept past breakfast, you'd not wish to sleep past luncheon also. Moreover, I'm needing to look again at that knee of yours.'

So he did, expressing satisfaction at its condition before rebandaging it. We talked of small matters while he gave it attention. When he was finishing, I asked idly: 'What are the plans for today, then, Rahir?'

'Why, we'll be finishing our task by riding on Cat Crags. While that evil roost remains undestroyed, there's too much chance of other carrion birds settling in these hills; so we go to lop it away. The task should not prove a great one, with Casimir the Cat and most of his kittens accounted for already.'

Our riding forth was cheerful. A small garrison, under the charge of Alban Daintree of Owlsgard, was left in Alunsward. The wounded were sent away to Becketsward, in charge of two of the Ralphsland men who had themselves suffered slight injuries. The rest of us, wizard's men, men of Owlsgard and Ralphsland, all set off together up the track northwestward.

We made no great haste, since we knew that Cat Crags was already invested by the men of Pochardsvale. Nor, indeed, was it a track on which haste was desirable, for it was of the very roughest and led through the most difficult country I had yet experienced. The rocks appeared to be shales or slates, sometimes hard and sticking upward in irregular masses, sometimes crumbly and decayed to form pools or sudden, deep bogs that had to be skirted with care. Within the pools and bogs, myriad frogs, toads and other slimy things seemed to have their habitation; their cachinnating choruses sounded loud in our ears. In sheltered places, thorny bushes grew in profusion and a few misshapen trees reminded us of the strength of winter winds hereabouts.

We made many descents and many climbs as we followed the winding track but, in general, we were mounting ever higher into the hills. After nearly three hours of riding we saw before us, upon the highest crest of all, the fortress of Cat Crags.

It was a simple enough structure, a circular tower-keep set upon a high, narrow ridge; but its situation made it almost impregnable. On its southern and western sides and, as I was to learn, on its northern side also, the ridge fell away

318

into steep cliffs, crowned by tall, machicolated walls that were overseen by a single western tower. On the eastern side, where the ridge narrowed, it had been excavated away into a deep slot, crossed by a drawbridge beyond which loomed twin defensive towers. The whole fortification was constructed of slabs of purplish-grey slate. Rising as it did from cliffs of similar character, it seemed more a natural phenomenon, a rugged growth from the rock itself, than a product of man's labour.

On a flat place some way to the east of the gatehouse, and safely out of arrowshot, the men of Pochardsvale had made their camp. There the main group of Sir Cuthbert Reddlestone's force was waiting at leisure. However, they bore arms and were ready to leap into action at any call from the guards watching the castle.

As we approached, the Lord of Ralphsland, the wizard, Sir Robert and Sir Samuel moved into the lead. It was Sir Cuthbert himself who came forward to meet them. He was a large man, clad in chain armour from head to foot, with a surcoat of white bearing the device of a black tower atop a scarlet rock (the latter in punning reference, I presumed, to his surname; 'red rock', Reddlestone). Swinging from his waist, in a silver-chased scabbard, was a massive sword of the two-handed type which was now becoming rare but which his mighty thews permitted him to wield with ease. His hair and moustache were silver grey, his cheeks rather jowly, and he had a look of arrogance that I misliked. However, his greeting was courteous enough.

'My Lord of Ralphsland, Sir Samuel and Messer Obiran, welcome to you! We have prepared some small refreshment for your men and yourselves; may I beseech you to join us? My soldiers will ensure that the residual rats in this bleak rathole do not venture forth while we eat; but indeed, they show little evidence of courage.'

A considerable feast was awaiting us, laid out on great wooden platters on trestle tables. There were roasted ducks; great fishes of a sort unknown to me, each cooked, boned and skinned; haunches of some sort of venison; and a variety of fruits and vegetables, some familiar but most unfamiliar. Though Sir Cuthbert had made his way in haste to Cat Crags, he had managed to arrange an ample provisioning!

We ate better than we had done in many days, the men of Pochardsvale serving us and cross-questioning us eagerly about the downfall of Casimir. They were jubilant at this, for he had been a menace to all who desired to live peacefully in or about the Stoney Mountains.

They were contemptuous about the garrison remaining in Cat Crags Castle. 'Only a handful of soldiers, most of 'em old or feeble; and mayhap a few women and children. Your master the wizard will frighten them out briskly enough. There's no courage in 'em.'

That latter judgement was soon to be tested. As the afternoon was ending, Drakht Belineg was sent as emissary, to speak to the men in the fortress. He was conducted up to the castle by two men of Pochardsvale, one bearing the triangular white flag which, throughout Rockall, signifies a desire for peaceful parley and the other carrying a slim trumpet. As they neared the moat before the castle gate, the trumpeter blew five shrill blasts, then lowered his instrument and waited.

There seemed some hesitation within the castle. It was only after a moderately lengthy delay that the drawbridge was lowered and two men ventured forth. Each wore, over chain mail, the yellow surcoat with the leaping cat that Casimir had chosen as his device. Otherwise, they were very different. The first was as broad and swarthy as the generality of Casimir's men but the second, who seemed the more senior, was thin and clerkly. It was he whom Drakht addressed.

'I speak for my lords of Pochardsvale, Ralphsland and Owlsgard and for the mighty wizard Vedlen Obiran. Know that your Lord Casimir is dead and his men slain also, in just retribution for their treacherous ravaging of Owlsgard. As you must perceive, your castle is closely invested by forces overwhelmingly greater than those remaining to you. You may choose between surrendering peacefully, in which case your lives will be spared, or being forced out from this last refuge, in which case you are in gravest peril. Which do you choose: to yield or to be destroyed?'

I did not hear the response, but I gathered it must have been a request for time for consideration. The two men withdrew onto the drawbridge. The thin man seemed, from

320

his gestures, to be urging surrender; the other, to be urging resistance.

At length they returned over the bridge. Unexpectedly, it was the burly man who spoke, in a growling tone that carried almost as well as Drakht's mighty voice. I cannot attempt to reproduce his accent, but his words were clear.

'We defy you! You cannot seize Cat Crags and we are amply provisioned. You may lay siege, of course. However, you will become weary as the days pass and you spend your time profitlessly. Be wise and leave now! Cat Crags has never been taken, nor will it be taken.'

Drakht laughed. 'You are quite wrong. Not only will it be taken, but taken swiftly! Very soon you will be ceasing to wish to stay in that wretched bolthole. When you desire to capitulate, you must come forth bearing a brown flag — and perhaps, even then, your lives may be spared. Adieu for now!' And he turned away.

The thin man seemed disconcerted and again hesitant, but his burly companion seized him by the arm and hurried him back into the castle. They vanished from view and the drawbridge was lifted swiftly.

As Drakht and his companions walked back toward us, I chanced to be standing close enough to Sir Cuthbert Reddlestone to hear his words to Vedlen Obiran. 'Are you quite confident that you can do this thing, wizard?'

'Oh, yes.' There seemed a gleam of amusement in Vedlen's brown eyes — for honey-brown they seemed, in the setting sun's light. 'With a wind blowing steadily from the southwest, as now it is, and with the help of your men, I can guarantee that those brigands will soon be eager to forsake their refuge.'

The task we were set was one that surprised most of us, though Drahkt and the three Ravatsengs — Hebehir, who had ridden to Rewlenscrag, had rejoined us now — knew well enough what the wizard had in mind. We were instructed to collect all the dead branches that we could obtain from thornbush or tree and bring them to be heaped on the southwestern side of the castle.

Since there seemed only the slightest of chances that any flames would reach high enough to trouble with their heat those within the castle, and none at all that so solid a stone structure could be caused to burn, I did not understand this.

I comprehended it even less when I saw that the burnable materials were being piled, not immediately beneath the castle walls but on the further side of the narrow Swiftling valley. Certainly the smoke from the burning would carry into the castle; but what would that avail, save to cause some small annoyance to its inmates?

However, like the others, I worked with a will at collecting the branches. We hacked through plant-stems and tree-roots with our swords, cursed as thorns pricked our fingers, and carried back as much as we might manage, on journey after journey, while the sun went down behind the southern hill-ridges and the light dwindled.

The combustible materials we had assembled were arranged into two piles. A long, hayrick-high mound was made on the upper slope of the southern flank of the Swiftling valley and a much larger mound of reserve fuel piled on the ridge-top behind, from which the fire would be fed as it burned down. After heaping up all the branches we could bring, we rested awhile and flasks of beer were circulated. Our throats were so dry by then as to make this refreshment particularly welcome.

I had wondered if the wind might drop with the coming of night, but it did not. Instead, it waxed stronger and gustier. This was the time of the dark of the moon, but the stars were bright and the clouds few. I glimpsed a nighthawk overhead and, remembering Sandastre, thought it a good omen.

Then, suddenly, I saw a series of pinpoints of light. Sparks were being struck from flints to set the fire alight. Soon the heaped-up branches were beginning to burn. However, they were damp and green; they would produce much smoke, but little flame.

In the slight extra brightness of their burning, I noticed that four men were walking along the lee side of the smoking pile and casting onto it handfuls of some sort of powder. Surely the lean one must be Narel Evateng and the burly one Hebehir? Then the other two must be Hebehir's two cousins.

As they passed by, the smoke from the burning seemed to increase and to take on a yellowish tinge. It was blowing across the valley in ample billows and reaching the castle, for sure; yet the change in the smoke's colour was not spectacular and I did not believe it would frighten those within.

After a while, the flames burned brighter as they used up their fuel. I was one of those who carried more branches over to feed the fire. I passed Rahir who, with the other three, was ambling leisurely along and throwing more powder onto the burning twigs; he gave me a smile and a wink.

As I cast my load into the flames, one branch fell short. I bent to pick it up and toss it after the others. Just at that moment the wind shifted and the smoke eddied a little. I caught a whiff of it and instantly began gasping and coughing. What a revolting smell! Hastily I ran back upslope, coughing and coughing till my eyes were streaming.

As I did so, the wizard's words of last night came back to my mind. Had he not said he would smoke out the remaining robbers? I had thought he had been speaking figuratively; but no, he was proclaiming the exact truth!

After blinking several times I contrived to clear my running eyes, though I was still shaken by coughs. As I looked back, I saw that Drakht Belineg and the wizard himself were both walking along the line of smoking branches, each casting into them some different, lighter-coloured powder.

The result, this time, was much more spectacular. Each grain was transformed into a brightly burning, almost agonizingly white spark, to be carried with the smoke and to rain down into the castle. Soon it seemed as if a torrent of light was flowing across the Swiftling valley, to bathe the castle walls and towers in a radiance brighter than the full moon.

This strange, magical method of attack was having its effect. Even here, across the valley, I could hear desperate cries and the noise of frantic movement from within the castle. Did I hear the sound of fighting also? I was not sure. Then, as I returned downslope bearing more of the dead branches, I heard a trumpet sound once, twice, thrice from the hilltop behind me. Instantly the wizard raised and let fall his right arm in signal; and he and his five men stepped back from the fire.

A man-at-arms of Pochardsvale was running down toward us. 'They have yielded!' he shouted, hoarsely but exultantly.

323

'The drawbridge is lowered and they're showing the brown flag. They'll be coming forth in a moment — if they can manage it, for I've never heard such coughings and gaspings!'

After that whiff, I could sympathize with them. Yet I found myself laughing at the ease with which the impregnable Cat Crags Castle had been taken. I waited till Rahir caught up with me and found he was chuckling too.

'Simple enough, wasn't it, Simon?'

'Simple indeed! But how was the trick worked, and why could we not have used it in the taking of Alunsward?'

'Ask me not how 'tis done! Aye, we performed a similar trick once before, long since, to rout out a murderous band of thieves from their forest hiding-place in Dakalet; yet I've no idea what potions we were using. Some strange, alchemical preparations, I don't doubt, and from the Trident Mountains. The first needs a strong, steady wind to carry its odours, while the fuel must be green and moist. Mayhap that's why we couldn't employ the same trick at Alunsward, for there'd been no recent rain; as you'll recall, the rain came afterward. The second preparation you have to be much more careful with. It's strange stuff indeed; if your fingers are wet, it'll burn them! We keep it very well wrapped and very dry, you may be sure. But no, I don't know at all what either of those powders contains. I'm not even certain our master does, wise though he be.'

As the Pochardsvale men had deduced, the garrison of Cat Crags Castle was not large; some twenty-five men, fifteen or so unhappy and worn-looking women and a few ragged children. All of them were coughing as if their hearts would burst and, once again, I felt sorry for them. I trusted that neither the Owlsgard people, nor any others, would desire to wreak vengeance upon such pitiful figures and I was glad to find that they did not.

The burly man was not among those who surrendered. I was to learn later that, attempting to prevent the capitulation, he had been struck down and slain by his frantic comrades. That was no source of regret for, though courageous, he had been one of the Cat's closest henchmen and very evil.

The others were treated well enough. After the lean man, Casimir's seneschal — and chosen for that office, I think, because he was too weak-spirited to be disobedient to his

324

master — had surrendered the keys and he and the other men had set down their weapons, each was allowed to seat himself on the ground and was given a cooling drink. Afterwards, however, the men were fettered and marched away.

In contrast, the women and children were given moistened cloths with which to lave themselves and invited to eat and drink at will, from the ample remains of our feast. Though three or four of the women seemed as wild and wicked as the reivers themselves, all were treated with like courtesy. Some, who had been captured from settlements in the hills or villages in the forests and plains, were weeping with joy at their release. The tales they told of what had been done to them made us furious again at Casimir's crimes; it was as well that the last of his cohorts had been removed already from our reach.

About their ultimate fate, I should perhaps write briefly. Needless to say, the women and children were all freed, to go wherever they wished; though most chose to go at first to Becketsward. As for the surviving reivers, it was decreed that all — including the six captured earlier — would be taken in chains back to Owlsgard and made to labour in its rebuilding. When that work was done, they would be compelled to assist for two further years in tilling and planting the fields of Owlswatch and harvesting its crops. Then, if they had worked well, they would be allowed to go their way in freedom. It seemed to me, remembering the sentences of execution meted out in our realm of England for crimes much less than theirs, a very merciful treatment; but that is the way of Rockall.

As for the rest of us, why, we built a large bonfire on the hilltop with the other branches we had collected. We sat about it, drinking or eating, singing or talking, men of Pochardsvale and Ralphsland, Owlsgard folk and wizard's men all intermingled, till the first hues of dawn were tinting the southern horizon. Then we slept well and long.

Chapter Thirty-three

THE DAYS IN RALPHSLAND

'Whatever can have become of Amos Sloly?'
We were riding down the Swiftling track, on our
way to Becketsward at last, when I voiced that
question. 'At last', I write, for three full days had elapsed
since the remainder of Casimir's robbers had been smoked
out from their roost. The first day had been an idle one,
for the castle had remained too odoriferous to be entered.
Our only solemn occupation had been a thanksgiving for
victory, Sir Samuel Saville leading our prayers; afterwards,
there had been more feasting and singing. Brisk overnight
winds having done their cleansing work, we had entered Cat
Crags on the second morning and searched it very thoroughly.
Though Casimir's brigandage had gained for his men and he
many unmerited luxuries, it seemed to me a dismal place. It
was very dirty and afforded nothing of the sense of prideful
community that characterizes any ordinary English castle. Of
its dungeons and the sad relics they contained, I will not
speak, though it is in vain that I have tried to put them
from memory.

The castle could not readily be burned or levelled and
was too important a strong-point to be left unguarded.
Moreover, there was reasonable pastureland for rafneyen in
the Swiftling valley and good prospects for hunting and the
planting of crops in the terrain to the north. It was decided
that families from Becketsward, Pochardsvale and, yes, even
Owlswatch be invited to settle there and form a new community. For the moment, it would be garrisoned by men
from all those three places, under the charge of John Stanton
of Owlsgard, who was unmarried and willing to become its
seneschal.

The loot that Casimir had accumulated was divided up,

327

much of it being allocated as compensation to the Owlsgard folk, the rest apportioned between Sir Henry Harbayne of Ralphsland and Sir Cuthbert Reddlestone of Pochardsvale for the use of their communities. Here in Rockall, nobles did not seize such plunder for themselves, as would have been usual in France or Britain.

Sir Cuthbert and the majority of his men were returning to Pochardsvale, whilst most of the men of Owlsgard had set off directly homeward on rafneyen that had once been Casimir's, taking with them the twenty-five prisoners. Moreover, the Lord of Ralphsland had sent some of his men, with the women and children from Cat Crags, off to Becketsward two days earlier. Hebehir Ravatseng travelled with them, to provide medical attention if necessary.

Only a comparatively small party, therefore, rode down the Swiftling valley that day. There were some thirty soldiers of Ralphsland and six men of Owlsgard, Bernard the archer and Sir Samuel's son among them. All of them, plus two dozen laden pack-rafneyen, were following behind Avran and me. Beside us were the Ravatseng brothers and, in the van, the Lord of Ralphsland, with the wizard, Sir Samuel and Sir Robert.

The three knights were talking lightheartedly, but the wizard was silent and seemed asleep in his saddle. Indeed, since his mount was entirely trustworthy and since he had a capacity for complete relaxation when opportunity occurred, it is probable that Vedlen Obiran *was* asleep.

'Amos Sloly?' Avran was echoing my question, his surprise evident. 'Why of course, he and the pack-rafneyen should have caught us up long since. Mayhap he stayed at Alunsward; we left a small garrison there, didn't we?'

'Aye, we did.' Rahir Ravatseng was speaking now and sounding unexpectedly grim. 'But Amos is not there, for our master sent Narel back yesterday to ask. And so, this morning, our master ordered a proper search to be made. Narel and Drakht are riding back toward Owlsgard, to see if they can find our absent friend.'

Those last words had so ironic a ring that I asked: 'Why, Rahir, what could be wrong? Likely enough Amos has stayed close to Owlsgard; perhaps he felt it safest. Whatever else *could* have happened?'

As I spoke, however, I was recalling my last glimpse of Amos and his strange secret smile. What had it meant?

'Well, 'tis possible that he and all our belongings might have finished up in Blackhill Castle; Sir Gabriel Jacklyn wouldn't mind putting his hands on other folks' property. Yet I hardly think so. For myself, I believe Amos has taken the most valuable of our goods and skipped away with his loot.'

Avran was as shocked at that idea as I. 'Oh, surely not, Rahir! Why, Amos is such a cheerful soul; always smiling, always so eager to help.'

'And always so careful not to miss anything that might give him a bit of profit for himself,' Rahir added dryly. 'For my part, I've never been so sure of that one.'

'He was wholly self-seeking.' Delhir's observations were so few that they came always as a surprise. 'He did not merit our master's trust.'

I found myself resenting these unexpected criticisms of one who, after all, was an Englishman like myself. 'Why, then, was he employed? Surely our master would not have taken into his service someone who was false-hearted? And surely he would not have left his tents, his gold and his other possessions in the charge of a man upon whom he could not rely?'

'Amos Sloly was useful to our master, of course.' It was Rahir who was answering. 'He spoke the English of your people who have settled here in Rockall. He could gain their trust easily and he gave them confidence when we were treating their ailments or injuries. Yet, as to Amos being left in charge of the packs, you must remember that our master sets little value upon such material things. Consider instead that, when he was seeking to rescue the Owlsgard folk and needed comrades whom he could trust, our master preferred to leave Amos Sloly behind.'

Such an inversion of my argument was disconcerting, yet it appeared perfectly plausible. I had come to understand and respect Vedlen Obiran's dedication and selflessness; though he enjoyed his luxuries, they were not important to him. Avran was impressed also, yet he remained unconvinced.

'Yet Amos is so jovial, so willing, so good-natured . . . No, I cannot believe him to be a thief, Rahir. He must have encountered some mischance — some accident or raid — surely?'

'I pray that you're right and I'm wrong, Avran friend. Our master can ill afford to lose so much. I don't think Sir Robert would be best pleased, either, to find his armour and his store of gold gone. Well, no doubt Narel and Drakht will discover all that's to be learned.'

We rode on for a while in silence. Soon we were passing on our left the stone bridge that spanned, in a double arch, the waters of the Swiftling and the Marolane just above their confluence. To the right of the bridle-path was the thicket where the men of Ralphsland had waited to ambush Casimir's men, yet had succeeded only in turning them back. It was formed of bushes of a type I had not seen, with dark green, shining leaves of oval shape, dense enough to afford excellent concealment. The tip of each twig had opened into a seven-petalled flower, each petal having a blush-pink base and a white tip.

The sight of these blossoms caused a stir of excitement among the Ralphsland men. Apparently these bushes, which were called saints-wreath, flowered only rarely. The men were sure that the flowers had opened in celebration of Casimir's downfall. Eagerly they broke off branches to carry to Becketsward.

Beyond the bridge, the bridle-path climbed slowly up the hillside between irregular crags of slate. Our rafneyen's hooves skittered perilously on the broken shards that had fallen from these crags onto the path, though none of the beasts lost balance. After an hour of difficult riding, the slaty terrain ended, the bushes faded out and we passed onto a swelling, grassy hillside, much like the ridge on which we had ridden from Owlsgard. There were rafneyen feeding among the few, low bushes, under the watchful eyes of herd-boys who shouted cheerful greetings to us.

With arrival home imminent, the Ralphsland men began chanting a carol of joy and victory. The chorus was simple; I joined in and Avran, producing his pommer, managed to tootle the tune also. Thus cheerfully were the last few leagues passed, as we rode over the round hill and down to Becketsward.

Its castle was, like the two others we had seen in the

Stoney Mountains, relatively recent in date and simple in structure. A square tower-keep was set centrally in a bailey of no great size and quadrate plan, with mural towers at the four corners. On the northern side, the castle was protected also by granite cliffs and by the swift waters of the Belden Brook below; on the southern and eastern sides, by a deep, dry moat whose further flank had been set hedgehog-like with pointed stakes. A drawbridge led over this to the southeastern tower, which served also as gatehouse.

As we approached, still singing, there were responsive sounds of music and cheering. A crowd of men and women, with children excitedly cavorting and prancing among them, surged out over the bridge to welcome us. Happiest of all were the wives, sons and daughters of Owlsgard, many of whom were weeping with joy.

Soon the knights and the wizard — wide awake now and beaming — were garlanded with flowers, while posies were thrust beneath the front saddle-straps of each of us. We were riding slowly by then, as the press of people about us increased. Suddenly a garland was tossed over my own head and I saw that Lauretta was among the crowd.

'That is for you, my angel!' she cried. 'Halt your mount for a second; I am coming up beside you.'

As Galahad stopped at my thought and I made place for her, she scrambled up onto his back. She sat side-saddle before me, clinging on to me in a fashion that half-delighted, half-embarrassed me and chattering away to me in a babble of pleasure, as we rode through the arching gateway into the bailey of Becketsward.

Sir Samuel turned in his saddle to look back at us, but gave us only his smile. Avran, however, raised his eyebrows and winked at me, thereafter staring steadfastly ahead.

That evening we feasted in the great hall of Becketsward keep. Not such a large party was present. Many of the Ralphsland men had returned to their farms and families in the valleys west of Becketsward, while most of the Owlsgard folk and their new-found friends were celebrating around bonfires burning outside in the bailey. Apart from a few servants, therefore, there were only seventeen of us at that feast — the Lord of Ralphsland and his Lady, tall, grey and grave; their two handsome daughters (they had no son); the seneschal of Becketsward and his lady; Sir Samuel, Dominic and Lauretta; Vedlen Obiran and the three Ravatseng cousins; Sir Robert Randwulf, Avran and me; and, to our great pleasure, Felun Daretseng, whom we had not seen for six hectic days.

With him, during the earlier part of the evening, was the small boy whom he had adopted or who had adopted him — it was hard to tell which, for they showed great mutual affection. Later Felun took the boy off to bed and returned, a little sheepishly I thought, to rejoin us.

While we ate the talk was merry enough; but, when the dishes had been removed and the wine was circulating, Sir Henry Harbayne spoke more gravely.

'For the destroying of your village and castle, Sir Samuel, I am in part to blame, as you are yourself in part to blame. Yes, yes, I know we have just obliterated an evil; but that evil was allowed to fester too long. Each of us has ruled his own small feoff in the Ferekar Naur and been content with that. Oftentimes we have disputed our boundaries with neighbouring feofdoms, often we have traded with each other and sometimes we have enjoyed each other's hospitality; but that has been all. When Casimir made his first small raids on farms or barns, we chased the reivers away and watched our own bounds more carefully; we did no more. When he seized and devastated Alunsward, we expressed shock but we took no action. We learned of his other fell deeds in the lands to eastward and northward, but still we did nothing.'

'All true enough,' said Sir Samuel, 'but what could we have done?'

The fist of the Lord of Ralphsland smote the trestle table so mightily that goblets and flasks danced. 'Why, we ought to have co-operated then, as we are doing now! Alone, none of us was strong enough to extirpate the evil of Cat Crags; but if we men of goodwill had acted together, we could have done it long since. Yes, I recognize that Messer Obiran and his men have given us great assistance' — he inclined his head politely to the wizard — 'but if you, Sir Samuel, and I had combined our forces with those of Sir Cuthbert and our neighbours to west and north, we would have been easily able to destroy Casimir and his knaves. The Lord of Wildfell and Sir Hugh ap Llewellyn of Merlinward — they have suffered much from Casimir and would certainly have joined us. Sir Gabriel Jacklyn I mislike and mistrust — I know he traded with Cat Crags and I suspect that, on occasion, he lent aid to Casimir's misdeeds. Yet he would not have dared rally to the support of the Cat, had we others decided to act in concert. But no, we thought only of our own concerns. Thus it was that Owlsgard burned. Had that deed gone unavenged, Becketsward might have been next put to the flame, set as it is betwixt Cat Crags and Blackhill.'

As Sir Henry paused and sipped from his goblet, Sir Samuel nodded his head. 'Aye, you are right. And now we *are* acting together, a fact for which we of Owlsgard are profoundly grateful. Yet how must we proceed?'

'Why, we must form a league, an alliance of those willing to take action against future evils! We must establish a system of rapid alert against danger. We must agree to rally, not merely when all are threatened but when any one of us is threatened. Yes, I know we have our disagreements about land and water, grazing and hunting rights, but those can be settled readily enough, given goodwill. Casimir the Cat is dead and, I trust and believe, in Hell; but there are other Casimirs that will prey on us, if we afford them opportunity. We must ensure that they are given no opportunity. Such men must learn that evil deeds are followed by swift vengeance.'

Sir Samuel was nodding again. 'Your words are most wise, my friend. What, then, do you propose?'

'That we must gather to confer — and quickly. This day fortnight, let us say? I shall propose to Sir Cuthbert that we meet at Rewlenscrag, not here in Becketsward. You must understand, I do not wish to seem to be setting myself up as leader — and Sir Cuthbert can be, let us say, rather sensitive. If he concurs, then messages shall be sent out to the rulers of all the feofdoms in these hills; not just our western feofdoms, but to Falconward, Starkward and even to Amsetch, though I suspect the Lord of Amsetch may feel his feofdom too remote either to be aided by us or to aid us.'

'Even to Blackhill?' enquired Sir Samuel.

'Even to Blackhill; though I question whether Sir Gabriel will come or, if he does come, will wish to co-operate.'

The wizard had been listening intently, a smile on his face.

His eyes looked honey-brown and benign in the firelight. Now he spoke.

'My lord of Ralphsland, your idea is excellent; I congratulate you, most sincerely. If what you propose is carried through, then out of the evil of Casimir's deed there may spring a lasting good.'

In the days that followed, Avran and I enjoyed a pleasant and relaxing time in the lordship of Ralphsland. We continued to give aid to the wizard and his men in their physicianly or chirurgical tasks whenever it was required. However, that was seldom; the people of this realm were mostly healthy. Moreover, the folk of Owlswatch were recovering well from their ordeal. Indeed, the rest of them set off back to Owlsgard on the third day, under the charge of young Dominic Saville and with some skilled masons and carpenters along to aid in the rebuilding of the village and castle. Lauretta, Avran and I rode with the group to the Marolane ford three leagues upstream from Blackhill. There we were bidden an affectionate farewell. If Sir Gabriel Jacklyn's men witnessed the crossing — we were within his lands — they gave no sign, and we returned unmolested to Becketsward.

That evening, we learned that Sir Cuthbert Reddlestone had agreed to stage the gathering of the lords of the Ferekar Naur and proposed to celebrate it with a tournament. He had asked especially that Vedlen Obiran be present, a request immediately granted by the wizard.

That was good news, but the other news received that evening was much less so. It was brought by Bevis, Sir Samuel's rafenu-master at Owlsgard, who had arrived with five pack-rafneyen. These were bearing the wizard's tents and tent-furniture, found abandoned in a gully of the Stoney Mountains not far north of Owlsgard. Drakht Belineg and Narel Evateng had made that discovery. Unfortunately, since the storm that had followed our taking of Alunsward had washed away most traces, neither they nor a skilled hunter from Amsetch whom they had recruited to their service could make clear sense of what had happened.

Had Amos Sloly been captured, along with the pack-raf-neyen and the other possessions of the wizard and Sir

334

Richard, or had Amos jettisoned the more unwieldy items and fled with all he might conveniently steal? They could not decide. However, they were sure the rafneyen had gone away eastward, down into the valley of the Brunflow and away toward Riotte. Drakht and Narel had taken the recovered items to Owlsgard, then had ridden away to continue the search for Amos Sloly.

Avran was still inclined to give Amos the benefit of what small doubt remained. 'Perhaps he was ambushed,' my friend argued. 'The scouring of Cat Crags does not mean we have driven all evildoers from these hills.'

However, the discovery shook further my own diminished faith in my fellow countryman. I remembered again that strange smile of Amos's and recalled also that Trayad-in-Riotte was a trading post of the Mentonese, where a thief might dispose of whatever goods he had for sale. As for the Ravatseng brothers, they just nodded their heads in sad unsurprise.

A much more pressing problem for me was Lauretta. She regarded me as a romantic figure, a sort of knight-errant who had saved her from a cruel fate. Well, I didn't mind that. The trouble was that, quite evidently, she assumed a marriage between us to be the only proper ending to such a romance. In consequence, she was regarding me in an almost proprietorial fashion, a fact I found increasingly disturbing.

Now that we were ensconced in the castle, she was unwilling to allow Rahir Ravatseng to tend my still-troublesome knee, nor would she permit any servant to do so. Instead, each morning, she came to my chamber high in the keep and insisted on re-dressing it herself. I was grateful that Avran, who shared that chamber, was present on those occasions; I was not sure, however, that Lauretta was equally grateful.

An additional problem was that I found her both attractive and amusing. She was slim and graceful in movement, with brown eyes set in an oval face that was rarely in repose. Much more often it reflected vividly her mood of the moment — interest, enquiry, attention or, most commonly, a bubbling enjoyment of life. I liked Lauretta very much. However, though Sandarro might be far away, though I knew well that I might never see Ilven again, it was she who had my heart.

Yet I found it hard to repulse Lauretta's attentions and, weakly I fear, I made little attempt to do so.

Avran might justly have been angry, had he not known that my feelings for his sister remained unchanged. As it was, he was merely sorry for Lauretta and rather annoyed with me for not having the courage to break off our developing relationship — a relationship of which, to make matters yet worse, her father and mother so evidently approved.

Thus it was that I spent much of each day with Lauretta, while taking care never to be left alone in her company. On some days we went out riding, though always with Avran, Sir Robert or some others along; up onto the hill behind Becketsward, northward along the steep valley of the Belden Brook or westward into the broader vale of the Marolane, with its little riverside farms. At other times we would join groups of musicians under the castle walls. Lauretta and I would sing the old ballads and carols of England and she would teach me some of the new ones of Rockall, while Avran persuaded his pommer into following the melody and musicians of Ralphsland strummed citole and cittern or played plaintively on psaltery. On Saturday we wandered round the town's weekly market, inspecting the stalls of food and wine, admiring the cloths and tapestries brought from England and Gascony and the hawks and falcons sitting hooded and stiff in the sunshine. Once I was persuaded into a game of chess with Lauretta and had her laughing at my ineptitude. On another occasion, we sat in a crowd about a travelling storyteller, enthralled by his tales of ancient valour and entertained by his scandal from the courts of Herador and Kelcestre.

It was on the day before our departure to Rewlenscrag that I found myself at last alone with Lauretta. Somewhere outside the castle walls, Avran was again trying his skills of swordsmanship with Sir Robert and, no doubt, again finding himself outmatched by that wily warrior. The wizard was engaged with a difficult delivery, of which the Becketsward midwife had despaired; the Ravatseng brothers were aiding him. Of the whereabouts of our other friends I was not sure, but they were not in evidence.

So it was that I found myself sitting with Lauretta up on a stone seat atop the northwestern tower of Becketsward

Castle, looking out over the green valley of the Marolane, with the deeper green of the Great Marshes in the distance. Though the castle was humming with preparations for to-morrow's expedition to Rewlenscrag, we were not involved and the prospect before us was tranquil. I remember that Lauretta was looking at her most attractive, in a dress of green velvet, tight-bodiced and high-belted, her long dark hair combed to sleekness and capped by a crisp, white coif. She had been unusually quiet as we climbed the stair, but now she spoke with a sort of earnest desperation.

'Simon, it is time for a decision. You know that I am yours if you want me. My father likes you and knows he is in your debt. Should you choose to come to Owlsgard, you are certain of high honours from him. If you prefer to go on with a wandering life, well, I would go with you, with or without my father's consent; but I believe he would agree even to that. Whatever you want, I want, so long as I may be with you.'

I looked at her sadly. 'Lauretta, I have been afraid of this. My dear, I like you very much and I enjoy your company, you know that. However, things between us can go no further, for I am affianced to the sister of my friend Avran, to Princess Ilven of Sandastre.'

It was as if I had given her a buffet across the face. 'Say not so!' she faltered. 'Tell me it is not so, Simon: I cannot — I shall not — believe it!'

'Yet it *is* so, Lauretta. If you credit me not, then you must ask Avran.'

'If you so assure me, then I must believe you,' Lauretta said sadly, then, desperately: 'But you cannot truly love her, when you have left her so far behind; and oh, Simon, I love you so much. Cannot you forget her and . . . and be kind to me, even if you do not love me?'

Poor Lauretta's voice had a catch in it now and her eyes were a-brim with tears. She had dropped to her knees before me and was clutching my hands. My heart went out to her, yet what could I do?

'Oh Lauretta, I am so sorry,' I said. 'Be sure that I have no desire to hurt you. However, I'm afraid I do love Ilven and most certainly I did not wish to leave her. Were it not for a vow made ere I met her, I would never have left Sandastre.'

337

I tried to explain my quest for my father and brother. However, I do not think Lauretta understood, or even tried to understand. Suddenly her hands slipped from mine and she rose to her feet. When she spoke, her voice held a profundity of desperation that was heartrending.

'Well, you do not want me or need me, that is clear. Farewell – my angel!' Lauretta turned and ran sobbing down the stair, out of my view.

Indeed, I was not to see her again. She did not appear at dinner that evening. Next morning we learned that, along with two servants, she had fled away back to Owlsgard.

Chapter Thirty-four

THE QUARREL AT THE BUTTS

The castle of Rewlenscrag was the most impressive I had seen in the Stoney Mountains, not so much because of its design, for the keep was simply a square tower, as because of its position and colour. That keep was set upon a crag isolated by a deep, narrow ravine from the hill behind. The crag was so small in extent that the keep occupied its whole summit. The only approach was by a steep stair, without balustrades and cut straight into the rock. A broad terrace below the crag was enclosed by high, machicolated walls to form the bailey. Beyond that, the ground fell steeply again to the meadows of the Pochard River.

This was a splendid defensive site, sure enough; but, as I have remarked, the colour also was striking. The keep and fortifications were built of blocks of white marble veined with green, but the cliffs under the keep and beneath the curtain wall of the bailey were of a black rock in which tiny green crystals sparkled in the sunshine. Add to this the verdant green of the grass of the meadowlands and the sward and shrubs within the bailey, plus the brown of the wooden houses set against the bailey walls, and you have a scene of considerable colour. Nor was that an end to it. In and about the castle there were numerous tents, most dyed in bright hues and many with the banners of their owners displayed upon poles alongside. Nine tents, for the eight lords and the wizard visiting Rewlenscrag, were set in the bailey, whilst the many smaller tents that housed the lords' following were distributed about the meadows below. All in all, I have rarely viewed so brilliant a scene.

Eight lords I say; for indeed, the Lords of Amsetch and Blackhill had both elected to attend this rallying of the rulers of the Ferekar Naur. Soon I learned the heraldry of the eight realms and could pick out, by his surcoat, whence any man came.

The arms of Amsetch were simple enough; argent, a fess doubly cotized azure — a silver field traversed by a broad horizontal line of blue, with two narrower blue lines parallel to it on either side. The others were all more elaborate. The men of Merlinward bore the old Welsh symbol, which I read as gules, a dragon sejant erect or — a golden dragon on a field of red, and a fierce enough beast it looked, with barbed tail and protruding, forked tongue. The green surcoats of Wildfell depicted a wild man, naked save for a wreath of green leaves round his loins and very fierce-looking, brandishing a massive black club. The blue surcoats of Falconward depicted, fittingly enough, a falcon in jesses and bells, hoodless and with a writhing lizard clutched in its claws. That was more difficult to blazon, but I thought it must be azure, a falcon argent belled and jessed gules, preying on a lizard or. In similar canting fashion, the black surcoats of Starkward showed a silver castle set on a green hilltop, its stones neatly indicated. (Sable, a castle argent masoned sable, upon a hill vert.)

The friendly arms of Ralphsward, green again and bearing a running rafenu in gold, were familiar enough (vert, a rafenu courant or). The silver surcoats of Blackhill I regarded with proper mistrust, being moreover rather puzzled by their charge. Yes of course, the black mount meant Blackhill, but why was it surmounted by that unusual emblem of a scarlet lion stretched out horizontally, as if in sleep? Even when I had blazoned it carefully as argent, a lion jacent surmounting a mount sable, I missed the laborious canting reference to the name of its owner till Sir Robert pointed it out – 'jacent lion', Jacklyn. The lion, though stretched out, seemed to be watching through narrowed eyes; if its nobility did not make it a suitable emblem for Sir Gabriel, that shifty glance suggested him well enough!

The arms that caused me most pain, however, were the three owls on a blue field that symbolized the Savilles. Since his daughter's abrupt departure, Sir Samuel had continued to be perfectly courteous to me, but without the warmth of cordiality he had shown hitherto; and who could blame him? For my own part, I was missing Lauretta acutely. At one

340

moment, I was condemning myself as all sorts of a fool for allowing her to go out of my life. (After all, was it likely I'd ever find my way back to Sandarro and Ilven?) At the next, I was chiding myself for my lack of consideration in permitting her hopes to rise as they had done. Why had I not told her earlier of Ilven? What a brute I had been to her!

All the time, I was thoroughly unhappy, sometimes wanting to pour out confidences to my friend, at other times too surly to speak any word. For poor Avran, it must have been a difficult period; but he bore my ill-nature very well, as only the truest of friends will.

The wizard's men and we had another cause for unhappiness, in that we looked so tawdry amid all this splendour. For sure, the wizard's tent stood proudly amid the others in the bailey, its multitudinous cabalistic signs evoking awe in its beholders. However, the splendid purple livery we should have worn had been stolen, along with so much else. For Avran and me, it was not too bad; our Doriolupata cloaks, worn yellow side outermost, looked sufficiently colourful, even if they bore no charge to indicate our allegiance. The wizard's men, however, had only their worn brown jupons and hose to wear and were made decidedly dispirited thereby.

This was especially so because most folk at Rewlenscrag seemed to assume that a real wizard might, if he so cared, magick his followers into a more impressive garb. One who did not, their glances implied, must be only a second-class operator, a mere charlatan!

To add to our problems, Avran and I had too little to do. Vedlen Obiran and the eight lords of the Ferekar Naur were closeted together all day in a chamber high in the keep, while they argued out plans for a league of mutual defence. Before this could be done, they had need to agree on the fate of Cat Crags and Alunsward, now become a no-man's-land; on the exact boundaries of their lands; on hunting rights and fishing rights; and oh! on so much else . . . Felun Daretseng, who attended with the wizard, considered that Sir Cuthbert's invitation to Vedlen Obiran had proved a crucial factor in the negotiations. Again and again, the wizard was appealed to as adjudicator and was able always to find an acceptable route around an apparent impasse.

Our evenings were pleasant enough, for then we would all join together. Sometimes we met at banquets in the castle, sometimes to prepare and eat our own meals before the wizard's tent and sometimes, when the wizard was not present, to dine and drink in the cook-shops and ale-houses that had been set up in the meadow. During the daytime, the Ravatseng brothers had enough injured or sick people applying for treatment to keep them occupied, while Sir Robert was heavily involved in the planning of the tournament. Avran and I, however, were quite without tasks.

What we should have done, of course, was to set forth again on our quest. Our difficulty was that we were still without any clear idea where we should be heading. Beyond the northern mountains, yes; but by what road and in what direction? Those mountains, we had been told, were greater both in extent and altitude than those of the south and passes through them were few and difficult. It seemed advisable to wait till the Rewlenscrag council had ended and then, if all went well, to travel north to Reschora with our good friends the wizard and his men. Yet, if Amos Sloly were not found, would Vedlen Obiran be travelling north? We could not be sure.

So we occupied our hours as best we might. Though Avran cannot have found me an agreeable companion, depressed and irritable as I was, he stayed with me loyally throughout most of those long days. In view of the atmosphere of martial endeavour that prevails anywhere prior to a tournament, it was natural enough that we should exercise with our arms. Avran sought patiently to improve my swordsmanship, trying to impart to me the tricks Sir Robert had taught him. Indeed, my skill with that weapon did increase, though it would never match his own. I practised also with my throwing-knives, an exercise all the more necessary in that I had not done so for many weeks; and both of us went daily to the butts, to refurbish our skills with the long-bow. It was there that we ran into trouble.

The great hall of Rewlenscrag castle was large enough for most normal occasions, but much too small to contain the host that had assembled this time. After a first evening when Sir Cuthbert entertained only his fellow lords and the wizard, he had bidden to his table each night two or three of the lords, along with their principal followers. Since the combination of invitees had been varied nightly, we came quickly to meet men and women from each of the little realms of the Stoney Mountains; and pleasant enough most of them were.

There were exceptions, however. One of them, most unfortunately, was Fulk Reddlestone, Sir Cuthbert's eldest son. He was quite as big a man as his father, with huge shoulders that hunched forward, a mane-like mass of yellow hair, light blue eyes as bright and unfeeling as sapphires, and full lips set into a perpetual curl of contempt.

When introduced to me, Fulk was merely uninterested and faintly condescending. However, when Avran was presented under his proper title of Prince of Sandastre, Fulk registered a sort of angry surprise. His handclasp had been of the briefest and most token kind. Afterwards, I heard him whisper to his neighbour some comment about the ease with which one might claim high rank in a realm of which no-one had heard. Unhappily Avran was listening also, for I saw his flush of anger.

On subsequent nights when we dined in the castle, Fulk addressed not a word to Avran and me, but his whispered comments about us to his neighbours at table, their amused glances and their titters, had several times irritated me and brought my volatile friend dangerously close to losing his temper.

For Fulk had his own particular associates among the sons of the lords of the Ferekar Naur and their followers. His younger brother Berenger seemed ever in fawning attendance upon him, while Humphry Stethren, scion of the Lord of Starkward, and Aldwyn Ennerling, the son of its seneschal, were almost as constant and admiring.

A more surprising associate, and certainly a new one, was Hubert Jacklyn of Blackhill. He was a youth as dark, lean and ever-smirking as his father and, in my judgement, quite as untrustworthy. He seemed at once to irritate and to amuse Fulk, stirring the bigger youth into brief anger at one moment and, at the next, pacifying him with honeyed words or provoking him into laughter by some barbed witticism. I felt that I disliked Hubert even more than Fulk. Young Reddlestone was merely a boor, but young Jacklyn was evidently a self-seeking mischiefmaker.

Thus it was that I felt disquiet when, on the eighth day at Rewlenscrag and the seventh of our archery exercises, I noticed that Fulk and his four cronies had joined the watching crowd. Most of the archers, from whatever lordship, were friendly enough and, on that day, we chanced to be matching our skills with those of two archers of Starkward. We had shot at the target already from a relatively short distance — about eighty yards — and had all shot well, our four arrows clustering about the gold. Now we were trying again from double that distance.

Just before the first man of Starkward, a grizzled veteran with a face as lined as an onion-slice, set his arrow at the nock, I heard Humphry Stethren cry out: 'I'll wager five gold marks that my man will outshoot the wizard's man!'

'Nay, I'll not place my money on such a long chance,' Fulk Reddlestone responded contemptuously.

Yet Hubert Jacklyn said laughingly: 'Taken; I believe always in betting on a dark horse — and that one is dark enough!'

Thus it was that, when I stepped up to the mark, I knew that five gold pieces of Blackhill money were depending on my skill. That was a tiresome thought for, while I cared not a jot whether young Jacklyn won or lost his wager, nevertheless I felt impelled to strive my utmost — for the honour of our master, if for no other reason.

The old archer had shot well; his arrow had struck only just outside the gold. It would be a hard shot to match and harder still to excel.

Take it easy, I bade myself; back straight, chest open, arrow at nock — good, now draw slowly. Watch the wind; there are gusts from the right, but the grass is not rippling, so the air should be still. Aim a little higher, so the arrow will drop right, and . . .

I was about to loose when there was a cry of 'Fast!' I relaxed as a small boy chased his wooden ball onto the grass just in front of the butt, seized it and, with the remonstrances of the bystanders ringing in his ears, ran back among them. Again I set arrow to nock, but now the rippling of the grass warned me of a wind-gust and I waited a moment to gauge its intensity. Yes, I must aim more to the right, to compensate . . . Pushing into my bow, I anchored for a second, then loosed just before the gust died away.

344

It was a good shot, yet not quite good enough. When men went to measure whether my arrow had hit target closer to the centre than that of the Starkward archer, they judged it a tie.

Humphry Stethren, sure that his man had won, flung his hands skyward in irritation, but Hubert Jacklyn merely chuckled and said: 'Let your wager ride on your other archer, Humphry, and mine on the prince from the south. Indeed, I'll double it, if you care to cover me.'

'Nay, I have not the gold,' young Humphry muttered embarrassedly.

'But I have,' Fulk Reddlestone announced. 'I'll take you, Hubert, and I shall have your money. The blackavised youth may know something of archery, but I question whether that self-styled princeling' — he jerked his chin contemptuously toward Avran — 'can even tell the fletching of an arrow from its point.'

This set his followers laughing sycophantically; all but Hubert, who merely smiled and said: 'We'll see, friend Fulk.'

As for Avran, he had so tensed and reddened in fury at Fulk's derisive words that I whispered urgently to him: 'Be calm, Avran! If you allow yourself to become annoyed, you'll never shoot well.'

He nodded and strove to relax, moving away so as to be out of earshot of Fulk's jibes.

The wind was blowing across the butts more steadily now and clouds were massing above the spur of hills behind the castle, causing shadows to advance across the sward. I shivered, not in cold but in anticipation of trouble to come. Yet, for the moment, all seemed well.

The Starkward archer, a younger man with a mop of brown hair and only a wisp of beard, took up his position, drew and loosed. He had not allowed sufficiently for the wind; his arrow struck only in the outer ring of the target.

Fulk and his associates groaned and I heard Humphry mutter to them: 'I'll settle with that bungling young fool, be sure!'

The question was, could Avran do better? He stepped up to the mark, looking less angry but still more tense than I would have wished. I saw him breathe deeply; then he set arrow to nock and drew back his string.

345

At the very moment when he was about to loose, young Berenger Reddlestone, who had been in his usual stance of admiration by his brother's side, coughed loudly and then gave a braying, embarrassed laugh. Avran, distracted, shot too much to the left and, at the anticipation of a miss, a ripple of chuckles spread among Fulk's cronies.

They laughed too soon. By some freak of chance, the wind was changing in strength and direction even as Avran shot. His arrow, which ought to have missed the target amply, veered in its flight and, instead, embedded itself close to the centre; not quite in the gold, but near enough.

There was an awestruck mutter among the crowd, then hesitant applause. I noticed that Vedlen Obiran was standing a little way further up the hill, smiling and silent; and I wondered . . .

Humphry Stethren was stamping in anger. 'That arrow should have gone wide. That was witches' work!'

'Nonsense, Humphry,' responded Hubert Jacklyn coolly. 'Just good shooting. You owe me five gold marks, friend; and so do you, Fulk.'

'So I do, Hubert; so I do,' said Fulk calmly. 'I deserve to lose, for I was foolish. I was assuming that the redhead was really a prince. Of course, no prince would trouble to teach himself skill with a bow, so I had expected him to lose handsomely. I should have known better. No true prince would be content to travel in the rag-tag of a wizard's train.'

He turned as if to go back up the hill; but Avran, scarlet with fury now, seized him by the arm and spun him about.

'You will apologize for those words', he demanded, his voice hoarse with anger. 'You do not know of what you speak. My father is ruler of a land that is greater than these whole hills and of an ancientry that you cannot even conceive. I will not allow my land and my lineage to be thus insulted.'

In comparison with my friend's anger, Fulk seemed dangerously cool. He was much bigger than Avran, looking like a wolfhound beside a terrier.

'Odd, then,' he answered contemptuously, 'that it should be a realm of which no-one has heard — your dark-haired friend, of course, excepted. If we were all endowed with such rich imaginations, we might all be scions of such realms!'

This renewed insult set his friends chuckling, but it caused Avran's fury to rise to fever pitch. 'Do you dare again to call me a liar? Then you must back your claim by the strength of your arms!'

He drew off the glove with which he had held his bow and flung it into Fulk's face.

The big man recoiled in shock, his face flushing with colour — partly as a result of the buffet it had received but largely in responsive anger.

'By God, this insolent mountebank dares to challenge me!' His voice evinced as much surprise as fury. 'Humphry, will you serve as my second?'

'Of course,' answered young Stethren with gratified alacrity.

Fulk was stroking his bruised cheek. 'Well, then, it is for me to choose weapons, is it not? Normally, I would suggest that we meet during the tourney with lances, as gentlemen should. However, since I hear you strangers ride rafneyen on such occasions and not horses, I am not sure whether that would be an equal match. It might allow too much opportunity for tricks of wizardry, perhaps. And of course' — he inclined his head in mock-courtesy — 'I cannot match you with the bow, as I freely admit.'

This oblique renewal of insult set his friends chuckling again. Fulk paused till their amusement had died down, then went on very deliberately: 'So I choose that our weapon be the sword and that we meet on foot. May I request also that your second be *not* your friend here' — he jerked his head at me — 'who is perhaps a little too knowledgeable by now in the arts of necromancy, but rather Sir Robert Randwulf, whom I know to be a gentleman?'

Avran had flushed anew at this insult to me, but he said merely: 'Very well. We shall leave it to our seconds to arrange time and place.' Without further word, he picked up his glove and turned away to retrieve bow and quiver.

Fulk and his followers went away up the hill, chattering as excitedly as starlings. The two Starkward archers, who seemed to feel some responsibility for the scene, muttered words of embarrassed apology and hastened away, while the crowd broke up into eddies of gossip. As for Vedlen Obiran, he came up to me, shaking his head from side to side in a sort of grim amusement. His eyes were black and inscrutable.

'Your friend can be fiery, can he not? Well, he has had provocation. Both Sir Cuthbert and his son are becoming uncomfortably arrogant; it can do no harm for them to suffer a rebuff. Yet I could wish that this incident had been postponed a little. Our negotiations are near to completion — so near, indeed, that I have been able to leave the lords at their task for a while without fearing acrimony. It would be unfortunate if the prospect of peace in these hills were to be destroyed by such a trivial incident.'

Avran had rejoined us, with dragging steps and a hangdog look: evidently the flare of his fury had burned out already.

'I am sorry,' he said, with a sincerity that could not be doubted. 'I've been an utter fool; but that Fulk, he is so — so absolutely infuriating . . . Nevertheless, I cannot allow my stupidity to wreck your plans. I will apologize to him and withdraw my challenge if you wish, though I confess it will go hard . . .' He relapsed into an embarrassed silence.

Vedlen Obiran looked at Avran steadily for a moment. Unexpectedly, the wizard's eyes had a light of amusement in them.

'No, you must not do that. Not only would it inflate further that young man's already overblown opinion of himself and confirm his ideas about you, but also it would reflect adversely upon all who are my followers and my friends. Be sure, instead, that when you meet him in battle, you emerge as the victor; but — er — try not quite to kill him!'

Avran's back, which had been bowed, straightened. He breathed deeply in relief. 'Thank you,' he said simply.

The wizard eyed him again, speculatively this time. 'However, it will be politic if I appear not to approve your actions and if I set myself a little apart from them. Sir Robert, Felun and I are to dine this night in the great hall, but it would be preferable that you and the Ravatsengs found some excuse for absenting yourselves.'

Seeing my puzzlement at his mention of the brothers, he

smiled and explained. 'Rahir and Delhir are your good friends, you know, and they do not like Fulk Reddlestone very much.'

The wizard paused, then went on: 'Nor, for that matter, do I.' After which, he walked away uphill without any further word.

Chapter Thirty-five

TIDINGS AND TREPIDATIONS

Drakht Belineg and Narel Evateng arrived at Rewlen-scrag that evening. They reported first to the wizard, then came down to join us for dinner. The Ravatseng brothers had elected to prepare that repast, for they were weary of the limited fare of the cook-tents. We ate in the castle bailey, beside the great pavilion of the wizard — a good meal of stew made from the meat of some rabbit-sized creature, flavoured with herbs and slivers of shallot and accompanied by hunks of good wheaten bread and flagons of strong ale.

Our two newly-returned comrades were both very weary and, while we ate, content to listen passively to the gossip of the castle. Our conversation was in Reschorese, good practice for Avran and me, for at Rewlenscrag most talk was in English. Only when Drakht, having thrice emptied his great beaker, had visibly relaxed did Rahir address to him the question we were all desiring to ask.

'Well, Drakht, you didn't bring Amos back with you, that's evident enough. So what happened to him? Was he victim or was he rogue?'

'Aye, that's the question,' Drakht sighed heavily. 'Would that we might answer it, but we cannot. Ours was a vain search.' He fell silent, staring unhappily into his beaker.

'Could you not trace him, then?'

'Did you find no trail?'

These two startled questions, one from Rahir and the other from me, were uttered simultaneously. It was Narel who replied.

'In honesty, friends, I am not sure. I could wish you'd been with us, Simon, or you, Delhir; Drakht and me, we're not trackers and the man from Amsetch had left us. Indeed, we'd not expected to have to rely on tracks. We thought to pick up information from people we met, hear of sightings maybe, for Amos is not a man to mistake.'

'That he is not,' growled Rahir.

Narel smiled at this, then continued: 'To cover the ground better, we elected not to travel together. Drakht went to Amsetch and thence into the skirts of the forest, but he gained no news of any strange travellers, either on rafenu-back or on foot. I searched the hill ridges south of Falconward. It is dry ground and stoney, affording little chance of discovering tracks. Yes, sometimes I did find a few fresh hoofmarks, but I could make little sense of them. So I headed eastward, out onto the dusty plains of Lukeyne — a harsh land, that, and with few settlers. I heard tales of men fleeing on foot from the phantom terrors of Alunsward' — he smiled briefly — 'and, yes, of rafenu-riders. Yet always they'd been glimpsed from afar, in the mists of morning or the gloom of evening. Nothing definite.'

He drank deeply from his beaker, then went on: 'Well, in the end I traversed Lukeyne and swam my beast across the All Saints River into Riotte. At Trayad-in-Riotte I encountered Lady Saville, her son and their escort, trading their gold for supplies to aid in the rebuilding of Owlsgard. However, no other strangers had come there. The Mentonese will not discuss their deals, of course; yet I am sure that my questions evoked no responsive echoes in their minds. Our master's and Sir Robert's possessions have not passed into Mentonese hands, of that I am convinced. Indeed, that was the only fact I gleaned in my long ride.' He sighed and shook his head sadly.

'So we cannot tell whether Amos is alive or dead.' Avran sounded almost relieved.

'Aye, that's so.' Drakht was speaking again now. 'Alive or dead, you ask; and Rahir asks, victim or rogue? I cannot answer either of you properly; yet my belief is that Amos is alive and a thief. Together Narel and I scoured the hills east of Alunsward and then I searched Amsetch, from the Hillebren Pass in the north to the banks of the Brunflow in the south. Yet we discovered only the jettisoned tent, nothing more. If Amos were dead, then surely we should have found his body.'

'But what if he be alive and a prisoner of thieves?' Avran

was still battling to retain his good impression of our former friend.

'That does remain possible,' Drakht responded heavily, but his disbelief was patent. Though Narel said nothing, a downward curve of his lips told me that he also could not accept Avran's idea.

'And what next? Will we search further for Amos?' Rahir was eager and indignant.

Narel sighed again and answered: 'Drakht and I, we would like to do so. Our master, though, says we've wasted enough time chasing after lost trifles, that other and more important tasks lie before us. He will not permit us to spend any more days questing for Amos.'

Quite evidently Narel was disgusted by this decision and, as for Drakht, he was nodding sombrely.

Delhir Ravatseng had been sitting under the shadow of the tent, as usual so quiet that almost one forgot his presence. At Narel's words, however, he leaned forward and struck his left palm with his right fist. His eyes were bright.

'Why, that *proves* Amos to be alive and a villain! Do you not see? If Amos were an innocent captive or if he were lying dead in some rocky place, would not our master strive to rescue or to avenge him? Of course he would!' Nodding to himself, Delhir sat back and fell again silent.

Delhir's deduction was so evidently correct that all of us tensed at his words. Drakht's nostrils were flaring and his eyes smouldering in wrath.

'Aye, Delhir, aye! You don't say much, my friend, but there's times when you're quicker in thought than any of us. So we must not seek our departed friend. Yet it may be that, some day, our paths will cross again. If so — why then, Amos will rue that day!'

From the fashion in which Drakht's great hands were twisting together, I believed him.

After that, the current of our talk shifted into other channels. To my surprise, the duel was not mentioned, though all knew of it — or all, it seemed, save Sir Cuthbert Reddlestone. It was certain that he would have been angry at such tidings; it was probable that he would have stopped the encounter; so word of the duel was being kept carefully from his ears.

The time had been set already: for the morrow, at one hour after noon. The place had been decided also: a dingle on the north flank of the Stoney Mountains about three hours' ride from Rewlenscrag.

After eight days of waiting while their masters negotiated, the followers of the lords of the Ferekar Naur were becoming as bored as Avran and I had been. If any nearer stage had been set for the encounter, a large crowd would certainly have assembled to watch. Wisely, the seconds — possibly Humphry Stethren, but more probably, I thought, Sir Robert — had chosen that more distant locality in hopes of preventing any such gathering. Moreover, they had been careful not to let either time or location be known widely.

For my part, I viewed the prospect of the duel with such deep disquiet that I was tempted to tell Sir Cuthbert about it myself. Only the knowledge that Avran would never forgive such a betrayal prevented me.

Yes, my friend was an excellent swordsman, his skills enhanced by his practising with Sir Robert; but, by reputation at least, Fulk Reddlestone was quite as good. Moreover, Fulk was much bigger — and, I assumed, much stronger — than Avran, with a reach that was considerably longer. Could my friend survive such an encounter without injury? I doubted it. Would he survive it at all? My mind flinched away from that question. Though I sought my blankets early, I slept little that night and rose hollow-eyed to a day that seemed unfairly bright and sunny.

Avran had risen before me and was as full of energy as I was listless. Already, I learned, he had been exercising with his sword for an hour or more. He devoured a large breakfast with enthusiasm, chaffing me because I would eat so little. If he guessed at my fears for him, he made no remark; and if he suffered from any disquiet himself, it was not evident.

Normally the wizard breakfasted in his tent. On that day, however, he surprised us by joining us. Yet he was not in talkative, but rather in pensive, mood. His strange eyes were as deeply brown as a peaty pool in shadow, while his face was as lacking in expression as a carven saint's on a Celtic cross. Only when his meal was done did he bestir himself, rising to his feet and addressing Avran.

'I cannot be with you today, my friend,' he said. 'The lords of these hills are meeting as usual and I must be with them in their discussions. They have decided their new boundaries and divided up the disputed lands. Whilst all their realms save Amsetch and Starkward have gained some new territory, the greater part of those lands has been placed into two new lordships. Alunsland, about Alunsward, will have Alban Daintree of Owlsgard for its lord. It seems he is to marry the daughter of the Earl of Amsetch, a union that should make for peace and strengthen his authority. A new realm, to be named Peakland, will be centred on Cat Crags. John Stanton will serve as its governor for five years, under the joint overlordship of Sir Cuthbert and Sir Henry. After that, its settlers will choose their own lord. That is good, but better still, the idea of a league for mutual protection is accepted by all — yes, even by Sir Gabriel Jacklyn, though he has been wriggling somewhat under the pressure of his peers' opinions!'

He paused and surveyed us searchingly before continuing. 'So it seems we have redrawn the chart of these hills into a new and, I trust, happier shape. We can take much content in that. In such a balance, the loss of our gold and possessions weighs lightly.'

Vedlen Obiran was smiling now, his brown eyes gleaming like a pool upon whose surface the sunlight is playing. His pleasure was reflected in our own countenances; yes, even in mine, dispirited though I had been. Then the wizard addressed Avran again.

'Sir Robert will be waiting for you down by the river, beyond the tents. Drakht, Delhir and Rahir will ride with you — and Simon also, of course — but I am afraid Felun, Narel and Hebehir have tasks to perform that will detain them here in Rewlenscrag. Be watchful for treachery, each of you! One cannot trust all those young men who follow Fulk to observe the ordinances of chivalry.'

He paused again, then gazed at my friend and me. 'My thanks and my blessings go with you, Avran and Simon, on this day and on all days. The road ahead of you is long and you will each encounter many problems and many dangers. Sometimes you will be afraid, sometimes almost overwhelmed by doubt, but you must never allow despair to take you in

355

its black embrace. If you employ your mind, Simon, and if you keep your skills, Avran, you will surmount every obstacle and attain all your desires.'

Solemnly he clasped hands with Avran and then with me. His words and this action pleased me, but they disconcerted me also, for they seemed so like a ceremonious adieu to friends setting forth on a long journey. Yet surely, if all went well in the duel, we would be back in Rewlenscrag that very evening?

If Avran was equally disconcerted, it was not evident. Probably he was too preoccupied with the thought of the duel to read any particular meaning into the wizard's words.

In contrast, Vedlen bade only the most casual of farewells to our other comrades before striding away up the hill. Hebehir followed him hastily; Narel had gone already and Felun had not been seen by us that morning. After ministering to his boy, Felun would no doubt be attending the meeting in the castle; but what, I wondered, had been the tasks found for Narel and Hebehir?

Speedily Delhir and Rahir cleared up after our repast, refusing any aid from Avran or me. For my part I checked over my throwing-knives, making sure that those concealed in the sheaths in the shoulders of my jacket and the spines of my boots could still be extracted readily at need. Then I fetched my bowstave and arrows from the bundle by my bed, advising Avran to do likewise.

To his surprised protest I responded: 'Quite evidently, Master Obiran anticipates trouble. Yes, I know you'll be wielding your sword in the duel, but we cannot tell what may transpire afterwards. We had better be prepared, don't you think?'

Within minutes, we were walking down the steep path from the castle bailey toward the meadows. Never had Rewlenscrag seemed more beautiful than it did in that hour of departure. The grasses were freshly bedecked with flowers, some as coolly blue as cornflowers, others as flaringly scarlet as poppies. The tents seem to glow with colour and the clothes of the people we passed seemed new-dyed into brighter hues. The very sky was the limpid blue of a songthrush's egg and speckled, not with black, but with white woolly puffs of cloud, too few and too innocent to hint at changing

356

weather. A gay scene, indeed; and since, in my altered mood, I wondered if I might be seeing it for the last time, I gazed about me almost wistfully as we descended the slope.

We had been warned not to seem to be leaving in a group. Drakht had gone ahead, while the Ravatseng brothers were sauntering along behind. Even so, we received many curious glances and traversed the meadows on the crest of a tide of interested comment.

In a glade half a league or so beyond the tent town, Sir Robert and Drakht were waiting with the six rafneyen: Fulk and his followers would be riding to our destination by a different path. As soon as the Ravatsengs had caught up with us, we set forth, following the Pochard's banks downstream for two more leagues and splashing across where its waters shallowed at a rock bar. Through a thicket and up a long hill we rode. The ascent was not continuously steep, but intermittently so, as if we were climbing a series of poorly made steps with shaly clifflets as risers. There were marshy patches on the flatter places, the treads of those steps; even after several days of sunshine, our rafneyen's hooves sometimes sank deeply into the mud.

It was hot; I slipped off my cloak and folded it across the saddle before me. Galahad, who was as hot as I and, in his usual fashion, sharing my uneasy mood, tossed his horns irritably.

The ridge crest, once reached, proved broad and fairly flat. Moreover, there was a welcome stir of air to cool us. Soon we could see beyond the ridge. The viridian hue of the Great Marshes extended into the distance over to our left. Below us, in a broad valley, there flowed a great river, bordered by lush green meadows and intermittently concealed by clumps of trees. Beyond it, a range of lesser hills humped the horizon.

All of us paused at this sight. 'Those are the Ferekar Rokanair, the Rockaine Hills,' said Sir Robert quietly. 'Gascon territory. They're a tempestuous folk, but most are good and chivalrous. Evil men like Casimir are as few among them as among the English or the Reschorese. The valley is that of the Aramassa, perhaps the greatest of all the rivers of Rockall — unless you have greater streams in the south, Avran?'

My friend shook his head and Sir Robert continued: 'We've

left Sir Cuthbert's lands behind now, by the way; we're in the Wilderward, the feoff of Sir Amyas Aydenburgh of Wildfell. We thought it better that the duel be held on neutral territory.'

Then he gazed about him. 'Many years have passed since I was last here; I am a little uncertain of our way. Do you recall it, Drakht?'

'Not I,' responded the big man. 'Never been here before.'

Fortunately, Rahir said: 'I mind it well enough. Over to the left a furlong or so, and then down; have I it right, Delhir?' At his brother's nod, Rahir led the way confidently and our rafneyen followed his.

The dingle was certainly well concealed from above. It was a notch cut into the slope of the hill as sharply as if by some giant axe; only when one rode up to its very edge did it become suddenly visible. Perhaps some stream had flowed through it once, but now there was just a space of green sward between two dense banks of bushes.

Fulk and his party were waiting for us already — not just the five we had encountered at the butts, but also a score of other nobles' sons and their hangers-on. Someone raised a derisory cheer when we were sighted on the skyline. However, he was speedily hushed and, when we had ridden down among them, we were greeted with proper courtesy.

However, I noted with some disquiet that all the young men were armed with swords, axes or spears; Berenger Reddlestone even bore a shield on his arm, its highly polished surface shining in the sunlight. If the duel should expand into a general mêlée, we would be outnumbered five to one – not a pleasant prospect.

An ample space near the centre of the dingle had been already roped off as arena for the combat. Its polygon-patterned surface showed it to be a dried-out marsh, the crust of the mud so much desiccated that it had crumbled to dust wherever feet had stepped. Even as we dismounted, Fulk's followers were already serrying about the ropes. I hesitated whether to extract my bowstave from its sling beside the saddle, but decided reluctantly that to carry a strung bow might merely stir up animosity. Instead I picked up my cloak and, after instructing Galahad to stay reasonably close by, walked over with my friends to join the watchers.

358

Humphry Stethren had brought with him the two swords that were to be used and he and Sir Robert solemnly compared them. In that matter, at least, the contest would be even; each blade was exactly a clothyard in length and they were so alike in shape that they would have fitted into the same scabbard. It was Sir Robert who chose which should be handed to Avran and which to Fulk.

Before he took his weapon, Avran said: 'I do not wish to proceed with this fight, if it can be avoided without dishonour. Master Reddlestone, if you will withdraw your imputations concerning my status and my family, I am prepared to lay down this weapon and to take your hand in friendship. Will you do so?'

At that, there were hoots and catcalls from Fulk's supporters, but Fulk himself merely responded coldly: 'What I have said, I have said.'

At that, Avran sighed and accepted the sword. Weighing up the adversaries, I thought again that my friend was outmatched and felt anew the cold clutch of fear at my heart. Even if one ignored Avran's smaller size and lesser strength, he was at a disadvantage also in armour. Fulk Reddlestone was wearing a tunic of chain mail over a padded hauqueton; on his head was a steel helmet and his stockings and boots were studded with iron plates. In contrast, Avran wore only the padded jupon and the leather hood that Rahir had issued to him at Owlsgard; his stockings, though thick enough, had no plating and his boots were merely of leather. Add to this advantage of armour Fulk's other advantages in strength, height and reach and the contest seemed so manifestly unfair that I wondered how Sir Robert could allow it to proceed.

However, Sir Robert seemed to feel no disquiet and arrangements were soon made for its commencement. The contestants were stationed eight paces apart, their swords pointing at the ground; then Sir Robert turned to the crowd.

'This duel shall begin when Master Stethren throws down the kerchief he carries. It shall end when "Pax" is called, either by Master Reddlestone or the Prince of Sandastre or, if one of them be unable so to cry, by Master Stethren or me. You spectators, I charge you all to obey the laws of chivalry, not only in letter but also in spirit. You must neither intervene in this fight nor protest at its outcome, whatever that be.'

This stern command was received in a silence in which I seemed to detect some unease. Then, as the contestants raised their swords, I was startled to hear Hubert Jacklyn mutter to Aldwyn Ennerling: 'I have still my five gold marks and, once again, I'll wager them on the Prince.'

Aldwyn Ennerling responded surprisedly: 'Why, you've lost your senses, man! Still, if you're such a fool, you deserve to lose your money. Taken!'

So for a second time, as I watched my friend begin a contest, I knew that Blackhill gold was riding on him. Somehow, this time, the knowledge comforted me.

Chapter Thirty-six

THE DUEL IN THE DINGLE

Sir Robert stepped away now, to stand on the north side of the arena. His hand rested on his sword-hilt, but that was his right for, by the rules which govern such contests in Rockall, the second can intercede on his principal's behalf whenever a foul blow be struck or any other base deed attempted. After Humphry had dropped the kerchief, he would take up a similar position on the arena's south side and be similarly ready to intercede if necessary.

Presently Humphry was standing in the centre of the rope-bounded space, his eyes bright and his lips parted; his excitement was evident. The kerchief, gaily coloured in green and no doubt borrowed from some girl of Rewlenscrag, was clasped in his right hand. Slowly he raised that hand and, with all eyes upon him, released the kerchief before backing away hastily to the ropes.

As the kerchief fluttered to the ground, the two contestants advanced toward one another, not directly but somewhat crab-wise, each with sword at the ready and eyes watchful. Fulk made a half-stroke, then checked himself; and, for what seemed a considerable while but was probably no more than a minute, the two circled each other warily.

Predictably it was Fulk who made the first onslaught, leaping at Avran with a suddenness that startled me and striking downward in a series of powerful hacking slashes which, it seemed to me, my friend parried only with difficulty. Avran was backing away and Fulk's friends cheering lustily.

However, as Fulk's blade flashed back and forth in strokes from left and right, Avran's continued to meet and block it. Moreover, though Avran was continuing to give ground, he did not do so directly, with the risk of being trapped in an angle of the ropes, but rather in a broad circle that kept him never far from the centre of the space. His strategy was perceived by the onlookers and the cheering died away.

Fulk halted, his sword drooping as if his wrist was weary; but, when Avran thrust at him swiftly, Fulk was ready. His sword swept upward with such force that Avran's blade was turned back. Indeed, such was the strength of that counter-stroke and the speed with which Avran's blade was carried upward that I feared my friend had lost his hold on his weapon.

There was a collective gasp from the watchers. However, somehow Avran kept his grip on his sword hilt. Though he was backing again, his blade caught and deflected Fulk's mighty downward sweep.

After that, for several minutes, there was such a quicksilver sequence of thrust and parry that their two blades seemed to be weaving a meshwork of light. Always it was Fulk who was on the attack, employing his greater strength to try to break through Avran's guard. Always it was Avran who was on the retreat, but that retreat was ever a calculated, never a precipitate, one. Their footmarks in the mud crust made a circle whose centre was very close to that of the arena. The dust thrown up by their rapid steps powdered their legs and hazed the sunlight.

The sun was at its height now and the dingle quite without cooling draughts of air. Even for we onlookers, to be enclosed in that sun-baked space was a cause for perspiration; the contestants must be becoming very hot indeed.

Fulk was both the bigger and the more heavily armoured; predictably, it was he who began to tire quickest. By almost imperceptible degrees, the fury of his onslaught was dimin-ishing. Instead of striving by sheer strength to break through Avran's guard, he was trying instead to benefit from the asset of his longer reach. The massive sweeping strokes at short range were being succeeded by probing thrusts and wrist-flick counters.

Yet, as Avran's blade blocked each thrust and avoided the flicks and twists of Fulk's sinuous-seeming sword, the bigger man seemed to be advancing, and the smaller to be retreating, more and more slowly.

Momentarily the two were at a stand, their blades criss-crossing. Fulk was facing toward me; I could see that he was breathing fast and that the sweat was coursing down his brow. Then he took a deeper breath and, calling upon his strength, launched a fresh onslaught that forced Avran again into retreat. However, as the dust eddied about them, the circle of their movements was closing tighter about the arena's centre and Fulk's massive hacks seemed ever more effortful.

Then, suddenly, we onlookers realized Fulk was on the retreat. There was a general insucking of breath and much excited comment. Hubert Jacklyn, standing behind Humphry on the far side, was nodding in satisfaction, his dark eyes a-gleam, while Aldwyn Ennerling registered resentful astonishment.

As it chanced, Berenger Reddlestone was standing just to my right. It was a choice of position that had surprised me, not only because his other close friends were all standing behind Humphry but also because it meant that he was looking south into the sun. The shield was still on his arm; I was puzzled why he had not set it down. Berenger had been shouting in delight during the first few minutes of the combat, but his cockcrows had faded into silence as it proceeded. Now he gave vent to a long moan of dismay.

Fulk was contriving to block all of Avran's thrusts, but that he was doing so with difficulty was more and more evident. As their paths changed again I realized that Fulk was backing, and Avran advancing, toward us.

At this, Berenger tensed. His slight movement caught my eye. Glancing toward him, I noticed that he was gazing at his shield-arm and raising the shield with care, at a curious angle.

In sudden enlightenment, I perceived Berenger's purpose. Why, he planned to use the highly polished metal of the shield to reflect the sun into Avran's eyes and, by dazzling my friend, expose him to big brother Fulk's thrust!

Well, of course that could not be allowed. How fortunate it was that I was carrying my cloak on my arm! Quickly I stepped behind Berenger and, as the sun's rays shone bright on the rising shield, I slung my cloak over it, green side outermost.

Berenger started in astonishment, then turned on me with a snarl; but I spoke loudly enough for all about me to hear.

363

'Sorry to do that, friend, but I feared you might dazzle the swordsmen. Quite inadvertently, I'm sure!'

Berenger looked at me furiously, but other eyes were upon him now. Seeing his ruse exposed, he muttered: 'Oh, yes, of course. Foolish of me; I should have put my shield down.'

'Then why not do so now?' I asked sweetly. As I drew back and folded my cloak, he set the shield on the ground with the illest of graces.

Sir Robert had heard my words and looked toward us. At this, he gave me a quick brief smile of approval and turned back toward the ring. My gaze followed his.

Thus it was that I witnessed Avran's feinting thrust, checked at the last moment, which drew an unnecessary counterstroke from Fulk and left him open to Avran's blade. I watched that blade slide inward and upward in a strange, spiral twist that sent Fulk's sword spinning from his hand; and I witnessed the mighty thrust that, had it not been checked, would surely have pierced Fulk's coat of mail and slain him.

As it was, it caused the big man to collapse backward onto his knees. Then, with Avran standing over him, eyes ablaze, and Avran's sword hovering about his throat, Fulk grunted hoarsely the reluctant word 'Pax!'

Since Humphry Stethren seemed too stupefied for speech, it was Sir Robert who stepped forward and shouted to the crowd: 'Victory and honour are to the Prince of Sandastre!'

There were delighted shouts from Rahir and Drakht, while even quiet Delhir was clapping his hands in joy. As for me, I was jumping with delight; and, though Aldwyn Ennerling, Berenger Reddlestone and a few others were glumly silent, the greater number of those watching were sporting enough to applaud my friend's victory. Realizing this, I perceived also that we were in no danger of any mass assault and felt a second surge of relief.

Avran had sheathed his weapon already and had fetched Fulk's sword. Now, with characteristic courtesy, he handed it to Fulk, hilt foremost.

The big man, who was still sitting back on his haunches, took it and got laboriously to his feet. He looked white and was breathing heavily, the perspiration coursing down his cheeks. For a moment he stood still and unsteady. Then he thrust his sword into its scabbard and held out his arms to Avran. As they clasped hands, Fulk spoke for the first time.

'Prince of Sandastre — wherever that is — you may be. A prince of swordsmen most certainly you are! I withdraw my words but, since they have brought about this bonny fight, I am not so sure that I regret them!'

From that moment, I knew that Fulk could not have been aware of his younger brother's treacherous devices. So honourable an antagonist would never stoop to such base practices.

Avran laughed joyously and responded: 'A bonny fight indeed! I am fortunate to have encountered so fine a swordsman and doubly fortunate to be victorious.'

Thus, with fair words, did an unhappy affair end in the best of fashions. Those words brought more applause from the onlookers and much favourable comment; but there were still some who were unhappy. Aldwyn Ennerling, reluctantly paying his forfeit of gold to Hubert Jacklyn, grumbled: 'More wizardry! Just as Humphry was, I'm a fool to wager against any of Vedlen Obiran's men.'

But Hubert Jacklyn responded lightly: 'Did you notice any evidences of wizardry, then? Did you see any strange green fogs, hear any weird chants, or witness any dragons emerging from the earth to eat up the combatants? Nay, my friend, I fear you're just a fool!'

As he turned away, Hubert noticed my amusement and winked at me before going to join Humphry and Fulk.

Sobbing in furious humiliation, Berenger had seized his shield and, summoning his rafenu, had fled away already toward Rewlenscrag. Others of the onlookers were soon riding away also, but Sir Robert and our other friends, though having also summoned their mounts, seemed inclined to linger. Indeed, after bidding a properly courteous farewell to Fulk, Humphry and the others, we were the last to remain in the dingle. I wondered why.

I was to discover swiftly enough. Sir Robert mounted his rafenu, then faced it about toward Avran and me. 'Well, friends, that was a worthy victory; and I am glad, Simon, that you anticipated yon young villain's stratagem in time.'

To Avran's surprised question, Sir Robert responded with a brief explanation which gained me a grateful smile from my friend. Then, before Avran could speak, he went on: 'Yet

365

you cannot return to Rewlenscrag, you know. Very soon, sweet little brother Berenger will be pouring out the story of this afternoon — or his own special version of it — into his father's ear. Even though Fulk has accepted defeat well, his father will neither forgive nor forget what he will view as being a smirching of his precious family honour. Sir Cuthbert has his good points, but he has a stiff neck and an ill temper also. I am afraid you're going to have to be sent on your way toward Lyonesse, Simon and Avran.'

Seeing our expressions of dismay, he smiled and went on: 'Yet you must not worry; Vedlen foresaw this, of course, and all is prepared for you. Your possessions are waiting for you, down the hill in the Aramassa valley. Vedlen had hoped to escort you to Reschora himself but, following the loss of his gold and goods, he cannot afford to do that. He must return instead to his work in the forestlands. However, he has charged me to set you on your way. As far as Reschora, at least, I shall travel with you, and maybe further if you'll welcome my company. I've long thought of traversing the Northern Mountains, to discover what lies beyond.'

This tiding softened for both of us the blow of knowing that we would be leaving behind our friends. To our protestations of relief and pleasure, Sir Robert answered merely: 'Splendid! Then let us be riding down to the river.'

So, instead of retracing our tracks toward Rewlenscrag, we rode together across the dingle, over its abrupt lowest rim and down a moderately steep slope into the Aramassa valley. As we jogged along, my friends made unduly much of my scotching of Berenger's little scheme. Drakht outlined in some detail what he would have done to that young villain, had it succeeded. Then the flow of our talk dried up, as each of us became regretfully conscious of the imminence of parting.

We rode through the belt of trees that hugged the lee of the slope and out into a broad meadow of green grasses, as colourfully flower-flecked as that at Rewlenscrag had been. On the very bank of the river was a hurst covered by well-grown trees whose dusty, arrow-shaped leaves showed them to be evergreens. The trees grew so densely that I was surprised when Sir Robert led us straight toward this grove: but indeed, there was a bridle-path winding among the trees, along which we were able to pass in single file to the riverside.

There, waiting patiently for us beside the broad flood of the Aramassa, were seven persons. Four were short, dark men in faded blue tunics and light cloth shoes, whom I did not recognize. The others, however, were delightfully familiar — Felun Daretseng, his small boy from Owlsgard, and big Hebehir Ravatseng. They were sitting in the shade of a tree, but leapt to their feet at our approach and hastened forward to greet us.

Hebehir actually lifted Avran from his rafenu and hugged him with delight. 'Why, man, you're in fine fettle! Surely you must have vanquished that arrogant young cub Fulk?'

'Careful, Hebehir! You're squeezing the breath out of me! Ah, that's better. Yes, I defeated him; but he's not so bad, you know. He's a fine swordsman.'

'Magnificent! Why, we're proud of you!' Hebehir hugged Avran again, beaming with such unalloyed delight that I realized again how fortunate we had been to make such friends. Alas! that we would be saying farewell to them so soon.

Felun's pleasure, if less violently demonstrated, was no less great; and, as for the little boy, he was hopping with joy. They added their congratulations to Hebehir's and received from Rahir a highly-coloured account of the combat, in which my own small service gained fuller mention than it merited. Meanwhile, the four strangers watched and listened inscrutably.

When that account was ended Felun introduced them, speaking in Reschorese. 'Sir Robert, Simon and Avran, I would like you to meet Etvan and Dazlan Garavet and Ulim and Terim Lazadel, boatmen of the Aramassa.'

We exchanged the clasped-hands grip of friendship and he went on: 'To ride in so small a party to Reschora would be difficult and dangerous, for perilous lands lie between. Our master the wizard has arranged that these men should take you there more speedily, by boat. It will mean your leaving behind your rafneyen, I fear; but then, rafneyen would be of small service in the mountains.'

'Thank you indeed!' responded Avran surprisedly. 'That will be splendid!'

I contrived to echo his gratitude. However, recalling my

past ineptitude in boats, I felt little enough enthusiasm for any prolonged voyaging.

Then Felun solemnly conveyed to us Vedlen Obiran's farewell and repeated his blessing, adding: 'Our master regrets the loss, not only of your company, but also of your services. He asked me to tell you, however, that he is recruiting a new assistant — young Henry Ellis here, who prefers to stay with us than to return to Owlsgard.' The small boy blushed with pleasure, then turned a couple of somersaults in glee. 'Narel Evateng, who took my place today in the council chamber, sends his blessings also, regretting that he cannot express them personally. He will be as overjoyed as we at the tidings of your victory, Avran. But now we must, I fear, be setting you on your way and returning to Rewlenscrag. You'll find the rest of your possessions stowed in the boats. Our master has made payment already to the boatmen, so you have no anxieties in that regard.'

Yes, that parting was as painful as I had expected. Not only was our gratitude to the wizard profound, but also our affection for his men had become very great. Especially did I find it hard to say goodbye to Rahir and Delhir, those two brothers who had saved our lives at Nekhalések. My farewell to my rafenu, the noble Galahad, was almost as difficult.

All too soon we were ensconced in the two boats that had been moored in the trees' shade, Sir Robert with the Garavet brothers in the first, Avran and I with the Lazadel cousins in the second. The boatmen pushed off from the sandy shore and paddled out onto the broad, slow-flowing river, using strange, long-shafted and long-bladed oars. All too soon, they were rowing upstream in a steady, effortless-seeming rhythm. All too soon, our friends and the beasts who had served us so faithfully were lost to sight in the shadow of the trees.

Once again, I felt, a part of my life was fading from reality into dream. In the shadow of that parting, I felt daunted and depressed. What lay ahead? More perils, surely, among those greater mountains we had yet to traverse. Was I destined ever to find Lyonesse, to meet again my beloved father and brother? Would I contrive ever to return to Ilven, my newer and more passionate love?

I glimpsed Sir Robert in the boat in front, gazing eagerly

about him; and I became conscious that Avran, sitting behind me, was dozing relaxedly in the aftermath of his exertions. Suddenly I was ashamed of my fears. Blessed as I was with these two strong companions, both of them willing, from a spirit of adventure and in friendship, to share all the risks with me, I should be feeling humble and grateful. Moreover, the words of the wizard came back comfortingly to my mind. Maybe there *were* perils ahead, yet somehow Avran and I would survive them and, some day, we would find Lyonesse!

GLOSSARY OF ROCKALESE WORDS

All Rockalese words are defined when first used in this account. However, for the convenience of any reader who finds them hard to remember, they are brought together here for ready reference. Four Rockalese languages are represented, of which the three principal ones are Sandastrian, herein {Sand.}, Montrion {Mont.} and Reschorese {Resch.}: where words are common to two or more languages, this is indicated.

A   **aftal**, *n.* one hundred {Sand.: Resch.}

agiru (*pl.* **agireyen**), *n.* nobleman {Sand.: but *not* used in Sandastre itself}

akhled (*pl.* **akhledai**), *n.* chief of a Montariotan tribe {Mont.}

akhledan (*pl.* **akhldanai**), *n.* consort of the chief of a Montariotan tribe {Mont.}

akhledet (*pl.* **akhledetei**), *n.* chief town of a Montariotan tribe {Mont.}

aldreslef (*pl.* **aldreslevei**), *n.* princess of secondary status {Sand.}

asalbek (*pl.* **asalbekai**), *n.* short-trunked deciduous tree with branches forming an upwardly-directed cup; leaves lanceolate; berries black and sour; used as a laxative {Sand.}

aseklin (*pl.* **asekleyin**), *n.* arrowslit window of a fortification or castle {Sand.}

ashlesar, *v.* to chain {Mont.}

askatal, *n.* one thousand {Sand.: Resch.}

aspadarn (*pl.* **aspadin**), *n.* component unit of a **padarn**, *q.v.* {Sand.}

astre (*pl.* **astrei**), *n.* land, nation {Sand.}

atim, *adv.* near, nearby {Mont.}

atra, *n.* or *adj.* southwest {Sand.}

ava, *n.* or *adj.* one (numeral); first {Sand.}

Avbalet, *n.* January {Sand.}

azesse (*pl.* **azessen**), *n.* marsh, swamp {Resch.}

B   **bavalin**, (*pl.* **bavalneyen**), *n.* rhinoceros-like herbivore of southern Rockall; hide brown; two immense, cone-shaped brown horns, bases almost confluent, tips sharp {Sand.}

belineg (*pl.* **belnegen**), *n.* blacksmith {Resch.}

bevnu (*pl.* **bevneyen**), *n.* beast [used of domesticated quadrupeds only] {Sand.}

biek, *conj.* placed between personal name and surname of a convicted criminal {Sand.}

D   **dakheslef** (*pl.* **dakheslevei**), *n.* king {Sand.}

dakheslevat (*pl.* **dakheslevatai**), *n.* kingdom {Sand.}

Dakhvardavat, *n.* Ruling Council of Sandastre {Sand.}

danatel (*pl.* **danatelen**), *n.* antelope-like herbivore of hare/jackrabbit size, with simple, short horns, forwardly directed (*cf.* muntjac) {Resch.}

deva, *n.* two {Sand.}

Devbalet, *n.* February {Sand.}

dort (*pl.* **dortan**), *n.* ward of a fortified city {Sand.}

370

dr, dri, *pref.* to verbs indicating a reversal of action [equivalent to English 'un-'] {Mont.}

drahakhal (*pl.* **drahaklen**), *n.* sacrificial victim {Mont.}

drashlesar, *v.* to unchain, unbind {Mont.}

E ebelmek (*pl.* **ebelmekai**), *n.* deciduous tree with flowers of bright orange hue {Sand.}

embelin (*pl.* **embeleyin**), *n.* musical instrument of half-melon shape with four strings (*cf.* citole) {Sand.}

eng, *suff.* man of . . . {Resch.}

enor (*pl.* **enten**), *n.* spot, blotch {Sand.: Resch.}

eslef (*pl.* **eslevei**), *n.* ruling prince {Sand.}

eslevar (*pl.* **eslevaren**), *n.* consort of ruling prince {Sand.}

estelen (*pl.* **estelnai**), *n.* yellow-flowering deciduous tree of northern Sandastre: the symbol of Estantegard {Sand.}

F faraslef (*pl.* **faraslevei**), *n.* earl {Sand.}

faraslevat (*pl.* **faraslevatai**), *n.* earldom {Sand.}

felbra, *n.* or *adj.* southeast {Sand.}

ferek (*pl.* **ferekar**), *n.* hill, mountain {Resch.}

feslar, *v.* to keep, maintain, hold {Sand.: Mont.}

festikier (*pl.* **festikieren**), *n.* water bird of southern Rockall {Sand.}

fil, *pref.* inner {Sand.}

G gahe (**gahé**), *adj.* streaked {Sand.: Resch.}

galikhu (*pl.* **galikheyen**), *n.* water-hog: amphibious riverine herbivore with short tusks and a grey hide; related to the pigs but only of piglet size and proportions; gregarious; resembles a pygmy hippopotamus in habits, but smaller {Sand.}

gard (*pl.* **gardai**), *n.* ruling family (of Sandastre) {Sand.}

H halések (*pl.* **halésekar**), *n.* temple, holy place {Mont.}

hasedu (*pl.* **hasedain**), *n.* heavy antelope-like herbivore; pelage dark brown; having two spiralling, lyre-shaped horns. Used as a beast of burden and source of meat and milk throughout Rockall; by the Montariotans, used also for riding {Sand.}

I iga, *conj.* and {Sand.: Mont.}

ikhoras (*pl.* **ikhoranai**), *n.* tree whose branches are used for arrow-making {Sand.}

indrakhled (*pl.* **indrakhledai**), *n.* heir to a Montariotan chiefdom {Mont.}

indreslef (*pl.* **indreslevei**), *n.* prince of secondary rank {Sand.}

isitelen (*pl.* **isitelnen**), *n.* starling-sized bird with azure blue plumage {Sand.}

K kal, (*pl.* **kalai**), *n.* etched sphere of quartz, used as a low-value monetary token [equivalent to a penny or cent] {Sand.}

371

kalvak, (*pl.* **kalvaken**), *n.* rhinoceros-like forest herbivore of central Rockall; brown, small-eared and with a single, Y-shaped nasal horn {Resch.}

kha, *pref.* imperative prefix {Mont.: equivalent to Sand. **ksa**}

koiru (*pl.* **koirneyen**), *n.* merchant, tradesman {Sand.}

ksa, *pref.* imperative prefix {Sand.}

'Ksakeren!', *imp. v.* 'Move!' [to a person or animal] {Grey Riders}

'Ksashassat!', *imp. v.* 'Be still!' [to a person or animal] {Grey Riders}

L lad (*pl.* **ladar**), *n.* fur {Resch.}

lan, *pref.* lacking, without {Resch.}

M marnis, *n.* or *adj.* south {Sand.}

mekret (*pl.* **mekreyet**), *n.* rascal {Sand.}

N naradat (*pl.* **naradaten**) *n.* republic {Sand.}

narat (*pl.* **naratai**), *n.* ruler (or president) of a republic {Sand.}

naur, *adj.* stony

nekh (*pl.* **nekhai**), *n.* sun-tree; large deciduous tree, with spreading branches. Survives in isolated hill situations in central and southern Rockall, but flourishes only in Vragansarat {Sand.: Mont.}

nendra, *n.* or *adj.* northeast {Sand.}

nos (*pl.* **nosan**), *n.* heart {Sand.}

not, *diminutive suff.* {Sand.: Resch.}

O obiran (*pl.* **obiranar**), *n.* seneschal, castellan {Resch.}

osumlet (*pl.* **osumleten**), *n.* aquatic wildfowl [general term] {Sand.}

P padarn (*pl.* **padin**), *n.* circular house {Sand.}

pevenek (*pl.* **pevenekar**), *n.* huge coniferous trees; bark creamy brown, punctate, resistant to impact and fire; cones very small, with tiny seeds (*cf.* sequoia) {Sand.}

R rafenu (*pl.* **rafneyen**), *n.* antelope-like forest herbivore having one nasal and two brow horns; nasal horn directed forward, brow horns five-tined with three foremost tines curving and moderately long, two rear tines shorter and straight; pelage walnut-brown, flecked with creamy spots; used as a mount and capable of simple telepathic exchanges with its rider {Resch.}

ramora (*pl.* **ramoren**), *n.* large forest herbivore having a long, straight nasal horn, a pair of long, straight brow horns and a pair of coiled, ram's-horn-like horns behind the ears; a line of erectile spines along the back and a spiked tail; pelage of almost Prussian blue hue; telepathic abilities exceptional {Sand.: Resch.}

rewlen (*pl.* **rewlnen**), *n.* grey, raven-like bird of central Rockall {Resch.: English}

rokh (*pl.* **rokhei**), *n.* warrior {Sand.}

ruan (*pl.* **ruanan**), *n.* hour {Sand.: Resch.}

S **sadnar**, *v.* to approach {Mont.}

salis, *n.* or *adj.* north {Sand.}

sasayin (*pl.* **sasayinar**), *n.* catapult-like weapon set between the brow horns of a **sevdru** {Sand.}

sasialin (*pl.* **sasialinar**), *n.* the dart propelled from a **sasayin** {Sand.}

selth (*pl.* **selthen**), *n.* nocturnal scavenging carnivore, gaunt, with long, flat-topped skulls; forelimbs longer than hind; canines pointed, first premolars converted into carnassials for shearing, other cheek-teeth strong, for bone-cracking; fur dull yellow with longitudinal grey or brown streaks {Sand.: Resch.}

senetar, *v.* to give or bestow {Mont.}

sevdru (*pl.* **sevdreyen**), *n.* antelope-like herbivore having two forwardly-directed nasal horns and two brow horns, branching twice symmetrically in Y-fashion so that each horn has four tines; pelage grey, with white underparts and central white line down neck and back; used as a mount and capable of simple telepathic exchanges with its rider {Sand.}

skarn (*pl.* **skarnar**), *n.* deciduous tree of central Rockall; bark honey-brown, pitted, overlapping in chevron-like layers; leaves pale green with yellow flecks and scalloped edges (*cf.* oak); bark used for tanning, branches for fletching {Resch.: English}

soven (*pl.* **sovenei**), *n.* stranger, foreigner {Sand.}

T **tal**, *n.* ten {Sand.}

tala (*pl.* **talnan**), *n.* village or hamlet, usually a cluster of **padin** {Sand.}

Taltegis, *n.* Sunday {Sand.}

tavelnek (*pl.* **tavelnekar**), *n.* deciduous tree with dark green foliage opening in fan-like fashion above a short trunk: bitter yellow berries, used as purgatives {Sand.}

thassak (*pl.* **thasskeyen**), *n.* sabre-tooth carnivore of central and southern Rockall; lion-sized; fur silver-grey, with darker patches {Sand.: Mont.: Resch.}

tsoned, *n.* strength, fitness {Mont.}

U **uen** (**wen**), *adj.* or *suff.* broad {Sand.: Resch.}

ukhur (*pl.* **ukhuren**), *n.* large, long-legged hog-like omnivore of the grasslands; cheeks warty; ears with swollen tips; tushes short and sharp; nocturnal and gregarious, capable of rapid running {Sand.}

uld, *pref.* outer {Sand.}

urut (*pl.* **uruten**), *n.* small, shaggy-furred, rotund insectivore of southern Rockall, with strong claws for opening up anthills {Sand.}

ushazar, *v.* to condemn {Sand.}; to praise {Resch.}

ustres, *n.* or *adj.* west {Sand.}

V **vakhast**, *n.* ejaculation of surprise ('My goodness!') {Sand.}

vard (*pl.* **vardai**), *n.* family-clan {Sand.}

vardaf (*pl.* **vardavai**), *n.* chief of a family-clan {Sand.}

vasian (*pl.* **vasianar**), *n.* small, tarsier-like arboreal primate of southern Rockall, large-eyed and with grey pelage; capable of moderately extensive telepathic inter-

373

changes with its owner; very faithful {Sand.}

vekra, *n.* one-third {Sand.}

vekruan, *n.* twenty minutes [one-third of an hour] {Sand.}

X **xalihu** (*pl.* **xaliheyen**), *n.* horse-like herbivore of the Eastern Mountains, with long, spiralling brow-horn; cloven-hoofed, otherwise *cf.* unicorn; pelage grey or silver-grey to white; used as a mount and capable of limited telepathic interchanges with its rider. {Sand.: Resch.}

Z **zembel,** *adj.* dark in hue {Sand.}

zikadath (*pl.* **zikadathen**), *n.* venomous, arboreal snake of southern Rockall; skin patterned in yellow and green {Sand.}